HUNTED

ALEX KNIGHT

ORION

Herefordshire Libraries

An Orion paperback

First published in Great Britain in 2020
by Orion Fiction,
This paperback edition published in 2021
by Orion Fiction,
an imprint of The Orion Publishing Group Ltd.,
Carmelite House, 50 Victoria Embankment
London EC4Y 0DZ

An Hachette UK Company

1 3 5 7 9 10 8 6 4 2

Copyright © Alex Knight 2020

A CIP catalogue record for this book
is available from the British Library.

ISBN (Paperback) 978 1 4091 9364 7

Typeset at The Spartan Press Ltd,
Lymington, Hants

Printed and bound in Great Britain by Clays Ltd,
Elcograf S.p.A.

MIX
Paper from
responsible sources
FSC® C104740

www.orionbooks.co.uk

To Karen and Gerry

'God makes some men poets. Some He makes kings, some beggars. Me, He made a hunter.'

– *The Most Dangerous Game*, Richard Connell

I

Now

The banging on the door was the second indication of the morning that Jake Ellis's life was about to collapse around him. He put the laptop down on the couch and walked quickly through to the cramped hallway of his third-floor apartment.

The banging continued, hurrying him along.

'I'm coming,' he yelled. He was wearing only jeans, so he grabbed yesterday's T-shirt from the floor and pulled it on as the banging was joined by a voice. Urgent, panicking.

'Jake, it's Molly. I think Mom is dead.'

The words hit him like a physical blow. He unlocked the door and threw it open. If Jake had any lingering disbelief about what he was hearing, it would have been dispelled by the sight of her.

Molly was thirteen years old, tall for her age. Her face was flushed, her long red hair in disarray, some of it matted to the sweat on her forehead.

She was wearing black leggings and a gray long-sleeve T-shirt with an anime character printed on it. No coat, even though it was an unusually cool April in San Francisco. The T-shirt, along with her forearms, were covered in blood. A lot of blood.

Rachel's blood.

He put his hands on Molly's upper arms to steady her and guided her inside, closing the door.

'What...' he began, not knowing what to ask first. 'Was there an accident?'

He dismissed the idea as soon as the words left his mouth. He could see Molly was in shock, but not just that. She was scared. He thought back to what he had just read on the screen of his laptop and knew that it was no sick joke.

'Who did this? Where's your mom?'

She shook her head. 'I don't know who it was. She was driving me to gymnastics club. We were parking and – and the window—'

'The window...?'

'It just exploded.'

'Was she shot? Did somebody shoot her?'

As he talked, he was scanning Molly's upper body and arms for a wound, but there didn't seem to be one. None of the blood was her own.

'Where is she?' The urgency in his voice came out like a bark and she flinched back.

'She – she...' Molly was shaking, her pupils slightly dilated. Jake had dealt with dozens of people in shock during his career. Hundreds. Just like this, covered in blood, disoriented. Stunned that, out of nowhere, a previously benign world has decided to turn around and bite them. But this was different, because he was in shock too.

He put his hands on her shoulders, gently. The fabric of her shirt was damp from sweat. She must have been running for a while. He forced his voice into a semblance of calm professionalism.

'It's okay. Molly? It's okay. You're safe. But I need to know where your mom is. If she's hurt...'

She swallowed. Blinked a couple of times. Her nostrils flared as she calmed herself enough to get the words out.

'I think she's dead. He shot at me too. I just kept running. I knew you lived here and...'

Jake felt his stomach dip. He guided her over to the couch, having to gently push her down to get her to sit.

He knew there was no point pushing her for details. It had to be related to what he had read on the screen of his laptop a few moments before. And that meant maybe this was all his fault.

'Wait here, I'm going to get help,' he told her.

Jake ran back through to the bedroom. His phone was right where he had left it, on the nightstand.

But before he could touch it, he heard a sharp, keening tone and the screen lit up with a message.

It wasn't a text or an email. Before he had a chance to read the words, he recognized the distinctive notification: the rectangle with the rounded edges, the exclamation point inside a triangle, like a road sign warning of unspecified but imminent danger.

The notification was an Amber Alert.

Like everyone in the Bay Area and across the country, Jake had received more than a few of them in the last few years. He had even been involved in the process a couple of times in the course of his job. But this one was very different.

He scanned the message, part of him knowing what it would say before he had time to absorb the details.

A missing child. Molly Donaldson, thirteen years old.

The suspect was male, Caucasian, forty-one years of age. Considered armed and dangerous.

The suspect's name was Jake Ellis.

2

Fifty-eight minutes before

'You know,' Molly said to her mother, 'they've carried out studies that show some people are genetically predisposed to being night owls.'

'Predisposed,' her mom murmured as she slowed for the left turn off Market, waiting for a gap in traffic. 'Good word.'

'Uh-huh. So it's actually discriminatory for you to force me to get up at this time.'

'Life is discriminatory, Molly.' Rachel Donaldson raised an eyebrow at her daughter and took a sip of coffee from her reusable ceramic go-cup while she waited for a slow-moving bus to pass them, before hurriedly dropping it back into the cup holder as the driver waved for them to go ahead.

She waved thanks and made the turn.

'See?' Molly continued, eyeing the clock on the dash. 'Plenty of time. I told you.'

'We were lucky with the traffic.'

Molly rolled her eyes and looked out of her window. Bad enough that Mom acted like this every school day. Saturday mornings should be for sleeping in. But it was this class or nothing. Rachel worked late Tuesdays, which was the only other time available. Molly had offered to take the bus there herself.

She was thirteen, not a baby. But Rachel had given that suggestion a hard pass. 'Maybe when the evenings get lighter,' she had said, in an unconvinced tone of voice that suggested she meant when the evenings got lighter in the year 2028.

Molly heard her mom take a sharp breath, then felt her seat belt catch tight. She lunged forward as the brakes slammed on hard. Their bumper stopped six inches from the man who had stepped out into the road. He was wearing a stained gray hoodie and carrying a bundled-up sleeping bag under his arm. He glanced at the car with disinterested eyes and held up a dirty hand in acknowledgment as he continued on his way to the opposite sidewalk.

Rachel muttered a curse and, after asking if Molly was okay, pulled away again. They drove two more blocks and reached the turn onto Sullivan Street. She pulled to a stop behind a truck making a delivery in the narrow street.

'I can walk from here, you know.'

'Just be patient,' Rachel said. The tone of voice put that in the 'do as I say', not 'do as I do' category.

Something was on her mind about work. Molly could always tell. She had a Saturday morning meeting, which was why they were even earlier than usual.

The buzz of a phone notification cut across the sound of the Ariana Grande song on the radio. Molly felt an involuntary sinking feeling in her stomach as she reached for her phone. She hoped Kaitlyn Logan hadn't commented on another one of her Instagram posts, calling her a carrot-top or whatever. But then she saw that it was the screen of her mom's phone that had lit up.

'Check who that is for me?' Rachel asked, without looking down.

Molly put her own phone on the dashboard and picked up

her mother's. The caller ID said, *Jake*. Mom's new boyfriend. Only, he wasn't that new anymore.

'It's just Jake, want me to take it?'

She shook her head. 'I'll call him back.'

Molly heard the rev of a motorcycle engine from behind them and watched as the leather-clad biker slowed to pass them and the truck on her side of the window. Perhaps because she was looking out at him, the rider turned his head to look in the car as he passed by. He was going slowly enough for her to see her own distorted reflection in the blacked-out visor of his helmet.

She was only assuming it was a he, of course. In all that leather and the full-face mask, it could be somebody's grandma riding that bike. Nicole would have reprimanded her for that, for treating the male gender as the default. She would have called it unconsciously reinforcing gender stereotypes. Whatever. The person on the motorcycle turned *their* head back to the road as *they* squeezed past the hood of her mom's red Ford Escape. She noticed a custom decal on the back of the bike – flames and devils. Possibly not a grandma, but then who could say for sure?

She looked back at Rachel, who was sighing in exasperation as the overweight delivery guy made his leisurely way back to the driver's seat, giving her a half-hearted wave of acknowledgment without making eye contact. He got in and the truck pulled away.

'Finally,' Rachel muttered, following the delivery truck for another block before making a left into the parking lot.

The Elite Center was a one-story brick building with a couple of windows either side of the door, one of which seemed to be permanently shuttered, and a sign over the door that read 'Elite Gymnastics'. Molly thought the place looked like

6

a crack house, but it was much nicer on the inside. Appearances can be deceiving.

The lot was virtually empty, but Rachel made for the parking spot she habitually chose. Molly unclipped her seat belt and reached for the door release, ready to pop it open and go as soon as the car came to a stop. The caretaker opened the building at seven, and she didn't mind Molly hanging around inside until the start of class.

'You got your water bottle?' Rachel asked.

Molly didn't answer, because she was distracted by the sound of the motorcycle engine approaching again. The revving sounded angrier, more urgent, the engine working hard. She glanced out at the road and saw the bike emerge from the direction it had gone and turn sharply into the lot.

'Molly?'

Molly turned around as she watched the bike arc around the lot to Rachel's side of the car. He seemed to be slowing. Rachel turned away from her and watched as the biker approached her window.

'Oh shoot, I hope I don't have a tail light out ag—'

Molly wondered why she had stopped and then she saw the gun in the biker's right hand. Pointing straight at them.

'Molly—' Rachel said. She didn't have time to complete the sentence.

The driver's-side window disappeared, and Molly felt something wet spatter her face. It seemed like it took an eternity for the sound of the gunshot to catch up. The gloved hand redirected the gun, the biker leaning into the car to improve his angle. Molly saw the muzzle of the gun and flinched back as she saw a searing-white flash. She was falling backwards as she heard the sound of the second shot, this one duller than the first in her ears. Dimly, she realized that she was falling out of the door. It had opened as she flinched with her hand still on the handle.

She scrambled to her feet and moved to the rear of the car, keeping low. She screamed as another shot rang out and the window above her head shattered. She kept moving to the rear fender as she heard the engine rev again. Oh Jesus, her mom, was she ...? She forced herself to focus. The easiest way to corner her would be for him to get off the bike. She heard a curse, muffled by the helmet, and there was another shot. This one blew out the back window.

She glanced around frantically. About twenty feet away, there was a narrow alley between the Elite Center and the row of units that lined the street outside. She froze.

She couldn't risk it. But she couldn't risk staying put, either.

And then she heard the strident blare of a horn. A blue pickup truck had stopped on the street outside the parking lot. A big, bearded guy with a black-and-red Giants cap was staring out of his window in disbelief at the scene.

'Get away from there!' he was yelling. His voice was commanding, but his eyes looked terrified.

Molly didn't waste any more time looking.

She took off at a run for the alley, not looking back as she heard a gunshot. Then there was another, but she was already in the alley.

3

Forty-two minutes before

It always starts with chaos.

Later on, when a full picture of the situation emerges, things settle into a groove. Manpower and technology and tested strategies can be deployed to the greatest effect. Sometimes there's a happy ending, sometimes not. But no matter what, the first hour of an abduction case is a whirlwind. Everything can go right, or everything can go wrong as those first few precious minutes tick away.

Special Agent Catherine Lark was reading through her monthly reports in a coffee shop on Van Ness Avenue when her phone rang. It was her SAC, Anthony Finn. She flipped over the page she had been reading and scratched down brief notes on the back as she listened to Finn's voice on the other end. He needed her to go immediately to the scene of a double shooting. The clock had already started ticking. SFPD were on the scene and had requested FBI assistance. They had two gunshot victims and a missing child.

She looked up the address on her tablet as her boss was speaking. 'I'm close, I'll be there in five minutes.'

She abandoned her espresso on the table, directing a rueful raise of the eyebrows at the barista as she made for the door. It wasn't the first time she had had to leave breakfast in a hurry, which was why she had gotten into the habit of paying in advance everywhere she went, on duty or off.

Weekend morning traffic was quiet. Finn had told her one male was dead at the scene and a female victim was en route to the hospital. That would most likely be Zuckerberg General, named after the Facebook guy when he kicked in seventy-five million dollars for the building.

As Lark reached the scene on Sullivan Street, she saw the flashing lights of the two San Francisco Police Department patrol cars on the scene. They were parked outside a low-rise brick building. Some kind of community center.

She saw a blue pickup on the street outside the parking lot, the large-built male driver draped over the steering wheel, freshly shed blood misting the inside of the windshield. The lot was almost empty, just four vehicles aside from the pair of police vehicles. Three of them, two sedans and a silver SUV, were tucked neatly into the spots nearest the door of the center. The other, a red Ford Escape, had come to a stop askew, as though the driver had swung around to reverse into one of the open spaces, and then gotten distracted.

Lark knew exactly what had distracted the driver. She parked on the street and got out. The officer standing at the edge of the taped-off perimeter around the lot waited for her to show her ID before he stood aside.

'Special Agent Lark, FBI,' she said, looking beyond the cop at the red Escape. 'We have a missing kid?'

He nodded and turned to yell at the group of officers by the car.

'Greg!'

One of the officers turned at the shout. He was black, in his early thirties, tall and slim. He jogged over to the perimeter.

'Feds,' the first cop said by way of introduction. There was none of the animosity she occasionally encountered from rank-and-file cops, just matter-of-fact.

The second cop raised a finger to his temple in acknowledgment. 'Officer Wilkins, good morning, Agent.'

'Catherine Lark,' she said, looking beyond Wilkins at the car. 'You were first on the scene?'

He shook his head. 'Davis and McCormack got here at oh seven forty, I was a couple of minutes later.'

'Nine-one-one call was seven thirty-six, that's a pretty good response.'

'My partner and I were pretty close by. How's the other vic?'

'Still breathing, last I heard,' Lark said. 'May I?' She gestured at the tape.

Wilkins lifted it so she could duck under. He kept talking as they approached the car. The open passenger side door was closest as they approached. The rear window on this side was blown out.

'The lady was in a bad way, Davis and McCormack thought she was DOA as well at first. If they hadn't been looking after her, they would have seen it first.'

The driver's window was blown out as well, crystals of glass scattered over the dark gray upholstery of the front seats. There was a lot of blood, most of it in the driver's seat and headrest, but Lark could see spatter on the felt of the ceiling and all the way across to the passenger side window. The blood distribution on the window was more concentrated toward the edges. Something had been blocking the path of the spray. Something, or someone.

'Seen what?' Lark said as she drew level with the car. And then she saw it, too. There was a pink canvas backpack lying on one of the back seats. It was small, with some kind of cartoon character on the front. The bag of a teenage girl, not a thirty-nine-year-old woman like the victim.

'Yeah, the backpack,' Wilkins said as he watched her eyeing it.

'Victim's name was Rachel Donaldson, right?' Lark said, realizing she was using past tense prematurely. 'Who's missing? Daughter?'

Wilkins nodded. 'A teen girl's clothing and a pair of sneakers in the bag, size four. We checked and the victim has a thirteen-year-old kid, name of Molly.'

'Father?'

'Deceased.'

That at least eliminated the most likely suspect.

Lark glanced at the blood in the front seat, not even dry yet, and reflected that it was amazing how quickly you could start to gather information these days.

'Boyfriend?'

'We're looking into that.'

Lark leaned in the window, being careful not to touch any of the fragmented glass still in the frame. There was a leather purse in the driver's footwell. A mugger would have taken the purse. Clearly the motive wasn't carjacking, because the car was still here.

'So this may or may not have been a targeted attack, and either way, we have a child abduction.'

'Agent Lark!'

She looked up at the sound of her name and saw the first cop approaching her, holding a cell phone.

'We got a suspect.'

4

Six minutes before

Sometimes it's the little things.

The hairline crack in the ceiling plaster that turns out to be major structural damage. The snapped retort that's the harbinger of the end of a marriage. The mole that will develop into a melanoma in a few short weeks. In this case, it was a coffee ring. Or, more precisely, the absence of a coffee ring.

Jake's laptop was a basic Hewlett Packard workhorse. Nothing fancy, but good enough. He had bought it from Amazon three years ago, and it had served him well in that time. It had a very slight crack in the top-right corner of the screen, and the bottom-left control key stuck from time to time. There was a sticker on the middle of the back of the screen, covering the HP logo. The sticker showed Elmo from Sesame Street inside a crossed-out red circle, like the Ghostbusters logo. An inside joke with the guys, after he had busted an overly aggressive Elmo impersonator who had been harassing tourists in Union Square last year. He had noticed that a lot of people had stickers on their laptops. Some people did it to personalize their device, he supposed. He mainly did it because someone else at his local Starbucks had the exact same model laptop, and they had almost been mixed up, once.

He didn't know what made him look at the Elmo sticker at that moment, but he knew at once that something wasn't quite right.

The edge of a coffee ring, about a quarter of the full circle, had been visible on the edge of the sticker for almost as long as the sticker itself had been there. He could have switched the sticker out for a fresh one, of course, but he liked the crossed-out Elmo, and the coffee stain made it extra-personalized.

Over the months, the stain had faded to a light tan, but it would never disappear. It was dyed into the fibers of the paper.

And yet, somehow, the coffee ring had disappeared.

He opened the laptop and examined it. The little crack in the top-right corner of the screen was still there. Then he tried tapping the control key. It didn't stick any more.

He scratched the morning stubble on his cheek while he thought about the conundrum. He logged in and opened a browser window.

Everything looked normal at first. His bookmarks were there. He was still logged into Amazon and his Google account. His email inbox looked the same as it had yesterday. His browsing history contained all the websites he'd visited recently.

Only, not quite. Where was the site he had visited last night, the rare vinyl place? It didn't show up on his history. Neither did his Google search for the nearest place that would sell a turntable.

He looked back in his emails. There was the purchase confirmation for the record: an old R.E.M. single, signed by Michael Stipe and Peter Buck. For Rachel's birthday in a couple of weeks.

So why was that search missing from the history? The most recent page visited before this morning was an op-ed in the *Chronicle*. It was about the city's spiraling homelessness problem. He remembered reading it yesterday lunchtime, before the start of his shift. His browser history only went up to around 2 p.m. yesterday.

A glitch, perhaps.

But he was immediately thinking back to a case he had assisted on last year involving a small-time cybercriminal. The perp had hacked his victims' devices when they thought they were logged into public Wi-Fi and had been able to access their online banking. This wasn't quite the same, though. Now that he was really looking, the laptop itself felt slightly different. The control key might have loosened of its own accord, he supposed. But the machine just felt a little newer, a little less-used. And, of course, there was the missing coffee ring.

This wasn't his laptop. But it was in his apartment.

He closed the browser window and checked his emails again. All as he remembered. That didn't mean anything, though, since emails synced across devices.

Wait – the emails weren't quite as he remembered.

The draft folder had a number one in brackets next to it. He couldn't remember saving a draft.

He opened it.

The subject line was: *I'm sorry*.

The intended recipient was his girlfriend, Rachel. The sender was his own email address.

It started: *I had no choice. I had to kill you and Molly.*

That was when the banging on the door started.

5

Two minutes before

The San Francisco field office of the Federal Bureau of Investigation was housed on the thirteenth floor of the Phillip Burton Federal Building at 450 Golden Gate Avenue. There was a beautiful view of the city from that height. At least, there was a beautiful view on days unlike today, when the view was obscured by low cloud. On days like today, it was like being inside a frosted glass jar.

Lark had a morning ritual when she was on duty. She would arrive early enough to grab a cup of coffee from Peet's, then take the stairs, not the elevator, for a burst of cardiovascular exercise. Along with the caffeine, it got her physically and mentally ready for whatever the day ahead would bring. When she got to the thirteenth floor, she would take a minute to look out of the window, either at the view or the silhouettes of the buildings in the gray, and sip her coffee, organizing her thoughts.

There was no time for the ritual this morning. She rode the elevator up, no coffee. The office was filling up fast, a well-rehearsed operation springing to life.

Special Agent Kelly Paxon met her at the elevator. She was thirty, a diminutive five feet one, with strawberry-blond hair and glasses with thin, dark red frames. She had transferred in from the Chicago field office at the end of last year, and Lark was already wondering what she had done without her before.

'SFPD are at Ellis's apartment; he's not there. Finn wants the Amber Alert out now,' Paxon said.

Lark gave a resigned nod. Her instinct would have been to wait just a little longer, but she understood why her superior didn't want to be seen to have hesitated if this went bad.

'So who is this guy?' she asked. 'He's a cop?' An eyewitness had called in shortly after the shooting with a description that had quickly led to one likely suspect.

Paxon was carrying a neat stack of printouts. She nodded without consulting the papers. 'Officer Jake Ellis. SFPD for the last fifteen years.'

'What's his record like?'

'Unremarkable. Until last year – he was involved in some kind of beef during a traffic stop. There was a police brutality claim, he was suspended; eventually it was settled.'

'Okay, we're looking out for his vehicle, and SFPD are at his apartment. Doubtful he'll go back there.'

Lark's phone rang before she could ask anything else. It was Grier at the authentication center, confirming the details for the alert.

There were strict criteria for authorizing an Amber Alert, but there was no question that this case checked all the boxes: first of all, the subject of the abduction was under eighteen years old. Second, the child was certainly at serious risk, given the perpetrator had already shot her mother and one other person. Lastly, they had an identified suspect, along with his vehicular details.

Because she had Paxon right in front of her with Ellis's file in her hands, Lark read the details out while holding eye contact with her. 'Caucasian male, forty-one, Jake Ellis.' She spelled both names, and then read out the address and the license plate of

17

his personal vehicle, a 2015 Subaru. Paxon nodded and Grier confirmed on his end. She went through the same with the kid's details.

'Good to go?' Grier asked.

She lifted the phone from her ear for a second to take a note of the time: *8.27.*

'Okay, do it,' Lark said.

She hung up and folded her arms. She looked over at the window, seeing the silhouettes of the high-rise buildings through the fog. She imagined the message spreading between the buildings. Surging through the main streets and the alleyways, like a flood.

She knew the Amber Alert was something of a gamble: it would get the word out, in a way that couldn't have been imagined even ten years ago. But it would tip off the target that they were on his trail.

Paxon looked nervous too. She let out a sigh and took her phone out of her pocket.

'Okay everybody,' Lark said, raising her voice to take in the rest of the office. 'The Amber is going live now, so be ready for the rush.'

No sooner had she finished the sentence than it began.

The first notification was a sharp tone from the phone lying on the desk of Rick Telfer, the silver-haired veteran agent working two desks down from where they were standing. Then Paxon's phone lit up. Then Lark's. As she looked down at her screen, more and more phones sounded. All with the same piercing sound effect. The same message appearing on the screen of every phone in the office.

And not just in the office.

AMBER ALERT: San Francisco,CA
CHILD:13 Cauc F 5'0 110 Donaldson, Molly
1SUSP:41 Cauc M 5'10 185 Ellis, Jake
VEH: LtBlu 4drSubaru
Suspect armed, do not approach
415-553-0123

6

At a stroke, the alert went out to every media, law enforcement and partner agency contact on the database via email and text message. It was automatically formatted and posted to the major social media channels. Within the hour, the pertinent details would be broadcast over local radio and television. The description of Molly Donaldson and her abductor would appear on news websites around the same time, and on the front pages of the *Chronicle* and the *Examiner* tomorrow morning.

But the message delivery to phones would beat all of these other means of communication. In fact, it would render most of them redundant.

The Amber Alert used the Integrated Public Alert and Warning System, or IPAWS for short. Within thirty seconds of the button click in the investigation center, the details of the suspected abduction of Molly Donaldson flashed up on the screens of just under four million smartphones across the Bay Area. Unless your phone was turned off, or you were out of range of any cell tower, or you were one of the statistically insignificant number of people who had bothered to opt out of the program, you got the message along with everyone else at 8.27 a.m., Pacific Daylight Time.

The Department of Justice's statistics on child abductions made a compelling case for the importance of getting the word out. The vast majority of children reported missing in the United States were eventually discovered safe and well. However, in the small minority of cases where the child was killed, the murder usually took place within the first three hours of the abduction. Time was of the essence. Accurate information was vital. And four million pairs of eyeballs could make the difference between life and death.

The alert flashed up on the phones of joggers braving the morning chill in Golden Gate Park. It interrupted coffee shop loiterers scrolling idly through their Facebook feeds. It appeared silently on the nightstands of those who were enjoying a lazy morning in bed, waiting to be the first thing to greet them when they opened their eyes.

Chrissie Chung would rather have been doing any of these things at 8.27 a.m. on a Saturday, rather than being where she was.

Chrissie was working on a short-term contract for a company that styled itself as an 'agile marketing and communications agency', based in a high-rise office building at the southern end of Montgomery Street. She had only just gotten to her desk. Technically, her shift started at eight, but Marc, her boss, was almost never in the office on a Saturday morning.

As soon as she got logged in, she took a quick look at the local crime news. Two people had been shot in an attempted carjacking in the Mission District this morning. It had to be pretty recent, as the article wasn't much more than a stub. Other than that, it seemed to be all quiet on the Western Front. She closed the window and opened her case log. There was a list of new cases awaiting her, but before she scanned them to organize by order of urgency, she did what she usually did: she checked the progress on the new episode of the show.

Sean, her producer, had created a slightly fussy project-plan template for each episode of *Untraceable*, the podcast they recorded and published weekly. It had different columns for all of the various elements: credits, interview snippets, narration, incidental music, advertising. Though there was precious little of that, of course.

Everything looked shipshape. Monday's episode, a follow-up show to a case they had covered in season two, was pretty much in the can. Just then, Chrissie's phone emitted an unusual high-pitched tone. She reached for it, wondering who the message was from.

Only it wasn't a text message. As she was picking it up, she heard other phones around her go off with similar tones and knew at once what it was.

She took the details in and put the phone back down. She opened Google and started typing in the names from the Amber Alert. Her fingers flew over the keys. Donaldson. Ellis.

The *Chronicle*'s page came up first. The article from earlier about the shooting had been updated. It didn't look like a carjacking any more. It was one dead, one injured, and the abduction of a minor. It hadn't yet filtered through to the other news sites, or even the San Francisco Police Department's website, but already she could see more information here. She picked up her phone again as she was scanning the details, thumbed into recent calls without taking her eyes from the news story. She hunched down below the top of her cubicle so no one would see that she was making a personal call.

She finished reading the article as the phone started ringing. Still very sparse information, so far. But then this case was less than an hour old. Oven-fresh. Soon there would be much more information. Photographs. Sightings.

'Hello?' She could tell from Sean's bleary voice that she had woken him up, and he was not pleased about it.

'Sean, did you see the alert?'

'What... what are you talking about? What time is it?'

'How the fuck much did you drink last night? Look at your damn phone.'

'I'm on my phone.'

She lowered her voice and enunciated slowly. 'Take the phone away from your ear, and look at the screen.'

There was a pause. 'Oh.'

'Oh. This is it. I think this is related to the shooting in Mission. Can you get down there now?'

'Sure, just let me—'

'No, go now. Go in your jammies, if you have to. This is exactly what we've been looking for.'

She scribbled a couple of notes and then looked down at the pile of documents that her boss believed would take her the whole shift to process. In reality, she could have it done in ten minutes, leaving the rest of the morning clear.

She went back to the *Chronicle* site. It had been updated with photographs already. The pic of the girl was pretty much as expected: smiling, in a Warriors baseball hat and a light-blue T-shirt beneath a deep-blue sky. Disneyland – Sleeping Beauty's castle was in the background. What was more interesting was the picture of the suspect in her abduction. He was white, with sandy-colored hair and a mustache, and a serious look around his eyes, but none of that registered at first.

What was unusual was that he was wearing a uniform. A San Francisco Police Department uniform.

7

'What is it?'

Jake looked up from the phone. 'I have to—' He stopped in the middle of the sentence.

Molly was still looking back at him with that blank, shell-shocked stare, waiting for him to do something. There was a vertical line of dried blood on her cheek, like a crimson tear.

A hail of competing imperatives assailed him. Keep calm. Focus on the most important actions. He had to get away. He could leave Molly here. The guys responding would help her.

But could he be certain of that? Right at this moment, the only thing he could be sure of was that someone had planned all of this, right down to a fake confession on his laptop. A fake confession that had referred to Molly's death. That meant both of them were in imminent danger.

He made a decision: stop thinking, start doing.

'We have to get out of here, right now.'

He half-expected Molly to argue, to refuse to leave the false safety of the apartment, but she just nodded. How long did he have? Minutes at most. Maybe seconds.

His badge and department-issue SIG Sauer were lying on the coffee table. He picked up the gun and went to the window, in time to see a patrol car rounding the corner at speed, headed in this direction. Did they know he was here? If so, why had the Amber Alert been triggered already?

Jake slipped his bare feet into his sneakers and grabbed his jacket from the hook at the side of the door. He opened it a crack. There was no one out on the landing. He stepped out and heard the main door downstairs opening. They couldn't leave from the ground floor, which narrowed the options. Molly followed him out of the door, looking at him, not speaking. He glanced over the rail.

Multiple officers, ascending the stairs with purpose. No way out in that direction. He pointed in the direction of the other flight of stairs, the one going up, and the two of them hurried up. By the time he had reached the next landing, he remembered he had left the laptop on the couch. The one with the draft confession and God knew what else on it. Not that it mattered. Whoever had set this up had obviously worked very hard at putting Jake in the frame. Switching his computer would be the tip of the iceberg.

'Keep close to the wall,' he whispered as they climbed to the next level. He tried to focus on the now, but he couldn't stop thinking about Rachel. Rachel, dead. Who had done this? Why?

They were halfway between floors four and five when he heard the sharp knock on his own apartment door, followed by his name being spoken by a gruff male voice.

'Police. Open up and keep your hands in full view.'

He had given that warning so many times. He knew exactly how the cop downstairs was feeling, that queasy knot in your stomach that never goes away, no matter how many suspects' doors you knock on. Because every time is different.

They reached the next landing and kept going up. He heard the voice call his name, quieter this time, which meant that the cop had tried the unlocked door and was now inside his apartment. His one-bedroom apartment, which would take all of five seconds to search.

Top floor. Two doors flanking the top of the stairs. Jake's heart sank as he saw one of them open. An elderly man peered out over his horn-rimmed glasses. He was short, with gray hair and a pale complexion. Jake had exchanged hellos with the man a couple of times in passing. He didn't know his name, and he guessed it was too late to wish he'd made more of an effort with the neighbors now.

He glanced in the direction of the stairwell, and then at Jake. 'Do me a favor, pal?' Jake said. 'You never saw me, okay?'

The old guy looked at Jake, then looked at Molly, then looked at the gun in Jake's hand. His pallor changed from pale to white. He nodded, too quickly, and hurriedly shut the door.

'Why are we running?' Molly asked as Jake tried the roof door. He heard footsteps on the stairs again. He hoped they would take the time to check each apartment, but that might not take long.

As usual, the door was locked. As usual, the key was under the pot plant in the corner of the landing.

The cops had reached the floor below now. They had seconds. He put the key in the lock and gritted his teeth when it stuck. He remembered there was a knack, pushed his full weight on the door and tried again. The key turned and the door swung inward. He stood aside to let Molly go through first.

He was closing the door behind him when he heard a yell. Couldn't be helped. They would have worked out where he had gone no matter what. He just hoped they wouldn't shoot through the door. He turned the key in the lock and left it in the keyhole to buy them a little more time.

He scaled the short flight of concrete steps and found Molly waiting on the flat roof. The buildings were a hundred years old, close together. The gap between this roof and the roof of the next building was less than five feet. They could cross that and jump an even narrower gap to the roof of the President Hotel.

He looked back at Molly. She was standing close behind him, already sizing up the jump. She had stopped shaking, didn't seem to be as stunned as she had been in the apartment. There's a lot to be said for having a physical task to take your mind off something.

He pointed across the nearest building to the roof of the President. 'There's a fire escape on the other side of that building,' Jake said. 'We can get down to the street. Do you think you can...?'

Rather than answering, Molly turned, took off from a standing start, crossed the twenty feet to the parapet, and launched off her left foot, sailing across the gap and landing on the next roof. She made it look easy.

Jake backed up a couple of steps and ran toward the edge.

8

Paxon drove as Lark talked over the phone to Sergeant Fleck of the San Francisco Police Department. He was one of the officers setting up the perimeter outside Ellis's building and was relaying updates as they came through from the team inside.

Somebody had fucked up. The message relayed from SFPD was that officers had already called at the suspect's apartment, and he wasn't home. A couple of minutes after the Amber Alert, the story changed. Officers had arrived at the apartment shortly after the alert, to discover they had missed Ellis by seconds.

Paxon rounded the corner and Lark saw an officer ushering pedestrians back with one hand as he strung a length of crime-scene tape across the road with another. There were two black-and-whites parked across the street, a third one arriving from the opposite direction.

She could see a uniformed officer standing opposite the front entrance. Gun in his right hand, phone held to his ear in his left. She watched his lips move in sync with the voice in her ear.

'Stand by, we have someone coming out.'

'It's okay, I'm here,' Lark said, hanging up.

Paxon pulled to a stop ten feet from the sergeant.

'Special Agent Lark?' he asked as she got out.

She didn't waste time acknowledging. 'How many people do you have in there?'

'Four men, more on the way.'

She had been hearing approaching sirens since she had gotten out of the car, and more were joining in all the time. Another officer emerged from the front entrance, approaching them quickly. Young, early twenties. Black hair and blue eyes. He had his gun in his hand.

The cop shook his head. 'Looks like he was there very recently, Sarge. Could be somebody tipped him off.'

'You could say that, Officer,' Lark replied, thinking about how exactly that had happened.

Fleck's radio crackled and he pushed the button, telling the sender to go ahead.

'We got the Subaru.'

Lark felt a surge of hope. Did that mean they were in pursuit of Ellis, or that they had actually managed to pull him over?

'You stopped it?'

'Negative, it's parked over on Eddy Street.'

The sergeant exchanged a frustrated glance with Lark. 'All right, stay in position, maybe he'll come back for it.'

'Sarge!'

The three of them looked up and back toward the apartment building, where a second officer was waving for their attention.

'We got something.'

Lark told Paxon to go and check out the Subaru, while she followed the sergeant through the main entrance door and climbed the stairs. It was an old building. The kind of place that would have been cheap to rent a decade or two ago. From the tired look of the communal areas, and the modest cars lining the street outside, she was guessing most of the current residents had been here longer than that, and were only still around thanks to rent control. They passed Ellis's door, which was open with one of the uniforms guarding it. Sergeant Fleck kept going, leading them up another two flights. Lark worked out the story as soon as she saw the open door to the roof, a couple of large bullet holes punched around the lock.

There was a man on the landing, talking to another cop. He looked consternated. He was in his seventies, if not older. He had wispy gray hair that was swept back and hung down beyond his ears; thick-rimmed glasses with thick lenses that made it hard to tell what color his eyes were.

Lark pointed at the door, addressing the cop who had led them up the stairs.

'You got someone up there?'

Before the cop could answer, a pair of boots appeared on the stairs, followed by the rest of another cop. 'He's not on the roof, as far as I can see,' he said.

'As far as you can see?' Lark repeated. She didn't expect Ellis would have hung around.

Sergeant Fleck cut in before he could answer. 'Get back out there and make sure, Donnie.'

'But—' Officer Donnie began, before thinking better of it. He disappeared back up the stairs.

Lark turned to the old guy now. 'You saw him go up there?'

He took his time answering, shaking his head slowly. 'He told me to forget I'd seen him.'

'How long ago was this?'

He glanced at the cop as though he might have the answer. 'A few minutes? Just before you people got here.'

'Did he have anybody with him?'

'Yes, the girl. The one you're looking for.'

'The one we're looking for?'

The old guy held out his palm toward Lark, showing her his iPhone, the Amber Alert visible on the screen. The same message that had no doubt motivated Jake Ellis's sudden exit from his apartment.

'Can you describe her?'

The old guy took a moment to carefully tuck the phone into his pants pocket, then held his hand at shoulder height. 'Yay high. Red hair. There was blood on her.'

'Blood?'

He nodded.

'Was she hurt? Could you tell if it was her own blood, or someone else's?'

'Well, I don't know.'

'Did she seem upset?'

'I guess...'

'Thank you, Mr...'

'Rosenberg. Ronald Rosenberg.'

'Mr Rosenberg. Were you on speaking terms with Ellis?'

He paused again. 'I didn't really know him too well. You know how it is.'

Lark could still hear more sirens converging on their position. The open roof door made it sound like they were coming from above. By the time she got back downstairs, she knew the street would look like the parking lot at police headquarters. She took out her phone and called Paxon, turning away from Rosenberg.

'Where are you?'

'We're at Ellis's car. Parked and locked. No sign of him out here.'

Lark resisted the urge to curse out loud. 'All right, keep your eyes peeled. He has the kid with him, she's covered in blood. Somebody will see them.' She turned to Sergeant Fleck. 'He can't have gotten far.'

He nodded. 'We're locking the whole area down. In ten minutes, every cop in the city is going to be down here.'

Lark bit her bottom lip. Ten minutes. A lot can happen in ten minutes.

'Somebody will see them,' she said again. Fleck nodded again. She wished she felt as confident as she sounded.

9

Jake didn't recognize the young officer covering the mouth of the alley three blocks from his building. He looked nervous. Kept glancing around this way and that. Up and down the street and the park across the road. The officer's right hand kept wandering to his holster and patting it for reassurance. He performed the check a couple of times a minute. Fresh out of the academy, Jake guessed.

His level of experience didn't matter all that much, though. All that really mattered was that there was an alert man guarding the only way out. A patrol car flashed by on the street. Other sirens drifted in from farther away, discordant and disparate, like an orchestra tuning up. Jake knew the drill all too well. Every minute that passed meant more boots on the ground. They would nail down a perimeter, and they would expand it block by block, and they would kick over every rock until they found him. It was only a matter of time.

He hunched down behind the short wall they had taken cover behind. Molly turned back to him, looking like she wanted to speak, but not daring to. She looked out of breath. They had covered a lot of ground in a short space of time, but the run might end here.

If only he could think of a way to get the rookie to move, there was a clear run across the park. If they could make it to

Marcus's place over on Washington Street, there was a possibility that they could get out of here on wheels rather than on foot.

No time left for hesitation. If he didn't recognize the rookie, then that meant the reverse was also true. He reached inside the pocket of his jacket to check that his badge was there. Force of habit, he had picked it up when he left the apartment.

'Stay down,' he whispered.

He stood up. He took his badge out and positioned his thumb over the picture on the identification. Then he started running in the rookie's direction.

'Hey!' he yelled, even though the rookie was already turning around at the sound of the footsteps. He was banking on the fact that this had all happened too fast for them to circulate his picture. The rookie was reaching for his gun again, hesitating as he saw the running man was waving a badge.

'Ed McCrossan, Bayview Station,' Jake said, lowering the badge before he got too close. Odds were he had to be with one of the Metro Divisions. Hopefully he wouldn't be too familiar with the rosters in Golden Gate. 'What's your name, Officer?'

'F-Friedrich,' the rookie said, his startled eyes moving from Jake's face to the position on his jacket where he had replaced his badge.

'What the hell are you doing over here, Friedrich?' Jake yelled. 'What's your division?'

'Northern, sir, I'm covering the—'

'Who's your sergeant?'

'My, I mean...'

'I said, who's your goddamn sergeant?'

'Sergeant Fleck, sir.'

'Jim Fleck. That asshole is still around?' He groaned and adopted a kinder tone. 'Look, this is a massive fuck-up. The suspect was seen heading south on Leavenworth. I need you over there, okay?'

Friedrich's eyes followed the direction he was pointing, and Jake knew it was working. 'But Sergeant Fleck...'

'I'll talk to Jimmy, it's my call. Don't worry about it, Friedrich.'

'Okay, sir.' Friedrich turned to go, and Jake was already sizing up the run across the street when the officer hesitated a second and looked back at Jake. Looked down at Jake's feet. Sneakers. No socks.

'Sir...'

Friedrich reached for his gun, but Jake already had his drawn and pointed square at the officer's chest.

'I'm sorry about this, kid,' he said. 'Give me your cuffs.'

Three minutes later, the engine of the old VW SUV started up with a cough. Jake hoped Marcus, the owner, was insured. Then again, he had advised him against leaving it unlocked. He told Molly to hunch down in the spacious passenger footwell. She slid down and brought her knees up in front, fitting snugly into the space as though it had been built for the purpose. There was a scratched pair of sunglasses on the dashboard. Jake slipped them on and pulled out of the lot behind the bar. He turned right onto Hyde, and had already passed two patrol cars before he reached the turn onto Bush Street. He didn't glance at them, and they continued on their way without looking at him.

Molly spoke in a whisper from the footwell. 'Couldn't we just have talked to the police?'

Jake shook his head. 'No.'

'Why not?'

'Right before you arrived, I found something on my computer. A confession, like I was the one who did this. Somebody planned this, and they planned for me to take the fall.' He was about to say that what he had seen suggested that both Rachel and Molly were supposed to die, but stopped himself. 'Until I know who and why, I can't risk it.'

He had glanced down at Molly as he said the last part, and when he looked up again, he saw a tall, thin man in a gray suit was crossing dead ahead, looking in the opposite direction. Jake slammed on the brakes and the SUV came to a stop, its hood a couple of feet from the man in the suit.

He had heard the engine at the last minute, had his hands up in a useless attempt to protect himself.

A mutual intake of breath, and then the man kept going, casting words to the effect of 'Look where you're going, jerk,' in his wake without looking back.

Jake pulled away again. He followed Bush until he reached the turn for 1st Street. He passed another three police cars. Sooner or later, one of the cops in those cars was going to take a closer look at him. He resisted the urge to exceed the speed limit, even though traffic was quiet.

Jake suddenly remembered something. 'You have your phone?'

'No,' Molly answered. 'I mean, yes. I have Mom's phone. Do you want me to call—'

'No, give me it.' He reached his hand down without looking.

She handed him the phone and he glanced down at the screen. The Amber Alert was there too, of course. It was every-where.

He wound down his window and was pulling back his arm ready to pitch it out when he felt Molly's fingers close around his wrist.

He glanced down at her.

'No, it's ...' Her voice cracked a little. 'It's Mom's.'

He relented and lowered his hand. He held the power button until it switched off. It was a Samsung, one of the models that still had a removable battery. He handed it back to her and told her to take the battery out.

They reached the ramp for the 80 after what felt like an eternity, merging into the other morning traffic bound for the Bay Bridge.

'Who did this?' Molly's voice came from the footwell.

Jake didn't look down this time. *Who did this?* That was the sixty-four-thousand-dollar question. A couple of hours before, three lives had been proceeding as normal. They had time to be concerned with coffee and gymnastics classes and birthday gifts. And now somebody had ended one of those lives and thrown two more into the abyss.

He glanced in the wing mirror and then ahead again. He hadn't seen any police vehicles in a few minutes. They had made it out. They were on their way.

The next question was, where were they going?

10

Three hours later, Chrissie Chung was at her producer's apartment, listening to her own voice. Her eyes were closed, concentrating on every word:

> *'This morning, a woman named Rachel Donaldson and her thirteen-year-old daughter Molly woke up, got ready and left their home in Bayview, thinking this was going to be an ordinary Saturday. Somebody else knew better.'*

It was a decent opening. The rest of the episode was in good shape too, especially considering it had been less than four hours since her phone had buzzed with that Amber Alert. Chrissie slipped the headphones down around her neck and opened her eyes. She turned to look over at Sean. He was crouched over his laptop in the opposite corner of his cramped living room, making an adjustment to the new version of their cover graphic. He was tall and very skinny, though he tried to hide it under the baggiest band T-shirts known to man. Today he was wearing a black KISS T-shirt with the band's grease-painted faces leering out across his back, tour dates superimposed on top.

'Sean.'

He turned around and swept a wave of light brown hair out of his eyes. 'All okay?' he asked.

Chrissie made a face. 'I sound a little tinny, like I'm recording inside a can of beans.'

Sean considered this, biting his thumb gently in the way he habitually did when thinking about a technical issue. 'The Samson is on its way out. I was going to replace it before next time, but...' He shrugged. He hadn't expected next time to be today. 'You want to go again?'

'Nah. It's fine. We can stop by Best Buy later and pick up a new mic for the next show.' Sean frowned, but she cut him off as he was opening his mouth to suggest something else. 'This one is different – fast is more important than polished. People will get it.'

He looked unconvinced.

'Really,' she said. 'It'll... add to the immediacy. Trust me.'

He rolled his eyes, but she could tell he was amused. 'If you're sure, then we're pretty much good to go.'

'Excellent, do it.'

'You are sure about this?'

'Yep. I told you, it's not that bad.'

'Not the sound. I mean... this. It's different.'

'That's the point. Different is good.'

'What if people don't like it? What if the *cops* don't like it? What if—'

'What if everybody loves it?'

He stared back at her, still not convinced. He'd go along with her anyway. He always did.

'Come on, Sean. Publish and be damned.'

A final sigh and a raise of the eyebrows. 'You're the boss.'

He clicked the button to upload.

Untraceable

Excerpt from Untraceable – Season 4, Episode 1, April 18

Untraceable is brought to you by QuickFix Business Cards. Direct to your door with next-day delivery. Choose from hundreds of beautiful designs or create your own. Go to quickfixcards.com and use the code Untraceable10 for a ten percent discount.

Welcome to *Untraceable*, the podcast that goes deep into the most fascinating missing persons cases. I'm Chrissie Chung, and every season, we'll be taking you through a missing persons case from disappearance, to resolution.

This time around, we're going to be doing something a little bit different, and I hope you guys will stick with us, because I think this has the potential to be a really interesting case. This story isn't like any we've covered before. You're not going to be able to go and read up on it in a true crime book. There's no Wikipedia page – at least, not yet. Chances are, you know about as much about the case as we do at this point. And if you're one of our listeners in the Bay Area, you may even know more than us about it already.

Because the case we're focusing on this season is... well, it's very recent. Current, to be exact. As in, it's going on right now.

This morning, a woman named Rachel Donaldson and her thirteen-year-old daughter Molly woke up, got ready and left their home in Bayview, thinking this was going to be an ordinary Saturday. Somebody else knew better...

II

'What the hell happened?'

Special Agent in Charge Anthony Finn didn't wait for Lark to close the door of his office before he spoke. Finn was standing behind his desk, in front of the window looking out on Golden Gate Avenue. The thick fog from earlier had mostly lifted but still lingered around the tops of the tallest buildings, fading them into the gray sky. Finn was tall, in his mid-fifties, with hair that was still suspiciously jet-black. He wore a two-button dark gray suit over a striped shirt.

'Somebody screwed up,' Lark said simply as she closed the door behind her.

Finn blinked at her abruptness. She almost thought he was about to smirk. Instead, he cleared his throat and sat down behind his desk.

'Somebody screwed up,' he repeated. 'I would say so.'

'We were informed that SFPD had already checked out his address. Turned out they were just en route. So it looks like the first person to react to the Amber Alert was our suspect. He escaped across the roof. SFPD's blaming us, we're blaming them. Standard.'

Finn considered for a moment. 'The suspect is a police officer. Could this have been deliberate?'

Lark had given the matter some thought over the past couple

of hours. She shook her head. 'Possible, but I don't think so. We have witnesses. And our people found what appears to be an email confession on his laptop. From what I've picked up so far, he's not one of the most popular guys on the force, even before this. They want him nailed as bad as anyone.'

'How do we fix this?'

Lark sighed and composed her thoughts before answering. It had been a long morning. It wasn't unusual for things to go wrong in the initial confusion of an active manhunt, but this was a blunder that would take a great deal of explaining if the full details got out.

After interviewing witnesses from Ellis's apartment building, they had been able to establish that the SFPD had missed their opportunity to capture Jake Ellis and rescue his prisoner by a matter of seconds. He had made his escape across the roof, jumped the gap to a neighboring building, and slipped through the cordon while it was still being established.

Allowing for the communication screw-up that led to the Amber Alert being triggered prematurely, the task force and the SFPD had operated well from that point, under the circumstances. The perimeter had gone up quickly, and, as it turned out, in time to enclose their target. It hadn't been good enough. Ellis had gotten the jump on a twenty-two-year-old rookie named Daniel Friedrich, taking his gun and leaving him bound with his own cuffs. The kid was lucky to be alive.

Despite everything, Lark couldn't help but feel a twinge of sympathy. Getting that close to a suspect and letting him slip through your fingers? A tough thing for a first-year cop to get past. Maybe impossible. These days, he wouldn't be openly punished for it by his peers, beyond some dirty looks and some kidding-on-the-square jibes, but it wasn't the type of bad-luck episode to be forgotten about.

'We're pursuing a number of lines of inquiry,' Lark said.

'Usual procedures in place, we have all hands on deck on the tip lines, we're chasing down known associates. We're lining up interviews with people who knew the victim, too.' Her tone was completely confident, like everything was under control.

Finn nodded, looking a little more reassured. 'Okay. Anything you need on this, you got it. If we don't find that kid soon…'

'I know, sir. We're on it.'

Lark closed the door behind her, avoiding the sidelong glances of the agents outside in the main office. Finn's unfinished sentence lingered in her ears. Because there were a lot of ways of completing that sentence. If they didn't find Molly Donaldson soon, they might not find her at all, or they'd find her dead. But she knew that wasn't the only thing on her superior's mind. If Ellis killed the girl, and it came out that the FBI and the police had between them blown an opportunity to apprehend the suspect before he had a chance to harm her, there would be hell to pay. And she had a strong suspicion Finn would prove to be the take-everyone-else-down-with-you type.

She took a moment to look out of the window as she gathered her thoughts. To the north, the buildings on the hill started to look hazy and indistinct the farther away they were. The Bay was invisible. Days like this, she believed San Francisco revealed its true self. It was like the city didn't fully exist all at once, and parts of it became real only when you approached them.

She crossed the teeming open-plan office, headed for the main conference room. Phones rang and were immediately answered. Keyboards clattered. There was nothing like the hum of activity when everyone in the place was focused on one live case. Despite herself, she relished the buzz.

It was obviously contagious. She heard the murmur of cross-cutting conversations as she opened the conference-room door. Varying in volume and tone, united in urgency. The chatter immediately died away as she appeared in the doorway.

There were five people in the room, arranged around the oval boardroom table. The primary team she had assembled to lead on this. Kelly Paxon was standing by the smartboard, adjusting something on the touchscreen. Agents Adrian Garcia and Mitch Valenti were standing by the window that overlooked the California Supreme Court building across the road, examining something on a tablet screen. La-Vonne Taylor was standing too, leaning over a pile of documents that had been methodically fanned out on the desk in a wide rainbow shape. Only Colette Osborne was seated. The youngest member of the team, she was tapping away at her laptop while holding a conversation on the cell phone she held in the crook of her neck.

Everyone looked up as Lark entered.

'How was Finn?' Garcia asked.

Lark offered a humorless smile. 'He impressed on me the importance of a quick resolution to this investigation.' Before anyone could ask for more details, she clapped her hands together. 'Okay, we're collating new tips as they come in, and we're looking for likely places for Ellis to go, people he might reach out to. We've got a watch on his credit cards and bank accounts. If he turns his phone on, we'll know where he is one second later. But we're not going to find him by waiting for something to drop into our laps. So let's just take a minute to lay out what we have so far. Kelly, you've got the background on Ellis?'

Paxon tapped on her phone. A second later, a picture of Jake Ellis flashed up on the big screen. It was a typical San Francisco Police Department profile pic: you've seen one, you've seen them all. That was bad, Lark knew. They would need to dig out some more candid shots of him in civilian clothing for the media. It was difficult to tell much of anything from this picture, other than he was white, had a mustache and was in decent shape.

'Officer Jake Lewellen Ellis,' Paxon continued. 'Forty-one years old, been with the San Francisco Police Department fifteen years. For the most part, his record doesn't raise any red flags, up until last year, when things got rough during an arrest and he found himself on a police brutality investigation. Suspended on full pay for a few weeks, no charges filed on investigation.'

'Let's find out what really happened,' Lark said. 'What about the victims?'

Valenti answered, not looking up from his tablet. 'The dead bystander is Steve Holdcroft. He was a cable engineer, looks like he just got in the way. The target was the woman, Rachel Donaldson. She and Ellis have been seeing each other for the last few months.'

'Any prior incidents in the relationship?'

He shook his head. 'No nine-one-one calls, not much of a build-up to this.'

Lark expected that would change when they spoke to friends and family. There's always a build-up. It doesn't always leave an official trail.

'Where's the kid's father?'

'Died in 2009. Suddenly.'

'Suddenly?'

'Natural causes. Heart attack.'

'Did any of our people speak to the eyewitness yet?' She recalled the name Officer Wilkins had given her at the scene. 'Da Costa, right?'

'Edward Da Costa,' Osborne said, looking up from her laptop. 'I sat in while SFPD questioned him. He lives close to the scene. He teaches at the City College. Environmental Horticulture or something. He was out for his morning walk and saw the two shootings. He ran in case he was next. He described a uniformed cop shooting Ms Donaldson, then Holdcroft, then dragging the daughter into a blue car. They had a look at cops matching the description, and it turned out one of the ones that fit was dating the victim.'

'All right, I'd like to speak to him too.' Lark crossed her arms and looked back at the face on the screen again. 'Last question. How the hell are we going to find this guy before it's too late?'

12

Chrissie had visited crime scenes many times before, but this was different.

The difference wasn't hard to explain. Those other ones had all been historic crime scenes, the place where a terrible act had been committed months or years or even decades before. The blood had long since been hosed away, the broken glass swept up. Usually there was no outward sign that the house or park or alley in question was any different from any other. The community center on Sullivan Street would be like that too, a year from now.

Not that you could see much of anything from this distance right now. Chrissie stood a little way down the street and watched as the red Ford Escape was hoisted onto the back of a flatbed truck. It was mostly covered in a protective tarp, so she couldn't see what kind of shape the car was in. Whether there were bullet holes or bloodstains. When the removal operation had finished, she could try her luck with the young-looking cop manning the barrier. In the meantime, there was someone she very much wanted to speak to.

She crossed over the street and walked to the building at the corner. She took her phone out to check the apartment number and the name of the man she wanted to talk to. She had been pleasantly surprised at the response to the new episode so far.

Sean had just texted her to say they had broken their first-hour record for downloads and streams, and that was matched by the chatter online. A listener had DMd the show's Twitter account with a very useful piece of information. He had seen one of his neighbors being interviewed by several police officers shortly after the shooting. The listener wondered if he was a suspect, but Chrissie knew he had to be the witness.

The building was more modern than its neighbors, with a parking garage below street level. She pushed the buzzer for Edward Da Costa's apartment, wondering if she would be able to get him on record. She took her phone out and hit record. If nothing else, she would be able to use a clip of him refusing to talk.

But there was no answer. She pushed the button again, holding it for longer this time. She glanced back along the street. The truck driver was still securing the car on the flatbed, attaching various clamps and chains. The cop at the perimeter was regarding the activity with disinterest.

She turned to try the buzzer one more time and heard quick footsteps approaching from behind her. She turned to see a woman in her thirties, blond hair pulled back in a ponytail. She was wearing a red coat. She looked upset, like she had been crying. Chrissie saw that she was looking at the notebook in her hand.

'We're not interested in saying anything,' the woman said before Chrissie could react to her approach.

She thought quickly. The woman had assumed she was a reporter. A trad one.

'Mrs Da Costa? I just wanted to—'

'No. We don't want to speak about it.'

'Is your husband home?'

She stopped at the bottom of the steps. 'If you don't move from my property, I'm going to call the police.'

'Well, this isn't actually—'

The woman moved up the steps and shoved her out of the way before using her key to open the door.

'Can I give you my number?' Chrissie asked. She held out a card toward the woman.

The woman ignored it as she pulled the door shut behind her. 'No comment.'

Chrissie sighed and stopped the recording. Kind of an over-reaction, but perhaps she hadn't been the first journalist to drop by. Maybe the last one had been really pushy or something. Perhaps she would be able to catch Edward Da Costa separately later. She could tell that any approach going through his wife would fail. She wrote 'Any info about shooting today' and the date on the back of the card and slid it under the door. One of their few sponsors had provided free business cards in lieu of actual money, so she had a couple thousand of them to use up.

She stepped back onto the street and started walking back toward the police perimeter. There was a guy sitting in a door-way, wrapped in a sleeping bag, cross-legged on top of a big sheet of damp cardboard.

'Good afternoon, ma'am.'

Had he been there when she came past? Chrissie supposed he had to have been, given how settled-in he looked. She had walked within a couple of feet of him without noticing.

She reached into her pocket for some change, dropped it into the paper cup beside him. She saw that behind him was a narrow flight of steps down to the basement level of one of the buildings. There was a door into the building and a small space where trash had collected. There were vents from the heating system blowing out steam. Perhaps that was why she hadn't seen him, maybe he had been warming himself at the vent.

'God bless you,' the man said.

She tapped on her phone to start the recording app again before she continued.

'Say, have you been here long?'

'Three years now. Ever since——'

'No, sorry, I meant as in right here,' she said, pointing down at the sidewalk. 'Did you see what happened this morning?'

He stopped, looking a little disappointed that she hadn't been asking for his life story. She felt a little guilty, made up her mind to give him a little more money in a minute.

'No, ma'am,' he said, looking suspiciously in the direction of the cop at the barrier, who had taken an interest in their conversation. 'I try not to go near that.'

'Near what?'

He glanced over at the cop and beckoned her in closer. She crouched and moved in. The poor guy reeked. She tried not to let the discomfort show on her face.

'The cops,' he whispered. 'They'll fucking kill you, man.'

'Oh,' she said, giving an understanding smile after a second. 'So you didn't see the shooting this morning.'

'That what it was?' He shrugged. 'I was down at St Anthony's this morning. Tuesday's a good day. Real good day.'

'Oh.' She guessed he was talking about a soup kitchen. 'This is Saturday, though.'

'It is?' He pondered this for a minute.

'Well, thanks anyway,' Chrissie said, and put a couple of dollars in his cup, earning another 'God bless you.' As she stood up, the man shot a suspicious glance at the cop again.

'Serious. Be careful.'

'I will be.' She smiled, humoring him.

The officer at the barrier watched her walking toward him. He wasn't quite as young as he had looked from a distance. Maybe in his early thirties. She could see his jaw tense as she approached.

49

'You'll have to go around by the diversion, ma'am,' he said, pointing at the alley before the barrier.

'I was actually wondering if I could ask you a couple of questions,' she said, smiling.

He started to shake his head. She dug out another business card.

'I'm Chrissie Chung, I present a podc—'

He stepped back and held up a hand like he was stopping a stream of traffic. 'Go through media relations.'

She put the card back in her pocket. 'Do you know the guy who did it? He's a cop, right?'

The officer took a step forward and leaned into her personal space. From the look in his eye, Chrissie wondered if she had been a little too quick to discount the homeless man's paranoia about the police. The cop had looked unapproachable to begin with. Now he looked positively infuriated that she required two tellings.

'Get the fuck out of here, little girl,' he said. 'You can quote me on that.'

Her eyes went to the badge on his shirt. 'I'll make sure to, Officer.'

She waited until she had gotten a reasonable distance from the barrier before she took her phone out to check the recording had captured that.

13

In theory, the multi-level saturation of the hunt for Jake Ellis and Molly Donaldson meant that they might be located at any second, with no additional effort from the authorities.

A civilian could spot one or both of them somewhere and call it in. One of the hundreds of traffic cops looking out for vehicles with a male driver and a female teenage passenger could pull them over. Sometimes that's how it works: the suspect getting unlucky can't be underestimated as a way of resolving the toughest cases. But Lark wasn't relying on it.

In the absence of confirmed leads, there was plenty of material to sift through in the backgrounds of the key players. The crime-scene people were going over Jake Ellis's apartment, looking for anything that might give a clue to where he might run. They had removed every electronic device, to be examined by their digital counterparts. The next thing on Lark's list was a visit to the home of Ellis's victim. Rachel and Molly Donaldson lived in Bayview, a suburb south-east of the city. It was likely that Ellis had spent time there. Lark had picked Kelly Paxon to accompany her out there to talk to the investigators on the scene.

She stepped out onto the street outside the federal building and took out her phone as she walked to the corner with Larkin Street. She stopped when she got to the cornerstone with the dedication to John F. Kennedy, who had been president when work on the building had commenced, but dead by the time it had opened.

Paxon was bringing the car around from the basement lot, and suggested meeting her outside in five minutes. That gave Lark time to check in on what the media was saying.

The news sites all had variations on the same material: the shooting, the abduction, pictures of stony-faced police officers and crime-scene tape outside the Elite Center, the photographs of Ellis and Rachel and Molly, and now of Steve Holdcroft, the bystander. There were a couple of references to Ellis's police brutality case, which had been settled a few weeks ago. A co-incidence?

'Change, lady?'

Lark looked up to see a woman in her late twenties with washed-out blond hair underneath a grubby white baseball cap. She was wearing a blue wool sweater a couple of sizes too big for her, with sweatpants and shoes that looked as though they had been found in a dumpster. Her right hand was held out, a dirty bandage across the palm.

Lark dug into her pocket and found only a quarter and three nickels. Like a lot of people, carrying cash was a habit she was gradually losing.

'Sorry,' she said, dropping the meagre offerings into the woman's palm.

'Hey, I take all major credit cards,' she grinned.

Lark grinned gamely and stepped away to look down at her phone again as the woman moved on to the next sidewalk loiterer.

The *Chronicle*'s site had a civilian picture of Ellis now, which it ran alongside the uniform shot. Lark was pleased to see this made him look more like an identifiable human being. It was a photograph of him with Rachel in a bar somewhere. He wore a light-blue cotton shirt and had sandy hair that matched his mustache, which had grown out a little compared to the in-uniform pic. He reminded Lark a little of Anthony Edwards in *Top Gun*, back when he had hair. In the picture, Ellis had his arm around Rachel's shoulder. She had red hair like her daughter's and was wearing a white strap vest. Both were smiling at the camera. Lark felt a shiver as she looked at Ellis's hand on Rachel's arm, thinking about how the same hand had attempted to end her life a few hours ago.

'Special Agent Lark?'

Lark looked up from her phone and saw a cop approaching along the sidewalk. He was wearing the SFPD uniform: dark-blue short-sleeve shirt, a radio clipped to his lapel beside the polished metal star over his heart. He had striking blue eyes and the hair under his hat was dark and looked close-cropped. He put his hand out and she shook it.

'Hartzler, out of Mission Station.'

'Good to meet you,' she said, a note of caution in the pleasantry.

'You're looking for Jake Ellis,' he said. A statement. Getting right to it.

Lark nodded slowly, sizing him up. There was an extra dimension to the inter-departmental complexities on this one, and she wasn't thinking of the wrangling over who had screwed up on the timing of the Amber Alert. Eyewitnesses or no, evidence or no, Ellis was one of them. She scanned the street for Paxon. There was no sign of her or the car.

'That's right,' she said. 'Mission is Ellis's station, isn't it?' she asked, knowing the answer already.

He put a hand up. 'Look, I'm not here to—' He stopped and started again as Lark folded her arms, ready to go on the defensive. 'There's no way Jake did this. I don't believe it.'

She managed not to roll her eyes. 'I don't need you to believe

53

it, Officer Hartman. We have an eyewitness who saw him shoot Rachel Donaldson. We have another who saw him with the child he abducted. She was in distress and covered in blood.' Mr Rosenberg had been very convincing. As had Edward Da Costa, the witness who had described seeing Ellis shoot two people. Lark had just watched the video of his interview. Both accounts had been entirely credible.

'It's Hartzler. Marty Hartzler.' Hartzler looked down at the ground and shook his head. 'I'm sorry, Agent. I'm still ... It's a lot to take in, you know?'

'You're a little off your patch, Officer,' Lark said, turning her head to look south, in the direction of the Mission District. 'Did you come all the way out here to try to intimidate me? Because—'

'No!' Hartzler cried out. 'No, God no.' He took off his hat and glanced around at the people walking past. He lowered his voice. 'I'm here to help.'

'Help?'

'I know you gotta find Jake. *We* gotta find him. I don't know what's happened or who saw what, but I know somebody needs to get to him and talk to him soon.' He folded the fingers of his right hand into a fist and jutted the thumb back at his chest. 'I know the guy. I can help you. If I can just talk to him, I can—'

'Talk him down, huh?' Lark said.

'He's my buddy,' Hartzler said. 'He'd do the same for me.'

Lark could sense that her expression was unwittingly conveying her skepticism. With an effort of will, she straightened her face into a more neutral setting. Perhaps it wouldn't be a bad idea to keep this guy onside. Like she had just been thinking, a resolution wasn't going to fall into their laps. They needed to explore every avenue, check everything.

She saw the gray Chevrolet Impala make the turn onto the street at last, Paxon behind the wheel, the dull sunlight glinting off her sunglasses. Lark reached into her jacket and produced a business card.

'Text me your number, okay? If I have time, it would be good to know more about Ellis.'

Hartzler took the card. 'Thanks, Agent. It's going to take all of us, isn't it?'

She answered with a thin smile as she opened the passenger door and got into the car.

14

'I left her. I just left her.'

Jake glanced down at Molly. Sunlight glinted off the track of a tear down her cheek. They had found out the good news twenty minutes before, when the one o'clock update on the SUV's radio had reported that Rachel Donaldson was undergoing emergency surgery. Critical, but not dead after all. There were no other details for now.

'You can sit up now, if you want,' he said, after glancing back at the road.

They were headed north on the old Route 99. What used to be known as the Golden State Highway, before the interstate had come along and literally sidelined it. Jake had decided on a destination a couple of hours before; the 5 would have gotten them there a lot faster, but he wanted to keep to quieter roads. The near miss back at the crosswalk was weighing on his mind. The guy in the gray suit had looked right at him. The man hadn't seemed to recognize him at the time, but when he turned on the news and realized that the police were looking for someone who looked just like the driver of the SUV, that might change.

Molly climbed up onto the passenger seat, clipping the seat belt in. The spatters of blood on her shirt had dried to a rusty brown. She would need a change of clothes as soon as they could manage.

'I just left her,' she said again.

'None of this is your fault,' Jake said.

'I shouldn't have left her. I thought she was dead.'

'You did exactly the right thing. Number one, if you had stayed, he would have hurt you too. Number two, you distracted him long enough that he didn't have time to make sure—' He stopped before he said something overly blunt. 'You got him away from your mom. And the paramedics would have been on the scene really fast.'

Molly avoided eye contact, brushed a lock of hair out of her eyes. 'I just keep thinking about how much we've been fighting. I was so...'

Jake knew exactly how she felt. After the initial shock had subsided and they had cleared the city, it had been one of the first things he had thought about too: that big blow-up between him and Rachel on Wednesday night. He had been under a lot of pressure, coming back off suspension, but that was no excuse. Some ridiculous thing that he couldn't even remember had sparked off a fight. *Everything isn't about you, Jake*, Rachel had snapped at one point.

'Don't think about that. None of it matters,' he said.

Molly turned to look out of the window.

Good advice. Easy to give, hard to take. So he forced himself to think about something else. First things first, they had to get rid of the SUV. Surface roads were slower but safer than the interstate, less chance of encountering highway patrol. But less chance didn't mean no chance. Every cop in the state would be looking for them. He wished he could listen in on the police bands, to find out if they knew about the SUV yet. Hell, he wished he could risk switching Rachel's phone on, just to find out exactly where they were.

He wondered what Diehl would do when they showed up on his doorstep.

A couple of hours ago, a few miles west of Stockton, he had thought of the one person who might be able to help him. The more he thought about it, the more it seemed like the only option. Jake hadn't seen Walt Diehl for a while. He didn't know what Diehl would be making of the news, if he'd seen it, but he did know one thing: he would give him a chance to tell his story.

Diehl would be in his late seventies now, maybe early eighties. The truth was, he had always seemed like the old man. The irascible owner of a dive bar named The Belle, where Jake had worked. Jake had come to believe that, in a quiet, unspectacular way, Diehl had saved his life twenty-two years ago. Jake had to drop out of college in his junior year to care for his mother when she got too sick to look after herself. When she had eventually passed, Jake would have lost his home, had Diehl not kept paying him through the last three weeks when he had been unable to leave his mom's side.

He had waved off Jake's gratitude when he came back to work. 'Ahh, anyone would do the same thing.' That wasn't true. Not by a long shot. He hoped Diehl was still the kind of man who would go out on a limb for a friend.

Every minute behind the wheel felt like a trade-off. He wanted to put as many miles behind him as possible, expand the search radius as much as he could. But the longer he stayed in this vehicle, the more likely it was that he would be stopped. They needed to find another car.

The road started to sweep around in a long, lazy curve, and a sign came into view. A couple of seconds later, it was close enough to read: DUNNIGAN 2 MILES. Okay, that gave him a better idea of their location. He thought Dunnigan was about forty or fifty miles north and west of Sacramento, which meant that they still had a long way to go. He thought about it for a minute, and then took the turn.

They thumped over the tracks at a railroad crossing and kept going. The road was lined with evenly planted fruit trees on either side. In the distance, Jake could see the arcs of irrigation spray glinting in the afternoon sunlight. They passed a dirt track on the left. Jake took a note of the read on the milometer, in case he wanted to backtrack. The town itself was another three quarters of a mile along the road. He slowed as they reached the first houses, scanning for people and vehicles, police vehicles in particular. The place wasn't much more than a wide spot in the road, but it might just be big enough for there to be a police station. He told Molly to hunch down again.

Low houses, wide yards, mature fruit trees. He passed by an old couple ambling along the sidewalk. The man loosely holding a leash, a gray beagle scampering along ten yards in front of them. Neither of them gave Jake or the SUV a second look. He started glancing at the cars in the driveways as they passed, looking for an older model, something easy to break into.

Then he rounded a corner and saw the bell tower of a small church rising above the leaves of the nearby trees.

A line of cars parked outside the church. A hearse right in front of the door. People filing inside. All dressed in black.

He kept going, turned at the end of the road, and headed back the way they had come, picking up speed as they left the edge of town behind. He slowed and took the right onto the dirt track. He followed it for about half a mile. The track became more and more rough, the bushes encroaching more from each side as he got deeper into the woods. The track passed by a wide clearing with some more trees on the far side. He pulled onto the side of the road and turned the engine off.

Molly started to get up from the footwell again. He told her to stay put; that he'd be back soon.

15

The house where Rachel Donaldson lived with her daughter was on a quiet street in Bayview, about twenty-five minutes' drive from Golden Gate Avenue. The same story as Ellis's neighborhood: affordable a decade or two ago, prohibitively expensive now. Same as Lark's neighborhood in Bernal Heights. Sometimes, on the rare occasions where she had time to think about things other than work, Lark wondered how the transformation the city was undergoing was going to end.

As they approached the house, Lark could see that there was a police car parked outside, with a uniformed officer guarding the short, steeply sloping cement driveway in front of number 84. The house was a narrow Victorian, with off-white wood siding and three squat floors: a garage on the bottom and a set of wooden stairs up to the door on the front deck, then a top floor with a single window below a sharply peaked roof.

The police officer wasn't the only person on the street. Several of the neighbors were out in their front yards, all watching the car as they slowed down on the approach. There was a woman in a turquoise blouse at the window of the house next door. She put a hand to her mouth in a nervous gesture and turned away as she saw Lark looking back at her.

Paxon parked next to the police car and the two of them got out. Lark glanced at her phone to see if there were any updates.

Nothing that stood out on the various team Slack channels. A couple of emails from their liaison at Highway Patrol and a text from Joe, her husband. She checked the emails first. Nothing new, no confirmed sightings. A lot of tips on the back of the Amber Alert, but apparently nothing promising enough to stand out.

She opened Joe's text.

Guess I'm on dinner detail tonight. Pizza?

She smiled and texted back.

Don't wait up x

The cop at the foot of the driveway, a thin guy in his late forties with graying hair, watched them without expression as they approached and glanced carefully at their identification.

'ERT still inside?' Lark asked.

'Finished up twenty minutes ago,' the officer said. 'All yours, Agent.' Neutral tone, so it was likely he wasn't another friend of Ellis. Or hid it better.

Lark let Paxon take the lead and they climbed the creaking wooden steps up to the front door, both of them snapping disposable gloves on. It was ajar, having been opened by the locksmith, and Paxon used the back of her hand to push it inward, so as not to touch the handle. The door opened onto a narrow hallway, with the living room on the left-hand side and a bedroom on the right. The two rooms at the back were a dining room and a relatively spacious kitchen, with a narrow flight of stairs climbing steeply to the rooms on the top floor.

Lark noted some of the traces of the evidence response team: powder on the touch surfaces, the faint smell of luminol in the air. Other than that, the place looked — well, it looked completely normal. Clean and tidy, but not obsessively so. Lived in. It looked exactly like someone had gone out for the morning and expected to be back soon. They moved from room to room. The living room had a beige leather couch and a coffee table and a television. The window looked down on the houses across the street. Those were lower down the hill, so the roofs topped off fifteen feet or so below those of the houses on this side of the street.

Lark gestured in the direction of the stairs. 'You want to take upstairs?'

Paxon nodded and made her way up to the top floor.

The kitchen was clean and tidy, but again, not too tidy. There was a light dusting of crumbs on the counter next to the toaster, and a pound of frozen hamburger was defrosting on a plate next to the cooker top, thawing out for a dinner that would never be served. Lark had to ignore the urge to put the meat in the refrigerator.

Looking at the refrigerator itself, there were the usual notes and pictures attached. Photographs of Molly; some alone, some with friends, some with Rachel. A list of groceries to stock up on. A certificate from the gymnastics club on Sullivan Street. No pictures of Jake Ellis, but then she didn't know exactly how long they had been dating. Not long enough to have moved in together, at any rate.

Rachel's bedroom was small and neat. Double bed, floral wallpaper on one wall. Lark climbed the creaking stairs to the top floor, where Molly's room was. It had sloping walls with anime posters and a map of the world pinned to them. The carpet was pale pink and there was a single bed. Clothes and piles of books were strewn over the floor, standard for any teenager's room. Paxon was by the window, holding a small notebook in her gloved hand.

'Journal?' Lark asked.

'Yep. Looks like standard teenage girl stuff.'

Lark thought about her own leather-bound journal that she had kept as a teenager. 'If someone had gone through my diary at that age, I would have died. Sorry,' she added, as Paxon winced. 'Bad choice of words.'

Lark moved over to the window. They were above the roof level of the houses opposite now, and there was an unobstructed view of the bay. She could see all the way across to Alameda.

'Nice view.'

'Yeah,' Paxon agreed. 'I'm guessing she bought a while ago.'

Lark nodded. The feel of the city had changed out of all recognition in the couple of decades since the tech boom. San Francisco was now home to more billionaires than any other city on the planet. But it felt like there were more homeless people than anywhere else, too. It was like living in two cities. Unimaginable wealth floating above unimaginable squalor. The gap in the western world between the haves and have-nots was at its very widest right here in the City by the Bay. For tourists and newcomers drawn by the tech gold rush, it was disconcerting enough. For those who had lived here long enough to see the changes, it felt like being part of an experiment that hadn't fully played out yet, and you had the gut feeling that something was very wrong.

She thought about the lady on the street a half-hour ago. *I take all major credit cards.*

Paxon put the journal down and started opening the drawers of the dresser. It was a pale pink with a big oval mirror. There was the normal clutter across the surface: a hairbrush, various cosmetics, an inhaler, a notepad with doodles on it, a phone charger.

'No other devices?' Lark asked, looking around. 'Phone, tablet?' No phones had been recovered from the car, which suggested that Ellis had taken them.

'ERT took a laptop and a desktop,' Paxon said without looking up.

Lark always felt unsettled when she visited places like this. Dwellings frozen in time, waiting for someone to come home. To eat hamburgers for dinner, scrawl an update in a diary, brush their hair in front of an oval mirror. Too often, they didn't come back. She hoped this would be one of the exceptions.

They finished up and descended to the living floor, then made their way out of the door and onto the front porch. Rachel Donaldson's house hadn't thrown up any surprises, which was disappointing in some ways, but Lark knew there might well be evidence that they couldn't see yet. Both of the forensic kind in the house, and on the electronic devices they had taken. If something could provide a clue as to why this had happened, or why it had happened *now*, they might be able to work out where Ellis might have gone.

'Excuse me?'

Both women turned at the sound of the voice. It was the lady from the adjoining house, the one with the turquoise blouse. She was on the other side of the fence separating the properties, one hand resting on it.

'Yes, ma'am?'

'You're the police, right?'

'FBI. You live here, I take it, Ms ...'

'Clarke. Amy Clarke. I've lived here for thirty-five years,' she said with an odd, defensive look. 'Such a terrible thing. That poor little girl.'

'Did you know them well?'

'Not well, only saw them in passing.'

The same as Mr Rosenberg back at Ellis's apartment, Lark thought. She wondered if their job had been easier in the past, when everybody knew each other.

'We're looking for a male suspect—' Lark began.

'That's right. The cop. I've been watching the news.' She added the last with a slightly guilty tone, as though she didn't want to acknowledge how exciting this all was. 'And I got the Amber Alert too.'

'You ever see him around?'

'Couple of times.'

'Ever speak to him?'

She wrinkled her nose. 'He parked in my space once. I had to ask him to move. He's actually what I wanted to talk to you about.'

'Oh yes?'

She nodded and put a finger to her mouth, her brow knitted as she tried to recall something. 'Let me see now, this is Saturday, so it would have been Thurs— no, Wednesday night.'

'What happened on Wednesday night?'

'Well, there was a commotion in there.'

'You mean like a fight?' Paxon prompted.

'Well, yes. Like a fight.'

'Could you tell if the altercation was physical?' Lark asked.

'Sounded that way. I couldn't make out words, but I heard raised voices, both of them, and then he yelled about something. I heard something break, like a glass or something. I almost called you guys. I mean, those guys,' she said, a note of contempt in her voice as she shot a glance over at the uniform cop.

Lark nodded. 'To be honest, Ms Clarke, I wish you had.'

The woman registered the edge of disapproval in her voice and pursed her lips. Lark gave herself a mental kick. Never get on the wrong side of a potentially useful witness.

'Well,' Amy Clarke continued, 'it calmed down after that. And what would they have done? I've been calling them about those kids hanging out at the end of the street for weeks and they don't do anything.'

'We appreciate your cooperation,' Lark said. She handed over another card, making a mental note to stock up from the box in her desk drawer. 'We may need to speak to you again, but if you think of anything at all in the meantime, I want you to give me a call right away, okay? I'd like to find the little girl as soon as we can, and to do that we need all the help we can get.'

Ms Clarke accepted the card and seemed to be mollified. 'Well, what with the Amber Alert, I'm sure somebody will have seen them.'

Back in the car, Lark checked her phone as they strapped in. There was a text from Valenti back at Golden Gate Avenue. Rachel Donaldson's employer was at his office today and had agreed to meet them there. That would kill two birds with one stone, because she wanted to see where Rachel worked. She read the address out to Paxon, who tapped it into the GPS on the dash.

'You don't know how to get there without that?' Lark said, raising an eyebrow.

'Of course I do, but this'll tell us if—' She paused and a smile that was oh-so-slightly smug appeared as she read out the message on the screen. '*Much heavier traffic than usual on US-101* – we'll go by Bayshore.'

Lark raised a skeptical eyebrow. It would save them a whole three minutes, according to the estimate. 'Pity that thing can't just tell us where Ellis has gone.'

When she looked up, Paxon was staring back up at the house. Rachel Donaldson's neighbor was still on her porch, looking back down at them. 'What do you think?'

Lark thought about what she had seen in the house, and what the neighbor had said. 'I think Ellis sounds like a piece of shit. And I think Ms Clarke up there has more faith in the alert than I do.'

16

Jake jogged all the way back to town. He didn't pass the elderly couple with the beagle on the return trip. He didn't see any other people on foot. Perhaps everybody in town was at the funeral. He hoped so.

If they could just make it to Diehl's place, it would buy some time. The only problem was, it was a long drive. They couldn't risk traveling all the way in the same vehicle they had left the city in. It would be linked to him sooner or later, if it hadn't been already.

He slowed his pace as he got closer to his destination. The church building was Gothic-revival-looking: arched windows, a modest three-story louvered bell tower rising above the entrance. He counted more than a dozen cars lining the road outside. The entrance doors were open on a small vestibule, with another pair of sturdy oak doors leading into the main church hall. There was a wooden bench and a noticeboard, advertising town events. According to one of the signs, today's service was for Emmeline Ware, October 12 1945 to Tuesday last week. There was no coat room or office. He would have to risk doing this the hard way.

Carefully, he pushed open the door, trying to make as little disturbance as possible. He hoped the attendees would be too focused on the funeral service to notice the incomer in casual clothes.

The church was perhaps two thirds full. The mourners were seated, most of them toward the front, on a half-dozen pine pews on either side of the aisle. The minister stood at the lectern, alongside a casket festooned with white lilies. He glanced briefly at Jake as he entered, before looking down at his reading again. Nobody else turned around.

Jake took a seat in the last pew. The church smelled of sawdust and old books. The reading was from a Bible passage that Jake didn't recognize, something about when the perishable has been clothed with the imperishable. Then again, there would be very few Bible passages he would recognize. He turned his attention to the clothes of those gathered in the room. The row in front of him held five people. Three of them were still wearing their coats, two had draped theirs over the back of the pew.

He tried not to think about the fact that every one of these people currently had a device displaying his name and description in their pockets, whether they knew it or not.

He shifted along on the pew, careful not to move too quickly and attract attention. Slowly, carefully, he reached into the pocket of the first coat.

One thing about being a cop for fifteen years: it teaches you a few tricks from the other side of the law. A charming lowlife named Pete King used to specialize in this. Jake had busted him for misdemeanor possession a few years back, but when they searched his house, they found meticulous records of his sideline selling used cars. The list of used cars matched up perfectly with dozens of vehicles reported stolen from churches and gyms and school plays all over the Bay Area. A simple operation: King would sneak into a gathering, go through the coat pockets and disappear as soon as he found a set of keys.

Nothing in the first pocket.

He moved to the next one, a man with gray hair sitting up straight, listening intently to the words of the service. His black overcoat had been folded neatly and draped over the back of the seat, but the bottom of the coat protruded from the gap between the back and the seat of the pew. Jake reached into the pocket and felt his hand close around exactly what he was looking for: a key and a hard plastic fob. As he shifted, his pew creaked audibly. The man with gray hair glanced around. Jake was ready for it. The man couldn't see where his hand was at that angle, not without standing up, so Jake played it cool, kept his head down as though in prayer. The guy turned back to the service.

Outside, Jake walked the line of cars, clicking the button on the fob until the lights of a white Ford Fusion flashed back at him. California plates, a few years old. Perfect. Not too new or flashy, but not eye-catchingly decrepit either.

He glanced around to reassure himself that there were no onlookers before opening the driver's door and getting in. He turned the key and felt the engine come to life, running smoothly. A quarter of a tank. He put the car into drive and pulled slowly out of the space and onto the road, headed back to where he had left Molly and the SUV.

Untraceable

Excerpt from Untraceable – Season 4, Episode 2, April 18

Rachel Donaldson is an accountant with a firm based in San Francisco. She's thirty-nine years old, and she grew up in Napa, before going to college at UCSF. She has a thirteen-year-old daughter named Molly. Molly's dad, Richard, died a few years ago.

This morning, Rachel was shot in the head at point-blank range as she was parking her car outside her daughter's gymnastics class. Another man, named Steve Holdcroft, was killed, apparently as he tried to intervene. The police already have a suspect: a forty-one-year-old man named Jake Ellis, who's reported to be Rachel's boyfriend. Molly was with Rachel at the time of the attack, and she hasn't been seen since.

Regular *Untraceable* listeners will know just how crucial it is that Molly is found soon. All police investigations are time-sensitive. Homicide cops talk about the importance of the first forty-eight hours. After that, the odds of catching the perpetrator drop off. Child abduction investigations are even more time-sensitive, because the victim is – you hope – still alive. But they may not remain that way for long.

Four hundred and sixty thousand children are reported missing in the United States every year. The overwhelming majority of those kids are found safe and well. But in the cases that don't have a happy ending, the stats bear out the importance of a quick resolution. Of the abduction cases that result in homicide, seventy-five percent of the time, the victim was killed within three hours of being taken.

Regular listeners will know all of this, so why am I talking about it?

Because we don't know how this investigation will end yet. The attack on Rachel Donaldson and abduction of Molly Donaldson happened this morning. The police are searching for Jake Ellis right now. And time is of the essence.

An Amber Alert was issued at eight-twenty-seven this morning. It gave us the known details about Molly and her abductor. She's white, with red hair, approximately five feet tall, a hundred and ten pounds. Jake Ellis is also white, fair hair with a mustache, five-ten, a hundred and eighty-five pounds, forty-one years old. They were last seen in the Tenderloin. That was almost five hours ago as I'm recording this. They could still be in the city, or they could be anywhere within a search radius that grows by the minute. The police and the FBI need all the help they can get, so if you see anyone answering this description, call it in.

There's one more wrinkle to this case that I haven't mentioned yet. This abduction has a complicating factor. Because Jake Ellis is actually *Officer* Jake Ellis, of the San Francisco Police Department. Which means the cops are hunting one of their own.

17

McMurtry & Dane, the accountancy firm where Rachel Donaldson worked, was on the sixth floor of an office building on Van Ness Avenue. It was right across the street from a diner Lark liked. She decided they would get an order to go after they had interviewed Rachel Donaldson's boss. As she looked over at the diner, she noticed a black town car parked outside. The driver was wearing sunglasses, and he immediately looked away when Lark looked at him. She took a mental note of the license plate as she and Paxon crossed the street.

'Have you seen this?' Paxon said as they reached the entrance to the building.

Lark turned and looked at the screen of Paxon's phone as she held it up. It showed the banner image for something called the *Untraceable* podcast. The image showed a lone female figure from behind, walking into a dark, oppressive-looking forest. The text announced: NEW SEASON: THE MOLLY DONALDSON CASE, AS IT HAPPENS.

Lark blinked in disbelief. 'Holy shit. They don't wait around, do they?' She had fielded inquiries from this new breed of armchair detective before, but as far as she could recall, this was the first time anyone had started a podcast on a case the day it happened. It was almost impressive.

Paxon put her phone away and they entered the foyer. The

building dated from the 1920s, the vibe was elegant, but faded. The floor was tiled in worn black-and-white marble, and the doors and skirting were dark wood. The upper floors were served by an old-fashioned cage elevator. Lark and Paxon rode up to the sixth floor, listening to the machinery clanking away, catching glimpses of people through the shutter doors as they passed each floor.

McMurtry & Dane Accounting's floor was decorated in a more modern style than the foyer and the glimpses of the other floors Lark had seen. The furniture was expensive, three of the walls painted a bright white, with one in a deep olive color. The receptionist was an older woman with gray hair and glasses. She wore black and a solemn expression. Lark didn't know if that was because of what had happened to Rachel, or if this was her usual garb and demeanor. She escorted them down a thickly carpeted corridor and knocked lightly on a door at the far end. The name on the door was William J. McMurtry.

'Come in.'

The receptionist turned the handle and pushed the door inwards and stood aside, smiling briefly at Lark and Paxon.

McMurtry was behind a desk opposite the door. He had stood up to greet them as they entered. He was in his sixties, with thinning salt-and-pepper hair. He wore a light-blue shirt with the sleeves rolled up and a blue tie with white dots. He held out his hand to shake across the desk; Paxon first and then Lark. He looked from one to the other, trying to work out which of them was in charge.

'We appreciate you giving us some of your time, Mr McMurtry,' Lark said. 'I'm Special Agent Lark, this is Special Agent Paxon.' She reached into her jacket and produced the wallet displaying her badge and ID.

McMurtry didn't even glance at it. He collapsed back into his chair, like it had been an effort to stay on his feet. 'No problem at all. This is so awful. Is there any news about Rachel?'

Lark shook her head. 'She's still in surgery, we won't know anything until later.'

'And her daughter?'

'Well, I'm hoping we can do something about that. Any information you can give us could help us to find her.'

McMurtry opened his hands, resting his elbows on the desk. 'Ask me anything.'

Lark put her phone on the desk between them. 'You okay if we record this?' She had gotten into the habit of doing this with all interviews; it was both quicker and more accurate than writing notes. But the real advantage was she could watch the person she was interviewing the whole time.

'Go for it.'

She tapped record. 'Thanks, Mr McMurtry. Let's start with the last time you saw Rachel.'

'Last night. Here in the office; she left at around six. I was working late.'

'Filing deadline last week; must be busy,' Paxon said.

'It's always busy. We had an audit on one of our clients. That's why I'm here on a Saturday, instead of the golf course.' He raised a rueful eyebrow at Lark, expecting a sympathetic response. Lark kept her expression neutral.

'Did Rachel seem different in any way?'

'Different how?'

'Any kind of different. Worried or stressed, maybe. Quieter than usual.'

He shook his head slowly. 'Not that I noticed. Although I have to say, I was pretty busy, so ...'

'And she didn't mention anything you think could be relevant? Concerns about her home life, perhaps.'

'She tended to keep herself to herself. I didn't even know she had a boyfriend until I read the news.' He looked from Lark to Paxon before tentatively adding, 'He's a police officer, right? Why would a cop do this?'

Lark felt Paxon's eyes on her. 'We're not speculating right now, Mr McMurtry. All we know for sure is that he appears to have Molly, and we'd like to get her back safe. How about Molly, did you ever meet her?'

'Rachel likes to— liked to keep herself to herself. I just said that, didn't I? She didn't talk much about her home life.'

They asked him some more questions: background on Rachel, how long she had been with the company. When they had covered everything on Lark's list, she asked if they could see where Rachel worked.

McMurtry led them out of the door and opened the door to the neighboring office. Rachel's office was the same size and layout as her boss's, but the chair looked cheaper and the desk was smaller. The desk was clear except for her keyboard and screen and a small stack of documents in a tray. Lark picked them up and leafed through them.

'Client accounts,' McMurtry explained, looking like he wanted to take them out of Paxon's hands.

'Can you give us a list of her current clients?'

He hesitated for the first time. 'Is that really necessary? I mean, you know who did this.'

'I just need a list of names and contact details. We're not interested in their files. Unless, of course, you want me to come back with a warrant, because—'

He sighed. 'Okay, okay. Some of our clients get a little precious about confidentiality, but I guess you're the FBI, so ...'

They rode down in the creaking cage elevator and walked through the foyer and stepped out onto Van Ness. The sun had come out since they had been inside, and there was a pleasant warmth in the air. Lark observed that the black town car had moved on. At that moment, her phone buzzed. It was Mitch Valenti. Lark exchanged a glance with Paxon as she answered.

'News?'

'Yes,'Valenti said. His tone of voice didn't fill Lark with hope. 'Good and bad.'

'Don't keep me in suspense.'

'Rachel Donaldson is out of surgery.'

'What's the bad news?'

'They can't tell us when, or if, she's going to regain consciousness.'

Lark sighed. 'All right. How we doing on the tips on the alert?'

'We've taken over eight hundred so far.'

'Anything?' She wasn't hopeful. If any of the tips had been confirmed or even promising sightings, he would have called her already.

'Couple of false sightings of Ellis – one on the Wharf and one at a strip mall out in the cuts. Neither checks out. A maintenance worker called in to say he might have seen Molly in the Tenderloin around eight this morning...'

'Really?' Lark cut in, although she knew from Valenti's weary tone that it wasn't anything to get excited about.

'...But he couldn't be sure. Just remembers a girl with red hair skulking in a doorway. He didn't notice what clothes she was wearing or anything else. And he said she was alone.'

Around eight would place it after the shooting, and before she had been seen by the witness at Ellis's apartment. If the girl was alone, it was unlikely to have been Molly. But the maintenance worker's call would be checked and added to the list, anyway.

'Okay. We're going to grab something to eat and head back in, see you soon.'

76

They ordered burgers to go from the diner and ate them in the car. After they had finished, Lark took out the printed-out list McMurtry had given her. Rachel Donaldson's current client list. Four columns: name, company name if applicable, phone number and email where available. There were fourteen clients on the list, and there was at least one way to contact each of them.

'Think any of that will be any use?' Paxon asked.

'Doesn't matter, you—'

'…Have to check everything,' Paxon finished, completing a mantra Lark had made a point of drilling into her team.

Lark smiled. She took out her phone and took a picture of the sheet of paper, examining the image to make sure the text was in focus. She wished she had thought to ask McMurtry to email her the document instead, but he had been unhappy enough about giving her the names without a warrant anyway. She Slacked it through to La-Vonne Taylor back at the office, asking her to contact each name and ask the basics on their recent contact with Rachel: when they last saw her, if she mentioned anything of concern, anything else that they might know.

Paxon took the burger wrapper from Lark and stuffed it into the paper bag the food had come in. She got out of the car to dump it in a nearby trash can.

'Who's next?' she asked as she got back in.

'That's her home and her workplace crossed off the list. If we were going to get a good lead, chances are it would have come from one of those. Let's hope we catch a break soon.'

Paxon started the engine up, pulled out onto the street and made a right onto Post Street, heading back to Golden Gate Avenue. Lark watched the people walking the streets as they passed, wondering if Jake Ellis was still somewhere in the city. This was always the most frustrating part of any case: spinning your wheels, feeling like you weren't getting anywhere. And the worst thing was the knowledge that it wasn't *just* a feeling. You could keep hanging in there, waiting for a break, and often it would come. But sometimes there never was a break and, eventually, you just had to move on to the next case. She hoped this wouldn't be one of those times.

Lark's phone buzzed again. She felt a sinking feeling as she saw Valenti's name on the caller ID again. He was calling to tell her that Rachel Donaldson had died, she knew it.

'What happened? Did the hospital call?'

Valenti's voice sounded completely different from the last call. The defeated tone had evaporated. 'We have a good sighting of Ellis, and a vehicle.'

18

Molly watched Jake as he drove. Occasionally, he would glance over at her, as though to make sure she was still there and hadn't evaporated since the last check. The landscape was flat, the expanse of sky seeming enormous after the city.

She could see how hyper-aware he was; scanning the road ahead, checking out the driver of every oncoming car. She noticed that every time they passed a vehicle in the other lane, he would take one hand off the wheel and hold it up to partially obscure his face, making it look as though he were massaging out a headache.

She closed her eyes and immediately found herself in the passenger seat of a different car, a different person in the driver's seat.

'Molly—'

She opened her eyes again and forced back the tears. Her name. Her name had been the last word her mom spoke, perhaps the last word she would *ever* speak.

She looked out of the window, in the useless hope that she might see something that would make her think about something else. Anything else. They passed signs directing traffic to places Molly had never heard of, like Bluegum and Grapit. Some stating the long distances to places she knew were farther north. She wondered how far they had driven since the town where Jake had stolen this car. It was difficult to tell how fast they were going. A little faster than the other traffic, going by how many cars they had passed, but not so fast as to attract attention. Come to think of it, she had no way of knowing how long they had been driving, since she didn't have her phone, and she couldn't turn on her mother's.

'What time is it?' she asked.

'It's three-thirty,' Jake answered, without even glancing at the clock next to the speedometer.

Molly sat back in the seat. She opened her mouth to ask the question a couple of times before she decided how to phrase it. In the end, she went for straight and to the point.

'What were you fighting about?'

He glanced back again. 'What?'

'You and Mom. Last week.'

'I didn't know you had heard that. I'm sorry.'

She didn't say anything.

'I don't really know, is the honest answer. I had a crappy day at work, and I think your mom did too, and – it just happens sometimes. People fight, even people who like each other a lot.'

'It hadn't happened before.'

'You're right, it hadn't.'

There was silence for a while. They passed a sign saying they were entering Red Bluff. It was bigger than the other towns they had come through. They passed rows of ordinary-looking houses with nice lawns and trees, a park with a stretch of water following alongside the road, a red-brick church framed by twin towers, like a miniature version of Notre-Dame in Paris.

She took a sharp breath as a police car turned out into the road ahead of them, heading toward them. Jake kept going, staring straight ahead, and the police car passed them without slowing. A minute later, they reached an intersection and waited at the lights before turning left onto the road running across.

80

How far was Red Bluff from where they had started out? Two hundred miles? More?

Whatever. Home was a long way in the rearview mirror. She didn't have to know exactly how far they had come to know that.

People fight.

Jake was right. That was just a fact of life, wasn't it? So why did she resent him so much for that raised voice, the sound of the smashing glass? She hadn't even been worried at the time. Hell, she had had an argument with Mom even more recently than that, so maybe she was being a hypocrite. Jake was probably feeling as bad about the fight with Mom as she was about complaining about getting up early.

The more she thought about it, the more she decided the difference was that she really didn't know Jake. Not like she should. He and her mom had begun dating in January, and Molly really hadn't made the effort to find out much about him below the surface. Of course she cared about her mom, and it wasn't like there had been a lot of boyfriends, but it all seemed ... fine. Jake had seemed like a nice guy. Pleasant and conversational toward Molly, but not like he was trying too hard. She could tell he wasn't trying to ingratiate himself, perhaps instinctively knowing that would have been the wrong approach. And Mom had known him since before she was born, of course, so it was easy to be reassured that there was nothing to worry about.

Maybe she should have been less accepting. Maybe she should have made the effort to find out more about Jake. But no, she was caught up in all her usual bullshit: homework and gymnastics and gaming and the ever-changing politics of school. It all seemed like such a waste of time, now. She should have been making an effort to spend time with Mom, taking an interest in her life. And now it was too late, and she was stuck with this guy whom she barely knew, going who knew where.

She turned back to look at Jake. He was doing that thing of casually shielding his face again as they passed a big truck in the other lane. She realized he had taken a deliberate decision to take this new road rather than staying on the straight road they had been on for a while.

'You have somewhere to go now, don't you?'

He didn't look back this time. 'I have a friend who might be able to help us. It'll be safe, give us some time to think, try to work out what happened.'

'How far?'

He thought about it. 'A few hours. The farther we go, the better.'

She sat back again as they passed the driver of the truck. She put her hand up to the side of her head to shield her face.

19

A lead, finally a good lead.

Lark was back in the office, listening to an update from Garcia on what looked like confirmation that Ellis had managed to acquire a vehicle and leave the city.

A man named Jerry Yorke, who owned a small chain of restaurants specializing in something called French-Fusion, had called the tip line an hour before. He said he had almost been hit by a guy driving a gray Volkswagen SUV at the corner of Bush Street and Powell Street at around nine o'clock that morning. He had gotten the Amber Alert along with everyone else, of course, but he hadn't paid it much attention. He had been in meetings all morning. It was only while grabbing a late lunch that he had seen Jake's picture on the news and thought he looked a lot like the driver of the SUV.

Yorke hadn't bothered to look at the plate, but they had run the description of the vehicle through the system to see what was in the area and had come up with a hit. There was a gray VW SUV registered to a Marcus Bolton, who lived above the bar he owned on Washington Street. The bar on Washington was a few blocks from Ellis's apartment building, and on a direct line between his route of egress and the spot where he had assaulted Officer Friedrich. Jerry Yorke's brush with death on the crosswalk at Bush and Powell had come about ten minutes after Ellis had gotten past Friedrich, and about half a mile from the bar on Washington. The timing and the location all matched up perfectly.

They looked into Marcus Bolton, who was currently overseas and therefore hadn't noticed that his vehicle had vanished from the lot behind his apartment. When they got him on the phone, he confirmed he knew Ellis, and that he was a regular at the bar. Last year, he had closed down one of his other bars, and Jake had helped him move some of the kegs.

So now they had an all-but-certain sighting of Ellis, and they knew what vehicle he had been driving, and the license plate. Unfortunately, they were finding this out more than six hours after the fact.

Garcia consulted his notes. 'Cameras picked up the SUV on I-80 at nine-sixteen, headed across the bridge into Oakland. He drives through the west side of town after that, then he takes Park Boulevard at nine-forty-eight. After that...' He spread his hands apart to show all they had after that.

'Nothing at all?'

'Depends what you mean by nothing. We've had no more sightings of the SUV. Nothing on cameras, nothing from highway patrol anywhere in the state. Of course, we didn't know we were looking for a Volkswagen SUV until a half-hour ago. Meantime, we've had a ton of other tips from the public.'

'A ton?'

'Nine hundred and forty-three unique interactions logged on the system, as of ten minutes ago.'

'Any in that area?' She looked up at the map and the area around Oakland. Her gaze moved east, along Ellis's last-known direction of travel. 'Vallejo? Stockton?'

'Sure. But it's white noise.'

Lark knew exactly what he meant. They would take a closer look at tips in that area later, but if there had been anything immediately credible, such as a sighting that mentioned the SUV, it would have stuck out. No, the tips from Oakland and points onward would be the same as the tips from here in the city, or from Monterey, or from Sydney, Australia. Possible sightings, helpful suggestions to find the suspect using his phone GPS, sightings where the person reporting was a hundred percent sure ... until it turned out that the person or people they had seen had nothing to do with the case.

The frustrating thing was, there were very few tips that could be immediately written off. The truly crazy ones, involving aliens or government conspiracies, were almost welcome. Most of them fell into the gray area. Almost certainly dead ends, but each one had to be checked out. You have to check everything.

'Who's this guy?'

Lark looked up at Kelly Paxon's murmured question to no one in particular. She was perched on the edge of a desk, her eyes on the television on the wall, tuned to the local news. A man with a grave expression on his face was being interviewed outside of City Hall. He looked in his mid-thirties, was wearing a dark suit and a blue tie. The graphic on the bottom of the screen said he was George G. Driscoll, Board of Supervisors.

'I've spoken with friends and family of Rachel Donaldson and I've also been in touch with our fine police department and the FBI, who are assuring me that everything possible is being done to find Molly.'

'I must have missed that important summit,' Lark said, dryly.

The interviewer prompted Driscoll on speculation that the police might go easy on Ellis because he was one of them.

'That's not my perception of the situation at all, Jen. Every cop I've spoken to wants to resolve this situation and catch this guy. He's shot two people already, and in my view we need to bring Ellis in. Dead or alive.'

85

'Dead or alive,' Lark repeated, shaking her head as the news cut to another story. 'Thank you very much, Mr Driscoll.'

Paxon's jaw was set. 'That's all we need. Like this isn't volatile enough, he wants people acting like it's the Old West.'

'Ignore it,' Lark said. 'We can't be distracted by all of this crap. We focus on the facts.'

As Paxon moved away, Lark wondered at her own words. *Focus on the facts* sounded good. But was it really possible?

20

With a final turn, the last screw from the license plate came loose, and Jake lifted it off, placing it on the ground beside where he was crouched. The compact tool set he had bought along with a couple of other items in Red Bluff was cheap, but it had been up to the task. He took a moment to look around the lot to make sure nobody was watching, before picking up the plate he had removed from the Ford and screwing it into place. It wasn't an ideal substitution. The two numbers were nothing alike, but at least they were both California plates. The owner might notice the switch if he happened to glance at the plate. But how often do you look at your own license plate?

Jake didn't know if they had tied Marcus's SUV to him yet, or how long it would take before it was found. If they linked him to a report of the stolen Ford, this could buy him a little extra time. Of course, the substitution would become clear the moment a traffic cop had reason to run the plate, but it was better than nothing.

He picked up the new plate and walked quickly across the deserted lot to where the white Ford was parked. Molly was in the passenger seat, ready to crouch down if anyone came by. She was holding up amazingly, all things considered.

After fitting the stolen plate to the stolen car, Jake got back in and turned the key in the ignition. He pulled out of the lot and headed north.

'It's nearly time,' Molly said quietly. The sweater he had bought along with the tool set was baggy on her, but it looked a lot better than her bloodstained shirt.

She was right about the time: the clock read two minutes before the hour. He glanced over at her. Her face was composed, though he could still see the streaks of tears and the remnants of her mother's blood on her face. They would need to clean up somewhere. Do something about that very noticeable red hair, too.

He turned the volume up on the radio. It had retuned to a new local station every thirty miles or so, and they had been waiting for the on-the-hour news bulletin. Jake wished he could listen to it without Molly being there. They needed to know if the police had released any updates on the hunt, which could give him an idea of how much they knew. But he knew Molly wasn't thinking about that. She was waiting to hear if her mom was dead.

'Alone' by Heart started to fade out and was immediately replaced by a fast-talking ad for a car dealership, then one for a new food-delivery app. Then it was the news.

Jake saw movement in the corner of his eye: Molly's fingers were gripping the edge of her seat, making deep indents in the faux leather. He realized he was holding his breath.

They were the lead item. Police in San Francisco on the lookout for a man suspected of... yadda yadda. Nothing new on that front.

'The surviving victim, a thirty-nine-year-old woman, is being treated at Zuckerberg Hospital...'

No new information, then. Which was good, wasn't it? But Jake didn't feel reassured. He knew how long it would take for information to filter out from the hospital, to the police, and on to the media. But he saw Molly's fingers relax a little. No matter what, it wasn't what she had been dreading. It wasn't confirmation.

He wanted to tell her it was going to be okay, that Rachel was going to be just fine. He couldn't do it.

The next item was about a system-wide closure of the BART, caused by a software patch issue, followed by a story about a proposed ballot measure to creating affordable housing for teachers, who were being priced out of the city. Jake turned the radio back down again, so it was just background chatter.

'No news is good news,' he said, hoping he sounded more confident than he felt.

'I thought she was dead,' Molly said. 'I mean, when it happened. There was — there was so much blood, and she wasn't moving and I—'

Jake felt a human urge to tell her not to talk, not to put herself through this. It was overwhelmed by his cop's urge to let her keep going, let a witness reveal information.

'I just... I mean, I don't understand why. Did he want to steal the car?'

Jake didn't answer. Sooner or later, he would have to tell her that, in all likelihood, this was his fault. His fault her mother was lying in a coma, that she might still die. His fault Molly herself had almost been killed. His fault she was riding in a stolen car, hiding from the people who should be able to help her. He promised himself he would tell her, but not yet. Not until they got to where they were going.

'What did he look like?' he asked after a moment, changing the subject without making it too obvious. Molly had related the basics. A guy on a bike. A gun. An exploding window. He hadn't wanted to press her earlier, when she was still at the sharp end of the shock.

She didn't answer right away, and he took his eyes off the

road ahead to glance over at her. Her brow was furrowed, as though she hadn't considered this yet.

'I couldn't see his face. The helmet...'

'The motorcycle helmet?'

She nodded. 'Yeah, the visor was down, so...'

'What did the bike look like?'

She nodded again, looking confused. 'Just... a bike?'

He kept nudging with questions, giving her time to think, trying to reassure her, while telling her it was important to try to remember any detail she could, no matter how insignificant. She was a pretty good witness, considering.

The attack had come when her mom had been parking the car. As far as she could remember, the build of the shooter wasn't noticeably bulky or skinny. Not tall or short. She had seen the rider pass them a minute before, and he had looked in her window. He had checked out the target to make sure Rachel was in the car. Maybe he had known she was about to reach her destination and would be cornered in the parking lot. That would make sense. A pro? If so, there would be a way to find out who he was, and who might have hired him.

When Molly had finished speaking, she rubbed her eyes and looked away. Jake watched the road. There was a truck parked on the shoulder up ahead, its hood up. A wide-built man with a do-rag standing over the engine looked up at them as they passed. Jake stole a glance in the mirror to check the guy hadn't turned to watch as they passed, but he was bent over the engine again, engrossed in the task. Nothing to worry about, he hoped. Random strangers make eye contact with you a dozen times a day. You just don't usually have cause to be concerned about it.

The attack on Rachel and Molly had to be a message to him, somehow. The only question was why? Why kill Rachel and frame him, rather than cutting out the middleman and just killing him? He had made enemies, that was true. But he couldn't think of any who would be in a position to do this.

Every time a car passed in the opposite lane, Jake watched the driver and any passengers, looking for any glance in their direction, anyone paying attention to them. No one did. But it would be different when they left the safety of a car. They couldn't stay wrapped up in their metal-and-glass cocoon forever, so some things would have to change. Jake slowed as he saw a sign for a gas station ahead, hoped it would have a convenience store attached.

'What if we just call the police?' Molly said. 'Explain everything? I mean, they know you wouldn't do this.'

He grimaced. He wasn't so sure about that, even if someone hadn't gone to extreme lengths to convince them otherwise.

'We will do, as soon as it's safe. In the meantime, I think we're going to have to change a couple of things.'

He glanced at her again and saw her holding a strand of her long red hair, understanding immediately.

'Okay,' she said.

21

Lark called the hospital for an update just after five o'clock. Rachel Donaldson was in a stable condition, though still unconscious. That was one piece of positive news. Another was that SAC Finn had personally called George Driscoll, the Board of Supervisors member who had been interviewed on TV earlier. He had asked him, politely but firmly, not to make any more demands for their suspect to be brought in dead or alive. The task force had enough problems without men in positions of power tacitly advocating vigilante action. There was a database full of sightings of Ellis and Molly that had mostly turned out to be erroneous. What if somebody decided to act on one of those sightings before it had been ruled out?

The more Lark thought about the TV interview, the more it irritated her. She had a lifelong aversion to clear-eyed soapbox orators, burning with moral fervor.

'The guy has form,' Finn explained. 'He's taking every opportunity to paint himself as the true-blue law-and-order guy. The dead-or-alive thing is a dog whistle to his base. I think he's angling to run for governor in a few years. Let's hope he burns out before then.'

Now she'd had time to think about it, Lark recalled seeing Driscoll interviewed before, back when there had been a controversial new homelessness center proposed in his district.

Investigations like this one were challenging enough without politicians and media personalities and now, apparently, pod-casters trying to make it about them.

Lark closed the door on her office and sat down with the file on Ellis's police brutality case.

It had been a routine traffic stop on November 12 last year. Ellis had been patrolling solo. Not an unusual state of affairs; a legacy of years of cuts to the department. He pulled over a car doing double the speed limit on West Pacific Avenue. It was a blue Mercedes-Benz S-Class, and in the report, Ellis said he assumed it was stolen, on account of the way it was being driven.

He was mistaken about that. The driver was Linton Martin Jr, the twenty-two-year-old only child of the previous Linton Martin, who himself came from a long line of San Francisco old money. There was still some of that around in the city, if you looked hard enough.

What happened next was the point of contention. Ellis claimed Martin tried to hit him, resisted arrest. Martin claimed Ellis hit him first. Ellis wasn't wearing a bodycam, so the con-trasting accounts of the two men was all there was to go on.

What wasn't in doubt was who had come out of the encoun-ter worst.

Officer Ellis came away with a slight scratch on his cheek, Martin had a black eye, a cut across his forehead that required four stitches, and two cracked ribs. He yelled police brutality, and his father's legal team made sure the complaint was upheld. Ellis was suspended, pending investigation. The fact that Martin had been way over the blood alcohol limit didn't help his case, but it was hard to argue he hadn't taken a beating. In the end, the department had reached an agreement with Martin Snr's lawyers. Martin Jnr walked from the DUI charge with a slap on the wrist; Jake Ellis went back to work with a black mark against his name.

Lark looked up from the file as she considered its contents. On one level, she was disappointed there wasn't something more damning in here: something that pointed to a pattern of behavior. Were it not for the knowledge of what Ellis had done today, she would have been all the way on the cop's side in this account. But victims come in all shapes and sizes. Linton Martin Jr might have been an entitled little douchebag, but it was entirely possible he was telling the truth. Either way, the stress of the disciplinary process would have taken a toll on Ellis. Maybe it was one of the factors that had caused him to snap.

She put the file aside and picked up the other one on Rachel Donaldson. Thirty-nine years old, mother of one. She wondered if she would get a chance to speak to Rachel, to tease out the real life underneath the bare statistics, the work history and sparse family contacts that were all she had to go on. She hoped so, but the surgeon she had spoken to ten minutes before hadn't sounded overly optimistic.

Rachel had come from a nice, stable family in Napa. She had never gotten into trouble as a teenager. Majored in business administration and minored in drama at the University of California, San Francisco, before graduating and getting a job at an accountancy firm, marrying and having a kid. A very nice, normal existence, the kind most people wanted. Until her husband died when their daughter was an infant. Some kind of undiagnosed heart defect, out of nowhere. Both parents were deceased, too.

The details on her relationship with Jake Ellis were sparse, but she hoped some of Rachel's friends and neighbors might be able to give her more information.

All they had to go on right now were the occasional updates to Rachel's Facebook page.

A group photo in a bar on Market Street, posted at 22.44 on January 7. Five people standing around a table: three women and two men – the two on the right of the picture easily identifiable as Rachel Donaldson and Jake Ellis. Not that the human eye was necessary to make the identification, of course, since all five people were labelled. Either tagged manually or automatically by Facebook's sinister facial recognition algorithms. Lark hated that stuff. It was one of a hundred reasons she wasn't on social media.

All five were smiling. Rachel's hand was on Jake's shoulder. She was dressed in slacks and a cream blouse, he in jeans and a black short-sleeve shirt. A casual meet-up, not a formal event. They were all holding drinks of various kinds: Rachel holding a highball, Jake cradling a beer.

Caption: Great to catch up with the old gang.

The old gang. The other three were tagged as, left to right, Mike Apple, Jennifer Greer and Elaine Peel. They were trying to line up interviews with all three, had an appointment with two already. But Facebook actually filled in a lot of the blanks without the need to lift a phone. All five had been at UCSF in the late nineties. That and the comfortable way Rachel's hand was resting on Ellis's shoulder gave Lark a hunch as to what had happened. College sweethearts, or maybe just good friends. It hadn't worked out in the nineties, but they had come back into contact in the last few months and, somewhere along the line, had gotten together.

That was clear from some of the subsequent updates. Rachel wasn't a particularly prolific Facebook user, but she posted once or twice a week, usually photographs. In the weeks following on from the January 7 post, there were another five pictures featuring Jake. Another group shot with a different line-up on a different night, then one of him outside the house in Bayview with Molly, then one of Jake and Rachel over dinner in an Italian restaurant on Sacramento Street. Then the clincher: January 21: **Rachel Donaldson** is in a relationship with **Jake Ellis**. Nowadays, that's as official as it gets.

Lark looked back over the series of photographs, searching for hints of what had unfolded this morning. She knew it was a fruitless exercise. Even in unvarnished real life, she knew what people would say: they were such a nice couple... he seemed like a regular guy... you just never know...

If you could fool people in real life, it was child's play to fake it on Facebook and Instagram. Lark had put away a lot of bad guys over her fifteen years: fraudsters, bank robbers, murderers. Most of them could take a decent picture, or hold a conversation. Monsters can always hide in plain sight. That's how they get close enough to do harm.

Her phone buzzed with a message. It was Kelly Paxon, letting her know the report on the search of Ellis's apartment was in. She stood up and walked over to the window as she called Paxon. She looked down at the traffic passing by on Golden Gate Avenue as she listened to the ringtone. Where had Ellis gone after he took the SUV?

'Anything?' Lark said, wasting no words.

'Nothing immediately useful,' Paxon said. 'He left his phone in the apartment. That and his computer are with the computer science people.'

If there was anything useful on his devices, or in his internet search history, they would find it. But the very fact that he had left everything behind meant they couldn't use his devices to track him. Even with all the technology at their disposal, they would still have to lean heavily on the old-fashioned tactics: speaking to known associates, informed speculation about safe places he might run to, tip-offs from the public. At least that last thing was facilitated by the technology, not least the Amber Alert. When Lark had checked the update a half-hour ago, the tally of calls and messages from the public, volunteering information, had nosed into four figures. Most of that, if not all, would be garbage, of course. And the task of sifting through all of that grit looking for flecks of gold was a major challenge in itself.

'Anything else?'

'Nope. The guy has the most boring home life you can imagine. Even for a cop.'

Lark could imagine. She remembered how small the apartment had been. One bedroom, a kitchen, a living room. It wouldn't have taken long to give the place a thorough search. It looked as though he had left everything. They just had to hope he hadn't been carrying a lot of cash. He couldn't use his credit cards without being traced, and there had been no withdrawals from his bank account. That had all been checked already.

Something occurred to her. Officer Friedrich mentioned that Ellis had been wearing civilian clothes when he attacked him. No socks.

'Did they find Ellis's police uniform in the apartment?'

There was a pause as Paxon checked back through the report. 'Yes they did. In the closet.'

That wasn't the answer Lark was expecting. She had expected there to be no sign of it.

'Are there pictures?'

'Video from the walk-through. A set of blues, hung up, nice and neat. They took it in, obviously, but there were no visible bloodstains or anything on it, if that's what you're asking.'

Lark thought about it, said it out loud to see how it sounded. 'So ... he shoots his girlfriend, kidnaps her kid, then comes home and takes the time to change clothes and hang his uniform up neatly?'

Paxon paused. 'Maybe he thought it would be too noticeable. He thought street clothes would help him blend in.'

'And yet he didn't have time to put on socks?'

Paxon didn't have an answer for that. 'What are you thinking?'

'I don't know yet,' Lark said. It made no sense. If Ellis had been wearing his uniform when he carried out the shooting, as the witness had stated, it would have made sense to ditch the clothes somewhere, get rid of the evidence. If there hadn't been time to think about that, he would have kept wearing the uniform. It didn't quite add up. Perhaps it didn't have to, but ...

There was a knock on the door.

'I have to go,' she said to Paxon. 'Keep me posted.' She hung up and called, 'Come in.'

It was Garcia. He was jacketless and the sleeves of his shirt were rolled up. Lark didn't doubt it was his attempt at subtly drawing everyone's attention to how hard he was working.

'Jennifer Greer is in four.'

Lark waved an acknowledgment and gathered her papers as Garcia closed the door again. It looked like Jake Ellis's trail was hitting a dead end for the moment. Time to see if Rachel Donaldson's last few months held the key to finding her daughter. Along with her attempted murderer.

22

Molly watched as the ribbons of black circled around the drain. Last year, her mom had let her watch *Psycho* on TCM one night. She had read some online articles about the film afterwards; about how the shower scene was cut together, how they had to reshoot when Janet Leigh took a breath after dying. How they used Hershey's chocolate syrup for the blood, because it looked perfect in black and white.

She looked up from the sink, at the spot the mirror would ordinarily be. Except there was only dirty, cracked tiles and a slightly cleaner rectangle with four holes at the corners where the mirror had been. She couldn't evaluate her new look. Instead, she looked down again and took a lock of her newly black hair between her thumb and index finger. It wasn't just a different color, it actually felt different against her fingertips.

She didn't need a mirror to tell her that she looked different. Twenty-four hours before, she would have wondered about how it suited her. It seemed ridiculous now that she ever cared about anything so superficial. No doubt Kaitlyn Logan would have found something else to criticize, anyway.

'Not a carrot-top any more, bitch,' she said out loud.

There was a soft knock on the door. She called out, 'Just a minute,' and dropped the strand of hair. She picked up the stained towel and gave her hair a last rub to get it as dry as possible before stuffing it into the plastic bag, remembering Jake's warning that they had to leave nothing behind.

That was a joke. She had left everything in the world behind, except this ratty old towel from the trunk of a car her mom's boyfriend had stolen from a stranger.

She picked up the bag and walked out of the restroom and outside into the parking lot. This had been the third gas station they had tried, and the first one that had met with Jake's approval, because there were only a couple of other cars there when they pulled in, and the restrooms were housed in their own building. That was important. Not just because of the time it had taken to complete her makeover, but because exiting a bathroom with a different hair color to the one you had when you entered is the kind of thing that draws attention.

Jake was waiting by the door, keeping the gas station attendant in the corner of his eye. He didn't seem to be paying them any attention. Molly saw that Jake had undergone his own transformation. His hair was shorn to the skull with the clippers he had picked up along with the hair dye back in Red Bluff. He had lost the mustache too. It made him look older, somehow. Or maybe that was nothing to do with the hair. He scratched an itch on the top of his head and fitted the blue-and-white baseball cap he had bought over his head.

'Good job,' Jake said, stepping around her to inspect her hair. 'Big difference.'

She didn't reply, since there didn't seem to be anything more to add to that. Big difference. She hunched up her shoulders as a cold breeze drifted across her neck and the still-damp hair. Jake noticed and got that concerned look on his face again. He had been getting that look a lot. Like he was expecting her to throw herself off a bridge as soon as an opportunity presented itself.

'Let's get you back in the car. It's warmer.'

She sat in the passenger seat and watched as Jake crossed

the forecourt. He paid for the gas, and then came back out and started to make a call from the payphone. She guessed he was calling whoever they were driving to meet. Molly pulled the sun visor down and angled the inbuilt mirror a couple of different ways to inspect her new look. Jake had been right, it was striking how much of a difference it made. And it made her look older too.

She jumped as a set of beefy knuckles rapped on her window. She jerked her head up, knowing that it was going to be a cop. But it was just an old man, with a thin, drawn face that made him look a bit like a skeleton. He had watery blue-gray eyes, and wore a coat zipped right up to the neck, even though it wasn't all that cold. She looked back at the store for Jake, couldn't see any sign of him. She looked back at the guy outside. He was staring in at her, unsmiling. The door was unlocked. Should she lock it?

He kept looking straight at her, obviously expecting some acknowledgment.

She swallowed nervously and buzzed the window down a quarter of the way.

'Yes?'

'You have a problem, young lady.' She felt a cold chill and looked away from him so he couldn't keep inspecting her face the way he was doing. He had a low, raspy voice. Too many cigarettes, or maybe he had some kind of throat condition.

'Uh, no. No, I'm fine,' she mumbled. Added, 'Thank you.'

'No, you're not fine.'

'Everything okay here?'

She looked in the other direction to see that Jake had returned, holding a bag from the store.

The old guy stared back at Jake for a long moment.

Oh my God, he knows, Molly thought. *He knows.*

'No, everything's not okay, mister,' the old guy said. He started to walk around the car, then stopped before he got to Jake. He bent down and pointed at something at the rear of the car. 'You got a flat.'

Twenty minutes later, they were underway again. Molly had been a little unnerved by the way Jake seemed to snap into a whole different personality as soon as he realized why the old man had approached them. The pensive expression had vanished and his face had creased into a philosophical grin.

'Hey, if it's going to happen, this is the best place for it, right?'

Jake shook the old guy's hand and introduced himself without hesitation as Robert. The old guy, who said his name was Bill, waved away Jake's protestations and insisted on helping. It didn't take long to change out the flat for the spare, but Molly practically held her breath the whole time, wondering how the old guy managed to fit so many questions in as they worked. Jake didn't miss a beat. They were up from Oakland. Robert and Ursula Chambers. Mom was on the trip too: they had dropped her off to visit with a sick friend and had left the two alone to catch up for a while. The fiction sounded so convincing that Molly started to wish she could believe it herself. She was Ursula, not Molly. Her mom was only visiting a sick friend and would be right back to sit here in the car in an hour or two.

'He believed you,' Molly said, filling the silence that had enveloped them since pulling out of the gas station.

'No reason not to,' he said. 'People are lazy. You give them a plausible story, they won't go looking for problems with it. A lot of my job is remembering not to fall into that trap.'

Molly wondered if he was right. Their pictures would be on the TV. Sure, they had both changed their hair, but that was it. What if Bill saw them on the news and started to think about the man and the teenage girl he'd run into earlier in the day? What if that was enough to make him go looking for problems?

She glanced at the dashboard clock, realizing that for the first time today she had lost track of the time. It was just before the hour. She reached out and turned the radio up. The tuner had automatically picked up the next station along the dial. Some song from the eighties she vaguely recognized was playing, it had probably been on *Stranger Things*. Then an ad for an evangelist church, and one for windshield repair. Then the clock ticked over to seven.

'This is K-CVS serving Tehama County, I'm Kevin Jackson. We'll be back in three minutes, but right now it's over to CBS Radio for the news at the top of the hour.'

The first item started with her mother's name. She felt her chest clench and suddenly wished she had her inhaler. She was staring straight ahead at the road but could see Jake's fingers tighten on the wheel.

'Rachel Donaldson, the woman shot in an attack in San Francisco this morning is ...'

In the second before hearing the rest of the sentence, her imagination explored a lifetime where she was an orphan. Mom was dead. Whoever killed her would find them next. Or the police would find them, and Jake would go to jail, and no one would believe it wasn't him. No one would protect her from the man on the motorcycle.

Or try the best-case scenario. They would find new evidence and track down the man who did it. She and Jake would be safe. But her mother would still be dead. She would be all alone. Jake was a nice guy, but he wasn't her dad. Wasn't even a stepfather; it was all too soon for anything like that. There would be no one. Did they send you to a home at thirteen? Foster care? And, oh God, like any of that mattered. Why was she even thinking about it when her mother was ...

'... in a stable condition. Doctors carried out emergency surgery to remove a bullet from her head this morning.

Meanwhile, an Amber Alert has been issued for her daughter, thirteen-year-old Molly Donaldson, who authorities believe has been abducted by the suspected attacker, San Francisco police officer Jake—'

'Does that mean she's okay?' she said urgently, the rest of the newsreader's spiel disappearing from her awareness as smoothly as if the volume had been turned down.

'It's a really good sign,' Jake said, keeping his voice even. He was relieved too, though, she could tell.

'She hasn't woken up, though. They would have said if she had, wouldn't they?'

'Honest answer? I don't know. They don't give out everything to the media.'

She sat back in the seat, watching the road ahead. Despite everything, she felt a little lighter. Her mom wasn't dead. Not yet, anyway.

'When we get where we're going, can we try to call the hospital? We wouldn't have to say who we were.'

Jake didn't look at her, but she saw a pained wince.

'We'll see.'

23

Lark shook Jennifer Greer's hand and thanked her for coming in, and another agent escorted her toward the elevator.

Greer hadn't had anything useful to contribute: not surprising, as she seemed more acquaintance than close friend. The usual platitudes, about how Rachel was such a nice person, lots of examples of how she was a good friend and a loving mother. The kind of things people say after a friend at work dies. She even referred to Rachel in the past tense a couple of times, though Lark had been able to give her a positive update on Rachel's condition at the start of the interview: she was out of surgery and stable.

That was good news, though the doctors couldn't say how soon – if ever – the patient would regain consciousness. The next forty-eight hours were crucial. There seemed to be a lot of deadlines like that going around.

The doctors had been able to remove the nine-millimeter bullet from Rachel's brain, which was a good thing, in more ways than one. The ballistics people were running it now, to see if it could be matched to any guns that could be tied to Ellis. This was all stuff that would only be important if and when they caught up with Ellis.

She heard her name called from the other side of the office.

It was Colette Osborne, who was beckoning her over to her workstation.

'You're going to want to see this.'

'Something from his computers?' Lark asked as she approached. The confession in Ellis's draft emails had been found immediately, but the computer guys had been going through his devices since this morning to see what else was there.

She nodded. 'Well, from his social. Messages to the victim.'

She turned her screen around on its pivot for Lark to get a better look. It was filled with screen grabs from Facebook Messenger. She scanned the messages. Nothing particularly imaginative, but that didn't make it any less grim.

Bitch.

Whore.

. . . fucking kill you.

. . . kill the kid.

'Nice,' she said. 'How long does this go back?'

'Last few weeks,' Osborne said. 'Started turning nasty February 22.' She swiped at the screen and brought up one of the screenshots:

02.22.20, 01.18 – You really think I didn't notice you behaving that way? The whole bar saw you checking out that guy.

'Downhill from there. Last one sent this morning, an hour before he did it.'

04.18.20, 06.19 – Pick up. I swear to god I will not be responsible if you keep ignoring me you fucking bitch.

There was a preoccupied tone in Osborne's voice that Lark picked up on immediately.

'What is it?'

'It's just, they go in and out of it. It's not all like that. Like, one minute they'll be all happy couple, talking about dinner plans, the next he'll be threatening to kill her. The next morning, they're like it never happened.'

Lark held up a finger. 'First rule of domestic violence cases. Stop expecting either party to behave like rational people. The environment is toxic. Either they're too scared to provoke, or they get desensitized. The victim, as well as the abuser, starts to think it's normal. They brush off this kind of verbal like you would someone leaving a dribble of milk in the carton one morning. They stop thinking it's such a big deal.'

Osborne nodded. Lark suspected she was lucky. She hadn't been in one of those relationships, or raised in one of those families. It looked crazy to her, because it *was* crazy.

'Anyway,' Osborne said, tapping on one of the more unpleasant messages. 'This guy is a class-A son of a bitch. Anything I can do to help you nail him, let me know.'

Lark patted her on the shoulder. 'You already are. When you're sure you've got everything, give me screenshots of all the messages, okay?'

'You got it, boss.'

Lark noticed the shadows across the office had lengthened. The sun was going down. She straightened up and found the clock on the wall in her eyeline.

7.27 p.m.

Exactly eleven hours since the alert had gone out, and no closer to finding Molly.

24

'So,' Officer Hartzler said, taking a sip from his coffee cup. He winced; it was still a little hot. 'Thanks for reaching out.'

Lark had decided to give Hartzler a call after getting nowhere with Rachel's friends and co-workers. Jake Ellis's friends seemed to be thin on the ground, but perhaps this one could give her some kind of insight into the man she was pursuing. Hartzler was on duty but told her they could meet for a coffee if she could get away from the office. They met at a coffee stand in Union Square. Hartzler told his partner to go for a walk and they sat down on the steps facing the Dewey Monument.

She unfolded a sheet of paper she had been carrying in her jacket and handed it to Hartzler. It listed all of the known associates they had been able to establish for Ellis. It was a relatively short list. He had been raised by a single mother, who had died when he was nineteen. Most of the names on the list were cops, including Hartzler himself. Lark's team had already gone through the list, to no avail.

'Any of these stand out?' she asked Hartzler. 'Anybody missing?'

He studied the list for a minute and shook his head. 'Sorry.'

She took the paper from him and put it back in her pocket. 'Tell me about Jake Ellis,' she said.

Hartzler raised his eyes, seemed to study the monument and

the statue of Victory at the top, floodlit against the evening sky. 'Like I told you, he's a good man and a good cop. I've known him fifteen years, we came up together. Partners for three of those years.'

He took his phone out and showed Lark a picture of the two of them. It depicted Hartzler and Ellis with a female officer, all in uniform. 'That's us with Karen Hendricks, a couple years back. The day after this was taken she was shot by a dealer on Sixteenth Street. Jake risked his life to get her to cover.'

'She make it?' Lark asked. Ellis wasn't wearing his hat in the picture. He had a half-smile on his face, maybe in reaction to something one of the other two had said. He looked off guard, more human. It was much better than the SFPD profile picture.

Hartzler nodded. 'She wouldn't be here today if it wasn't for Jake.'

Lark asked if he would send the picture to her phone so they could add it to the website. He did so without complaint, and she prompted him to say more about Ellis.

He kept talking, sketching out an idea of the man. Lark could tell he was making sure to foreground Ellis's positive attributes: his focus on the job, his tenacity when pursuing a suspect, his willingness to stand up for others. But hints of something else slipped through: a guy with a quick temper, prone to impulsive acts.

'You still don't think he's guilty,' Lark said after he seemed to have finished speaking.

'I don't believe Jake would do something like this, not without a good reason.'

Lark narrowed her eyes. 'What "good reason" could there be for shooting two unarmed people?'

He shrugged. 'I mean, maybe the witness got confused. That happens, you know it.'

Lark said nothing. She had seen the tape of the statement

now. Edward Da Costa hadn't seemed confused at all when he identified Jake Ellis. He came across as unusually certain, if anything. She let Hartzler keep talking.

'I don't know; he's a good guy. He's good at the job.'

'That seems to be a matter of debate.'

Hartzler smirked and took a drink. 'Linton Martin is a rich-kid prick. I don't know who started that—'

'But he had it coming, huh?'

'I don't expect you to understand.' He lifted his gaze again. 'Your office is a little farther from the street than mine.'

Lark rolled her eyes. 'If we're going to run through all the salt-of-the-earth beat cop versus stuck-up Fed bullshit, can we skip to the end? I have a lot on at work.'

Hartzler waved his hand. A gesture either of apology or dismissal, Lark didn't know which.

'I want to help,' he said after a minute.

'Good. Because we're all in this together.'

'I can ask around. See if any of the other guys have an idea of where he might have gone. If he reached out to anyone, they'll tell me. If I hear anything that might be useful, I can come to you.'

Lark raised an eyebrow at the conditional wording. Can, not will.

'And in return, you want to make sure you're in on it.'

'That's all I ask. And you can use me, you know that.'

She thought about it. 'No promises. But to be honest, I'm not in a position to turn down any help at the moment, Hartzler.'

They parted and Hartzler strode off to rejoin his partner on the opposite side of the square. Hartzler's words stayed with Lark as she made her way back along the street toward the office. She took a slightly longer route around. Even carrying a gun, she wasn't comfortable walking Turk Street after dark.

She didn't know if what Hartzler had said was true, if he

really was the only one who could get through to Jake Ellis, or if he was just hustling to get a better seat at the table. Or perhaps there was a third possibility. He seemed convinced of his friend's innocence. What if he was hoping to run interference, throw them off the scent? Whatever Hartzler came up with would have to be consumed with a grain of salt.

She hoped that Ellis wasn't already too far gone to be reached. If he was, then she knew how this would end. Either by his own hand, or by forcing the hand of whoever managed to corner him.

She hoped Hartzler was right, and that Ellis could be brought in without further bloodshed. For all their sakes. But particularly for Molly's.

25

The Ford's radio gave no more updates on Rachel's condition over the next couple of bulletins as Jake drove north into the growing darkness, the gaps between the towns getting larger as the towns themselves got smaller. For the hundredth time, Jake reminded himself it was good news. If Rachel was dead, it would be all over the news.

The bulletins started to feed more information about his and Rachel's relationship.

How they had met in college. His checkered recent past. The newsreaders kept it factual, but it was clear from the tone that he was a 'suspect' in technical terms only. As far as the world was concerned, he was guilty as hell. In between the hourly updates, he would tune around, looking for other stations providing news updates. At one point, he happened on a talk radio phone-in. The Molly Donaldson hunt was the topic of the day. The callers were varied in their tone, but united in their assumptions about Jake's guilt.

'Oh, God bless that little girl. I just don't think I'll be able to sleep tonight thinking about her.'

'You know what the problem is? One word: death penalty moratorium. These animals think they can get away with anything.'

'Typical cops, man. I bet they won't even try to catch him. They close ranks.'

Every other ad break, every news update, the information from the Amber Alert was repeated. Their details read out. The appeal to call the tip line or go to the website. Changing their appearances had been the right decision, but they couldn't do anything about the fact that they were a man and a girl of the right age and physical description. Enough for people to give them a second look, if they knew about the manhunt. The only thing they had going for them was the distance they had covered. The search was still primarily focused on the Bay Area, by the sounds of things.

They stopped at a gas station outside of Willow Creek and Jake topped up the tank and bought sandwiches. He wore the baseball cap and kept his head down as he paid the clerk. She barely glanced at him as she took the money, but he wanted to make sure the camera at the register didn't get a good look at him. A more pressing concern was the fact he now had less than fifty dollars in cash left.

The food gave him an energy boost. He kept pushing Molly to eat her sandwich, but she had only managed a quarter of it. She had drunk most of her bottle of water though, which was the main thing. He wasn't surprised she lacked appetite.

As darkness fell, the cars became less numerous. Most people heading north from the cities would be taking the 101. Those people would have the luxury of not having to worry about cameras and tolls and highway patrol and would arrive at their destinations more quickly. Jake thought about the call from the payphone back at the gas station. Diehl's number hadn't rung out, it was disconnected. That didn't mean anything, really. Lots of people don't have a landline any more. No reason why Diehl would be an exception. Except he knew that was B.S. The cell reception where he was would be patchy at best. He suspected it had been one of the reasons Diehl had moved to the area. It was certainly one of the reasons they were headed there.

Jake had read a feature in a newspaper once about a place in West Virginia inside a federally designated zone where there was no radio, no cell coverage, no Wi-Fi. They called it the Quiet Zone. West Virginia was a little far to go, but perhaps this place would suffice.

Jake looked over at one point and saw that Molly had a strand of her long, newly dyed hair in her palm. She was looking at the black hair like she was about to start crying again. She sensed him watching her and looked quickly away, raising her hand up and sweeping the strand of hair out of her face.

'It looks fine,' Jake said, hoping that was the right kind of thing to say. 'And the pack said it comes out in three to five washes, you'll be back to normal in no time.'

'I might keep it like this,' she said, her voice flat. 'Brunettes get less crap.'

'Everybody gets crap,' Jake said.

There was silence for a while. A logging truck blew by them in the other direction and then the road was empty again.

'So, who gives you a hard time?' he tried.

'It's no big deal,' Molly said. 'Kaitlyn Logan, mostly. She stalks people on Instagram, comments on everything with her little digs. Her new thing is to call me a carrot-top. So original, right?'

'I'll tell you what. Next time she does that, next time *anyone* calls you a carrot-top, you know what to do? You get in real close, and you give them a solid punch, right here in the kidneys.' Jake tapped himself in the side for effect.

Molly was looking back at him with an expression he realized was one of sympathy. Like she appreciated him trying, but he was doing the world's worst job at bonding. 'Mom always says violence doesn't solve anything.'

'She's right. Always was smarter than me.'

It was just after nine when they saw the sign for the exit up ahead: FALSE KLAMATH.

When he had time to think about it, there had really only been one place to go.

He needed someone he could trust. Someone who had a safe place where he and Molly could hide out until he had time to get to the bottom of this. The difficult part was he needed that someone to be a person who would not be easily identifiable as an associate. Only Diehl fit the bill. But the truth was, there were very few other people he could trust in any case. He thought some of the guys from the station would back him up, but he wouldn't put them in the position of having to. It couldn't be anyone in law enforcement, and when you ruled that out, how many other people did he really know all that well? Precious few associates, and fewer friends.

He had never visited the place in person. The unusual name had stuck in his memory the last time he spoke to Diehl.

'You need to come up and visit, Jake. It's beautiful.'

Jake had assured him he would but had never gotten around to it. He smiled to himself in the darkness. *Here I am, just like I promised. Of course, I'm only here because it's the only place left to go.*

'Are we still in California?' Molly asked as the tree cover dropped away to their left and the expanse of the Pacific was laid out before them, a trail of moonlight shining across the surface.

Jake nodded. 'Barely. We're about fifty miles south of Oregon.'

The headlights picked out the sign at the edge of town when they were a hundred yards from it.

'False Klamath,' Molly read. 'What does it mean?'

'I think it's named after an old Indian tribe, or something.'

'Native American,' Molly said automatically.

'Native American,' Jake agreed, smiling. 'I don't know about the False part.'

'You're sure this guy can help us?'

'I hope so.'

26

A short line of stores and a gas station marked the edge of town, which was a cluster of one-story houses on generous plots of land. A little beyond the gas station was an old billboard, still displaying unreadable scraps of whatever the last paid ad had been. There was a space behind it that looked big enough for a car. If Diehl didn't have a garage, it might make a good place to stash the Ford.

Jake didn't have a precise address for Diehl, but he had gambled that there wouldn't be so many homes that it would be difficult to narrow it down from the details he had. Diehl had talked about a view out over the cove. About sitting on the deck out back and sipping a glass of Scotch as the sun went down. About a willow tree in the yard. The solar panels he had fitted on the roof.

The road circled around and then gained height, getting closer to the coastline. Jake slowed as he passed the houses until he saw one with a willow up ahead. No car in the driveway. Solar panels on the south-facing roof. He pulled off the road and parked at the foot of the driveway. He told Molly to stay in the car and got out. He took a moment to look back the way they had come. You could see a clear half-mile of the approach road from here.

The house was in darkness. Jake walked around the side.

There was a deck around the back that looked out over the cove. It would probably be a beautiful view, when you could see it. Right now, it was a black void. The sound of the ocean lapping against the shore drifted up. This had to be the place.

He walked around to the front of the house. It was number 22. No nameplate. He rang the doorbell.

Nothing. He tried knocking. Waited ten seconds. He tried the handle. Locked.

He stepped away from the door, looked back at the car. He could just make out Molly in the passenger seat, looking back at him expectantly. He beckoned her to come out.

'No one's home?' she asked when she got close enough to whisper.

Jake answered in a normal speaking voice. The nearest house was two hundred yards away. 'Doesn't look that way.'

'What do we do?'

Jake told her to wait there while he got back in the car and pulled it into the gravel parking spot around the side of the house. There were six-inch lengths of spindly grass jutting through the stones. He got out and, after looking around to check they weren't being watched, took the tire iron from the trunk of the car. Molly's gaze lingered on it, but she said nothing. They walked around to the back, where the deck was. There was a single rocking chair and a little table. He could picture Diehl sitting with his Scotch, thinking about old times.

There was a pair of glass-paneled French doors. They were locked too, but the lock looked pretty basic. Jake took the tire iron and edged it between the doors at the handle. Molly took a breath of surprise as she realized what he was doing.

'Won't your friend mind?'

Jake didn't answer, didn't want to think about why his friend might not mind. He tightened his fingers on the iron and pulled sharply. The wood of the frame splintered with a loud crack and the left-side door swung out toward them.

He stepped inside a kitchen. The furnishing was probably older than he was. Carved pine cupboard doors, good-quality but ancient linoleum on the floor. He remembered Diehl saying the house had belonged to some old geezer. 'I guess it still does,' Jake had joked, not really meaning it.

The house was completely silent. The far-off noise of the waves on the shore was audible.

'It smells like my grandpa's house,' Molly whispered. 'When we cleared it out.'

Jake didn't answer. She was right: the air smelled *old*. Like newspapers and stale cigar smoke.

In the course of his job, Jake had been inside all kinds of residences. This one had a very specific smell. The older relative's house, empty and waiting to be put on the market.

They left the kitchen and went into the hallway. The moonlight shone through the frosted-glass panel on the front door, making it light enough to see. He heard Molly cough behind him, then clear her throat. There was a heap of mail by the door. He crouched down and leafed through it. Mostly junk and flyers. It had been building up for a while.

He found a sheet of coupons for a place called Kris-Mart with expiry dates a couple of months ago, meaning they had been delivered weeks, or months, earlier than that. There was only one piece of real mail. A light-colored envelope with a window. His heart sank when he saw the tasteful logo of a law firm printed on the bottom corner of the envelope, and sank deeper when he read the addressee: *Heirs of Mr James Delaney Diehl.*

He ripped the envelope open and read the contents.

He heard Molly coughing again from behind him. She had a hand on her chest, looked like she was making an effort to breathe more shallowly. The place was dusty. Could use a good airing out.

'You okay?'

She stuck a thumb up, her gaze moving to the letter in his hand. 'What is it?'

'He's dead,' Jake answered. He scanned the contents of the letter. Three paragraphs: perfunctory condolences, a reference to Mr Diehl passing away on November 14, a request for contact details for heirs. They had probably sent this letter out to every address they had on record. Jake could have saved them the trouble. His wife had passed twenty years ago. He had no heirs, at least none he had ever talked about. Last of his line.

'So ... we can't stay here?'

Jake turned and saw she was shaking, even though her voice had been calm. He remembered why they were here. Molly had been coping so well that it was easy to take it for granted. She had been violently attacked. She had almost lost her mother. Could still do, come to that.

'The man who owned this place wouldn't mind,' he said. 'Let's get some rest.'

27

Chrissie's phone buzzed with the email as she was paying for a burrito at La Taqueria just after ten. A late dinner, when the rumbling of her stomach reminded her she hadn't eaten since breakfast. Episode three was in the can and due to drop later tonight, though she had a nagging feeling they were treading water. The live-case angle had certainly brought them some attention; the challenge was how to keep people interested.

She had tried again to get an interview with Edward Da Costa, the witness who had seen the whole thing. Even a quick soundbite over the phone. She had managed to get ahold of his home number, but Da Costa's wife had answered. She had declined again, and held firm against Chrissie's best efforts: it wasn't happening. That meant the only exclusive in the new episode was an interview with one of Jake Ellis's neighbors, Carl Lomax, who said he had helped his son out by talking to some neighborhood bullies. It didn't quite fit in with the image that was building of Jake Ellis so far, but that was one of the things Chrissie liked about looking beneath the surface on these cases. People are fascinating. Good people do bad things. Bad people do good things.

She paid with her card and almost walked away without her food, impatient to read the message. She hoped Sean wasn't having a technical issue. The downloads and new subscribers had gone through the roof since earlier in the day, and she hoped they could continue to keep riding that wave.

But it wasn't Sean, it was a Gmail account with the sender name *Tru Crime*. That was odd. Her personal email wasn't on the website. Email tips usually came through the generic address. The subject was:

Of interest?

An attachment, no other text by way of explanation.

She clicked on the attachment. It was a series of images. Screenshots of messages. She started to read through them, before tearing herself away with an effort of will and calling Sean. Could this be for real?

He answered on the second ring. 'It's just about to go live, chill ou—'

'No!' she yelled. A tall, skinny guy wearing headphones was walking past, and her exclamation was loud enough to cut through whatever he was listening to. He glanced at her and gave her a wide berth on the sidewalk as he passed.

'What do you mean "no", I thought you said—'

'I need to record a new intro,' she said, then thought again. 'Wait. No. An outro. A new segment at the end.'

'No,' Sean said. 'It's locked.'

'Oh, don't give me that shit, you're not working for NPR. The episodes can be whatever length we goddamn want them to be.'

He mumbled something about having to remix the outro music, but in the end he went along quietly, like he always did. 'You want to come back here?'

She looked at the time. She wanted to get this out before the messages hit the news. This time of day, it would take her forty minutes at least to get all the way to Sean's apartment, even if the BART wasn't suffering one of its regular delays.

'No. Hang on a second.' She turned and went back into the

restaurant, taking the phone from her ear and affecting her most dazzling smile. The server looked up, his brow furrowed beneath his white peaked cap. 'Hey! Can you give me the code for the restroom?'

'I'm sorry, the public restroom is out of use, ma'am.'

She didn't miss a beat. 'Then would it be okay if I used the staff restroom?'

He opened his mouth and hesitated. 'We're n—'

She let the smile drop. 'It's for a personal issue.'

Fifteen seconds later, she locked the door on the staff restroom and looked around. It was a small, unisex cubicle. Toilet, sink, dryer all within the same space. The walls were tiled. She guessed that would be okay for acoustics; she had once read an interview with some singer or other who talked about recording all her demos in the bathroom. She sat on the toilet seat and looked at her phone screen. The call was still in progress. She changed window to show the email attachment, scrolled down to see the ones she wanted to read out.

'Sean, you still there?'

'Yeah.'

'Okay, count me in. I'll do this, and then we can add some of it to the teaser.'

Sean counted down from five, leaving the last two silent, and she started talking. No script, she knew exactly what she had to cover and where this link would fit in: right after the interview with Carl Lomax.

'But there are other sides to Jake Ellis's personality. The same guy who would help fix your car, or run a home security check, was apparently capable of murder. The same guy who told Carl Lomax's son not to give in to the bullies was giving someone else advice too.

'Advice like, "If I see you talking to him again, I'll cut your

122

fucking throat." Like, "Don't speak to me like that. Who do you think you are, you fucking bitch?"'

Chrissie kept her voice completely neutral as she read out the text messages. It sounded more powerful that way: she didn't need to emote, to signal shock over the contents. The listeners would add that all by themselves.

'Advice like, "Who the fuck do you think you are? You disrespect me like that again and I'll put a fucking bullet in your head. You and your kid. Two bullets."'

28

Jake drove the Ford back around to the main road and parked it behind the old billboard. Then they made the return trip to the house on foot. Molly took clean sheets from the closet and went into the bedroom. Jake wasn't about to put money on Molly getting any actual sleep, but he hoped she would rest.

As for himself, he felt exhausted, but he also knew he wouldn't be able to sleep. He went out on the back porch and stood by the rocking chair where his old friend had liked to sit and drink Scotch. He leaned on the pine railing and listened to the sound of the waves lapping against the rocky shore at the bottom of the cliff for a few minutes.

He had found a flashlight in one of the kitchen drawers. He considered exploring the terrain around the house but decided it would be better to wait until morning. He would only draw attention with the flashlight. In the meantime, there was nothing else he could do but think.

Jake had always fancied himself as less dependent on technology than most people. His cell phone was almost three years old, and he had only replaced the previous one, a candy bar model that probably qualified as an antique, because the battery had finally given up the ghost. He didn't really engage with social media, had only reluctantly set up a Facebook account because people didn't text any more and he needed a way to receive messages. He still read books. He even bought news-papers, although less often, he had to admit, than he used to. He still maintained a landline, although it rarely rang and when it did, it was usually somebody selling insurance. He didn't have a Fitbit. He didn't have a smart refrigerator or lights you could talk to or a button that ordered toilet paper automatically.

All of that was an advantage in the current situation. There was less for the people hunting him to profile, less data on which to base predictions. But it wasn't nothing. His phone would still contain a lot of information about him from the calls he had made, as well as from the location data. Like most people, he had always meant to opt out of that stuff but had never gotten around to it.

That was the single most important reason for choosing Diehl's place as a refuge: he had never been here before. When he had last spoken to Diehl, it had been in person, at some dive bar in Russian Hill. He thought back and the last time they had spoken on the phone had been almost a year ago, via the landline. Diehl had called him. That was the one record of them speaking, and he hoped it wouldn't stick out among the other calls.

But there was a big downside to being as completely cut off from technology as he now was. He hadn't appreciated how much he had come to rely on satellite navigation, for instance, on having a friendly artificial person continually telling him the next move he needed to make to get where he was going. He had known roughly where False Klamath was, but buying a map, finding the town and working out the sequence of roads to get there, avoiding the interstate, had been like relearning a forgotten skill.

Access to up-to-the-minute news was the thing he missed most, of course. Like everyone else, he had gotten used to being able to find out what was happening in the world at any given moment via his phone. He couldn't do that now, and the fact that he *was* the news made it doubly unnerving.

And now he was in the middle of nowhere with a television that only got basic cable, a computer that wasn't connected to the internet and a cell phone he couldn't switch on. He had the TV on with the sound down, but so far he had seen very little on the progress of the manhunt. On the ten o'clock news, there had been a clip from a press conference earlier; an FBI agent named Lark talking about how dangerous their suspect was, and how he should not be approached.

He looked over at Rachel's small Samsung phone, lying on the coffee table, keeping its secrets. Perhaps it could give him the answers. Perhaps it could put his mind at ease, or warn him not to be so complacent. Tell him that the police were homing in at this moment. Tell him if his girlfriend was dead or alive. Tell him *why*.

But, of course, switching it on would only bring them here. It was like some *Twilight Zone* vision of a future society where the technology that could save you would kill you at the same time.

No. They had passed a gas station on the edge of town. In the morning, he could walk down there, see if it sold newspapers. He could get up to speed with what had happened today, if nothing else. In the meantime, all he had was peace and quiet and time to think. That was something.

His thoughts turned first to Rachel. The last few months had zipped by, and only now did he realize that that was because he had been happy. Finally happy. For a short time, despite the disciplinary action, it had felt as though everything had been going right. It was like they had fast-forwarded past dating and found themselves in a long-term relationship. They appreciated each other, enjoyed spending time with each other. Going to movies, cooking dinner at Rachel's place, planning weekend getaways that they hadn't got around to yet. Yet.

Maybe it was some kind of divine punishment. He wasn't supposed to be happy and carefree. Something always had to come along and fuck everything up.

Who had done this? That was the most important thing to establish. Everything else flowed from there. If he worked out who, he could work out what to do about it. A cop makes enemies, but not many with the will or the resources to do something like this.

The most recent enemies he had made had, of course, been the Martin family. He and his career hadn't exactly come away unscathed from the experience, but he knew Linton Martin Senior had wanted him off the force. That hadn't happened. Was he making it happen by other means?

Attempting to murder a woman and a kid and framing him was extreme, but was it out of the question? He didn't know. Martin was rich, and unquestionably an asshole, but Jake's instinct was that he wouldn't go this far.

But what other explanation was there? It was no carjacking gone wrong. That might explain the bare circumstances of the attack on Rachel, but not the attempt to frame him, too. No, this was targeted, and who had reason to target him like this? Sure, he had helped put some dangerous people away over the years, but always as part of a team. There was no well-resourced criminal genius out there who had been biding his time waiting for payback.

So think. Break it down. Make a virtue out of a necessity. No internet, no news, no way to contact anyone tonight. But lots of time to think.

Someone wanted to set him up. Why? No, don't think about that now. Think about how.

They build a frame and put you in it. They have you watched, build up a picture of your routine, your personal life, the people you love. They line up the frame, and then they send someone to kill Rachel and Molly. But the killer screws up. Rachel isn't dead, and Molly escapes. They're forced to adapt. The frame for a double murder still works for an attempted murder and a kidnap. The only way it doesn't hold is if the victims can tell the cops that you weren't the shooter.

Jake heard a creak from the bedroom as Molly shifted in bed. Not sleeping either. He leaned back on the old couch and closed his eyes.

The shooter. Forget about who hired him, for now. Molly had said the shooter was riding a motorcycle. He didn't think that had been mentioned on any of the radio bulletins. Tomorrow, he would check if it had been reported in the papers. Maybe that was an angle he could pursue. If the shooter was indeed a professional, it might be possible to narrow down a list of names. Normally, he would pick up the phone to one of the guys at the station, ask them to put the word out, but that wasn't an option. Or was it? He would have to think about the risks of doing that: both to himself and anyone he decided to trust.

What did they want?

That was tougher to answer. Why come at him through Rachel? Why not just kill him? It would have been far easier to have done that. So this had to be a message of some kind. Jake had to be alive to get the message. Whoever it was wanted something.

He had to find out what that was. Perhaps there was nothing Jake could do to prove his innocence, but maybe he could keep Molly safe long enough to figure this thing out. And then? Then he would find a way to get to the people who did this and make sure of two things: that Molly and Rachel were out of danger, and that whoever was behind this wouldn't draw breath after Jake had finished with them.

Untraceable

Excerpt from Untraceable – Season 4, Episode 3, April 19

By the time this episode goes live, it will have been around twenty-four hours since Rachel Donaldson and Steve Holdcroft were shot and Molly Donaldson disappeared.

The suspect, Jake Ellis, was last sighted driving a gray Volkswagen SUV at the corner of Bush and Powell Streets in San Francisco, at around nine a.m. yesterday.

This episode, we have some interviews with people who knew Rachel and Jake. We have the latest updates on the search to find Molly, and we speculate on where he might have gone. But make sure you listen right until the end, because, last night, I received an anonymous email from a source. There's no other way to say it: what it contained was seismic.

29

'You and your kid. Two bullets.'

Lark's eyes widened as the presenter's voice got to the last, most damning of the messages she was reading out. Paxon opened her mouth to say something, but Lark put her hand up to tell her to hold off. She wanted to hear it all.

'You can view the messages on our website, at UntraceableSF dot com, as well as other special features and extended interviews. Join us for the next episode of *Untraceable*, coming as soon as we have something new on this tragic case.'

The presenter's voice dropped the plaintive tone and slipped into rote for the next part.

'Don't forget to subscribe wherever you get your podcasts, and leave a rating – it really helps new listeners to find us. *Untraceable* is a Missed Opportunity production, written and presented by me, Chrissie Chung. The producer is Sean Tramel. Music is provided by . . .'

Lark closed the playback window and turned to Paxon. She didn't even need to ask the question, it was all in the look she gave her.

The morning sun was streaming through the windows of the thirteenth floor of 450 Golden Gate Avenue. On another day, it might have lightened the moods of those working there. Today it only reminded them how long the clock had been ticking.

'I don't know,' Paxon said. 'Nobody outside the task force knew about the messages yet.'

'Well, they certainly know now,' Lark said. 'How many people listen to this thing?'

Garcia was in the corner, staring at the screen of his phone. 'According to iTunes, half a million subscribers and climbing. Everybody is talking about the show on Twitter, too.' He flicked his thumb upwards on the screen, scrolling through the feed. 'Hashtag FindMolly,' he read.

'You know, this might not be a—' Paxon began.

'Don't even,' Lark said, cutting her off. 'No publicity is bad publicity, right? That's not the point. The point is we have a leak inside the task force. Which means we can't control the flow of information.'

Garcia raised his eyebrows. 'Welcome to the twenty-first century.'

Lark shot him a look that made him take a step back and murmur an apology.

'We can talk to them, see if they'll give us their source,' Garcia said.

Lark sighed. 'I imagine we'll get to it at some point.' She doubted they would get very far. In Lark's experience, chasing down leaks was like trying to nail Jell-O to a wall. If anything, citizen journalists with an inflated sense of their own importance were even more forthright about their First Amendment rights. And if they tried to come down hard on some little podcast, it could have a negative effect on their relationship with the real news outlets.

'Nothing on his credit cards?' Lark asked. It was barely a

question. Any hope that Ellis might be dumb enough to use his credit card somewhere and put a big pin in his location had long since evaporated. Garcia shook his head.

Ellis had left his phone in the apartment, so that couldn't be used to track him either. That reminded her that neither Rachel's nor Molly's phone had been recovered from the car or their home, suggesting that Ellis had taken them. Why? At any rate, neither was currently active. Two more dead ends.

Lark turned to look at the state map on the wall, slowly tracing the line of the road from the last point the gray VW SUV had been seen. Dozens of potential places to zig and zag, or perhaps to stop and hide. She rubbed her eyes. She estimated she had managed three hours' sleep last night.

'He can't still have the SUV. He needs money or he needs a friend.' She turned around. 'How are we doing on known associates?'

Paxon consulted her phone. 'We've been working the list of KAs. Covered all of the primary list. Nobody has seen or heard from him.'

Lark had a little more faith in those responses than she might normally have when looking for a wanted fugitive. The innocent victims, the child in peril, changed things. Jake Ellis wasn't just wanted for jumping bail or check fraud. She believed people would want to help if they could. Like Hartzler. He didn't want to believe what his friend had done, but he knew the best thing for all concerned was that he was found, and quickly.

'Start casting the net wider,' she said. 'We already know about the Facebook messages. Start talking to Facebook friends-of-friends, whatever it takes.'

'Not much social,' Garcia said. 'He barely uses it, has fewer Facebook friends than my great-aunt, and she doesn't even know how to add her profile picture. He isn't on any of the other networks.'

'Great,' Lark said. It was unusual, in this day and age. Most people are entangled with the big tech companies tighter than they suspect, no matter how careful they are about security settings. It's easy to forget how much information we hand over voluntarily. How many digital footprints we leave without even being aware of it. These days, it was common to catch a suspect not because of a misstep in the here and now, but because it hadn't occurred to them to take note of every online interaction they had made in the past. More than one criminal Lark had nailed was currently serving federal jail time because they had freely broadcast a clue to something they had done, or a place they liked to go, months before.

She stared at the map. Not for the first time, appreciating just how big California was. And, of course, it wasn't as though their quarry was hemmed in by state lines. Almost twenty-four hours gone. Ellis could be in Kansas by now. Someone had to have seen him and Molly, if she was still with him. She hated not knowing. That didn't change the fact they had to work on the assumption Molly was still alive. Alive and in danger.

'Agent Lark!'

She turned to see a junior agent in a light-blue shirt standing at the door, shading the sunlight out of his eyes with one hand.

'What is it?'

'We've got the SUV.'

30

Jake looked up from counting the contents of his wallet and pockets, laid out on Diehl's outsize mahogany coffee table. Molly was standing in the doorway of the bedroom. She looked pale, but a little better than she had last night. She glanced at the paltry collection on the table and gave a humorless smile.

'Mr Big Bucks.'

'Forty-seven dollars and thirty-nine cents,' he said ruefully. 'I hope you like ramen.'

'This help?' She was holding a battered brown leather wallet. 'I found it in the drawer in the—' She stopped and cleared her throat. It was still dusty, despite him opening the windows at the back. 'In the nightstand. There's some more money in it.'

She handed the wallet to Jake. He spread the bills section open. A hundred and two tens. A welcome boost to their finances, but they would need a lot more than that if they wanted to stay off the grid indefinitely. There were also some cards. Diehl's driver's license, a library card from his old address and three credit cards. Two were expired, but the Visa still had three months to run.

He would add the cards to the go bag he had been putting together, along with a couple of changes of clothes, a hat and a pair of sunglasses. Diehl had been a little shorter and a little wider around the waist than he was, but the clothes from his closet fit well enough.

'Thanks,' he said, waving the wallet and smiling. 'We won't starve to death after all.'

Molly looked down at the floor. 'I'm not hungry.'

'I know,' Jake said. 'You need to eat something, though. I'm going to—'

There was a knock on the door.

The two of them froze.

The silence stretched out. Molly took a step forward. Whispered: 'What should we do?'

Jake held a hand up. It could be a mailman, or somebody selling something. Perhaps whoever was out there would give up. They waited. Thirty seconds passed. Just as Jake was starting to believe whoever it was had gone away, there was another knock.

'Hello?' came a female voice. Then, 'I know someone's in there.'

Shit.

'Wait here,' Jake whispered. 'Stay out of sight.'

Jake turned the key in the lock and opened the door on a slim woman in her early fifties, her arms folded. Dark hair with flecks of silver. She wore blue jeans and a pink halter top. She had to live close by; it was still a little cold to be outside without a jacket.

'Good morning,' Jake said.

'Who are you?'

Jake decided to respond with bemusement. 'Uh, who are *you*?'

'Eleanor Grace,' she said. She glanced back in the direction of the house across the road. 'I was Walt's neighbor.' She said it pointedly.

'Oh,' Jake said. He held his hand out. 'Robert. I was a friend of Walt's.'

She ignored the hand, tightened her arms around herself. He let the hand drop when it started feeling awkward.

He cleared his throat. 'Walt's attorney contacted me to see if I could come up here and dig out some paperwork.'

Eleanor Grace's eyes moved from Jake to the door behind him, trying to see in. She looked back at him. 'I expected they would send his niece. Do you know Jennifer?'

Nice, Jake thought. Worthy of a cop. He furrowed his brow and tried to look puzzled. 'Ma'am, Walt didn't have any nieces. He had no brothers or sisters.'

She thought it over. 'What was Walt's opinion on the Forty-niners?'

Jake grinned. 'That's easy. He hated them. He was a Steelers man all his life.'

Eleanor held his gaze for a moment. 'Okay. I just thought you might be some random weirdo. Sorry, I guess.'

'No need to apologize. I'm really glad Walt had such close neighbors.'

'He was a nice old guy. Funny too,' she added. 'How'd you know him?'

'We worked together, long time ago. He always said I should come visit, that I would like it up here. Just wish I had done it earlier.'

She nodded, then glanced back at the empty driveway.

'Where's your car?'

'I got a ride with someone. They'll be back to pick me up tomorrow.'

There was another pause. He hoped she wasn't going to invite herself in for a coffee or anything. She seemed proprietary enough over the place to do it.

'All right,' she said finally. 'Well, it was nice to meet you.'

'Likewise.'

The friendly smile vanished from Jake's face the second he closed the door.

★

136

Jake told Molly to stay at the house and keep away from all of the windows while he walked into town. The two of them, a man and a girl, strangers in town, would have stuck out like a sore thumb. Even though they had done all they could to change their appearances, they would have been noticeable just by virtue of being newcomers in a place this small.

As it was, Jake was worried that he would stand out on his own, but he didn't have a choice. There was no food in the house. And he needed more than that. He needed information. He needed to work out exactly what was happening, before he could begin to work out how to fix it.

The town's modest center was about a mile and a half from Diehl's house. Jake had plotted the route on the map he had found in Diehl's desk drawer. He didn't like what the map confirmed about their location: there were only three roads out of town. It would be easy for them to be boxed in.

Main Street was a cluster of one-story buildings. The store-fronts were mostly shuttered. It was difficult to tell whether that was because it was Sunday, or because it was a couple of decades into the twenty-first century. Only two places were open: a fishing store and the gas station. There was one lucky break. Outside the gas station, there was an old-fashioned phone booth, the kind you barely see any more in cities, or anywhere with decent cell coverage. During the walk down from the house, he had made up his mind to call Marty Hartzler. He might hang up on him, but he figured Hartzler was his best shot. The other cops he knew were a little too by-the-book to entangle into this. But first, he wanted to take a look at the headlines.

He pushed open the door of the gas station. A little bell tinkled as he entered. Behind the register, a woman in late middle-age with tied-back gray hair looked up from her paper-back and quickly back down again. The place looked like it doubled as a general store for the town. There were shelves on every wall, tightly packed with everything from canned ham to paintbrushes.

He made a point of not glancing at the rack of newspapers right away. Instead, he moved around the three aisles of the store. He picked up a big bag of barbecue-flavor chips, some frozen dinners, some soda and some bottles of water. The water was coming out of the faucets at Diehl's place, but it was cloudy and brownish after months of not being run.

He glanced over at the woman, still absorbed in her book.

Casually, he circled back around to the front of the store and surveyed the headlines:

TAKEN

KILLER COP

FIND MOLLY

It looked like they had made all of the papers. He already knew the case had media traction from the radio news, but it still took him aback to see his picture splashed on every front page.

FBI HUNT COP IN SF SLAYING/ABDUCTION

FEW LEADS IN HUNT FOR MOLLY DONALDSON, 13

He picked up a copy of the *Chronicle* and took everything to the counter. He placed the paper so that his picture on the front page faced down, even though it didn't look much like him anymore. Or at least he hoped not.

The lady put her book down and smiled. No recognition in her eyes.

'Good morning.'

Jake returned the greeting. He gazed beyond her to where the cigarettes and batteries were stored, away from shoplifters, and saw what he was looking for. A rack of phones hanging in clear plastic packs. There were some basic flip phones at $17.99, and cheap Alcatel smartphones at $39.99.

He wanted to take all of them, and he would have done if he thought it wouldn't raise questions. He asked for one of each.

'We're not getting a signal up here. *Verizon.*' He shook his head as he uttered the word.

'Hmm,' the lady said. 'I'm with Verizon and it's usually okay.' She scanned the phones, bagging them along with the food. They came with five dollars of credit each, and he bought a top-up card with another ten.

Jake handed over the money, suppressing a wince as he did so. That left him with just over eighty bucks, and the cards in his wallet weren't worth the plastic they were made of.

31

The town of Dunnigan was already crawling with law enforcement by the time Lark, Paxon and Garcia arrived.

The gray VW SUV had been found by a local resident, walking his dog along a trail about a half-mile outside town. The vehicle had been well concealed, considering its size. Coming at the end of such a long drought of usable information, the discovery had been like an oasis in the desert. The SUV Ellis had stolen had been found. Therefore, he had definitely been in the area between the last sighting in Oakland and now. Therefore, there were two likely possibilities: Ellis was still in the area, hiding out, or he had procured alternative transport nearby. It didn't take long to identify which. Only one car had been reported stolen within a forty-mile radius: a white Ford, taken from outside a funeral in this very town, sometime between two-thirty and three-fifteen yesterday afternoon.

Lark slowed when they reached the turning for the dirt track. There were agents in navy-blue jackets moving traffic along. One of them approached the window.

'We've set up a local command center at the fire station; it's on Main Street.' He straightened up to point the way. 'If you head—'

'Okay if we take a look at the SUV first?'

He turned and looked along the dirt track. 'Sure. Lot of traffic down there, so I'd recommend leaving the car.'

The SUV was a couple of hundred yards down the track, in a stand of trees. Completely invisible from the road, so it was lucky that the dog walker had happened by and remembered the SUV being mentioned on the news. Lark flashed her badge at the cop who started to approach them. She spotted the forensics truck parked on the edge of the track.

'They got here fifteen minutes ago,' the cop said, following her gaze. 'Working on the SUV right now.'

She checked the time. Less than two and a half hours since the initial call to the tip line. She was grateful it hadn't been lost in the avalanche of data, but it only proved how important it was to have accurate intel. A person, or persons, who looked *kind of like* their suspect wasn't something they had the resources to move on every time one was suggested. An identifiable vehicle, not moving, with the license plate they were looking for: that was something that went straight to the top of the pile.

'We're lucky he didn't burn it out, I guess,' Paxon commented.

'Wouldn't have been a smart play,' Lark said. 'A burning vehicle would have been noticed immediately. If he'd torched it, we'd have known about this place and the stolen Ford yesterday afternoon. Sure, it would destroy the physical evidence, but we already know who we're looking for, so it would be pointless.'

The evidence response technicians were working on the SUV. One at the open driver's door, dusting the steering wheel and the other touch surfaces, two in the back. She already knew the most important thing. The answer to the question she had asked as soon as she heard the SUV had been found: Molly Donaldson's body was not in the vehicle. There were no visible bloodstains or any other obvious evidence of violence.

The next ten minutes would give them an idea if there was any evidence invisible to the naked eye. The cadaver dogs would be brought in soon to search the woods. She hoped they were wasting their time.

Meantime, agents and people from the Yolo County sheriff's office were knocking on doors in Dunnigan, canvassing to find anyone who might have seen Ellis or Molly, but also asking if the owners would consent to a brief search of their premises. Lark didn't hold out too much hope. Ellis had stolen a car for a reason, and that reason wasn't to lurk around a small town a hundred miles northwest of San Francisco.

No, Ellis was long gone from here. That was almost certain. They knew the vehicle he had been using now, which meant they had the next link in the chain. But, for the moment, the question foremost in her mind was unchanged. Was Molly still alive?

Lark caught the eye of the technician beside the open passenger-side door. He was crouched over, working on something in the footwell. It made her think about Rachel Donaldson's car yesterday. They had hoped to find prints or blood that could be matched to Jake Ellis there, but there had been nothing.

'Anything?' she asked.

He looked up at her in acknowledgment, and then back down at his work as he answered. 'Yeah. Too much.'

He didn't have to elaborate. An old vehicle like this would have had many people passing through over its lifetime. Every one of them would leave traces: shoeprints, fingerprints, skin cells, buttons, fabric fibers ...

Hairs.

The tech had stopped and was peering at a long strand of hair. He reached for a pair of tweezers and an evidence bag and lifted it up to the light. Lark moved closer, careful not to touch anything. The tech held the long strand of hair in a beam of sunlight. It was red, and looked about the right length for Molly.

Her phone rang. It was Taylor, back at headquarters.

'News on the Ford?' Lark said, mentally crossing her fingers.

'Looks promising. It may have stopped at a gas station outside Willow Creek at seven-thirty yesterday evening.'

32

Jake closed the door of the phone booth and kept his eyes on the road. He dialed the number. A Tennessee area code, although he had no idea, and indeed didn't care, if that was where it was actually based.

As he waited for the call to connect, he thought about the last time he had seen Marty Hartzler in person. They had been close in the past, but the regular drinks at O'Malley's had become less frequent over the last few years, like those with his other colleagues. Part of that was a natural consequence of getting older, he guessed. The last time they had been face to face was on the job – Jake had responded to a report of a body dump under the freeway where it crossed 10th Street. Hartzler had already been on the scene with his partner.

It rang three times and clicked into an automated response. A hiss on the line, an accentless female voice so devoid of personality that he wondered if it could be some kind of AI. Only the hint of a sigh before the first word gave it away.

'Please enter your credit card number to continue with the transaction.'

Jake took out Diehl's Visa card and keyed in the long number followed by expiry as requested. A pause, then:

'Please enter the destination phone number.'

For a direct number, Jake would have had to consult his

own phone, which he had left at the apartment, and which he couldn't have risked turning on even if he had it with him. But that didn't matter. An indirect call would provide one more layer of distance between him and the recipient of his call.

Instead, he tapped in one of the few numbers he still knew off by heart: the number of the Mission Station.

There was a long, silent interlude while the broker service did whatever it did to route the call through a bunch of other exchanges so that both it and the source of the call were hidden under layers upon layers of misdirection.

Finally, a ringtone, followed by the sound of a phone ringing at the other end. It was crackly, like making a call to Europe used to sound in the old days.

'San Francisco Police Department, Mission Station. How may I direct your call?'

This part at least would be recorded, so Jake changed his voice a little. He strained for a lighter tone and channeled the southern accent of a friend from the academy. He had spent three years working alongside him, so he had the voice down pat.

'Hi, can you put me through to Officer Martin Hartzler, please?'

'Let me see what I can do. Can I take your name, sir, and ask what this is regarding?'

'Hawkins, Cole Hawkins. It's actually kind of urgent. If you tell him I'm calling about the Marino case, he'll want to take the call.' Timmy Marino was the name of a particularly memorable drunk he and Hartzler had busted numerous times when they were partners.

'Let me see what I can do,' the voice said again.

Jake heard keys tapping in the background. He hoped Hartzler wouldn't be anywhere with a landline. Less chance of being recorded.

145

'Please hold.'

The PD had a hold message, repeated over and over, thanking him for holding and saying an operator would be available soon. No music. What would they use? The theme from *Hill Street Blues*?

Jake turned and surveyed the road running past the gas station through the sunglasses he had found in the kitchen drawer at Diehl's. He had been gone for almost an hour. He hoped Molly would be okay when he got back. Perhaps she would be hungry enough to eat something by now.

The message cut out halfway through its fifth or sixth repetition, and the voice of the operator came back on.

'Putting you through now.'

Another distant, crackling ringing. Jake wondered how many links in the chain this was. Two rings, and Marty Hartzler's familiar voice answered.

'Jake? What the hell are you doing?' His voice was low, like he didn't want to be overheard. That was a good sign, he hoped.

'Marty, I can't talk for long. I didn't do it.'

'You didn't do what? You didn't kill a guy? You didn't shoot your girlfriend, didn't kidnap a minor? Do you have any idea—'

'How is she? How's Rachel?'

Hartzler paused, and for a second Jake was certain he was about to give him bad news. News that hadn't made the radio or the papers yet. 'Docs say she's critical but stable. You know how that goes.'

Jake knew. It could go either way. Marty wasn't trying to sugarcoat it for him.

'Jesus.'

'Man, I'm telling you—' he stopped, and Jake could tell he was moving, probably walking away from anyone who could overhear him. When he came back on, his voice was quieter again. 'I'm telling you as a friend: you gotta come in.'

'Not an option.'

'Jesus Christ, Jake,' he hissed. 'I'm not fucking around here. You know what'll happen to me if it gets out I took this call?'

'I know,' Jake said. 'That's why you should tell them about it.'

There was a pause, and Jake could picture Hartzler's knotted brow, the vein that stood out on his forehead when he was pissed.

'Is the girl all right? Tell me the girl's all right at least.'

'Of course she's all right, Marty. As long as she's with me she's safe. I didn't shoot Rachel. I love her, I would never—' he stopped as he heard his voice crack a little.

'Okay, I believe you, buddy,' Hartzler said. 'But you need to come in. Tell me where you are. I'll make sure it goes smoothly. We'll get you a good lawyer.'

'No. We can't do it that way. I need to work out who did this first. They wanted to kill Molly too. As long as he's out there, she's not safe.' He paused. 'Molly said the shooter was riding a motorcycle. Did anyone report that?'

'I didn't hear anything about that,' Hartzler said. 'The witness IDd you, he said—'

'He's lying,' Jake said. 'Start with him; can you get to him?'

'Tell me you're kidding. What am I supposed to do, look up his address and go beat it out of him?'

Jake bit his tongue so that he didn't say 'Wouldn't be the first time.' Because he didn't know that for sure, but he certainly wouldn't have put it past his friend.

'Can you at least poke around at the story? Or look into this bike thing at least, see if there's anything in the system that rings a bell. I can't do anything while I'm up— out of the action.' He caught himself just before he said 'up here'. Had Marty noticed?

Marty gave no indication, other than a resigned sigh. 'I'll ask around. Meantime, at least tell me where you are. I won't bring anyone else in. I can help you.'

'Better for both of us if you don't know.'

There was a long pause. 'What about money, then?'

'Running a little light, but I'll manage.'

'Let me see if I can think of something. Do you have a number I can call you on?'

'I'll call you again this time tomorrow, okay?'

'Shit.' Jake could hear the exasperation in Marty's voice. 'All right. Play it your way. But call me on this number.' There was a pause and he read it out. Jake jotted it down on the back of his receipt from the store. His personal cell, presumably. 'I'll tell you what,' he continued. 'Get one of those pre-pay credit cards, text me the number and I can put some money on it.'

'I can't ask you to—'

'Don't worry, it won't lead back to me.'

'Well, thanks,' Jake said.

'You know me, Jake – whatever it takes, man.'

Jake grinned. He had forgotten about Hartzler's little motto. It summed up why, when he had been thinking of contacting someone with knowledge of the investigation, he had been the only candidate. Hartzler was a good cop, but he had never been overly troubled by niceties of procedure when they got in the way.

'When was their last confirmed sighting?'

Hartzler paused before answering. Jake knew he was having to weigh up everything he said. Every second of their conversation was embroiling him deeper in aiding and abetting a fugitive. Jake had meant it: Marty really ought to do the smart thing and report everything about this call. He knew he wouldn't, though, because he wouldn't do it himself in this situation. Not if he believed his friend.

'They know you stole a white Ford in Dunnigan, which I hope for your sake you've gotten rid of. And we just got word they have a sighting after that at a gas station outside of Willow Creek.'

There was an unspoken question in the way he said that, like he was waiting for Jake to confirm or deny.

'All right. Molly's fine, Marty. Just make sure her mom is looked after until we can come back, okay?' His throat started to tighten up again at that, so when Hartzler answered by telling him to take care of himself, he simply hung up rather than trust his voice.

Twenty-four hours until the next call. He hoped it would be long enough to work out who was behind this thing.

33

Molly sat on top of the covers on the single bed in the bedroom, her back against the headboard, knees pulled up under her chin. It was colder in here than in the rest of the house. There was a crack in the windowpane that let in the air. The cool air was helping her chest a little.

Doctors say the victim, thirty-nine-year-old Rachel Donaldson, is in a coma following emergency surgery.

Molly kept hearing that part of the last bulletin on a loop. That one line. That one word. *Coma.* She knew what that could mean. Brain damage. Maybe her mom wasn't dead, but it could mean she would never see her again, never talk to her, never be able to thank her for everything she did. She had been such a brat yesterday morning, now she thought about it. Not realizing it had been their last few minutes together.

Jake had been gone a while now. He had said he had to work out why someone had done this to them. To all three of them, if what he said was true. That he had been framed.

She had believed him. Why wouldn't she? She had decided to go to his apartment on her own, although it hadn't been something she had thought much about. She had no other friends or relations in the city, and Jake had seemed ... well, he'd seemed okay. And of course she knew he hadn't done the thing that the news was saying: he hadn't shot her mom.

But what if he was involved, somehow? Why couldn't he just talk to the other police officers?

And then there were the other things the newsreader talked about. Some podcast which had gotten hold of messages between Jake and Mom. They hadn't quoted any of them, but it didn't sound good.

She wondered what kind of things he had said to her. Or what they had said to each other. Her mom's relationship with Jake was new, but it seemed to be going well. Her mom had only had a couple of boyfriends over the course of Molly's life. Ty, the accountant she had dated for a few months last year, had always made a point of trying to ingratiate himself with her. He had a habit of crouching when he talked to her, like you might do to a really young kid, not a tall-for-her-age twelve-year-old. Jake wasn't like that at all. He was ... cool. As in, nice, polite, but not too eager to please anybody. When she didn't feel like talking, he didn't force it. Like he was doing now, in fact.

But she knew people didn't always reveal what they were really like.

She wished she had somebody else to talk to, but for the moment, that was impossible. Not just inadvisable. She had left her phone in Mom's car. It was probably lying in some evidence locker right now. A cold feeling at the back of her neck as she had a thought that momentarily displaced the thoughts about her mother. The cops would go through it for clues, wouldn't they? Just like they must have gotten into her mother's Facebook account to find those messages. She didn't like the idea of someone going through all her texts and messages.

But she had to admit, that was a pretty low-priority problem right now.

Her friends would be worried about her. Maybe they thought she was dead already. If only she could somehow get a message to Nicole.

34

Jake walked back up the road to Diehl's house, constantly looking out for anyone watching him too closely. The only person he passed was a small middle-aged woman in brown-tinted sunglasses walking a Pomeranian. He kept his face angled away from her as they passed on the sidewalk. It was safer here, he reminded himself. San Francisco was a long way away. The people here wouldn't have gotten the Amber Alert.

He was going to move the car from behind the billboard to somewhere safer later on, but he wanted to check in on Molly first. When he reached the house, he kept on walking, past the driveway, and took the path down to the clifftop, so that he could circle around the back.

When he started to open the door, he stopped and took a breath as he heard the low sound of conversation. He pushed it fully open and stepped inside.

It was the radio. On low, in the living room. He approached the door and Molly turned around as he entered, her face wet with tears. There was a male voice on the radio. Sounded like a talk station.

'...cases like this, unfortunately sometimes they never find the child, or they find a body...'

Shit. Rachel. 'Molly, is...?'

She wiped the tears away with the back of her hand and

swallowed. 'No. Last bulletin said she's stable. She still hasn't woken up, though.'

'Oh,' Jake said. 'Good.'

When he had seen her crying like that, the way she had jumped when he walked in, he had assumed the worst.

He held up the bag from the store. 'I got us some food. You like mac and cheese, right?'

'It's fine, I'm not hungry.'

He put the bag down and stepped closer. He reached out to put a hand on her shoulder, but she flinched.

'Sorry,' he said, standing back and raising both hands like she was holding a gun on him. Damn it, he wasn't used to dealing with a kid, never mind knowing what the hell to say to a kid who might still lose her mother.

Molly swallowed and glanced at the old radio. The station had moved on to a local weather update. A cold front sweeping in from the Pacific. Temperatures dipping lower than average.

She cleared her throat. Her voice sounded a little raspy. 'They said they found messages. On Mom's Facebook, I guess.'

'What kind of messages?'

'From you. Um. Angry messages. Bad things.'

'What kind of things?'

'They didn't say. Apparently some podcast put them out there.'

'Molly, whoever did this wants to make sure everyone thinks I was responsible. You know that, right? You know I would never...'

'Right,' she said. Not meeting his eyes.

'I'm going to find out who did this, Molly. I'm going to make it all right.'

She didn't say anything. Perhaps it was his imagination, but she looked paler than she had earlier on.

'Molly, you need to eat someth—'

'You can't,' she snapped, looking up at him. 'You can't make it all right. I mean, unless you're going to go and find something the doctors missed, wake Mom up from her coma. Can you do that?'

'I ...'

She sighed and put a hand over her eyes. 'I'm going to lie down for a while. Is that okay?'

'Of course.'

Without another word, she stood up and walked through to the bedroom, closing the door behind her.

Jake sat down at the table and ate a couple of chips from the bag, took a long drink of the soda. Salt and sugar and caffeine. He didn't feel much like eating either, but he needed fuel. He opened one of the burner phones, plugged it in using a charger he found in the desk drawer, and waited for the rudimentary browser window to load up. He set up a hotspot and connected Diehl's computer to it. The signal was weak, but after a tense minute, the familiar Google logo appeared.

He typed his own name and started to scroll through the endless list of headlines.

35

Chrissie had called her manager, Marc, first thing in the morning. She told him she was taking a couple of personal days. She would have called in sick, if it hadn't been obvious what she needed the time off for. Marc had okayed the request with a weary 'Fine.' Not even bothering to summon up a snarky comment. It was probably a relief to him: he wouldn't have to spend the next few days making sure she was actually working.

She was feeling so exhilarated that she actually thanked Marc sincerely and told him to have a great day before she put the phone down. The first two episodes had created quite a buzz, vindicating her gamble on covering a live case. Even Sean's natural pessimism had evaporated when he saw the numbers: a million and a half downloads, well over two hundred thousand new subscribers. They had always had listeners from all over, but their natural base was in California. The new subscribers were coming in from all over the world: Europe, Asia, Russia, everywhere. Submissions to the advertising form were piling up in the inbox – too many to schedule for the foreseeable future, even when they had weeded out the lower-quality offers.

That was all before the latest show. Episode three, with the exclusive on the Facebook messages, had gone viral. The previous two episodes had been doing extremely well on the novelty of focusing on a live and unfolding case. They had been able to surf the wave of media coverage. The fact that the case had appeared on everyone's phones as an Amber Alert had acted as a free ad for the show. Their scoop on the messages had put them ahead of the rest of the media, reversed the emphasis. Rather than merely contributing to the story, they were part of it now. All of the major national news outlets were talking about the latest development in the case, and referencing the show. All of which drove more subscriptions, more shares, more traffic to the website.

The site had crashed shortly after 9 a.m., in fact. Too many people trying to view the screenshots of the messages at once. Sean had spent a half-hour on the phone to their provider and negotiated a pretty good deal to increase their bandwidth. It was expensive, but scalable. And the new sponsorship they were lining up would mean cost wasn't a problem.

The traffic that had crashed the website was only the people going direct to the source, of course. On social media, it was even bigger. Her tweet trailing the show, with the attached screenshot of the 'two bullets' message, was at half a million likes, a couple of hundred thousand retweets. Her follower count had tripled. When her phone had started blowing up, she had felt a sick feeling in her gut. Like everybody was watching her.

She had gotten over that feeling pretty quickly.

The attention wasn't all good, of course, but she had always had a thick skin about this stuff. The nature of the case meant that she wasn't the subject of most of the attention. Most of the top replies were concerned with finding Molly Donaldson and nailing Jake Ellis. The usual stuff about Chrissie having an irritating voice, or giving her advice on how she could look more presentable in her profile picture, was way down the list.

To her surprise, part of her felt a little uneasy when she looked at the strength of the vitriol against Jake Ellis. Sure, the guy deserved it all, but she could see that there were a lot of people out there who weren't particularly concerned about him getting his day in court. She wondered if he would survive the experience if someone other than the police or the FBI found him.

Her phone rang and she glanced at the time. Ten forty-five, meaning it would probably be the reporter from the *Chronicle*. She answered and rattled through her prepared comments about the show, about the importance of focusing on the victims at the heart of the case, about harnessing the army of people listening as a force for good.

'No, I won't reveal my source, Mel, and I'm sure you wouldn't either in my position,' she said as she summed up. 'If you want to know more, the next episode will be out later today.'

Melanie Ryker thanked her for the interview. Chrissie heard the click but was so preoccupied that she didn't put the phone down for a minute. *The next episode will be out later today.* But how were they going to follow the last one?

She had blocked out the bones of the episode. With the experience of doing the show on solved and cold cases over the past couple of years, the fundamentals were essentially the same. Covering the known details of the case, the backgrounds of the principals, phone and in-person interviews. It was just that the potential for new information coming to light was so much greater. Even that was not a completely new factor. The show had always picked up new snippets of information from the listeners as it went out.

Sean had built a robust tip-management system which aggregated everything coming in via the website and social media, and it was scaling nicely to meet the increased traffic. They knew that the FBI had descended on a small town called Dunnigan almost an hour before it appeared on any of the news sites. Chrissie had arranged a phone interview with the guy whose car was stolen later in the day. The only reason they weren't headed up there in person was that she had another interview lined up with one of Rachel Donaldson's friends in an hour at a coffee shop on the Wharf.

She brought Sean's database up on her screen and scrolled through the incoming tips. There were different folders for each tip case: credible sightings, junk sightings, vehicle information, background, deep background, and so on. The tips could be manually sorted into each folder, but Sean had designed a very effective algorithm to assign each tip to a provisional folder based on a combination of keywords, IP address, quality of source, and probably a hundred other things. She shook her head as she scanned through the folders, impressed at how good the automated assignations had been. Sean really was wasted on the patchwork of IT shitwork jobs he paid the rent with.

She clicked into the vehicle folder, looking to see if there had been anything promising on the white Ford that had been stolen from Dunnigan. Nothing so far, though it hadn't been long since the first media reports about it. She was about to click back out when she saw one tip in the vehicle folder that caught her eye. It was the only one that didn't mention a car or the gray SUV. Three out of five stars quality rating, which was better than the average. She opened the case to have a closer look. It was a message submitted via the website from a user who had left only a first name: Al. The IP address was highlighted in a dark green, meaning it was close to one of the designated places of interest. Reading through the message, she saw that that place of interest was the initial shooting scene on Sullivan Street itself.

Al had apparently heard the shots fired. He had been two blocks away, too far to see what had happened, but he said a minute later a motorcycle came past his street, in a hurry. He didn't get the license plate but remembered that the motorcycle was black, with flames on it. He said he had told the cops, but they hadn't seemed to do anything with the information.

She frowned. Nothing in the media reports had mentioned a motorcycle. If the biker had been Jake Ellis fleeing the scene, how could he have taken Molly captive on the bike? Even if he had somehow forced her to ride pillion, the tipper would have mentioned it. They could follow it up, but she thought she knew why the cops hadn't done anything on it — it didn't fit. Just a coincidence. A motorcycle going too fast. Maybe just in a hurry. But what if he was fleeing the scene not as a perpetrator but as a witness? Someone scared? She scribbled down the case reference, making a note to follow up with Al later. If nothing else, it was another little exclusive for the show.

The calendar reminder pinged on her phone and she realized she only had fifteen minutes before the interview with Jennifer Greer. She was tapping on Sean's number to ask him where he was when she heard the familiar busted-exhaust noise of Sean's old Mazda pulling to a stop outside. She hurried downstairs.

'Sorry,' he said. 'Client call, couldn't get away.'

'I told you, we need to focus on this right now,' she snapped. Then she softened her voice. 'Did you see the numbers?'

'I do have other gigs besides this, you know. Some of them actually make money.'

'Sean,' she groaned, elongating his name. 'We have to strike while the iron is hot. Make hay while the sun shines. All that stuff.'

He rolled his eyes as he pulled out into the road, but she could see he was suppressing a smile. In his own way, he was enjoying this just as much as she was.

36

Jake sipped from a large coffee mug emblazoned with the Pittsburgh Steelers logo as he scanned the information on the Kidnappings and Missing Persons section of the FBI website.

It contained the basic information that had been sent out. The descriptions of himself and Molly. A brief summary of the scenario as it was understood. Pictures of both of them. Hotline numbers for the SFPD and the FBI field office. A link to the anonymous tip form. Very light on additional detail or speculation about what had happened.

For that, there were plenty of other sources.

He had spent the last hour going through the news websites, catching up on the reporting on the hunt. He forced himself to try and view the situation from a detached, professional standpoint. The good news for the people looking for him was that this was the lead story. The Amber Alert had gotten traction. The picture of Molly seemed to have activated the part of the public psyche that dictated that this was one of the cases they should care about. Everybody was talking about it. He wondered how much of it was visual. The pretty young girl at Disneyland on the left, the stern-looking picture of him in his uniform on the right. All it needed was the word 'abducted' and anyone could fill in the rest of the story. Some blowhard politician had gone on TV and practically demanded his head on a plate: no trial, no jury.

George Driscoll. Why did that name ring a bell? Had he been the one demanding answers from the chief when that activist had been found with a bullet in his head under the Central Freeway? Thinking about it, Jake thought he remembered seeing him on the news a few times, always demanding action on this or that, making sure he attracted the maximum level of attention. Maybe the familiarity came from knowing the type, rather than the specific name.

The bad news for the people working this case, and the good news for him, was that there was speculation all over the place. There had been reports of sightings of him and Molly, both together and separate, from all over the state. LA, Oakland, Bakersfield. They had been spotted farther afield: in Nevada and Oregon. South of the border in Tijuana. As time went on and the potential search area expanded, that list would only get longer. As a police officer, he knew that a million tips was much, much worse than no tips at all. For now, the main thing was that there had been no sightings of them farther north than Willow Creek.

He had a notepad beside the keyboard and was jotting down the information in the media that was accurate, to see what they had.

As he expected, they had linked the SUV to him after the guy on the crosswalk came forward. It had been late afternoon before the vehicle description had popped up in the news. If the man in the suit had called it in earlier, they might not have made it as far. He remembered the black-and-white that had passed them in Red Bluff.

They had found the SUV in Dunnigan this morning, which had given them the white Ford. That had been unavoidable, and he suspected that, given time, they would have made that link even without finding the SUV in the vicinity. There would only be so many stolen cars in the relevant time and geographical windows. The Ford was now unusable. That was the problem: how to break the chain of vehicles so that the discovery of one would not put them on the trail of the next. False Klamath was a tiny community. There was almost no chance he could steal another car from around here without it being noticed.

He looked at the list of bullet points of real information after he had read through all the main news sites. They knew he had taken the SUV. It had been spotted in Oakland. They knew he had dumped the SUV in Dunnigan and taken the Ford. The latest update was that the Ford had been picked up on a camera at the gas station in Willow Creek. That was almost a hundred miles south of here, and it wasn't a straight route. Not quite a dead end, but just about far enough for comfort.

It was more information than he would like them to have, even though it was hidden in all the rest of the data. He reminded himself that he was in a unique position to know what was real. They knew his direction of travel had been north. He hoped they wouldn't have any way of making the link to Diehl's place.

And on the bright side, there were no clear photos or videos of them. Nowhere that they as individuals had been caught on camera. They didn't know Molly had dyed her hair, and that the girl in the now-famous Disneyland image no longer looked quite the same. The uniform picture of him had been a poor choice by the investigators, even before he had cut his hair and shaved the mustache. People see a picture of a cop, they remember a cop.

He started looking beyond the facts. In the later reports, there was reference to abusive text messages, apparently sent from him to Rachel. The podcast Molly had mentioned had managed to get hold of screenshots and publish them. He hadn't focused on that at first. He knew he was being framed, and this would be one of the first and easiest things to accomplish.

When he finally clicked through to look at the screenshots, his heart sank. Forget about believing what you read in the papers; people today believed everything they saw on social media. It was there, in blue and white.

The most damning one was the 'two bullets' message.

You and your kid. Two bullets.

Again, with his insider perspective, he thought that was a little too obvious. The person writing it knew exactly what was going to happen. But he knew that was exactly what made it so damning to anyone else reading it. It made the crime he was suspected of look colder, premeditated.

How the hell had they done it?

A hundred possible ways, probably. He knew there were many ways to alter messaging information like this, but he thought they would have been smart. They would have gotten his password somehow. They would have made sure the messages were sent using an IP address he could be identified with, or at least one that would not rule him out. That would have been as simple as following him and making sure the message was sent from a location he was confirmed to be in. Ideally, they would have used one of his devices too. The forensic computer people would be all over it, but that would take time. Thanks to whoever had leaked the messages, the public knew all about it before the FBI even had a chance to verify them, assuming they would be able to find anything to rule him out as the sender.

In the meantime, the public had all the context it thought it needed. His name, and her name, and a threat of violence, followed by an act of violence.

He wasted a few minutes scrolling through the FindMolly hashtag on Twitter and quickly discovered that the stuff people were saying about him on talk radio was nothing compared to what they were willing to say on the internet. The fact of him being a cop only made it worse. A junkie or deadbeat dad who abducts a kid is basically, as far as the public is concerned, acting according to their nature. Terrible, of course, but to be expected, in a sad way. But a police officer? Someone entrusted with keeping the populace safe and maintaining order? That didn't play well to either side of the aisle: it was a betrayal to those who like cops, a confirmation to everyone who hates them.

He doubted whether many of these keyboard warriors posed a genuine threat, but it was a sobering experience just the same. He wondered how much difference it would make if he was able to prove his innocence. He might be able to satisfy a court of law, but public opinion was another matter. Maybe this nightmare would never really end, even in the best-case scenario.

The thread running through a lot of the more recent chatter was references to the podcast that had broken the 'two bullets' messages. It was called *Untraceable*. He went to the show website. They had links to download the episodes, of which there were three in this season so far. They were pumping them out fast. Weren't these things usually done retrospectively? He guessed the immediacy, and the scoop about the messages, was why this one had skyrocketed in popularity, tagging on to the existing virality of their case.

UntraceableSF.com was a professionally designed site. Not too busy, not too many pages. Besides the download links, there was an 'About Us' section on the team: presenter Chrissie Chung and producer Sean Tramel. There was a bonus material page, with the screenshots of the messages, more pictures of the principals: himself, Molly and Rachel, and maps showing the key locations. It was thorough and mostly accurate stuff. A better summation of the facts than he had seen on many of the news sites.

He downloaded the first three episodes onto the phone. He could listen to them later on.

Reassured that their location seemed to be secure for the time being, he turned his attention back to whoever was behind this. The witness was unidentified in reports, but, whoever he was, he was in on it. It was no case of mistaken identity. He had fabricated his story, describing a man who looked like him manhandling Molly into a car that looked like his. Since his call to Hartzler, he had been thinking more about that, and the man on the motorcycle, the one that was missing from the witness's description or any of the reports.

The more Jake thought about it, the more he was sure the guy had to be a professional. If he made a habit of using a bike, it would narrow the list of names down. There was one person in the city who would know every contract man that could fit the description and the MO. A man named Carl Dolan. The only problem was, he didn't make a habit of speaking to cops.

But he thought he knew someone who might be able to get a message to him.

He set up an anonymous Gmail account and composed a message. He wanted to get a message to Dolan, and if the recipient could help with that, he would make it worth his while.

He clicked send and sat back in the chair, hoping that an answer would come soon.

37

Lark stared at the wall-height map of California in the operations room. Specifically, the section around the gas station where Jake Ellis's stolen white Ford had been last seen. So many minor roads. So many small towns and stretches of open country.

They were as sure as they could be that this was a genuine sighting. Irritatingly, the forecourt cameras hadn't been good enough to confirm the license plate, but the driver hadn't been able to avoid the in-store camera. He had been wearing a hat and keeping his head down but was wearing a leather jacket that matched the one Ellis's neighbor and the cop he assaulted had described.

There had been nothing concrete since then. Wherever Ellis had gone after that, he had stayed away from major highways, security cameras and highway patrol. The focus of the search had moved to the area around Willow Creek. Valenti was organizing a base of operations in the area, and they would be on their way there soon.

The door behind her opened and she turned to see Paxon enter. 'I just spoke to the hospital. No change in Rachel Donaldson's condition.'

Lark frowned. She had hoped there would be more promising news by now. She couldn't help but think that Rachel Donaldson could be the key. Rachel would be able to tell them why this had happened. Or, better yet, where her boyfriend might have gone.

Lark's phone buzzed with a text message. It was from Marty Hartzler.

Might have something. I'm at O'Malley's on Hyde now.

She read the text and thought carefully about how to respond. Making her decision, she grabbed her jacket from the back of her chair. 'I'm going to get a coffee. Anything happens, call me.'

'I could go if you want,' Paxon said.

'Thanks, but I need some fresh air. Clear the cobwebs.'

Lark took the elevator to the ground floor and waved at the guy on the desk on the way out. She exited through the front doors, but instead of turning right, in the direction of the coffee house, she turned left and headed east for two blocks. O'Malley's was an Irish pub on the corner of Hyde Street. She had walked past it often over the years but had never been inside. She pushed through the oak door with a stained-glass window and let her eyes adjust to the dim lighting.

There were tables and booths on the right-hand side, before a wood partitioned area. There was a long bar down the left-hand side, Guinness and Irish lagers on tap. A wide array of whiskeys lining the shelf behind the bartender, a guy in his twenties in a black T-shirt. He looked up as Lark approached.

'I'm meeting someone.'

'That someone?' The bartender pointed a finger past her. She turned to follow his gaze and saw a door had opened in the partitioned area, and Hartzler was standing there. He was wearing civilian clothes: jeans, a blue shirt, a gray sport coat. He still looked like a cop. She wondered if Jake Ellis was any better at hiding that than his friend. She thanked the bartender and walked across the room toward Hartzler. She saw that the partition was actually one of a series of small snugs with leather benches facing each other across a small table. You could fit four people in one, assuming none of them had a body-mass index over 25.

Hartzler closed the door behind him and waited for her to sit down. There was a fresh pint of Guinness on her side of the table. One in front of Hartzler, half-empty.

'Cozy,' she said. 'This one of your regular haunts?'

She looked around the confined space of the snug. With the carved wood and the stained glass in the edgings, it reminded Lark a little of a confession booth.

'One of them,' he agreed. 'I like this place. It's good for a quiet conversation.'

'Maybe I'll try bringing suspects here.'

He raised an eyebrow. 'You could do worse.'

She took a sip of the Guinness. Early in the day, but what the hell, it was evening in Ireland. She had only tried it once before, on a flying visit to London chasing down a fugitive with the assistance of a heavy-drinking sergeant in the Met who hailed originally from Belfast. This didn't taste quite the same. It seemed thinner, less potent.

'So he was somewhere around Willow Creek yesterday,' Hartzler said.

'It's not a hundred percent,' Lark said. 'We didn't get a plate, but it looks like it was him.'

Hartzler looked up at the ornately carved wood-panel ceiling, as though he might find the answers to all of their questions engraved there.

'Not a hundred percent,' he repeated. 'Always the way. With what you and I do, we both know one thing, right?'

'You never really know anything,' she said.

He lowered his gaze to look at her. 'Exactly.'

'So what do you have? Is it related to the car?'

'Could be. One time, a few months ago, Jake mentioned this old guy he used to work with. Only reason it came up was I was getting solar panels installed, and I thought the guy was overbilling me for the work. Jake said a guy he knew had done the job himself, saved a bundle. He said the guy lived on the coast, up north somewhere. He said he could put me in touch with him.'

'Up north,' Lark repeated. 'You think he might have gone to hide out with this guy?'

'I don't know. I just remembered about it after you talked about how he had no family, how you'd checked out all of his KAs. I didn't see any addresses that far out on your list, figured it was worth mentioning.'

'So did he? Put you in touch with the guy, I mean.'

'Nah. I told the guy doing the job someone else had quoted me two grand less. Lo and behold, my guy managed to shave twenty-five hundred off the quote. I forgot all about it until this blew up.'

She opened her mouth to prompt him further but was cut off when her phone buzzed on the table. Valenti's name flashed up on the screen.

'One of your minions?' Hartzler joked, looking at the screen.

She didn't rise to that. Valenti was calling with an update on another list: Rachel Donaldson's work clients. He and Taylor had worked through it already and had crossed off every name but had come up with a big fat zero in terms of new leads.

'Some of the clients had never met her in person,' Valenti said. 'The ones who had, only in passing. This one's a dead end, sorry.'

'All right, thanks anyway. Let me know when we're ready to hit the road.' She hung up and put her hands on the table, the fingers knitted together. 'So how far did you get?'

'How far did I get?' Hartzler repeated.

She nodded. 'You didn't suddenly remember this solar panel guy, and' – she snapped her fingers – 'come straight to me about it. Did you?'

He shook his head. 'Jake didn't give me a name, or a town. All I know is it was up north, and it was on the coast. I assumed California, because otherwise he would have said "up in Oregon" or somewhere else. Do you know how many small coastal settlements there are north of San Francisco?'

'Off the top of my head? I'm guessing a lot.'

'"A lot" covers it,' he agreed.

Lark nodded. 'And every one of them has a lot of doors to knock on, so you realized you needed me.'

'We're all in this together, Agent Lark. Isn't that what you said?'

'I'm touched you took my words to heart.'

Lark considered. In the background, an Elvis Costello song started up on the jukebox, and she became aware of how quiet it had been. Unconsciously, both of them had been practically whispering this conversation. He was right. Whether or not this little nugget of information led to anything, Jake Ellis had very few friends and acquaintances. And here was one, seemingly willing to help. Assuming he hadn't made the whole thing up five minutes ago.

'All right,' she said. 'We'll see if we can find out who this solar panel guy is. If we get a line on Ellis, we'll bring you along.'

Hartzler smiled and put his hands up. 'Thank you.'

Lark stood up and straightened her jacket. She had only drunk a quarter of her Guinness. They shook hands across the table. As she opened the door to the snug, she thought of one more question.

'If we find him, you think he'd talk to you?'

'I hope so. If I can't get through to him, nobody can.'

Lark stepped out and let the door to the snug swing closed.

The bar had gotten a little busier since they had entered, a couple of drinkers at the bar forming the advance guard for the lunchtime rush.

Her phone lit up again. They were all set for the journey up to Willow Creek; booked on the 4.10 United flight to Arcata.

38

A second trip to the gas station. The same lady was at the register but showed no signs of remembering Jake from earlier. He bought some more water and a prepay credit card, as Hartzler had suggested. He left the gas station and kept walking until he reached the billboard. He cleared away the branches he had stacked behind the Ford and got in. He wound the windows down and listened until he was sure there was no traffic approaching. He had been passed by only one car as he walked back along the road, so he hoped it would remain as quiet while he moved the car from behind the billboard.

Sooner or later, he would have to dispose of the Ford, and he was looking for somewhere a little farther from town. There was a track marked on the map that looked as though it led down from the main road to the shore. He didn't want to abandon the vehicle just yet, but it would be good to have a disposal spot nailed down for when he was ready.

When he was sure there was no other traffic coming, he started up the engine and reversed out from behind the billboard. He turned in the road, put his foot down and covered the half-mile to the turn onto the beach road in under a minute.

The mouth of the road was wide and tarmacked, but it quickly turned into a narrow dirt track. The way the grass had grown over the furrows in the road told him it hadn't been used in a while, which was ideal.

He slowed a little, had to steer around three big potholes that looked like lunar craters. There was a tight turn, and then the road dropped down toward the shore. There was a kind of plateau halfway, and he saw that the ground dropped away even more steeply at the side of the road. He put the parking brake on, left the engine running and got out to give the slope a closer look.

It descended at an angle of forty-five degrees for about twenty feet, and there was a gap of about two car-widths between the nearest pine trees. He carefully picked his way halfway down the slope and took a closer look. Thick bushes covered the ground. It would be a good place to conceal the car when they found alternative transport. A well-directed push and five minutes stacking foliage against it would conceal the car pretty effectively, he thought.

But not yet. He wanted to make sure they had another vehicle before he got rid of this one. He left the car where it was and walked down to where there was a patch of gravel that gave way to the shoreline.

He looked both ways. Deserted as far as the eye could see. A long stretch of sandy beach and a low tide. The sand was a gray color, almost like moon dust. There was a wooden hut a little way down the shore, and beyond that, a rocky sea stack rising fifty or sixty feet up from the waves.

Jake glanced back up at the car, and decided to check out the wooden hut. He walked down the shore, staying on the dry sand so his footprints would not be noticeable. The windows of the hut were shuttered and he could see a padlock on the doors. It looked like it had been shut up for the winter. Maybe not even for this winter. The padlock on the door looked strong, but the wood of the door was old. It wouldn't take much to break in. Close up, he could see a small jetty extended from the far end of the hut out into the sea.

He lifted his gaze to the towering sea stack and beyond it the perfect horizon where the ocean disappeared. You could sail in a straight line from here and not touch land for five thousand miles. It put things in perspective. Maybe a little too much perspective.

The afternoon sky was beginning to darken behind him, and he realized he had left Molly alone for longer than he had intended. He walked back to the Ford and got in, guided it slowly back up the dirt track.

39

'You really think this will help?' the eyes of the older woman were plaintive.

Chrissie summoned her best customer-service smile and nodded encouragingly. 'I know it will. We have a responsibility to get all the facts out there, to a huge audience. And I think you have a responsibility to tell us everything you can. To get Molly back safe.'

They were in the small living room of the woman's cozy house in Bayview. It looked as though it had last been redecorated in the early seventies, but it was neat as a pin. The woman's name was Sally Nelson, and she had been Molly's babysitter when she was younger. This was the last of the personal contacts on Chrissie's list. It had been easy enough to get time with Rachel's circle of friends, the ones who hadn't told her to get lost, at least. She had been hoping to get some quotes from some of the kids in Molly's class, but the principal had appeared before she had a chance to hit record, had threatened to call the police if she didn't get off school property. She noted with some satisfaction that the mainstream journalists received the very same treatment.

There was some good stuff in the interviews, she thought, but it was all background, mostly atmosphere. She had been hoping for something that might help them start to untangle the whys and whens and hows of the case so far. And most importantly, of course, the *where*: where the hell were they?

Almost all of Rachel's friends had said the same thing: they hadn't seen this coming. None of them knew Jake all that well, but it seemed like a normal relationship.

She tuned back in to Sally.

'…always a bright young thing, always drawing on her pads or writing in her little notebook. She was poorly when she was little, you know, asthma…'

Chrissie smiled and nodded every so often, but she wasn't really listening to Sally. The recorder would do that for her, and she could whip through it on double speed later to see if there were any sound bites worth using. But it all sounded like background color. *Why would somebody want to do this? Such a lovely mother and daughter.* Et cetera.

If she was disappointed with the progress with Rachel's acquaintances so far, it was still streets ahead of the progress she had managed to make speaking to anybody with more than a passing acquaintance with Jake Ellis. If he had close friends, they were among the cops he occasionally drank with in O'Malley's bar. She hadn't gotten anywhere approaching the police direct. The best interviews she had bagged so far were with an old guy in Ellis's building, who had actually witnessed the abduction, and a phoner with the guy whose SUV Jake had stolen in the course of his escape.

The old guy at Ellis's apartment building, Mr Rosenberg, had given her some pretty good material for the previous episode: 'He had a gun,' 'He looked crazy,' 'Poor girl was terrified, had blood all over her.' The only problem was it was the same stuff he had told the other news outlets. Marcus Bolton, the owner of the gray SUV, had sounded long distance on the call: not the quality of the line, but his voice itself. Like he was talking about some half-remembered TV show he had seen ten years ago. He didn't seem too concerned about the situation with Jake on the run and an abducted kid. Not that Chrissie got the feeling he was in Ellis's corner, exactly, more that he had just decided it had nothing much to do with him. He wasn't even bent out of shape about Ellis stealing his vehicle. 'Nah,' he confirmed when Chrissie pushed him on it. 'Insurance'll cover it. I was looking to sell the damn thing anyhow, never got around to it.'

Chrissie realized Sally Nelson was staring at her, waiting for her to say something.

'Do you have any other questions?'

Chrissie looked up at Sally's worried expression. She had zoned out completely. How long had she been talking?

'This is perfect,' she said. Her thumb hovered over the record button and she thought of another question. 'Say, you don't remember Jake Ellis from before, do you? The news said they had dated a long time ago. Him and Rachel, I mean.'

She shook her head. 'I didn't know Rachel back then. I only met her when Molly was two years old.'

Chrissie clicked off and put the recorder back in her purse. She reached out to put her hand on top of Sally's. 'Thank you so much for your time.'

The older woman nodded. 'I just hope it helps. I feel so … so powerless.'

Chrissie took her phone out and called Sean when she got outside.

'You get anything good?' he asked.

'Same old, same old,' she said. 'Nobody knows why he did it.'

'One person does,' Sean reminded her.

'Well, hopefully we can get an interview with him, huh?'

'Send me what you got,' he said. 'You still want to get it out tonight?'

'Mhmm,' she agreed. 'We've got enough to go with. I'm still hoping I get somewhere with Edward Da Costa.'

Sean sighed. 'If he was going to talk to us—'

Chrissie finished the sentence for him. 'He would have already. Worth a try though, right?' Da Costa intrigued her. Other people were bending over backwards to talk to her, or the regular reporters, why was the one person who had actually witnessed the shooting so reticent? Thinking about Da Costa reminded her about the tip from the guy on Sullivan Street who had seen a motorcycle. She hadn't followed up on that yet.

She could hear the amusement in Sean's voice as he moved the subject back on track. 'I'll send you the rough cut in a half-hour. And, Chrissie? Try and—'

'Listen at regular speed,' she finished. 'So you keep saying. Fine.'

Her Uber pulled up as Sean was saying goodbye. She hung up and got in. The driver glanced at her with disinterest and tapped his screen to log the pickup. They pulled out onto the hill. The asphalt dropped away in front, like cresting the summit on a big dipper.

40

Lark's ears popped as they descended into Arcata. The low sun glinted off the ocean as they circled around for the final approach. They had another couple of hours of daylight, and she hoped they could make it to the gas station at Willow Creek before then.

The airplane Wi-Fi had let her keep in touch with the team back in the city for most of the duration of the flight, but she had reluctantly stowed her laptop after the second request from the steward, and she was now on the tenth minute of being cut off from information. She wondered if there would be anything new when she landed. So far, there had been no update from the people on the ground in Willow Creek. It was almost twenty-four hours since Ellis's car had been sighted here. She just hoped the trail hadn't gone cold.

She had her phone in her hand as the back wheels thumped on the tarmac. She had turned off airplane mode before the front wheels contacted.

41

Jake had been gone a while, now. Longer than last time. To pass the time, Molly had tried to read a couple of the books in the bedroom. Jake's dead friend had had good taste: lots of Stephen King, some mysteries, some vintage science fiction. She had given up when she realized her eyes were just passing over the words and taking nothing in. She replaced the books on the shelf and went through to the kitchen to get a soda. She wasn't really thirsty, just needed something to do to occupy herself.

On her way through, she made her obligatory check of the television, playing silently away on the news channel. A reporter was on a street in what looked like New York City, conducting man-on-the-street interviews on the issue of the day. She watched the news crawl along the bottom. It didn't even mention her mom or Jake or *The Molly Donaldson Hunt*. No news is good news. She was beginning to hate that mantra. When did no news start to mean not getting any worse but not getting any better?

She coughed shallowly. The living room was dustier than the bedroom had been. Her chest was feeling a little tighter, and she was starting to think about the inhaler she had left in her room almost as frequently as she thought about not having her phone.

It was a little less dusty in the kitchen. The door didn't quite close over where Jake had broken the lock, and cool, fresh air got in. It made this side of the house a little chilly for comfort, but it was easier to breathe in here.

She opened a can of Pepsi and sipped it, moving over to the window above the sink. There were venetian blinds over the window. Jake had told her not to go too close to the windows, but she figured the blinds and the fact that she was at the back of the house made it okay. The nosy lady from earlier couldn't see her on this side.

The sky had been overcast all day, but the clouds had broken up a little so that she could see glaring holes of sunset over the ocean. She had asked her mom if she preferred sunrises or sunsets a few weeks ago. It was for some dumb online personality test. 'Sunsets, definitely,' her mom had said, without even pausing to think.

Jake had been gone a couple of hours, now. He told her he might be a while, but he hadn't said exactly how long. It was so weird not being able to drop someone a text to check they were okay. That reminded her. She had been so worried about her mom not pulling through that she hadn't stopped to think about what her friends must be going through. As far as they knew, she had been abducted by the guy who had shot her mom.

She had been thinking. She could send a message to Nicole, just to let her know she was alive and okay. She knew Jake had said they couldn't afford to break cover, but if she swore her to secrecy...

She went back into the living room. The street interviews were over, and it had moved on to a financial segment, footage in the background of the stock market, sports results on the ticker along the bottom of the screen.

Jake had been working on the computer earlier. She guessed he had hotspotted it with one of the burner phones he had bought. She wondered if he had taken them both with him.

She switched the computer on, wondering what she would do if it worked. As before, there was no internet connection. She opened the browser just in case it was magically working and got the 'No internet' message with the little dinosaur and helpful advice to check network cables, modem and router, or try connecting to Wi-Fi.

The image on the television changed to a familiar scene. It took her a second to work out why it was familiar: it was the gas station they had stopped at last night. Somebody must have seen them. The headline was: *Molly Donaldson Hunt: Focus Shifts North*. When Jake got back, she would have to tell him they were getting closer.

She looked back down and opened the first of the desk drawers, coughing as it dislodged some more dust. It was stuffed full of junk mail. It was getting darker, so she turned on the desk light to see better. She dug around a little to see if there was anything else, but there was nothing underneath. She opened the second drawer and found one empty plastic pack and an unopened one containing the second prepay cell phone.

She stared at it for a minute.

'Screw it.'

After stabbing the pack a couple of times with a pen, she managed to rip it open, breathing a little harder with the exertion. She needed to go outside, get some fresh air. She promised herself she would do it soon.

She turned the phone on, feeling a slight shiver as she did so. She reminded herself there was nothing to worry about. Nothing about this phone that would connect to them. She opened a browser and, after a long pause, the web page of the phone manufacturer appeared. A working signal, if only just.

A minute later, the Google home page loaded. She smiled. Access to the world after what felt like a hundred years of being cut off. The little multicolored logo created an almost physical buzz. It was a little like the moment of anticipation before you drink a glass of cool water on a hot day. She had almost forgotten about the tightness in her chest. It would take no time at all to set up an anonymous email address and send Nicole a message. She could do it from the phone. No details, no information, just that she was safe and not to tell anybody she had been in touch.

But first, she wanted to check in on her mother's condition. She typed *Rachel Donaldson*. The first thing she saw was a picture of her own face on one of the news articles.

Molly Donaldson Suspect Facebook Threats

This must be about the messages they had talked about on the radio. Part of her didn't want to look at them, the rest of her needed to see what Jake had supposedly said. She was dimly aware that she was finding it harder to breathe. She needed a drink and some fresh air. No, she needed her inhaler. But she would go out on the porch in just a minute. After she had read this.

She tapped on the link.

42

As the credits rolled on a rerun of *Special Victims Unit*, Eleanor Grace glanced over at the house across the street, remembering about the guy she had spoken to earlier. Robert, he had said his name was.

With hindsight, it had been foolish to go over there like that, she supposed. What if he really had been a burglar or something? He might have turned violent. And it wasn't as though poor Walt could mind if somebody had broken in, anyway; he was long past that. But the man at the door had been on the level. Or he certainly had known Walt, at any rate. Passing her little tests with flying colors. He hadn't even seemed offended by her suspicion.

Although, wasn't that in itself a little suspicious?

'Eleanor Grace,' she said aloud to herself. 'You are the limit.'

The news came on. They were still looking for that little girl in San Francisco. She felt a tug of sadness as the images that had been playing for the last day and a half cycled through: the crime scene where the mother had been shot, the pictures of the girl and her abductor. The hunt seemed to be expanding north, beyond the city now. Willow Creek was only a hundred miles south of here on the 101.

She looked back over at Walt Diehl's house. She had seen Robert go out earlier, and he hadn't come back yet. Where had he gone? And what exactly was he picking up from the house? That had all been a little mysterious.

Just then, her phone rang. Landline, not a cell. Up until the last couple of years, they hadn't had any kind of reception up here to speak of, and she had never bothered with a cell phone. It probably put her in a one percent minority in the country, a distinction of which she was secretly proud. She went back to the kitchen, where it hung on the wall, to answer it.

A pause, and an electronic voice started up.

'We're calling you about the accident you were involved in—'

She hung up. Okay, so maybe there were some disadvantages in not having a screen that flashed up caller ID.

As she hung up, she saw a light wink on in Walt Diehl's house. Walt Diehl's supposedly empty house.

She stepped closer to the window and peered out at it.

Either Robert had come home without her seeing him, or somebody else was in there.

43

Jake had almost reached the house as his burner phone bleeped loudly in his pocket. He flinched and wondered if he would ever again be able to hear a phone ring or buzz or make any sound without worrying about what it meant. At first, he thought it might be a reply from his contact, the one he had asked to put him in touch with Carl Dolan, but it was from Hartzler, on the email address to which he had sent the details of the prepay credit card.

$500. Best I can do for now. Good luck.

Jake texted back a quick thanks. No names. He hoped Hartzler had been as careful about this as he had said he would be, but he couldn't deny he was relieved to have a little more of a financial cushion. If they needed to get out of here in a hurry, they had more options now.

Jake circled around and approached the house from the rear again. He navigated the twisting clifftop path, which snaked along, at times getting alarmingly close to the hundred-foot drop to the rocky shore.

The gable roof of Diehl's house was in sight when he started to wonder if he had remembered to move the bushes behind the billboard in front of the Ford. Surely he had done it automatically? He stopped, looking back the way he had come and calculating the time for a return trip. Twenty minutes, perhaps? The less he was out in the open, the better. The risk of being seen and recognized had to be weighed against the risk that someone might see the car and decide to investigate. That was what his existence was, at least for the moment. The balancing of small and not-so-small risks against one another.

He turned back to face the house. No. Better to go back after dark. He had left Molly alone for almost two hours, now. Maybe he was starting to take her resilience for granted. With her mom's life hanging in the balance, he needed to shoulder as much of the burden as possible, to give her space to deal with the situation as best she could.

As he stepped up onto the deck, he knew something was wrong. All of a sudden, he was moving toward the doors with urgency. He took his gun out and pulled the door open. Something about the air in the house felt wrong. It felt empty.

'Molly?' he called out as he moved through the kitchen. Empty, just like the living room. The front door was still closed. The bedroom door was ajar. He called her name again as he moved across the hall and urgently pushed the door open.

The first thing he saw was the second of the two phones he had bought lying on the floor, a diagonal crack across the screen extending out from the corner where it had hit the floorboards. The next thing he saw was Molly's navy-blue Converse sneakers, extending out from behind the bed.

He half dove, half fell across the bed and came down on the ground beside her. She was conscious, but only just. Her hands were loosely at her throat. She was white as a New Hampshire winter, beads of sweat standing out on her forehead. Her eyes were dazed, unfocused, barely registering his arrival.

Goddamn it, some kind of seizure? No ... he registered the wheezing sounds. Did she have asthma? He dimly remembered her taking a puff of an inhaler at Rachel's house a few weeks back. It can't have been a big deal because he didn't remember her using it any other time. Only that couldn't be so, because it clearly was a big deal.

'Molly, do you have an inhaler? Medication?'

She blinked twice, shook her head. Kept sucking.

He stopped thinking. Dredged up a memory from the first-aid course at the academy. This wasn't the kind of medical assistance a cop was usually called on to give, but they had covered it.

She was still conscious, which he hoped was a good sign. It had to be, right? He knelt and gathered her up in both arms. She was heavier than he expected. *Dead weight*, the unwelcome voice at the back of his head whispered.

He moved quickly through to the back of the house, where the doors were still open, telling her it was going to be fine. His voice came out the way it had been trained to in crisis situations. He was calm, he used her name a lot. He hoped he sounded more confident than he felt. He stumbled through the doorway, banging the second door out of the way with Molly's feet, and gently laid her down on the deck.

No, she had to be upright. Upright was important, he re-membered. He moved her so she was sitting up, back against the wood siding. Her breaths seemed to be a little clearer now, but still a long way from natural. He looked at her eyes. They were less dazed-looking. She wasn't looking back at him, though, she was focusing. Putting all of her concentration, all of her will, into encouraging her airway to stay open.

'That's it,' he kept saying. 'That's it, you're doing great.'

In another minute, she was taking careful, painstakingly gentle breaths. He could see from her face that she wanted nothing more but to try to gulp in the oxygen. But she was doing the right thing. She was getting there.

Her lips started to form into a word.

'Don't try to talk.'

She mouthed something. Her pale lips forming an O, which widened.

'Water?' he said.

She nodded her head weakly.

He ran to the kitchen and grabbed one of the bottles of water from the fridge. When he got back outside, she was breathing a little more normally. She raised a hand toward the bottle but stopped halfway, lacking the strength to lift her hand all the way after what the battle had taken out of her. Jake held it to her lips carefully, let her sip. Rivulets of water ran down her chin and spotted her gray hoodie.

'You're okay,' Jake said. He said it again. And he kept saying it, until he started to believe it was true.

44

'You saw the messages.'

It wasn't a question. It was what needed to be said. An uneasy silence had fallen following the hysteria of a few minutes ago. Jake had been stupid. He had wanted to protect her from seeing the Facebook messages, but he should have known that curiosity would have led her to read them. And now he looked guilty for not talking about it before now.

Molly hesitated for a moment, then nodded. Her eyes didn't meet his. She was sitting on the rocking chair on the deck, her knees bunched up under her chin, an old throw from the couch wrapped across her shoulders.

It was cold, but Jake felt a twinge of relief every time he saw a little cloud of her breath. It had been close, too close. They couldn't afford to let that happen again.

'I didn't write them,' he said after a minute.

She didn't say anything. She was looking away from him, out at the ocean, the slate-gray waves roiling away beneath a sky the color of ashes. The sun was setting behind the clouds, but the only way you could tell was a slightly lighter patch of gray where the sky met the waves.

'You don't believe me.' Again, a statement, not a question.

Molly took an intake of breath and then winced, massaging her throat with her right hand.

'I don't know. I don't know what I believe. Those things y— Those things I read...'

'They were horrible, I know.'

She glanced up at him now, but looked away just as quickly.

'Molly, you remember what I said before? Somebody went to a lot of trouble to frame me for this. The messages are part of that. It's not difficult to fake this kind of stuff; you know that, right?'

She seemed to be thinking it over. Wondering if she could believe him? After what felt like an hour, she spoke.

'This girl in my math class, Samantha Howard, nearly got expelled because someone snagged her phone when she wasn't paying attention at lunch. They, uh... they posted something they shouldn't on the school Facebook page under her name.'

'Really? What did they post?'

She hesitated. 'They posted "Mr Robinson fucks farm animals."'

Something about the cold, neutral way she said it made Jake issue an involuntary snort. He saw the corner of Molly's mouth curl upwards in response. It was the closest he had seen to a smile since yesterday.

'I'm sorry,' he said, straightening his face. 'Who's Mr Robinson?'

'He's the principal. He kind of deserves verbal abuse.'

'So what happened to Samantha Howard?'

'Her parents had to come in for a meeting. I guess somehow they talked the school out of kicking her out. Her dad is some kind of lawyer and there was talk that he threatened to sue them or something.'

'You know who really posted it?'

She raised an eyebrow. 'I have my suspicions.'

That chilled the moment of good humor for Jake. They all had their suspicions.

'All right,' he said. 'So, that was a fairly low-tech incidence of identity theft. Somebody physically got hold of her phone and ... fraped her? Is that what it's called?'

'We don't say that any more, it's insensitive.'

'Right,' Jake said. He wondered if he had made the adults around him feel as old as Methuselah when he was thirteen. He didn't think so, at least not to the same degree. There had been a lot less distance between the generations back then.

'Anyway, the point is, it's a good way to get somebody into trouble,' Jake said. 'People see your name and your picture, they're conditioned to assume the words are yours too. If somebody really knows what they're doing, they can cover their tracks pretty well, too.'

Molly said nothing but met his eyes this time. She was coming around, he thought, but she still wasn't entirely convinced. He couldn't really blame the poor kid, either. How much did she really know about him?

'Those messages, they weren't me. None of them. I promise.'

She considered it for a moment. He hoped she believed him. 'Whoever did it must have known ... must have known what was going to happen.'

He knew what she was thinking about. *Two bullets.* 'That's right.'

'They wanted us dead, and for it to look like you did it. But why?'

He owed her the truth. Should have trusted her to be able to make up her own mind about him before now. 'I think the people who attacked you and your mom wanted to get at me. And I'm so sorry about that.'

'What kind of people?'

He stood up and grasped the rail around the deck, straightening his arms and pushing his weight down. 'I don't know exactly. But I'm going to figure out who they are and what they want. I have a couple of ideas. I've reached out to some of my contacts.'

'Kelly Cosgrove,' Molly said after a moment.

Jake looked back at her, his brow furrowed. 'I'm sorry?'

She cleared her throat gently. 'Kelly Cosgrove. She's the one who stole Samantha's phone that day in the lunch hall.'

'She tell you that?'

'No. The message about Mr Robinson fucking farm animals – she put a period after "mister". She's in my English class. I always collect the papers, and she was the only one in school I ever saw do that.'

Jake was impressed. 'Nice detective work. But you didn't tell?'

Molly shook her head. 'I don't like Samantha, or Mr Robinson. I don't have a problem with Kelly.'

Her voice had started to sound a little raspy again. Too much talking.

'You left your inhaler behind?' He had almost said 'in the car', but stopped himself just in time.

'In my room. I forget it all the time. I used to need it a lot more when I was little. These days it's just if I'm somewhere smoky or dusty, or if it's hay-fever season.'

Diehl's house certainly fit the bill on the dusty count. Jake could have kicked himself for not paying more attention to the fact that her breathing had been a little more labored since they had gotten to the house. Inhaling dust and the old smoke over the previous few hours had marched her up to the edge, and a panic attack when she read the Facebook messages had pushed her right over it. She was lucky it hadn't been worse. They both were.

Jake took the other burner phone out of the pocket of his jeans. A perfectly blank screen, only one bar. He had set up the new email account on the phone, but the inbox was still empty. Perhaps the answer would never come. In any case, they couldn't sit here waiting for Molly to have another attack. He turned to look at her. She had gathered the throw around her again, shaking a little in the cold. She was rallying well, considering everything that she had been through, physically and mentally, but she seemed frailer, diminished since a day ago.

No. They couldn't just wait here and hope for the best.

'Are you okay to move from here?'

She took another sip of water. 'We're going away?'

'Not far, I hope,' he said, as he turned to go back inside. He would need to use the computer again.

He heard a faint scuffing noise as he turned and his head jerked around to its source. They weren't alone.

Eleanor Grace was standing at the foot of the steps up to the deck, looking like she didn't know whether to say something or run.

45

Lark had temporarily split the team, bringing Paxon, Garcia and Osborne with her to Willow Creek, and leaving Taylor and Valenti to hold the fort back in the city. They had taken over a motel just outside Willow Creek, a couple of miles from the gas station where Ellis's car had last been seen. The motel was an ugly sixties monstrosity that was practically falling down, but it had enough vacant rooms, and it wouldn't break the budget. They were working with the county sheriff's office to canvass other businesses and homeowners in the area to see if anyone else had seen Ellis or Molly. Her hope was that they hadn't gone too far from here.

Lark gave brief phone interviews to the *LA Times*, the *Washington Post* and the *New York Times*. They all had the same questions, more or less, and she supposed her answers left the reporters as dissatisfied as she was herself. Two of the three had asked about this goddamned *Untraceable* podcast, as if the interesting new wrinkle to a familiar story was something she would be as excited about as they were. The only thing she wanted to know about *Untraceable* was who had given them the screenshots. Paxon had found an address for the producer of the show. If there was time, Lark would be looking him up when she got back to the city.

She turned down a dozen more interviews from regional

outlets, directing them to the bureau web page for the latest updates on the hunt for Molly Donaldson. The case had gained national traction overnight. Lark couldn't decide if that was a bonus or a burden.

Either way, she knew there would be additional pressure on her and the team, and they needed that like she needed a hole in the head.

She had convened a conference call with the teams back in San Francisco at seven. No new updates. Following her conversation with Hartzler earlier, she had asked Garcia to find her some candidates for small towns on the coast that might have been the place Ellis had apparently told his buddy about. It wasn't much to go on, but like she always said, you have to check everything. She was actually a little more optimistic about that potential lead than she wanted to admit to herself. It fit with Ellis's last known direction of travel, for one thing. And it was exactly the kind of area she herself might go if she were on the run from the law. Remote, not too many people. Probably not the kind of place where people take much notice of the news from the city.

Then again, was it a little *too* plausible? Hartzler had made no secret of the fact he was in Ellis's corner. Could he be trying to throw them off the real trail? She couldn't shake the feeling that he knew more than he was letting on. But perhaps that wasn't only because he was friendly with their suspect. Each side knowing more than they let on was a long-established tradition of multi-agency investigations.

She put a call in to the staff nurse at Zuckerberg just after eight. No change in Rachel Donaldson's condition, too soon to say whether this would remain the situation indefinitely.

There was a big communal space in the room adjoining the motel's reception area where the team had set up. Somebody ordered in pizza and sodas. Once everybody else had fueled up, she wandered over to where the boxes had been splayed across a table and picked over what was left, taking a can of Pepsi and a slice each of pepperoni and anchovy and olive.

She carried the paper plate over to the window and looked outside. It had gotten dark while she had been making her various calls. There wasn't much to see in the pools of streetlight outside, just the highway and the thick woods on the other side. Getting on for thirty-six hours since the alert had gone out.

She wondered briefly how much the girl herself knew about the events of the past day and a half. Did she have any news about her mom? About the massive, statewide hunt to find her and bring her home? Maybe her abductor had kept her away from radios and televisions. Did she think she was alone? Halfway forgotten already?

Lark took her phone out and called Joe, just to check in. No progress, how were things back home? They were fine. She hoped she would be in her own bed tomorrow night. As she was speaking, she saw a black sports car cruise past, its waxed finish reflecting the lights like a mirror. It made her think of that other black car she had noticed yesterday, outside Rachel Donaldson's office.

'Babe, you still there?'

'Sorry, got distracted,' she said. They talked for another minute, exchanged 'I love you's and she hung up.

Lark took another bite of cold pizza and put the plate down, the second slice uneaten. She had lost her appetite, even though it was the first thing she had eaten since a bagel on the way into the office at 6 a.m.

'Not hungry, boss?' Garcia asked through a mouthful of pepperoni.

'You can finish it for me,' she said. She took out her phone and checked the note she had made of the black town car's license plate. 'Do me a favor and run this when you get a second?'

Garcia held the slice in his mouth while he patted himself down for a pen to transcribe the number. He accomplished the task and disappeared with the note and the pizza.

Lark sat down on one of the patched leather couches. She liked to keep an orderly workspace, even under pressure, but that was out of the window today. Every spare surface in the room was covered. Post-it notes were stuck to walls and windows. Maps and files and loose papers spread across the couches and chairs.

She pulled out Jake Ellis's file again, read over the story of his career since joining the SFPD fifteen years before. The police brutality thing seemed more trumped up the more she looked into it. Worst case, he had lost his temper. There didn't seem to be any line from that to what had happened yesterday. What had turned Jake Ellis into the person that would pull a trigger on an innocent woman and abduct her thirteen-year-old daughter?

Two bullets.

Two bullets had been fired into the car, as he promised. And then some; four in total. But only one of them had found its target. She thought about the scene that first morning, seeing the car with three of the windows blown out. It suggested Molly had sheltered behind the car at some point during the assault. The passenger-side windows indicated he had shot at her after the initial attack.

Why had he changed his mind? Why take Molly instead of just killing her along with her mother? Hadn't that been the plan? The unsent confession on his laptop certainly suggested that.

She stopped to think about this a little more. Along with everyone else, she had considered some of the reasons an un-balanced, violent male would have wanted to kidnap the child of his victim, and along with everyone else, she had come up with several plausible answers, none of which she particularly wanted to dwell on.

But thinking about the scene of the attack, not to mention the two bullets message, it had been clear that Ellis had meant to kill both Rachel and Molly. Why had he changed his mind? A spur-of-the-moment change of plan, or something else?

Too many whys. Every scenario she could come up with only cast up more questions.

'Got it.'

She looked over at Garcia.

'Got what?'

'That plate you asked me to run. It's an executive pool car, registered to the city council.'

'Okay.'

'What you expected?'

'I don't know what I expected.' She thought about it. The car had only caught her attention because the driver had seemed to stare at her and Paxon as they crossed the road. 'Rachel Donaldson's client list – anyone from the city on that?'

'I don't think so. How come?'

'No reason,' she said. In the back of her mind, she knew the reason: because you have to check everything. 'Tomorrow morning, get William McMurtry's office on the phone, ask him if they handle the accounts for any city departments.'

46

For what seemed like an hour, none of the three of them moved. Eleanor Grace looked from Jake, to Molly, to the gun lying on the deck where he had dropped it, back to Jake.

Eventually, he broke the silence.

'She had an asthma attack, she's okay.'

Eleanor shook her head and swallowed. 'It's you, isn't it? From the news.' She looked back at Molly, her eyes narrowing in concern. Then she looked back at the gun and took a step back.

'I'm not what you think,' Jake said.

Eleanor was shaking her head, perhaps unconsciously. She took another step backwards and started to turn.

'Don't go.'

It was Molly who spoke. Her voice raspy, barely above a whisper. Eleanor stopped and turned slowly.

'He didn't shoot my mom. He didn't kidnap me.'

Eleanor had stopped, but she didn't say anything. She looked down at the gun again. She couldn't possibly think she could get to it. And then Jake realized she was more worried about him picking it up.

He spoke without breaking eye contact with Eleanor. 'Molly, can you take my gun inside the house?'

She stepped forward and bent down, hesitating before she touched it.

'It's okay, it's safe to handle. Take it inside and put it in the kitchen drawer.'

Eleanor's eyes followed Molly as she kneeled, picked up the gun and took it inside the house. When she came back, she closed the door over and stood beside it, leaning against the siding.

'You should sit down,' Eleanor said. 'You don't look okay.'

'I'm good,' Molly said. 'I need to stay upright.'

Eleanor turned back to Jake. 'What the hell is going on?'

He held both hands up. 'We're not going to hurt you. By the time I could get to the gun, you can be halfway back to your house. If you want to call the police, I can't stop you, okay?'

She hesitated. 'Why shouldn't I?'

'That's what I'm going to try to explain, if you'll give me the chance.'

Eleanor's gaze shot from him, to Molly, to the door that led into the kitchen. She took a step closer.

Untraceable

Excerpt from Untraceable – Season 4, Episode 4, April 19

This episode of *Untraceable* is brought to you by one of our new sponsors, Golden Gate Cruises.

Welcome to *Untraceable*, the podcast that goes deep into the most fascinating missing persons cases. I'm Chrissie Chung, and every season, we'll be taking you through a missing persons case from disappearance, to resolution.

As we record this, Rachel Donaldson lies in a critical condition in the hospital. Shot down in her prime by a killer turned child abductor. As the manhunt for Jake Ellis moves north, we talk to a woman who knew Rachel and Molly like family.

But first of all, we got an interesting piece of information that doesn't seem to have been picked up on elsewhere. If the authorities know about it, they don't seem to have released it to the media. Perhaps it's nothing, but if there's one thing I've learned doing this show, it's that every detail matters.

[phone rings]

'Hello?'

'Hi there, am I speaking to Al?'

'That's right.'

'Chrissie Chung, from *Untraceable*. I understand you live on Sullivan Street, not far from the scene of the shooting on Saturday morning.'

'About three blocks down, yeah.'

'Can you tell us what you saw?'

'Well, first off, I heard the shots. I knew right away they were gunshots, no doubt. I went to my window to see if I could see anything, but nothing. A minute later, I heard a motorcycle engine, really going for it.'

'Out on Sullivan Street?'

'That's right, headed my way. A second later, he flies past my apartment. He's wearing leathers, the bike has flames and shit on the back of it. Now this guy has to be doing sixty at a *minimum*. I said to myself, either that's the guy who's getting shot at, or it's the guy doing the shooting.'

'And you called the police, Al?'

'Of course. By the time somebody got around to talking to me, they knew the cop had done it, though. I guess the guy on the bike was just trying to get away. Maybe he shot at him, too. I'll tell you something, though: those flames on the back of the bike were about right. That dude was riding like the devil was on his tail.'

47

The urgent care clinic was at the edge of Crescent City, about fifteen miles north along the coast from False Klamath. Jake went through the options in his head on the drive up on the dark highway as it snaked around the coast, plunging into stretches of total darkness as they passed through thick redwood forests.

Sending Molly in alone wouldn't work. It would raise too many questions: why was a thirteen-year-old out alone after dark? And yet it was a risk for the two of them to go in with a fabricated story. Everyone was looking for a man and a girl with their descriptions, give or take the cosmetic changes they had been able to make. Jake wasn't sure whether Amber Alerts were given an additional push to medical practitioners, but in truth it didn't matter. If the doctor, or the receptionist, or the night janitor had glanced at a news article at any point in the day, they would be aware of the story. And it would take only one of them to put that together with the man and the girl walking in on a quiet shift without insurance.

Which was why a woman and a girl were going to walk in. 'You sure about this?'

Eleanor Grace, sitting in the driver's seat of her Honda Civic, looked across at him. 'No,' she said. 'But I'm going to do it anyway.'

'We really appreciate this,' Molly said from the back seat, her voice still a little weak.

'I'm still thinking about what to do, okay?' Eleanor answered. 'That was quite a story you spun me back there. And I need time to process it. But, in the meantime, she needs that inhaler.'

Jake nodded and looked back at the road. He hoped she wouldn't decide to call the cops once Molly was safe. He didn't want to spell it out, but she had to have considered the fact that if Jake had really been the monster on the news, he would have killed her back at the house.

The blood-red neon sign of the emergency clinic came into view. There was one thing in their favor, at least: a quick medical examination would show that Molly needed what they were asking for. He had to hope that would take precedence over everything else.

48

When Molly shut the car door and saw her reflection in the window, red-tinged from the light of the neon sign, she almost didn't recognize herself. She had tied her hair back in the car, and she wore an old beanie hat Eleanor had dug out of her glove box. Between the hat and the hair and her hollowed eyes and pale skin, she looked almost nothing like the girl in the Disneyland picture.

They left Jake in the car and walked to the main entrance of the clinic. It led directly into a small waiting room with a desk and a door with a sign saying 'Exam Rooms'. There was a TV attached to the wall, showing a sitcom. The woman on the desk was in her sixties and wore a light green-blouse. When they got to the desk, she continued to stare at the screen in front of her for a good minute, as though she hadn't seen them walk in. Eventually, she looked up at Eleanor.

'Help you?'

'I hope so,' Eleanor said. 'We're on a camping trip and my bag was stolen. My daughter's Ventolin inhaler was in it, and she's not doing so well.'

Without moving her head an inch, the woman's gaze switched to Molly, then back to Eleanor. If she had noticed anything familiar about Molly, she didn't show it. She reached down behind the desk and produced a clipboard with a form on it. There was a ballpoint pen clipped to the board. 'Fill this in, ma'am. Do you have your insurance details?'

Eleanor gave her a rueful look and held up her empty hands. 'Well, that's the thing – my purse and all of our documents were in the bag, too.' Eleanor gently patted Molly on the back of her hat with her other hand. 'Can we buy an inhaler? I don't think she needs to see anybody. I just don't want us to be out here with nothing if she has another attack.'

The woman looked at Molly. Looked back at Eleanor. Eleanor blinked nervously. Molly could tell she was worried. This was going exactly the wrong way. They were making themselves memorable.

'She'll have to see the doctor. We accept cash or major credit cards.'

Eleanor took her Mastercard from her pocket and slid it across the counter. Molly noticed her hand was shaking a little. 'Lucky I keep this card separate.'

The woman took the card and looked back at her monitor, touch-typing something out onto the screen.

'Please take a seat.'

The doctor, a tired-looking thirty-something woman with blond hair and glasses, had had a slightly better bedside manner than the receptionist. She also showed no signs of recognizing Molly and seemed to take their story at face value. Perhaps it wasn't that out of the ordinary. She introduced herself as Doctor Mallory and asked Molly to lie down on the examination couch while she gave her a look over.

Eleanor told the doctor their names were Liz and Sally Morton, from Oakland. She mentioned the camping trip again, but Doctor Mallory didn't seem particularly interested. The doctor ran through some routine questions about 'Sally's' medical history – no allergies, asthma more severe when she was younger, not so much now. Active, healthy lifestyle. All good. Nothing too complicated. She asked Molly to blow into a plastic tube and noted down some readings.

She wrote out a prescription on her pad, tore it off and handed it to Eleanor. 'Pick it up tomorrow.'

Eleanor glanced at Molly. 'How you doing?'

Molly made a so-so face. 'I'm okay – Mom.'

Eleanor looked back at the doctor. 'I don't suppose you could give us something now? Only, I don't know if there's a pharmacy near where we are. I don't want to risk...' She tailed off.

Doctor Mallory looked at the two of them, and after a moment her better nature won out.

'All right. But you should make sure you keep your inhaler with you at all times, okay?'

'Yes, ma'am,' Molly said.

Doctor Mallory led them out into reception and told them she'd be a couple of minutes. She went into the back room again.

Molly exchanged a glance with Eleanor. Eleanor gave another of those nervous smiles that did nothing to reassure her. The receptionist had her head down, doing something involving removing staples from some documents on the desk. Molly looked at the clock on the wall. It had been almost half an hour since they had arrived.

Was Doctor Mallory back there calling the police? Or had the call been made while they were in the examination room, and she was just playing for time?

The second hand ticked around the clock face once, twice. The receptionist finished removing staples and tapped a sheaf of documents square on the desk. Molly looked at the closed door Doctor Mallory had used. It couldn't possibly take this long, could it?

The phone on the reception desk rang, loudly. Out of the corner of her eye, Molly saw Eleanor flinch. They exchanged another worried glance.

'Too long,' Eleanor said under her breath. She looked out at the parking lot. Molly wondered what was going through her mind. Probably just wondering how she had gotten herself mixed up in this.

Another minute ticked off. The doctor had been back there five minutes now.

'We have to go,' Eleanor said under her breath.

Headlights lit up the lot from behind them. Both of them turned around to look through the window that faced out onto the parking lot. Eleanor grabbed Molly's wrist and started to move, but she stayed in place. She had to blink to reassure herself that the light-colored sedan was not a police car. It circled the lot and drove back out again. She saw Jake get out of Eleanor's car and stand nervously by the driver's door, looking expectantly at the two of them.

'We have to go,' she said again under her breath. She pulled at Molly's wrist harder and this time she had to move as Eleanor stepped toward the exit.

'Not so fast.'

Molly turned around and saw Doctor Mallory standing by the door, holding a white paper bag.

'Sorry, I had to take a call.' As she held out the bag, she looked beyond them and saw Jake standing by the only car in the lot. 'That your husband?'

Eleanor smiled as she reached out to take the bag.

'Thank you, I don't know what we would have done without you.'

'Not a problem.' The doctor looked down at Molly. 'Try not to overdo it, but take a puff whenever you need to.'

Molly nodded.

'Take care of yourself. And take care of Mom and Dad too, huh?'

49

'... But that's the thing, isn't it? In investigations like these, maybe nobody knows anything. Tune in next time...'

Lark popped the earbuds out and rolled her eyes. 'Same Bat-time, same Bat-channel.'

'You say something?'

She looked back at Garcia. 'Just listening to this goddamn podcast.'

He grinned. 'Not much on today, huh?'

'Multitasking, Adrian. I'll tell you all about it, just as soon as you learn how to single-task.'

He took the barb with good grace. 'Any good?' he asked, gesturing at the screen of her Surface Book, where she had the podcast website up. She had found a section with a highlighted map of California with pins marking sightings the show had received from their rapidly growing listenership.

'They just concluded that nobody knows anything. Which probably gives them as much insight into this case as any of us.'

'They find anything we missed?'

'Nope. Not that they're broadcasting, anyway. It's interesting to listen to the interviews, though. People talk differently to her than they talk to us.'

'Different how?'

'I don't know.' She considered it for a moment. 'Like they're not in trouble, I guess.'

Garcia nodded. If you were a cop of any kind, people knew they had to talk to you. Wanting to didn't come into it. The girl on the podcast... Carrie? Chrissie. She actually seemed to have decent journalistic instincts. She could get people to open up. Just as importantly for what she was doing, she could tell a story. Lark hated to admit it, but even with no real fresh information, she had found it helpful to skim through the four episodes so far on double speed. It helped to have the events of the last couple of days laid out by a well-informed third party. It didn't mean she was any less pissed about the screenshots, of course.

The latest thing about the motorcycle was curious. She could see why the tip hadn't made it through to her. As the caller speculated, the biker had most likely been fleeing the scene. But in that case, why hadn't he come forward as a witness?

She checked #FindMolly on Twitter. The discussion was as lively as it had been earlier. 'Why are people so obsessed by this stuff these days?' she murmured. 'Podcasts, true crime shows on Netflix... is this normal?'

'You know who solved the code in the first Zodiac letter?' Garcia asked after a moment.

'Sure,' Lark said. 'A cypher expert, wasn't it?'

'A nice, middle-aged couple from Salinas who liked doing crosswords. Civilians.' He opened his hands as if to say 'there you go'. 'People are always interested in crime. They want to solve the case. Maybe we should be happy.'

She raised an eyebrow. 'Give me a nice crossword to solve over this any day.'

The clock on the corner of her screen clicked from 22.59 to 23.00. A day and a half gone, now. She wondered if another coffee from the machine out in the motel's reception would cure her incipient headache, or make it worse.

'Agent Lark?'

She looked up from the screen. It was Colette Osborne. Lark tried to read the younger woman's expression: it was difficult to tell whether she was anxious or excited.

'What is it? The hospital?'

She shook her head. 'No. I mean, yes. I mean, not that hospital...'

'Colette...'

'Sorry. I just spoke to a doctor at an urgent care clinic in Crescent City.'

'Okay?' Lark prompted. She was interested. Crescent City was about a hundred miles north of here, on the coast. Very much within their current area of interest.

'I put some feelers out for specific medical prescription issues statewide.'

'Specific prescription issues? I'm sorry, what does that have to do with—'

'Remember? You always say, "You have to check everything." So I did. The pictures from Rachel Donaldson's house. In Molly's room, there was an inhaler on her dresser.'

Lark caught on. 'And we were pretty sure she had nothing else with her but the clothes she was wearing when she was abducted, because her bag was still in the car.'

'That's right,' Osborne said. 'I figured if she didn't have it with her, and she's in this high-stress situation, she might—'

'Great work,' Lark said, feeling a little bad about cutting Osborne off in mid-flow. 'So where do we need to be?'

Osborne held up a torn-off sheet of notepaper with an address and the name of the urgent care clinic written on it. 'An adult and a girl in her early teens walked in half an hour ago and got an emergency inhaler for asthma. They paid upfront, no insurance.'

She looked a little uncertain as she spoke, and Lark picked up on it. 'An adult?'

'The person who accompanied her was a woman. But there was a guy waiting for them outside. A man in his late thirties, early forties.'

'What names did they give?'

'Nothing on the form they filled in checks out. We called as soon as it came up on the system, the doctor who saw them was still there.'

Lark felt a surge of excitement. An hour ago. Even if they had a car, they couldn't have travelled more than fifty, sixty miles from the clinic in that time. Who was the woman? Somebody they had missed on Ellis's short list of associates?

She stood up and yelled across the office to Garcia, who was going through the list of small towns and unincorporated communities that could fit Hartzler's description.

'What's up?'

She took the sheet of paper from Osborne's hand. 'How many towns on your list?'

'How many you want? Maybe fifty possibilities.'

'Narrow it down to the ones nearest Crescent City.'

He glanced down at his screen, at whatever he was in the middle of. 'Now?'

'No, let's pencil it in for Fourth of July weekend. Yes, fucking now.'

Something else occurred to her. She looked back at Osborne.

'How did they pay? They couldn't use insurance.'

She was assuming it had to be cash. Anything else was too good to hope for, and besides, they would probably already have heard about a ping on one of Ellis's cards. But when you catch a wave, you have to try and ride it, hope to stay lucky.

'I don't know,' Osborne said. 'I could—'

'Do it.'

Lark picked up the phone and called Finn. He picked up immediately, despite the hour. She started speaking before he had finished saying hello.

'We think we have a sighting. Crescent City.'

50

Jake told Eleanor to keep her Civic under sixty along the twisting coast road back down to False Klamath. It wasn't the kind of road you took at speed at night anyway. The inky blackness of the stretches through the redwoods hid the sharp turns on the undivided two-lane highway.

The whole way, he kept his eyes on the road ahead, waiting for the headlights to reflect off the black hood and roof-mounted lights of an oncoming California Highway Patrol car. Or, worse still, see flashing lights erupt into life in the rearview mirror as a bored cop decided to pull them over.

'You think she knew there was something wrong?' Eleanor asked, after they had been driving in silence for ten minutes or so.

'She would have tried to keep you there if she suspected something,' he said. It was a hope, rather than anything based on evidence.

A set of headlights appeared out of the curve a quarter-mile ahead and Jake tensed. He let out another breath as a silver SUV sailed past them, traveling at better than eighty. The wash made the Civic shudder a little in its wake.

Eleanor let out a long sigh. 'I must be nuts, letting you talk me into this.'

'We really appreciate it,' Jake said. 'She needed that.'

He turned around to look into the back seat. Molly was staring back at him, the soft lights from the dash reflecting in her brown eyes. She was cradling the inhaler in her right hand. As the doctor had ordered, she hadn't taken any more since the two puffs in the clinic. Just the knowledge that she had it was a weight off for him. He imagined she would feel the same way too. If only the other concerns weighing him down could be alleviated by a prescription.

'What if she knew it was us and let us go anyway?' Molly said quietly. 'Maybe she was scared.'

Jake opened his mouth to object. Did she really think people had to fear him? Was that the way Molly felt, after everything? He glanced across at Eleanor. She had been watching him out of the corner of her eye, and quickly looked back at the road.

51

When they reached False Klamath, Eleanor Grace parked her Honda outside her house. Molly waited by the car while Jake walked her to her door. She paused with her key in her hand, and her gaze moved beyond Jake to Molly. 'I hope you know what you're doing,' she said.

'That makes two of us.'

'You really think this is for the best? I could talk to them, make them—'

He shook his head. 'Can't risk it. Thank you for tonight.'

She bit her lip and then turned away to unlock the door. 'I need to do some thinking.'

'I understand,' Jake said.

She hesitated on the threshold, and then just looked back at him and went inside, closing the door. He stood there for a minute. He hoped she would keep quiet, even just for a day or so. He would have to trust her; it wasn't as though he had any choice.

They walked around the back of Diehl's house and entered through the French doors.

'You should get some sleep,' Jake said to Molly as they entered the kitchen. The light reflecting off the giant 1970s refrigerator facing them reminded him neither of them had eaten anything since late morning. Jesus, he wasn't shaping up to be much of a guardian. 'You hungry? You should eat something.'

She shook her head. 'I just need some water.'

He took two bottles of water from the fridge and handed one to her. She took it and turned toward the bedroom.

'I'll see you in the morning.'

He squeezed his own water bottle tight in his fist. She deserved better than this. He had to get her back to some sort of normality soon. Rachel would need her when she woke up. If she woke up. Whether the two of them would want anything more to do with the man who had brought all of this pain down on them was another matter.

He went over to the desk and booted up the computer, taking a long drink from the water bottle while the venerable old PC ground and whirred reluctantly to life. He felt every bit as tired and worn out as the computer. Caffeine might help with that, he decided.

By the time he got back from the kitchen with a fresh pot of coffee, the desktop had appeared. He poured a cup and took a sip while he waited another minute for the browser to cough up a screen. A minute later, he got into the inbox of the new Gmail account.

Which wasn't empty.

There was one message.

Re: your question

Jake put the coffee cup down and clicked into the message, cursing under his breath as the screen blanked and thought about giving up its secrets.

Eventually it did.

His contact had evidently come through. There was no name on the email. It had come from an account named 'Questions'. There were three short paragraphs, followed by a hyperlink to a news article. As Jake read, he began to wonder if the email had been written by Carl Dolan himself.

The email identified a likely candidate for the person who might have shot Rachel. A man named Wade Lang. According to the anonymous emailer, Lang fit the bill in a number of ways: he had carried out numerous hits for organized crime across the state, but was based in the Bay Area. He rode a motorcycle and was rumored to have used it in the commission of some of his jobs. He had never had anything pinned on him. The tone was playfully evasive; as though the writer knew all these things to be the truth but preferred to keep these details at an arm's length.

But there was one final piece of information that both reinforced the case against Wade Lang and caused a major problem: he had been found murdered. This morning.

The link took Jake to a brief news article about it. Lang had been found shot to death underneath the Central Freeway on Sunday morning. Police suspected it was gang-related and were appealing for witnesses. The article was short, and Jake suspected this would be the first and last time it would be mentioned in print. Gang-affiliated lowlifes don't command the front pages the way thirteen-year-old girls do.

This couldn't be a coincidence.

If the writer of the email was indeed Carl Dolan, he had to know more than the newspapers. Dolan was a broker of services, and it seems that had often included Wade Lang's services.

Jake sat back and stared at the screen for a minute. Then he opened a new message. This one, he didn't keep anonymous. He wanted to stop playing games, focus Dolan's attention.

My name is Jake Ellis

I know Wade Lang was the man who shot Rachel Donaldson.

He sat back and considered, then typed a last line.

What do you want?

He left the number of his burner at the bottom of the message and hit send.

At that moment, he saw headlights across the road and down. Eleanor Grace's house. A police car pulling to a stop outside. And then he saw a glint of light on the horizon, at the foot of the road that led up from town. More headlights approaching. Two sets of them. Traveling fast.

52

'Okay, got it,' Colette Osborne said, speaking into the phone. Lark craned her neck back to watch her in the back seat. Through the rear window, she could see the headlights of the CHP car that had joined them ten miles back. She listened and glanced down at the phone in her lap that was displaying the distance to the house in False Klamath. 'Sit tight, we'll be there in about three minutes.'

They had called ahead to let the sheriff's department know they were on their way and that there was a person of interest possibly holed up at an address on the edge of town.

The payment in Crescent City had been made by Mastercard. The name and address on the forms had been fake, but the card was registered to a Ms Eleanor H. Grace, who lived in a tiny community fifteen miles down the coast called False Klamath. Directly across the street from her address was a house owned by a Walter Diehl, who had died last year. The house had solar panels on the roof. Diehl's name had come up when they ran it through the database: he had been Jake Ellis's boss when he worked at a bar twenty years before. Not enough of a connection to show up on their checks for current associates, but it looked as though the two had kept in touch.

Osborne hung up. 'He says it doesn't look like anybody's home.'

Lark blinked. 'Tell me he didn't knock on the door.'

'He says not. He did a drive-by, didn't approach the house. No cars in the driveway, no lights on in the house.'

'What about the Grace house?'

'He's with her now. She isn't talking.'

Lark cursed under her breath. 'He was supposed to wait for us.' She turned to Paxon, who was driving. 'Can you hurry this up a little?'

They were already doing eighty along a road that would be a little risky at sixty. Paxon sped up by about five miles an hour. Lark had called in reinforcements before they left the motel at Willow Creek, but they were a long way ahead of them. She didn't want to wait another hour and risk losing Ellis again.

As Paxon slowed to a sedate fifty at the edge of town, the headlights lit up a disused billboard advertising a blank space. As they passed by, Lark thought she saw a glint of red. Like a taillight, as though a car was parked behind it. She thought about asking Paxon to stop the car but decided the house was the priority. If there was a car there, it was well within the perimeter and could be checked later. There were only three roads out of town. Lark had coordinated with Highway Patrol and set up roadblocks on all three, plus two more three miles north and south on the 101. They had put a box around the town, and if Jake Ellis was still here, he wasn't leaving it.

A couple of minutes later, they reached the road that led up to the house registered to the late Walter Diehl.

On Lark's instructions, Paxon pulled to a stop a hundred yards from the house itself. The four of them got out. The night was cold, cold enough to see your breath.

The house was set quite a distance back from the road, but there was enough moonlight to make out details. It was one story with wood siding, a slate roof and a covered porch over the door. A big willow tree dominated the yard on one side, its elongated leaves obscuring the ground beyond it. On the other side, Lark could see a short patch of open ground beyond the house and then the black void of the ocean beyond.

Even at this distance, it looked deserted, just as the local cop had said.

No vehicles in the driveway and blades of grass poked up from the gravel surface all over the place. The house was completely in darkness, too. If you were a salesman making door-to-door calls in the neighborhood, it was the kind of place you would pass by without bothering to check.

There were two large windows at the front. The moonlight was shining straight onto the house, so anyone standing close to the windows would have been lit up like they were in a spotlight. That reassured her a little about the approach. It didn't look like there were any other vantage points on this side of the house. The front door was solid wood with a small frosted-glass panel. No telling who or what was behind it.

She took her eyes off the house to survey the four members of her team. All had their guns drawn, held in both hands, pointed at the ground for now, but ready to move at a moment's notice to an offensive stance. They were all dressed for the occasion: Kevlar vests under navy-blue FBI-branded jackets and ball caps. No chance of one of them mistaking another for a target. On the other hand, if Jake Ellis was holed up here and didn't feel like going quietly, he would know exactly who to shoot at.

She looked at Garcia and Osborne. 'Cover the back, we'll take the knock. Be careful.'

The two of them acknowledged, glanced at each other, and wordlessly started to move off to the side of the house each was closest to, guns and eyes trained on the windows, looking for movement. As they got within ten feet of their respective corners, Lark and Paxon started moving quickly toward the front door. No way to approach completely silently over the gravel, of course, but it was hard-packed and Lark tried to step lightly. Unless someone was listening out for them, it wouldn't be immediately obvious.

Garcia and Osborne disappeared behind the north and south corners, circling around to meet at the back. There hadn't been time to properly evaluate the house from a distance, but from the satellite images, she knew there was a covered deck out back. She knew the two of them would keep their distance. Their job wasn't to approach, just to make sure their suspect didn't have an easy route out of the back door.

As they got within ten feet of the steps up to the door, Paxon stopped in place and trained her gun on the top half of the side of the door with the handle, so that she would have a clear shot if anyone opened it.

Lark covered the last few paces and climbed the steps. She rapped hard on the door, before standing to one side. 'This is the FBI. If there is anyone in here, please make yourself known immediately.'

Silence. So quiet she could hear the creak of the synthetic fabric of Paxon's jacket as she adjusted her aim on the door.

Lark raised her voice again. 'Be advised, we are entering the house. If you are armed, lay down any weapons or we will shoot.'

Lark took a breath. No matter how many doors you went through, no matter how sure you were that there was nobody behind it, it never got any easier. She reached forward and tried the handle. Locked, as expected. She tapped the button on her headset to communicate with the two around the back of the house.

'How's it look back there, guys?'

It was quiet enough that she barely needed the earpiece. She could hear Garcia's voice twice as she spoke. 'No signs of life back here. Back door looks like it's been jimmied.'

She glanced back at Paxon. If there was a point of ingress already, there was no reason to break the front door down.

'I'm coming around,' she said. She nodded her head at the door and Paxon acknowledged, staying in place with the gun trained at head-height on the front door.

Lark moved quickly round to the south corner of the house, the side Garcia had taken. At the edge of the house, the gravel gave way to rough grass. There was a single window on this elevation, about four feet off the ground. She kept low and watched it for signs of movement as she passed by. The moonlight picked out the strands of cobwebs in the inside corners of the window. She glimpsed a desk, a computer screen inside. There was a dull orange light at the bottom corner of the monitor, indicating that it was sleeping, not fully turned off. The first sign that the house might not be as long-deserted as it looked.

Garcia came into view as she reached the southwest corner. She was standing in a position that mirrored Paxon's around the front, several paces back from the building, gun pointed at the back door in a two-handed grip.

She could hear the gentle lap of the waves against the shore below. There was the outline of a rough path along the cliff edge, stretching for thirty feet before disappearing into thick woods.

The back porch came into view. A rocking chair and a circular table. There was an empty bottle of water on its side on the table. The back door was a set of twin glass French doors. As Garcia had said, she could see where the one on the right-hand side was splintered at the lock. She glanced at Garcia and Osborne to make sure they were covering her and stepped up onto the porch.

She felt better about approaching this than the front door. If anyone wanted to stand behind the back doors with a shotgun, they would be fully visible. She kept her gun pointed on the door as she reached out with her left hand and turned the handle down. The door swung out with a creak.

'FBI,' she called into the house. 'Be advised, we are armed. We're coming in.'

Without taking her eyes off the doorway, she gestured back to where she knew Osborne was standing and signaled for her to follow. Garcia would hang back and cover the door.

It didn't take long to clear the whole house. They moved quickly between the four main rooms and the bathroom.

Nobody home.

According to the records she had scanned on the drive up from Willow Creek, Walter Diehl had died in November last year. The house was tied up in probate, his only living relative lived in Canada and was planning to put it on the market once the legal issues were settled. The place didn't feel like it had been unoccupied for that length of time, though. There was an underlying musty smell, but it had been aired out recently. And the bed had been slept in.

She moved through to the room with the computer, the little orange light at the corner of the monitor screen the only sign of life. The chair was pulled out from under the desk.

'Who's been sitting in my chair?' Lark said to herself as she approached.

Definite signs of life, so where was Goldilocks?

She tapped the keyboard to wake the screen, feeling a faint warmth on her hand as she reached past the coffee cup that was next to it. She touched the cup. It was still hot.

'Son of a bitch.'

The screen woke up. Two tabs open on the browser: a Google entry for Crescent City Urgent Care and a news article about a murder in the city.

53

Louisa Martinez was so tired at the end of her double shift that she needed two of the plastic cups of machine coffee before she could work up the energy to make the last round of the ward.

She moved quietly, the soft soles of her sneakers padding on the floors. Most of the patients were asleep, only a couple reading with their bedside lights, or watching movies on tablets. She covered E wing quickly, checking the charts were all up to date for the rounds in the morning. As she crossed into F wing, she noticed a figure leaving by the door on the opposite side. He wasn't staff – he was wearing outdoor clothes. That was odd, visiting hours had ended a couple of hours before. She quickened her pace and pushed open the door the man had just used, coming out into the corridor. She looked up and down. There was no sign of him.

She shrugged and went back into F, making the same checks as usual. There was only one patient awake, a fifty-something guy with receding hair reading a Lee Child paperback. She glanced down at his chart. His name was Garrett, Michael A. Post-op recovery from removal of kidney stones.

He looked up from his book as Louisa approached.

'How are you feeling, Mr Garrett?' she whispered.

'Like I've given birth,' he said, making no effort to keep his voice low. The patient in the neighboring bed murmured a complaint and rolled over.

'Say, did you see that guy walking past just there?' She indicated in the direction the man had gone.

Mr Garrett looked blank. 'What guy?'

The neighboring patient made a louder grunt this time. Louisa smiled and moved on. The man she had seen had probably just been a relative, maybe he had been visiting the ICU in the next block, which allowed immediate family to visit at any time, so long as they checked in. Visitors who had become familiar with the layout sometimes cut through this way. It was a quicker route to the elevator that served the main parking area.

The ICU was her next stop, in fact. Louisa yawned as she walked through the link corridor and through the double doors. Only three patients in here, including their celebrity guest. She was looking down at her clipboard as she walked in.

'How's Sleeping Beauty?'

She put a line through the last-but-one item on her list and looked up when she realized her question had gone unanswered.

There was no one at the nurses' station. That wasn't good. She thought Shelby was on duty, and it wasn't like her to desert her post. Particularly when the ICU had to be monitored at all times. First things first, she checked on the patients. They all looked fine at first glance. Life-support monitors all ticking away okay, no lights flashing that shouldn't be. Rachel Donaldson was in the closest bed, so she went there first.

The top quarter of the patient's head was still bandaged from surgery, her red hair was shaven from her scalp underneath the bandage, but it fanned out on the pillow on the other side.

Louisa checked off the readings against the last notes on her chart. All the same. She shook her head as she looked down at the comatose patient. Her face under the bandage looked perfect and fragile, her skin like that of a porcelain doll. A shadow of bruising extended a little from beneath the bandage. Who would want to do this to anyone, let alone a young mother? She had been following the news with trepidation, the story hitting closer to home because one of the victims was here. She just hoped they would find that little girl soon.

She moved on to the next two patients. Johnson and Del Muerto. Neither were comatose, like Donaldson, but both were asleep. Charts all checked out.

She heard hurried footsteps outside and a second later the doors burst open. Shelby appeared. Her mouth opened when she saw Louisa.

'I am *so* sorry, I called down, but I just couldn't wait any longer. I was only away a minute, I swear.'

Louisa raised her eyebrow. She hadn't seen Shelby leave, so it had to have been longer than a minute. More like five or six minutes, at least.

'What happened?'

'I had to puke. All of a sudden I just felt so woozy.'

She did look a little pale, Louisa had to admit. And she was sweating like she had just run the San Francisco Marathon. As she watched, Shelby swayed a little on her feet. She helped her to sit down. She had been about to scold her, but she could see the other nurse really wasn't in good shape.

'It's okay, they're all fine, that's the main thing.' She held a hand up to Shelby's forehead. It was red hot. 'You need to be out of here, though. My God.'

She pressed the intercom on the desk. Someone acknowledged downstairs.

'Get somebody up to ICU four, stat, Shelby is sick as a dog and we need somebody in here.'

Shelby was bent over, her head almost touching her knees. ''M so sorry, I just feel...'

'That's okay. Let's get you into the corridor, though. We'll get somebody to take over here.'

They moved out into the corridor and she got Shelby sitting down. 'Now just wait here, I'll be back in a second.'

She went back into the ICU and washed her hands at the sink. Something made her glance back at Rachel Donaldson. There was something off about her drip. It looked like it was out of position.

She moved closer and saw what it was, with a sharp intake of breath. Her drip was set up to administer antibiotics at twelve-hour intervals. The next dose was almost due. But as she looked closer, she saw a tiny hole at the top of the bag, just above the fluid level. As though someone had injected something in there.

54

The night air was chill as Molly followed Jake through the woods. It felt sharp when she breathed in, like her throat and lungs were raw.

She could tell Jake was holding back a little, going slower than he wanted to. He glanced back at her, his expression saying he was worried she would suddenly drop dead.

'I'm okay,' she said.

They kept going along the path that wound down to the road. Her chest felt tight, but nothing like as bad as earlier. She didn't want to use the Ventolin up too fast, so she was trying to keep it until she really needed it. In the meantime, the pace was bearable. She wondered if Jake was wrong, though. Perhaps the best thing to do would be to wait for the police, explain everything. She could make them believe what she had seen; that Jake couldn't have been the one who shot Mom.

But then she remembered the gun pointed at her, the certainty that she was about to die. Jake said they could go to the police when he knew who had done it. As long as they thought Jake was the person they were looking for, the real attacker was still out there, and she didn't trust the police to keep her safe. Not when they would believe they had already caught the perpetrator.

Behind them, she could hear more vehicles arriving at the house. The sounds of voices.

'Do you think they'll have dogs?' she whispered. Molly had nothing against dogs, had always wanted a puppy, but the thought of police dogs pursuing them through the thick woods gave her shivers.

'I hope not,' Jake said. 'I think that was the advance party, but we need to get the hell out of here.'

'But how are we going to leave without the car?'

They reached a place where the trees thinned out and there was a slope of about thirty feet down to the road. Molly saw the lights of the gas station in the distance and realized they had curved around and come out on the road that approached the old house, doubling back on their pursuers.

'We're not,' Jake said, looking down the hill.

Molly followed his gaze and saw that they had come out just across the road from where the white Ford was parked, obscured behind the billboard. They stayed crouched down for a moment as the sound of an engine approached and they saw a police car flash past, lights blazing, headed for the house.

'This place is going to be crawling with Feds and cops in about five minutes,' Jake said. 'Wait here. As soon as I get in and get the engine running, come down and get in, okay?'

She murmured agreement, and watched as Jake carefully picked his way down the steep slope, scanning the road for more cars. It was quiet for the moment.

Molly let out a sigh of relief as he reached the road and approached the car.

And then realized the relief had been premature, as she saw the figure with the gun step out from beneath the shadows of the towering trees on the opposite side of the road.

55

The hunch had paid off.

The first thing Lark had done when she worked out how narrowly they must have missed their target was to take her phone out and examine the terrain around the house. There were a limited number of ways out. The most obvious was the road that led back through town, but they hadn't passed any vehicles on their way in for the last ten minutes or so.

Jake Ellis could have left before that and the coffee might still be warm, of course, but she was sure his departure had been sudden, and motivated by their approach. Which meant he, and hopefully Molly, might still be in the area. Maybe even on foot.

Rule out the road and the sixty-foot sheer drop to the shoreline, and you were left with the woods on the north side of the Diehl house. Looking at the satellite view of the area, she could see where the road curved around on the far side of about a quarter-mile square of dense redwoods. It was impossible to tell for certain, but the position of the gas station and the tight bend in the road gave her a good enough rule of thumb. She thought that if you drew a line from the house to the billboard where she had glimpsed the reflected taillights, it would be the shortest possible distance between the house and the road.

All of these calculations passed through her mind in a couple of seconds. She told Osborne to go to Eleanor Grace's house and check in with the cop detaining her, and Garcia and Paxon to start combing the woods from this side. Meanwhile, she got back in the car and headed around to the tight bend. A longer route than across country, but a lot faster by car than on foot. She covered the distance in less than a minute, cutting her headlights before she reached the bend and parking just out of sight of where the car was parked behind the billboard, assuming it was still there.

She got out and jogged along the roadside, keeping into the deep shadows cast by the moon and the thick pine trees. The old billboard loomed dark against the sky. The faded remnants of the last ad still showing. The car was there, and empty. A different license plate, but it was a 2012 white Ford Fusion. As she watched, a police cruiser appeared from past the gas station, lit up and proceeding at speed. The first of the reinforcements. She thought about flagging it down and then reconsidered. If that car was what she thought it was, she needed the coast to be clear for at least another few minutes.

Instead, she stepped into the deep shadows beneath the pines, keeping the reflective FBI branding on her back away from the road, covering the badge on her breast pocket with one hand, and keeping her head down so the brim of the baseball cap obscured her face in shadow. She held a breath as the police car flashed past, then let it out as it disappeared round the bend, pausing for a second to appreciate the irony that she had just found herself hiding from the police.

She moved closer to the bend again, keeping deep in the shadows, and watched.

She didn't have to wait long. After a couple of minutes, a figure appeared from the trees at the top of the hill on the side the house was on. Male, the right height and build to be Jake Ellis. He was carrying a small bundle, or bag. She narrowed her eyes and watched as he picked his way down the last twenty feet, almost stumbling once.

It was definitely him.

Ellis glanced up and down the road, but Lark knew he was looking for headlights and listening for police sirens. He wasn't looking for figures in the shadows. Even if he had looked directly at her, she doubted if he would see her. The contrast between the milky-white moonlight and the deep shadows was too great.

He stepped toward the billboard, his hand digging in his pocket and producing what had to be a car key. She stepped into the moonlight and clicked her flashlight on as she trained the gun on his chest.

'Hands on your head!'

Ellis froze. He dropped the bag. Slowly, he complied.

Was he armed? It was hard to tell. Nothing in his hands, but he was wearing a jacket that came down a little over his waist. Now she could get a good look at him in the flashlight beam, she could see that he had changed his appearance. Much shorter hair, and the mustache was gone. It made a big difference.

'Get down on your knees and lay down your weapon,' she said as she started moving toward him, keeping her aim on his upper body.

He turned around slowly, keeping his hands on his head. He had obeyed the direction to raise his hands, but not the one to kneel down, which made her uneasy. And no move to toss a weapon, which could mean he didn't have one, or it could mean he did and intended to use it if he got the chance.

'I didn't do it,' he said as she got closer.

'On the ground,' she repeated. 'What did you do with her?'

'She's safe, but whoever shot her mom is still out there, and—'

'Not any more, Ellis. Now I'm not going to ask you again...'

'Look out!'

Lark looked away for a second. She couldn't help herself. It was a knee-jerk response to hearing a cry from an unexpected direction. Maybe it was the fact that the voice belonged to the thirteen-year-old girl who had occupied her every waking thought for the last two days. She only glanced up in the direction of the cry for a second, *less* than a second. But by the time she looked back, her aim had wavered from Jake Ellis and there was a gun in his hands, pointed right at her.

'Drop it,' he said.

'Shit,' she hissed, furious with herself.

'We're getting out of here, Agent,' Jake said. 'Nobody needs to get hurt, but that's what's going to happen.'

We.

Slowly, she bent and put the gun on the ground. As she straightened up, out of the corner of her eye she saw another figure emerge from the same place at the treeline at the top of the hill. Smaller, leaner, lighter on her feet.

Molly.

She reached the road and glanced between Ellis and Lark, a pensive look on her face. She looked different too: hair dyed brown or black, instead of her natural red.

'Molly, stay away from the car,' she said. 'You don't have to go with him.'

'He didn't do it,' Molly said. 'He didn't hurt my mom.'

'Get in,' Ellis said quietly.

'Don't do it, Molly. I'll let him go, you can stay here with me, and we can work this out.'

Molly glanced at Lark nervously, then seemed to make up her mind. She opened the passenger door and got in the car. What the hell?

Ellis used his free hand to pick up the bag he had dropped and started to move back toward the door. He paused as he thought of something. 'The guy who did this was riding a motorcycle. Your witness is lying to you. Check out a guy named Wade Lang.'

He kept the gun on Lark as he stepped back. The door swung out as Molly opened it for him from inside. Ellis got behind the wheel, gun still on Lark.

She had lost her chance, now. If she had been going to risk shooting, she would have had to do it before Molly got in.

She saw Ellis's lips move, guessed he was giving Molly an instruction. She reached across him and the engine started up. Ellis put his left hand on the wheel, kept the gun pointed at Lark. The wheels spun and the car reversed out from behind the billboard at speed, before K-turning in the road and flooring it.

Lark bent and picked up her gun. Came up fast and lined up her aim with one of the rear tires. Started to squeeze the trigger, and then stopped. She couldn't risk it. As the taillights disappeared past the gas station, she lowered her gun and reached for her phone to call in the car and the new license plate.

If they were lucky, they could head him off before he reached the 101. If not, he would be stopped at one of the three-mile roadblocks.

If they were lucky. But why would their luck change now?

56

Jake thought the agent back there would probably have gotten a good look at the rear plate when he turned in the road. She would be calling in their location now. And any cop heading this way would stop any vehicle heading in the opposite direction, no matter what or who its driver looked like.

But they made it to the turn onto the beach road without passing another car. He didn't allow himself to hope, just tried to focus on getting where he was going.

Jake made a left and carried on down the road. As more and more cops descended on the area, he knew they would find this road and check it, but that was okay. With every minute that passed, they were increasing the number of routes that would have to be checked. All he had to do was hope they weren't seen until they got where they were going. They would be expecting him on the main roads though, not driving hell for leather down a dead end.

Down the beach road, much faster than he had taken it last time. He flicked the headlights on full, tried to remember the locations of the two or three big potholes he remembered from earlier. He successfully negotiated the first two, the third was closer than he had thought. The car thumped over it with a loud crack that he hoped wasn't the axle. He righted the swerve and they kept going. Just the bodywork.

Molly was turned around in her seat, watching the road behind them. They would need a few minutes.

'Anyone following?' he asked, keeping his focus on the pitted road ahead, trying to remember where the turn was.

She squinted into the darkness of the road behind. 'No. Do you know where you're going?'

He didn't answer, focused on the turn up ahead. He slowed and took it. Molly took a sharp intake of breath as the road fell steeply away from them at a deep incline. Jake followed the road around on the curve and then the shore appeared below them. He slowed and pulled to a jolting stop before the last slope down to the beach, angling the car so that it was pointed off the road and toward the other side of the drop, down to the trees. He turned the engine off and left it in neutral.

'Don't leave anything in the car,' he said.

Molly patted her pocket to make sure the inhaler was still there and got out, standing where Jake indicated, a little away from the car. He put both hands on the trunk lid, braced his feet in the dirt, and started to push.

Slowly, the car started to roll, picking up speed as it crested the small slope. When it started rolling faster, Jake let go. It rolled down the hill and disappeared into the undergrowth. No time to get fancy and arrange the bushes around it, but you could only make out the car if you were really looking for it. It would be easier to spot in daylight, but he was hoping they would be a long way from here by then.

'Don't we, uh ...' Molly began. 'Don't we need that?'

'There's no way in hell anything other than a police car is getting out of this area tonight. They'll have the roads blocked.'

'Then what do we do? Hide until they give up?'

'That's not what I said.'

He moved quickly down the rest of the hill toward the beach. The old wood hut was an angular black shape against the sky.

He took his gun out, but he didn't want to fire a shot if he didn't need to. First, he gripped the gap in the door by the padlock and gave it a good wrench. The wood creaked against the hasp. He gave it another pull and the damp wood popped apart around the lock, and the door swung open. He waited for Molly to catch up and then used his phone to shine a little light on the interior. When she looked inside, she nodded in understanding.

57

They could see the silent flashes of police cars speeding along the 101, lighting up the horizon like St Elmo's Fire. More and more joining the hunt. There would be roadblocks on all three of the roads leading out of False Klamath. Federal agents and men from the sheriff's office would be spreading out through the woods.

They were well out of earshot, but he waited until the current had pulled them out a couple of hundred yards before he turned the motor on. It coughed a couple of times and ground to life. Molly looked back at the shore apprehensively as the noise of the outboard motor shattered the calm of the night and the waves lapping against the hull. Jake wasn't worried. They were far enough out that the noise wouldn't be noticed unless one of their pursuers had reached the beach. With no lights, they would be invisible against the sea.

He moved the tiller and struck out in a straight line from the shore. They passed by the sea stack, a black void against the stars. Around a half-mile out, he curved around so the coast was on their left-hand side. It was easy to pick out Diehl's house, the point on the ridge surrounded by the biggest cluster of flashing lights. Tiny spears of light in the trees as the hunters moved through the woods with their flashlights.

The boat was old, but well-cared for. Maybe it belonged

to one of the homeowners nearby, or perhaps somebody who spent summers on the coast. He hadn't intended to use it for onward transport when he had seen it earlier, but it had opened up another possibility. Until he found the old hut and what it contained, he had thought of the shore as another boundary, not an avenue of escape.

'I guess Eleanor called them,' Molly said.

'Maybe,' Jake said. 'Could have been the doctor. Could have been something else I did wrong.' It was almost a relief, now that they had been found. Their eventual discovery had been an inevitability, weighing down on him since they had left the apartment. But now it had happened and, so far, they were dealing with it.

He flinched as the burner phone rang, the screen lighting up the inside of the boat. Jake glanced down at it. The number was withheld. He picked up the phone and answered the call, keeping his eyes on the dark coastline.

'Yes?'

'I'm speaking to Jake Ellis?' The voice had a slight accent. Carl Dolan.

'You're speaking to the man who gave you this number. You have something to say to me?'

There was a long pause, and Jake started to worry that he had pissed Dolan off.

'It's come to my attention you wanted to talk.'

'That's right. I believe Wade Lang was responsible for an attack on people close to me. He works for you. So you can answer me one question, Mr Dolan. What the hell do you want from me?'

Another long pause. When Dolan spoke again, it was impossible to tell from his tone if he was annoyed or amused. 'Will you have this phone tomorrow?'

'Not likely.'

'The email address your enquiry came from, then. You'll be able to access it.'

'Yes.' Jake was curious now. What did Dolan have in mind?

'Be in San Francisco tomorrow evening. You'll receive a message at five o'clock.'

'I'm done with games. I want to know—'

'Some things are best discussed in person, Jake. But perhaps you're not interested.'

Jake bit his lip and screamed all of the things he wanted to say to Carl Dolan inside his head instead. 'I'll pick up the email at five.'

The line went dead.

'Who was that?'

Jake looked over at where Molly was sitting in the prow. He couldn't see her expression, just her silhouette against the waves.

'The man who can tell us what the hell is going on, I hope,' Jake said.

The boathouse and the beach at False Klamath and the sea stack and the police cars and the spears of flashlight had all vanished behind them. San Francisco was a long way from here. He hoped he would be around to receive that email.

He kept watching the coast and held the tiller steady.

58

Chrissie thought the ringing phone was part of her dream.

She opened her eyes gradually and saw that the room was lit up by the screen light. She fumbled for her phone and found it a second after the caller had given up.

Sean's number. If he was calling in the middle of the night, it had to be big. She called back.

'What is it?' she asked, no preamble.

'Turn on your television,' he said.

She looked for the remote. 'What happened, did they find him?'

'It looks like it.'

She cursed under her breath as the TV took its usual leisurely five seconds to come to life. When it did, it was already tuned to the news. Chrissie saw aerial footage of what looked like a small town. Along the bottom, the ticker read: *Molly Donaldson Hunt: Federal agents swoop on town of False Klamath, Ca. No update on fugitive Jake Ellis...*

'Holy shit,' she said.

'I know. And there's something else.'

'What?'

'One of the locals wants to talk.'

59

'You okay?'

Lark nodded as she approached Paxon. She was standing in front of the door of the closest house to the Diehl place. Two more bureau vehicles had arrived. A couple of CHP vehicles too. There had been no word from any of the roadblocks.

Lark let out a growl of frustration. 'I had him. I fucking had him.'

'We'll get him. We've locked down every road out of here. They're not going anywhere.'

'I've heard that before,' Lark said. 'She in there?'

'In the kitchen,' Osborne said. 'With Garcia. Not being all that cooperative.'

Lark walked through the front door. The house was neatly kept. Of a similar period to the Diehl place, but with brighter décor and furnishings, and it didn't smell musty. Garcia was with Eleanor Grace in the kitchen, just like Osborne had said.

She shot a glance at Garcia, who was leaning against one of the worktops, his arms folded. He hadn't cuffed her. She was sitting at the table.

'Do you know the penalty for aiding and abetting a fugitive in California, Ms Grace?'

Grace looked nervous but defiant. She folded her arms and

stared back at Lark. 'I'm sure you're going to tell me, whether I like it or not.'

'Prosecutors and judges call it a wobbler,' she continued. 'Meaning the crime you've committed can be either a misdemeanor or a felony, depending on how they're feeling. If they decide to go felony, you're looking at three years.'

'You're looking for the wrong man.'

'Is that what he told you?'

'It's what Molly told me. She saw the whole thing. She told me a man on a motorcycle shot her mother and tried to kill her. Jake wasn't there.'

'She'll say anything Ellis tells her to. She's under duress, in fear for her life.'

'No she's not,' the woman said calmly. 'I just spent a couple of hours with them. She's not scared of him at all. She's more scared of you people.'

'Then the best thing we can do is find her,' Lark said. 'If Ellis has an explanation, let's hear it. You can help us end this with no more bloodshed by telling us where they're headed.'

Eleanor Grace looked down at her hands. 'I guess that would be something of a dilemma for me. I believe he's innocent, but I don't want to make trouble for myself. If I knew where they were going, I might be tempted to tell you.'

'You're telling me you have no idea whatsoever?'

'He could have killed me this evening if he wanted to keep me quiet. There was nobody else around. Nobody would have missed me for days.'

Lark kept her face expressionless. She didn't like the fact that what Grace was saying tied in with her own recent experience. Ellis could have shot her, too. It would have made more sense for him to have done so. Nobody would have the new license plate of his car if he had. And Molly had gone with him voluntarily, without hesitation. She didn't seem scared of him at all.

Eleanor Grace continued. 'That's one reason I trusted him when he said he didn't do it. The other reason is he made a point of not telling me any information I would have to feel conflicted about giving up.'

'Nothing at all?'

'He told me he didn't do it. I helped him get the medication for Molly. And then he just thanked me and went on his way, and trusted me not to call you.'

Lark leaned on the table and held eye contact with the woman. 'Where is he going?'

It was too late. The spell was broken. She could see it in Eleanor Grace's eyes. She was telling the truth, and she knew Lark knew that.

Eventually, Eleanor answered. 'Your guess is as good as mine, Agent.'

60

The boat kept up a steady fifty knots without complaint. Jake followed the coastline. They passed the mouth of the Klamath River and kept going. For a long stretch, the coast was completely dark where the highway dipped inland a couple of miles. Eventually the road came back into view and they saw occasional headlights moving between the small towns.

The map on Jake's phone picked them out as they passed: Patrick's Point, Trinidad, Clam Beach. Sleepy little dots on the map he would never visit. He steered in toward the shore when they were roughly a mile from McKinleyville. There was a small cove that cut in close to the highway. Molly took her shoes off and climbed out into the shallows as he guided the boat in. He moored it at a rickety wooden jetty that looked like it hadn't been used in thirty years. The short rise from the beach to the highway would keep it out of sight unless anyone came down here from the road.

From there, it was a short walk to McKinleyville. The boat trip had given him time to plan out their next steps. It almost seemed easier now that Dolan had given him a place to be and a deadline.

61

The roadblocks had been set up quickly at regular intervals within a hundred miles of False Klamath. The limited number of roads and the comparatively sparse traffic this far north and at this time of night meant that the task force was able to enact a full court press. Every vehicle headed north, south and east of the last known sighting was stopped and searched, some of them multiple times at separate stops.

Ellis and Molly seemed to have vanished into thin air.

The first indication that they hadn't was the discovery of the white Ford. It had been found just before 3 a.m., in the woods that lined an old beach road that dead-ended at the shore. Subsequent focus on the area had determined that it might not have been a dead end after all. The car was found within walking distance of an old boating house. It contained tools, cans of gasoline and back issues of nautical magazines. The only thing the boating house didn't contain was a boat.

It had taken a while to identify the owner, and a further thirty minutes to wake him up and confirm that, as far as he was aware, the building had been used to store his 1973 Luhrs 320 Flybridge Cruiser until some point last night. He said the boat had been in excellent working order when he had locked it up in early November. Which meant Ellis and Molly could be virtually anywhere on a hundred-mile stretch of the California coast by now.

Lark sat back from her laptop and massaged her temple with the index finger of her right hand. She had returned to the motel in Willow Creek with Osborne and Paxon at five, leaving Garcia to keep an eye on the ongoing search around the Diehl house. The plan was to get some rest, but no one had retired to their room yet. Lark planned to grab a couple of hours' shut-eye and then head back up to False Klamath. What if the boat was a decoy? What if Ellis had somewhere else in the area to hide out while he threw them off the scent?

Paxon got up from the table she was sitting at, yawned and said she was going to the coffee machine in reception, if Lark wanted anything.

'No thanks, I went into caffeine-overdose territory a while back.'

'There's decaf.'

'What's the point in that?'

'Fair point.' Paxon turned and headed off in the direction of the corridor.

An escape by sea. Ellis was smart. If there's one thing you don't want a suspect on the run to have, it's inside knowledge of the capabilities and limitations of a complex manhunt involving multiple law enforcement agencies.

In that respect, the hunt was going exactly according to her expectations. The truth was, even with all the manpower and technology at their disposal, even with the ability to reach out and touch almost every adult in the state using the Amber Alert, it was difficult to find an intelligent or even just wily suspect who didn't want to be found. Ellis's professional background only made him more challenging than your average suspect. It turned out a good cop makes a great criminal.

In fact, if there was any surprise, it was that they had gotten as close as they had to catching him. That he had been findable at all. If disappearing completely had been Ellis's goal, then, despite the challenges, she believed he would have been able to do it, at least in the short term.

And yet, he hadn't. He seemed to be driven by some sort of purpose, even if it was proving difficult to determine what that purpose was. The original flight north had made sense, because, as it turned out, he had somewhere to lie low in mind. The sparser population would also have been a factor: fewer eyeballs, fewer phones.

Where was he going now?

It was a safe bet that he wouldn't try to sail the small pleasure cruiser to Hawaii, so that meant he had to make landfall sooner or later. Where would he go from there? They had put a priority on any reports of stolen cars anywhere near the coast. Car rental companies had been sent an updated wanted sheet showing the digitally enhanced picture of Jake and Molly that had been produced following Lark's description. There was a watch on any credit cards linked to Ellis, Eleanor Grace or Walter Diehl. They had people at the major transportation hubs up and down the coast, although, of course, they might not use any of the hubs. Earlier, Paxon had suggested a way Ellis could steal a car without it being reported: by killing the owner and concealing the body. Without really considering why, Lark had discounted the idea immediately.

Now she thought about it, she knew exactly why. If Ellis was happy to kill so that they could make a clean getaway, he would have shot her back in False Klamath. Eleanor Grace, too. There wouldn't be a witness to his escape.

She realized she had been thinking about Ellis and Molly differently since the encounter on the road at False Klamath. *They.* Not Ellis and his victim.

There had been no doubt about it. Molly had had the chance

to escape but had gone, apparently willingly, with her captor. She had the chance to run and hadn't been tempted to take it.

Then there was what they had both said. That Jake Ellis didn't do this. And later, Eleanor Grace: *You're looking for the wrong man.* And that wasn't all. There were the other things that didn't quite add up. The early sighting of Molly on her own they had dismissed because it didn't fit with what they thought they knew. The number of shots fired around Rachel Donaldson's car.

Lark knew the relationship between an abductor and his victim could be a complicated one; particularly when they were already known to one another. But this seemed different, somehow. Molly looked entirely unharmed. Ellis had risked capture to get her medication.

And yet, there was the weight of evidence against Ellis. The relationship to the victim. The messages. And the eyewitness.

The witness was the main thing, of course. It had allowed them to focus on Jake Ellis from the moment the investigation had begun. And it was consistent with the laws of probability: the majority of violent attacks are committed by someone known to the victim. The fact that Ellis had gone on the run with the kid only cemented his position as not just the prime suspect, but the only suspect.

Lark had been in high school when OJ had gone for his ride in the white Bronco. She remembered watching the chase on television like everyone else. The case had dragged on for months afterwards, of course, but she remembered that that was the last time anyone truly believed he wasn't guilty. Not just because of the evidence, but because an innocent man doesn't run.

For her, that was just as important a factor as the eyewitness. But now she really thought about it; Da Costa's witness statement was the only thing that would stand up in court, in relation to the original shooting. A good lawyer would get the

Facebook messages and the confession email suppressed from any trial. So far, no fingerprints or DNA evidence from the scene of the shooting had been matched to Ellis.

The witness statement from Da Costa was the foundation on which the whole house of cards rested.

Your witness is lying to you.

She drummed her fingers on the table and looked up as Paxon returned from her trip to the machine with a small plastic cup.

'When we get back to the city, can we bring Edward Da Costa back in?'

Paxon's expression betrayed the mildest of bemusement. Lark understood why. It had been a good interview. He had been an extremely cooperative witness, giving detailed and consistent testimony. A perfect witness, in fact.

'Sure,' she said. 'What's up?'

Lark was trying to work out how to answer that question when Paxon's phone rang.

Paxon put her coffee cup down, took her phone out of her pocket, answered with her name.

As Lark watched, her eyes widened.

'Understood, thank you.' She put the phone down and stared at Lark with the look of shock still in her eyes.

'Have they found them?'

'No,' Paxon said. 'That was the hospital. They think somebody tried to kill Rachel Donaldson last night.'

62

The first southbound Thruway bus out of McKinleyville was scheduled to depart at 7 a.m. sharp. Jake bought the tickets at the office with the prepay credit card. Diehl's card was as useless to him as his own now. The sun was creeping up as Jake and Molly boarded at opposite ends of the line.

The bus wasn't even half full. Sleepy-eyed people shuffled on board, no one looking particularly alert, with the exception of a pair of senior citizens who sat up front and started peppering the driver with questions. Molly took a seat in the back third of the bus. Jake made eye contact with her as he boarded and took a seat three rows back and diagonally across.

He kept his eyes on the road as they waited for the doors to close. From time to time, he would look up at the illuminated clock above the driver.

6.58.

Not long now. The engine started up, and Jake relaxed a little as the seat shuddered and rattled beneath him.

A man with a green canvas jacket and a baseball hat boarded and showed his ticket to the driver. He walked slowly up the aisle, gazing from side to side. Jake turned his head to look out of the window as he passed. He walked all the way to the back of the bus, and then almost all of the way back again, before taking the seat immediately behind the chatty senior couple.

The clock ticked over to seven.

Time to go. Come on ...

One of the ticket staff was strolling over toward them, taking his sweet time. He approached the driver's window, started talking to the driver.

Jake looked over at Molly's seat. She was sitting up, looking over the seat back at him. He motioned with his hand for her to sit down.

A moment later, the driver laughed out loud, and Jake could see the guy from the ticket office break into a grin. He slapped the side of the bus twice, and the pitch of the engine increased, and the bus started to roll away. It turned out onto the road and started to pick up speed, heading south.

Jake sat back and waited for his pulse to slow down to normal.

63

Three hours later, Lark watched as Rachel Donaldson slept in her bed at Zuckerberg General. Her red hair pooled around her head on one side of the pillow, the surgical bandage covering the left side of her head. Lark wondered if there were answers somewhere underneath.

The various machines and electronic devices attached to the patient by tubes and wires hummed and bleeped along unremarkably, and if you looked closely, you could see Rachel's chest rising and falling in even, shallow breaths.

Lark rubbed her eyelids as she thought about the last four hours. A hair-raising drive from Willow Creek to the airport in time to catch the 6.15 early flight. An hour in the air, during which she had dozed off for twenty minutes. Another drive, made forcibly more leisurely by rush-hour traffic, from the airport to the hospital. It felt like she hadn't stopped moving for two days. She guessed that it felt like that because it was basically the truth.

'The neurologist says signs are promising,' the doctor on the opposite side of the bed said.

Lark had insisted on seeing Rachel in the flesh, even after being reassured that the faulty drip had been caught in time. *Faulty* – that wasn't really the correct word, was it?

'How sure are you this was deliberate?' Lark asked, without

taking her eyes from the patient. When the doctor didn't answer, she looked up. His expression was uncomfortable. The tip of his thumb was between his front teeth, as though he was wrestling with a tricky calculation. She knew exactly what he was worried about. The fact that the person responsible for the ICU had abandoned her post, for whatever reason, had serious implications for the hospital.

'I appreciate this is a sensitive situation, and I'm not interested in making life difficult for you or the hospital. But we need to know.'

'It was deliberate,' he said at last. 'No question. Somebody injected insulin into the bag. The only reason you would do that is if you wanted to kill the patient.'

Lark nodded. 'Thank you.'

It only confirmed what she already knew. Technically, the evidence of foul play was circumstantial – the nurse in charge had happened to be away from the ICU for a short period, and a few minutes later, a potentially life-threatening fault had been found with Rachel Donaldson's drip. The fault was immediately rectified. The log showed that the *fault* (keeping to that careful, noncommittal terminology) could have occurred at any time in the preceding four hours, not necessarily during the window when the ICU was unstaffed. There was no way to tell when it had been done, and until she'd asked the doctor the question, no one had given a firm answer as to whether the glitch could have been notched up to carelessness rather than malicious action.

But two other things had happened in that window. First: an unidentified civilian had been seen in the vicinity of the ICU, probably a male, and that person could not be traced. There was no way to tell if that man had been inside the ICU itself, because of the second thing that happened. Between 1.30 and 1.45 a.m., the hallway camera covering the entrance to the ICU had gone offline. Again, there might be other explanations for this technical failure. Lark didn't find any of them convincing.

So what they had was this: the overwhelming likelihood was that an unidentified suspect had entered the hospital in the dead of night, possibly drugged the duty nurse, and sabotaged the life-support equipment of the victim of an attempted murder. Somebody had tried to kill Rachel Donaldson for the second time in two days.

The only problem with that? The prime suspect in the first attempt on the victim's life was over three hundred miles away from the scene of the second.

Which meant that everything Lark thought she knew about this case was suddenly thrown into question. Another wrinkle, another puzzle piece that didn't fit. This was all she needed.

As though in response to her thoughts, her phone buzzed. Not a text or an email this time, but a notification that a new episode of everyone's favorite podcast had arrived.

Untraceable Episode 5 now available: They Seek Him Here, They Seek Him There…

Untraceable

Excerpt from Untraceable – Season 4, Episode 5, April 20

This episode of *Untraceable* is brought to you by Bay Mercedes.

Welcome to *Untraceable*, the podcast that goes deep into the most fascinating missing persons cases. I'm Chrissie Chung, and every season, we'll be taking you through a missing persons case from disappearance, to resolution.

'We can confirm the suspect was seen in the vicinity of False Klamath, Del Norte County, and that the suspect is still at large.'

'And what about Molly? Do you have any information on her?'

'According to our information, Molly is still being held by the suspect.'

'We've been told the FBI had the chance to capture Ellis and let him slip through their fingers. Would that, uh... would that be an accurate thing to say?'

'I'm not at liberty to say any more.'

'What about...'

'Thank you very much, I have to go.'

That was the voice of Lieutenant Ray Monzello of the Crescent City Police Department. As you can hear, things were still pretty much in flux when I spoke to him, less than two hours after Jake Ellis had apparently made his escape from the house of a former acquaintance.

Over the rest of the night, and this morning, a fuller picture began to emerge.

Reports say that it appears that Jake Ellis had been holed up in a house in a tiny community called False Klamath, for the past two days. It then emerged that the house was owned by a man named Walter Diehl, recently deceased, who turns out to have known Jake Ellis several years before.

Why didn't the FBI find this place earlier? I mean, maybe we should cut them some slack. After all, they're dealing with literally thousands of individual pieces of information coming in from all directions. They're hunting a guy who knows the rulebook, which has to make everything a lot more difficult.

And yet, when it came down to it, did they do everything they could to make sure they got their man when they had located him?

Unfortunately, it looks like the answer is no.

As usual, we're trying to keep up with a developing situation here. Initial reports coming out of the area suggested the authorities had Ellis in custody. Then it looked like that was a little premature, but they had him surrounded. It now looks like they did have him surrounded, but, somehow, he slipped through the net. And, unfortunately, it looks like they weren't able to find Molly, either.

We only found out about the operation in False Klamath at the same time as everyone else, when it hit the news networks. But at *Untraceable*, we have a big advantage, and that advantage is you.

As we scrambled to catch up on the situation, it turned out that one of our regular listeners, Nikki O'Connor, lives in the area. Actually, within a half-mile of the house where Ellis had been holed up all this time. We called her up and asked her if she would talk to us, and she said yes.

[phone rings]

'Hi Nikki, this is Chrissie from *Untraceable*. This is a pretty wild situation, huh?'

'Yeah, I mean I've been listening to the show and I never thought in a million years that the guy everyone's been looking for would be pretty much next door, you know?'

'I can imagine. So when was the first you knew things were happening up there?'

'First I knew, I heard the helicopters overhead. I mean, this is a pretty quiet little community; we're not even used to hearing sirens. Pretty soon, all I could hear was sirens.'

We talk a little more about what happened next. Nikki turned on the news, figured out what was happening. The next call she made was to her brother.

'So tell me about your brother.'

'My brother's a reserve cop. He told me to stay in the house because they didn't know where Ellis was, and I guess they thought this could turn into one of those mass-shooting scenarios.'

'So you just sat tight?'

'That's right, and eventually they started reporting that he had gotten away, that he was out of town. I drove down to the cordon with some coffee, but my brother wasn't there. I talked to the guys though, and one of them told me what had happened.'

I should just cut in here to say that this is unsubstantiated. This is a conversation Nikki had with a cop on the scene. She isn't a journalist and this conversation definitely wasn't on the record, and she didn't give me the cop's name. But what she said next shocked me.

'He said he must have driven right through the cordon in a police car.'

64

Jake dozed off somewhere south of the stop at Fortuna. He woke with a start, looking around his immediate surroundings.

No men in uniform, no guns in his face. Just the seats of the bus vibrating softly with the rotation of the tires on the highway. He shaded his eyes with his hand and looked out of the window. The sky was dull and overcast. Low hills covered with trees. A steady stream of oncoming traffic passing on the other side of the median strip. He straightened in his seat, just adjusting his line of sight enough to see diagonally across to where Molly was sitting curled up, the beanie hat pulled down over her hair.

He looked down the aisle. He could see the right arm and the shoulder of the driver. The man in the canvas jacket was slumped against the window. The chatty senior couple had left the bus while Jake was asleep.

He rubbed the sleep out of his eyes. The murmur of the tires on the road and the constant rush of the slipstream outside had blended into a soothing white noise that had lulled him to sleep, despite his best efforts. He looked up and saw the red glowing digits of the clock above the driver. It read 9.13. He had been asleep almost an hour.

He was angry at himself. But then, the sky hadn't fallen in while he dozed. He sat back in the seat and looked out of the window, trying to work out where they were. Inland somewhere, no sign of the ocean. After ten minutes, they passed a sign for Leggett. A long way to go, still.

He turned his thoughts to what was ahead of him. Dolan had told him to be in the city by five. Most likely, that meant he wanted to meet in person. A meeting that might well end with a bullet in his head. But he had to take the chance. If Carl Dolan could tell him who was behind this, he had to know.

Assuming they could make their way through the city without being seen, there was no way in hell he could take a thirteen-year-old kid into that lion's den. So they needed somewhere safe to wait until he received the email. He couldn't risk a hotel. The staff would have seen the Amber Alert along with everyone else, and it was standard practice that they'd be contacted separately with want sheets to look out for as they were checking in guests. Would they guess he was headed back to the city? They might consider it, in the absence of any other information. That was why it was so risky. That was why it was so stupid.

If it hadn't been for Molly, he would have cut his losses. Disappeared for a while until he could find out exactly who had ordered the hit and make sure they were paid back in kind. But he needed to end this for her sake, and for Rachel's. If that meant swallowing his pride and making a deal with Dolan, he could live with it. If it meant offering himself up as a sacrifice, he would do it.

The road widened from two lanes to four. He raised his hand to cover his face as a highway patrol car slowly pulled ahead of them, seeming to linger alongside his window. He only let out the breath he was holding when it finally disappeared out of his line of sight ahead of them.

He gave the other visible occupants of the bus another glance, to make sure that none of them were taking an interest in him or Molly. Satisfied, he sat back, looking out at the hills.

It was mentally exhausting; constantly having to evaluate every person he saw, every vehicle that passed by, evaluating every idle glance to look for a double take or the merest of recognition in the eyes.

He remembered being part of the task force hunting down six men who had escaped from the state prison at Solano back in 2012. All six had been recaptured, and five of them went quietly. He had always been curious about the strange look in the eyes of Jerry Cornell, the man they had found in a makeshift panic room dug beneath a shed in his brother-in-law's yard. He understood it now. It was relief. Jerry was going back to jail, but that seemed to be preferable to his existence for the previous four days.

Jake sat back in the seat and closed his eyes again, promising himself he wouldn't drift off this time. The cars passed by in the opposite lane in what seemed like a perfectly spaced rhythm. The tires hummed beneath him. The air rushed by outside, every second taking them closer to the city.

The chime of a phone notification shattered the calm. Jake's eyes snapped open. The woman three seats down from him held her phone up and peered at the screen. Jake tensed. He heard a mumbled curse, and she dropped the phone back onto the empty seat beside her. Just a text, or some social notification. Not another Amber Alert.

Jake straightened in his seat, eyes wide open, looking straight ahead as the road passed unceasingly beneath them.

65

Chrissie didn't bother trying to go back to sleep after the middle-of-the-night phone interview with the lady from False Klamath. At six, she had showered and gone down to the coffee shop below her apartment, early enough to snag the prime spot by the window with the power outlet for her laptop.

She barely noticed the place filling up around her as the sun came up and the time flew by. Before she knew it, it was lunchtime and the waitress was making comments about how they ought to put her to work in the kitchen in exchange for room and board. Chrissie ordered a grilled cheese and yet another coffee, switching to decaf.

She couldn't stop checking the numbers on the podcast in between making phone calls and tweeting links to new material on the site. Every time she was sure they had peaked, it just kept building. And the traffic was two-way. They were being swamped with emails and messages. Chrissie was working through the more credible tips Sean's algorithm had spit out: there was a woman who swore she had been sitting next to Molly for part of the journey on the Greyhound from Redding to Portland. The woman hadn't thought twice about it at the time, but when she had watched a news update later, she decided the girl looked a lot like Molly.

Chrissie wasn't convinced. The woman mentioned Molly's

red hair, but the latest composite image circulated by the FBI suggested that she had dyed her hair darker. Ellis had changed his look too.

The numbers were insane. The mainstream outlets were now leading with *Untraceable*'s latest scoop: that Ellis might have fled the area in a stolen police car. They were no longer just being credited as a source for these stories, they *were* the story in some cases. There were already a couple of think pieces in major papers about how *Untraceable* encapsulated the growth of citizen journalism, and perhaps this new real-time experiment was the harbinger of something else: citizen manhunts.

Chrissie wasn't sure what to think about that. Technology aside, they weren't doing anything that hadn't been done since the first sheriff nailed the first wanted poster to a tree. Giving the public the information they needed to be on the lookout for a criminal who had to be caught.

The authorities were doing that themselves, after all, only their wanted poster would now automatically appear in the pockets of millions of people. There was even a reward, just like in the old days. Fifty thousand dollars for information leading to the arrest and conviction of Jake Ellis.

And yet people still flooded *Untraceable*'s entirely pro-bono tip line. Did that mean the respondents were aware on some level that their information was unlikely to be useful? Chrissie thought it was more likely that fifty grand wasn't a big enough number. It would be a nice bonus for most people. A year's pay for some. But it didn't *sound* big. Not in the age of movies that make a billion dollars and technology companies valued in the trillions. In this case, the reward wasn't the thing that had captured people's imagination. In Chrissie's experience, it almost never was. It was the story: the poor, vulnerable girl who could yet be made an orphan. Nailing the monster who did this, saving her, bringing her home.

Chrissie hoped Molly would be found safe and well, she honestly did. But that didn't mean it wasn't a great story.

She went to get another refill of coffee and sat back down. The *Chronicle*'s page had added another story about the botched attempt to apprehend Ellis. She was pleased to see the show, her source and her own name mentioned in the second paragraph.

She was halfway through the article when she became aware of someone standing over her.

She looked up to see Sean. She had been expecting him in a half-hour or so. They were going to lock the narrative segments of the next episode at her place.

She smiled a hello and looked back down at the clock on her screen. 'You're early, I thought we said two-thirty?'

'Chrissie ...'

She looked up again as he said her name, and noticed that he had a guilty, haunted look about him.

'What is it?'

And then she looked beyond him and saw exactly what it was. Standing a couple of steps behind him, halfway between the door and her table. Special Agent Lark looked a little taller in person. She was wearing a gray pantsuit and a light-blue blouse. Her hands were planted on either side of her waist, making the jacket stretch back, exposing her gun in its holster. The look in her eyes said she was in no mood to fuck around.

Chrissie resisted the urge to stand to attention. She cleared her throat and tried to sound more confident than she sounded. 'Can I help you?'

'We need to talk. Now.'

66

'Special Agent Lark,' Chrissie said. 'Can I get you something? Maybe a mochaccino?'

Lark didn't move. Didn't speak. Didn't blink.

'The crullers are good ...'

Lark stepped forward and yanked the nearest chair out, sitting down across from her. Sean stayed standing.

'I want to know exactly who leaked you the screenshots of those messages, Chrissie.'

Chrissie folded her arms. 'You know, for a professional law enforcement officer, you don't seem to know a lot about the First Amendment. My sources are—'

'First Amendment? Give me a fucking break. You're a fleeting social media fad, not Woodward and Bernstein.'

Chrissie looked at Sean, who had shrunk back into the corner, avoiding looking at either of them.

'I get it. You're pissed that the show has more reach among the public than you do. You don't give a shit about finding Molly, all you care about is—'

'Listen to me,' Lark said, leaning across and jabbing a finger a couple of inches from her face. 'This isn't a game. I know to you, it's a great story, a way to get everybody listening to your podcast. But two people were shot, and one of them is dead.

The other could still die. And there's a thirteen-year-old kid who's in grave danger until we find her. You're not helping.'

Chrissie felt Sean's hand on her shoulder. 'Maybe we should ...'

No. Maybe nothing. She felt a surge of righteous indignation. 'The only reason Ellis got away in the first place is because your people screwed up, Agent Lark.'

'Excuse me?'

'You heard me. You let him slip through your fingers at his apartment, and then you lost him again last night. How did he manage to steal a police car, for God's sake? Molly's in danger because of your incompetence.'

'Our incompetence?' Lark repeated.

She held up her phone and tapped the screen to start a video. It showed news footage: an excited-looking woman with dark hair wearing a blue dress with a Peter Pan collar. The caption identified her as *Nikki O'Connor – Witness*.

'I saw him cut right through my yard,' she was saying. 'He pointed a gun right at me and told me I was dead if I talked.'

'Weren't you scared?' prompted the offscreen reporter.

'Well, I just thought this was too important to keep to my—'

Lark muted the sound and put her phone down on the table. Nikki O'Connor continued mouthing her breathless account of the action.

'Let me tell you something – your star guest is a fantasist. She's two interviews away from claiming space aliens were involved. This story about him stealing a police car? It's bullshit. We know how he got away, and that wasn't it.'

Chrissie winced. She was glad she had run the disclaimer that it wasn't official. It had sounded a little too good to be true.

Lark continued. 'You can bleat all you want about your First Amendment rights, you don't have the right to yell fire in a crowded theater. If you come anywhere near my investigation again, your next podcast will be an exhaustively researched

269

account of what it's like to spend a few months in a federal prison.'

Sean stepped forward and cleared his throat. 'We're sorry about the tone of the episode this morning. You're right, it wasn't fair.'

'Sean—' Chrissie started.

He held his hand up. 'We're sorry, but we're going to keep covering the case. We can do that without stepping on your toes.'

Lark folded her arms and waited for him to continue.

'We're not the enemy here, Agent Lark. We're another weapon in your armory.'

'How so?'

'If the best way to get this guy was doing it quietly, that's what you would have done. You wouldn't send out press releases, you wouldn't give interviews to the TV news, and you wouldn't have sent out an alert to every cell phone in California.'

'It was just the Bay Area, actually.'

'You want people to know about it. You want as many eyeballs on this case as possible. Not just eyeballs. Ears, word of mouth. Do you know how many listeners we've had on these five episodes? Almost four million. People from all over the world, and a nice big concentration right here in California.'

Lark cocked a skeptical eyebrow. 'A bonus. Best-case scenario, you're a bonus. When you're not getting in the way. You're providing extra publicity, fine. I'm not sure we need it. Anyone who watches the news knows about this case. Like you said, anyone who owns a cell phone knows about it.'

'Sure,' Sean replied, 'but knowing and caring aren't the same thing. That's what we bring to it. A show like this, people get addicted to the story. They want to know what happens next. Is that good for us? Of course. But this is in real time: people are obsessing about your case as it happens, while there's still a chance to affect the outcome. You really want to throw away an asset like that?'

Lark folded her arms and sat back. 'Good sales pitch.' She looked over at Chrissie. 'You should let him do the meetings.'

Chrissie resisted the urge to roll her eyes. The truth was, he *was* good at this. He got flustered if he had to get rid of a pushy cold call from an insurance rep, but when he was talking about something he was passionate about, he could make everyone else feel the passion too.

Lark looked back at Sean. 'So you're saying we should give you an easy ride because you're helping the … *virality* of the case. You think you're part of the reason it's still leading the news.'

Sean nodded. 'That, and for more concrete reasons.'

'Such as?'

Sean picked a tablet up off the table and swiped on the screen, bringing up a page.

Chrissie started to object. 'We can't just …'

Sean ignored her, holding up the screen for Lark to see. 'These are our tips. Every episode, we say if anyone has information, they should call you. But people send us their stuff too. Like, a lot of people.'

'Over two thousand unique tips since episode one went out on Saturday afternoon,' Chrissie said proudly, forgetting her desire to keep this quiet for a moment.

Lark looked thoughtful. 'Then you'll know that getting tips isn't the problem.'

'Right,' Sean agreed. 'It's collating them, filtering them.'

'Sean has an algorithm.'

'Oh?'

'That's right. I set it up a while back, for the season we did on the Devil Mountain case. It works on a bunch of different indicators—'

'It filters out the shit, basically,' Chrissie added. She could tell Lark was interested. Sean was managing to turn this around.

'Interesting,' Lark said. 'I'm sure there'll be a lot of crossover with what we have, but my people might be interested in comparing notes, see if anything you have fills the gaps.'

'We'd be happy to share it with you,' Sean said.

Chrissie stood up. 'Sean—'

'...And in return, I'm sure you'd be happy to give us an exclusive interview.' His voice only quivered a little. Chrissie was impressed. 'What do you say, Agent Lark?'

Lark looked down at the screen of the tablet as it lay on the desk. The feed refreshed in real time from the submission form. Names, emails, subject headers. Chrissie could tell she was interested.

'I say, the two of you have a set of balls on you.'

Chrissie opened her mouth, changed her mind, then changed her mind again. Perhaps it was time for a gesture of good faith.

'I can't tell you who sent me the screenshots.'

Lark started to interrupt, but Chrissie silenced her before she could get a word out.

'I can't tell you, because I don't know. Genuinely. I do have a contact who knows the investigation. He's not doing anything wrong, but he's been good for fact-checking. I assumed the screenshots came from him at first, but he says he doesn't know anything about it. And I believe him.'

Lark's brow furrowed. 'So who sent them?'

Chrissie shrugged. 'Somebody who really wanted to make sure the public knew what Jake Ellis is really like?'

'Or somebody who wanted to make sure everyone thought about him in a certain way,' Lark said quietly.

67

An hour later, Lark stood in the elevator as it climbed to the thirteenth floor, her head spinning with competing priorities. It had been easier than she had expected to manipulate Chrissie Chung into giving her exactly what she needed. If the witness who had seen the motorcycle fleeing the shooting scene had contacted the official Amber Alert channels with his tip about the motorcycle, it hadn't made it into the system. Thanks to Sean Tramel's database, she now had his details. If he had any more information, perhaps it could tie the sighting in with the name Jake Ellis had given her in False Klamath: Wade Lang.

The office was buzzing. Paxon was back at her desk. Lark wondered if she had even been home yet. Finn looked up from his desk as she passed by the glass wall of his office. He raised his eyebrows in a question that was easy to discern. The only question that mattered: *Anything?*

She shook her head. He nodded and looked back at his screen.

Valenti walked in with a coffee from the place downstairs. He was clean-shaven and alert-looking. 'Hey,' he said. 'You get any sleep yet?'

'About an hour,' Lark lied. She had gone back to her place after visiting the hospital. Her attempt at a nap had failed, but she felt a lot better having showered and changed.

Valenti looked down at the coffee in his hand and held it out. 'I think you need this more than I do.'

She took it with a grateful look and took a sip. It tasted like it was about forty percent sugar, but it was the thought that counted.

'You get ahold of Edward Da Costa?' she asked.

'On his way in,' Valenti answered. 'Said he was glad to co-operate.'

'Helpful fellow,' she said.

Valenti headed to his desk while Lark sat down at her desk and typed in her password. The Slack channel was busy with progress updates from the team members who were still at False Klamath and Willow Creek. There was no sign of Ellis or Molly, and no sign of the boat. She had a message from Garcia to say that he had spoken to a guy who swore he had seen Jake Ellis ahead of him in the line at a gas station outside of Eureka and was trying to see if they had security footage.

Suddenly she remembered she hadn't spoken with Hartzler since yesterday. His information about an associate somewhere north had turned out to be on the money. Perhaps she had been wrong to be suspicious of him... or perhaps she had been right, and he had more knowledge of Ellis's whereabouts than he was letting on. She took her phone out and dialed his number, wondering if he would be angry she hadn't checked in before now. She had agreed to keep him in the loop after all. But the number rang out. She left a short message, asking him to give her a call.

Then she sat down at her desk and read over the notes she had scrawled out while looking at Tramel's database.

She turned to a blank page and started to organize her thoughts into a list. Most of the thoughts took the form of questions. Number one on the list: who had tried to kill Rachel Donaldson last night, and why? The one thing she could be certain of – that it couldn't have been Jake Ellis – only complicated everything else about this case. It all boiled down to two possibilities: either Ellis had an accomplice, or somebody unrelated to Ellis wanted Rachel dead. She was leaning toward the second possibility, and part of the reason for that was the late Wade Lang.

She went into her emails and found the two documents she had read over before going out to talk to Chrissie Chung. The first was the scanned report that the SFPD homicide unit had sent through on her request.

The report provided a lot more information than the news article Lark had briefly seen on the computer screen at Walter Diehl's house. The victim's name was Wade Lang. He had been found in a quiet spot beneath the Central Freeway, the elevated road that carried the 101 deep into the city. A bullet in the chest and two in the head. Whoever had killed him wasn't taking any chances. The victim was wearing biker leathers, but no bike or helmet were found at the scene.

It wasn't the kind of homicide that was going to kindle a raging desire for justice in any investigator. If the San Francisco Police Department went in for TL;DR summaries, this one would read: 'Bad guy meets worse guy.' Lang was suspected of being a killer for hire, carrying out jobs across the state and several here in San Francisco. If the rumors were right, his clients included everyone from the Norteños to the Triads.

A bad guy, and one skilled and smart enough never to have been caught. What did that say about the person who had killed him?

Lang's body had been found by a city sanitation worker at around 9 a.m. on Sunday morning. Preliminary indications said time of death was a few hours before that. Which meant Jake Ellis was most likely out of the frame for that one too. Lang owned a motorcycle. Chrissie and Sean had interviewed a man who lived a few blocks from where Rachel Donaldson had been shot who had reported seeing a motorcycle fleeing the scene at speed.

It was difficult to resist the conclusion.

Your witness is lying to you.

There was something else about the report that rang a bell, and she couldn't put her finger on it. It was only when she read over the news article again that she remembered what it was. The location: under the freeway. It was a good spot for a killing, particularly in the sleepy pre-dawn hours on a Sunday. Sheltered, lots of shadows, no homes overlooking the scene. Not the first killing to take place around that location, and it probably wouldn't be the last.

Another man had been murdered there in February, in fact. It took her a matter of seconds to find the story. Michael Gregg, aged twenty-eight. This had been a sadder story: a community activist who worked with the homeless. Killed in a suspected mugging. Just as unsolved.

She opened the second document attachment. This one had come from La-Vonne Taylor. Lark had asked her to look into the background of Edward Da Costa, the witness who had supposedly seen Ellis shoot Rachel Donaldson. On the surface, it seemed the polar opposite of Wade Lang's summary. A clean record. Good, well-paying job as a college lecturer. Married for ten years. She knew that there could be other things going on beneath the surface; there always were. Financial troubles, addictions. The kinds of things it would take a warrant to uncover. And no judge was going to sign off on a warrant to intrude on the personal life of an upstanding citizen on the basis of a suspicion. She was going to need more.

The last page in the report was a list of calls to and from Da Costa's number on the day of the shooting, obtained from his cellular provider. Just the times of calls and texts, and the phone numbers where available. More detailed information, like the content of text messages, would, again, require a warrant.

Da Costa's 911 call was right there at 7.42 a.m. The call that had led to Jake Ellis being identified as the shooter.

Another call had been made four minutes before that one. An incoming call.

68

Jake and Molly changed bus at the Martinez Amtrak stop and then took another into the city.

They kept apart, avoided eye contact. Jake relaxed a little when he saw how much more anonymous the two of them were among crowds. His burner phone had run out of charge around noon, just after he managed to confirm their accommodation. A TV screen at the Martinez stop tuned to CNN told him that the hunt was still focused far north of here.

They disembarked at Powell Street and walked the rest of the distance across town. They kept to quieter streets, stayed a few paces apart. Jake didn't have enough cash left to take a taxi, and anyway, he didn't want to risk a driver recognizing the two of them. The buses had been a necessity, and a more acceptable risk. In Jake's long experience of questioning witnesses, cab drivers had good memories for passengers. It's a one-to-one transaction. Lots of things to remember: how well the fare tipped, whether he was chatty or too quiet, the exact addresses of their pickup and drop-off location. By contrast, bus drivers only remember the passengers who cause trouble.

Jake had found their quarters for the day and night on a new online apartment-share website. His hope was that it would be under the radar in comparison to more established sites like Airbnb. Diehl's credit card was compromised now, but he still had enough left from the five hundred dollars Marty Hartzler had added to the prepay card. He just hoped Hartzler had made sure the money couldn't be traced back to him.

The room was part of an old Victorian townhouse on Jackson Street that had been carved up into separate apartments. Jake found the key safe at the side of the door and tapped in the code. As the confirmation email had promised, there were two keys on a ring: brass for the main door, nickel-plated for the apartment. He glanced up and down the street one more time. No other pedestrians. A pickup truck passed by without slowing, the driver looking straight ahead. He turned the key, pushed the door open, and let Molly in. He felt a twinge of relief as he closed the door on the outside world.

The conversion had been done cheaply and badly, maximizing the number of units the old building could be divided into. They climbed to the top floor, and then up another short flight. The room Jake had booked was in the loft. The ceiling was barely six and a half feet from the floor at its tallest point and sloped down toward the eaves on each side.

There was a couch and a coffee table, and a bed in one corner. In the opposite corner was a cubicle containing a tiny bathroom with a shower. The angle of the ceiling meant that the foot of the bed was the only part you could sit upright on. There was a small TV fixed to the wall, the remote lying on the coffee table.

'Small,' Molly said, raising an eyebrow.

'Safe,' Jake countered. 'At least, I hope so.'

Almost without thinking about it, he picked the remote up and turned on the TV. CNN first. The latest White House Press Secretary was halfway through a morning briefing, saying something about an oil pipeline in the Ukraine. The ticker along the bottom was carrying last night's sports results. Nothing breaking. He switched to a local station. Midway through a weather report. Clear skies and above-average temperatures in the Bay Area all day. They watched the ticker until a familiar name appeared.

Molly Donaldson investigators following leads in Del Norte County, Ca.

Jake let out a sigh of relief and muted the sound, leaving it on the news channel. They were still looking far north of here; that was good. Coming back to San Francisco had been a big risk, but it did have the benefit of unpredictability.

'Why is it the Molly Donaldson investigation?'

Jake glanced over at Molly, who had taken the sitting place at the foot of the bed and was unlacing her high-tops. She was staring at the television.

'What do you mean?'

'They think you're the bad guy, right? Shouldn't it be the Jake Ellis investigation?'

He gave her an amused look. 'Sorry, Molly. You're the story.'

She didn't say anything for a minute, watching the silent screen as they moved on from weather and over to a newsreader, talking about the presidential race. The crawl on the bottom of the screen cycled through another couple of stories and the scores from last night's games in the NBA playoffs and back to the Molly Donaldson investigation. She got up and took the remote from Jake, changing the channel. He opened his mouth to object, then thought better of it. She flicked through the channels, lingering for a split second on each; far too rapidly for Jake to catch what was on any of them.

'So you think this Dolan guy will be able to help you?' she asked, not taking her eyes from the screen.

That was a complicated question, wasn't it? Jake thought. Perhaps not one to be answered with too much candor. 'I hope so,' he said.

'Who is he?'

'He's ... kind of a broker. Like the website where I found this place. He matches up customers with services.'

'Only he matches hitmen instead of hotel rooms?' Molly wasn't looking at him. She kept scrolling through the channels as she spoke.

'Pretty much, yes.'

'So he knows who hired the man on the bike.'

'I hope so.'

'Is he dangerous?'

'People like this guy don't go out of their way to look for trouble. It's bad for business. I'll be fine.'

A black-and-white movie appeared on the screen and Molly stopped, her finger hovering over the button. It looked familiar to Jake, though neither of the actors on screen was a big name.

'*Invasion of the Body Snatchers*,' he said after a second. 'I always liked this one.'

'Mom used to love this,' Molly said quietly.

'This movie?'

She shook her head. 'Just old movies. Sunday afternoons. Something black and white. We'd sit on the couch and watch them. Sometimes we'd make popcorn.'

He smiled. Rachel had loved old movies back in college, too. The two of them hadn't spent a Sunday together since they had gotten back together. They were still working things out, still juggling date nights and differing schedules and two homes. Given time, they would have settled down to watch a black-and-white movie on a Sunday. Given time.

Jake reminded himself that wallowing was both easy and pointless. Instead, he took a seat on the couch and started watching the movie.

'This is a classic,' he said. 'I liked the Donald Sutherland one too – that one was filmed right here in San Francisco.'

'I guess this movie must have come out when you were my age.'

He shot her an aggrieved look. 'This is from the nineteen-*fifties*, Molly, I wasn't even—' He stopped when he saw she was suppressing a smirk.

'You're too easy.'

He held his hands up. 'Fine, pick on the old guy.'

They sat and watched the movie in silence. Jake ignored the urge to ask Molly to switch back to the news. It had been a long journey, and they still had an hour to fill. For now it was nice just to let go for a little while, to let himself drift off.

69

'Thank you for coming in, Mr Da Costa.'

'I'm happy to help,' Edward Da Costa said. He was a wide-built man in his forties, with short dark hair. He wore slacks and a neatly pressed tennis shirt. The look and bearing was all very pillar-of-the-community. He would look good on the stand as a prosecution witness, if Jake Ellis ever came to trial. So why did Lark get the feeling he was a little nervous?

It wasn't unusual. People get flustered when they talk to law enforcement. It's perfectly understandable. But there was something about Da Costa's demeanor that made Lark wonder. He looked like somebody trying to get through something. Like he was the one being investigated. Which, Lark had to admit, was looking like more and more of a possibility.

'We're really grateful for your help,' she said. 'Seems like people would rather talk to a podcast than to us.' She rolled her eyes, making him feel like he was with them, part of an embattled team doing their best against difficult odds.

Da Costa seemed to loosen up a little. 'I heard about that.'

'Oh yeah? You listen to any of it?'

'No,' he said. Then reconsidered. 'Actually, a little bit, yeah.'

Lark watched him. 'You haven't talked to them yet though.'

He shrugged. 'Nobody asked.'

A lie. Less than two hours ago, Chrissie had told Lark that

she had contacted both Da Costa and his wife, Shelley, and had been brushed off. Interesting. Perhaps he just wanted to make sure Lark didn't think he'd been talking to *Untraceable* off the record, or perhaps it was something else.

'What did you think?'

'What did I think about what?'

'The podcast, *Untraceable*.'

'It was okay, I guess. Kind of exploitative, I thought.'

'Which episode did you listen to?'

The look of unease had come back into his face. He didn't understand why she was focusing on this.

'Um, I don't remember. Did you want to talk to me about something in particular?'

'We'll get to that,' Lark said. 'Episode four, you listen to that one?'

'Like I said, I don't remember.'

'Episode four, they interviewed another eyewitness farther from the scene, who saw a guy on a motorcycle come by on Sullivan Street a minute after the shots were fired. Did you happen to notice a guy on a bike?'

He shook his head. 'No.'

'You're sure?'

He looked over at Paxon for guidance. She stared back at him, unblinking. It had been the first question Lark had asked Chrissie's producer when he was showing off his algorithm. A witness a little farther down the street had seen a bike fleeing the scene right after the shooting. She had taken down the guy's details from Sean's database and sent Valenti over there to see if he could tell them any more.

'Yeah. No motorcycle.'

Lark let the silence fill the room. Kept her expression blank as she thought. The biker had been mentioned in episode four of *Untraceable*, and last night Ellis had told her the shooter had been on a motorcycle. Maybe he could have listened to the podcast, but he hadn't invented Wade Lang.

Lark opened the file in front of her and looked down at it, reading through the timeline she had compiled around the shooting. There was a new item she had added after requesting Edward Da Costa's phone records.

'You mind if we go through it all one more time?'

'Okay.'

She could see he was trying to get a look at what was on the sheet of paper she was looking at, without making it too obvious. She lifted the paper a little bit off the table to obscure his line of sight.

'You were walking along Sullivan Street at around seven-thirty a.m. on Saturday. You heard raised voices ahead of you, outside the Elite Center. You kept walking and saw a uniformed police officer standing at the driver's side of a red Ford Escape, yelling at the driver. You described him as white, around six feet, with a mustache. Wearing what looked like a police uniform.'

'That's correct,' Da Costa said.

'When the police interviewed you, you positively identified him from pictures as Jake Ellis.'

'That's right.'

'And you were completely sure.'

He glanced from Lark to Paxon and then back again. He nodded quickly.

Lark stared at him until he knew he couldn't get away with a non-verbal response.

'That's correct,' he said again. But this time, his voice cracked a little. He was lying. But there was no way yet to prove it. Thankfully, Da Costa didn't know that.

'You then saw the man fire shots into the car. It was then that a blue pickup truck stopped nearby and the driver yelled out. The man in the uniform shot him in the head and forced the girl from the car to get into a blue Subaru. What did you do then?'

'What would you do? I ran. I called nine one one.'

'You called nine one one at seven forty-two a.m.'

'If that's when it was, that's when it was.'

'There were other calls around seven thirty-six, not from eyewitnesses, just from people who heard the shots. The first responders were already at the scene by the time you called.'

'Okay.'

'Why did you wait?'

'I don't remember waiting. I ... maybe I was ... I mean it was a shock, you know?'

Lark looked down at her sheet and bit her bottom lip, as though trying to make sense of a problem.

'Who called you at seven thirty-eight?'

Da Costa went white. 'What?'

'There's a call to your cell at seven thirty-eight. It came from a phone within the same general area as you. The timing is interesting, wouldn't you say?'

'I ... I don't remember.'

'You don't? But you seem to recall the other events of that morning with such clarity. Isn't it a little odd that you can't remember answering a call?' She paused for effect. 'Or speaking to someone for two minutes, seventeen seconds?'

Da Costa sat back in his chair and took a deep breath. 'I'd like to speak to a lawyer.'

'Do you need one? You're not under arrest, Mr Da Costa. We're just asking you a question.'

'Then I'd like to go now.'

Lark stared back at him. 'If you need to tell us something, now's the time to do it.'

His lips pressed closer together and he looked over at Paxon. She returned his stare.

'You didn't see Jake Ellis shoot anyone on Saturday, did you?' Lark prompted. 'He wasn't there, was he? Were you there?'

Da Costa stood up and opened his mouth. Then he thought better of it and walked over to the door. Lark watched him go.

'We'll be in touch with you, Mr Da Costa,' she called after him. 'Keep that phone nearby.'

70

'Jake.'

He snapped awake. He had been dreaming of Rachel. The shadows had moved across the small room with the low ceiling. The TV was still on, switched back to the news channel, the sound on mute. Molly was shaking his shoulder gently.

'I'm sorry, I—' he started.

'I didn't want to wake you, you needed rest.'

Panic seized him. 'How long have I been out?'

'It's just after five.' She handed him the burner phone. There was a notification: one email. 'It just came in.'

He relaxed, and then remembered there was nothing to relax about. He tapped the screen to go into the email. There was an address in Chinatown and a time: six o'clock. He could make it there in time on foot. Nothing to worry about. Except for the hundreds of citizens out there who might recognize him, that is.

Jake checked the magazine in his gun and put it in the pocket of his leather jacket. 'You'll be okay for a couple of hours?'

Molly hesitated. 'I definitely can't go with you?'

'Sorry, not this time.'

'You will be back, though, won't you?'

He forced a smile. 'That's the plan.'

'Okay. I'll see you soon.'

'When I get back, I'll knock five times. If there aren't five knocks, it isn't me.' He opened the door and hesitated a second. He felt like he should say something.

'What's wrong?' she said after a moment.

'Nothing. I was just thinking your mom is going to be so proud of you when she wakes up.'

71

Chrissie's phone buzzed while she was in the back-room studio at Sean's apartment. Withheld number. She had been fielding a lot more calls lately, and even though her number wasn't publicly available anywhere on the show website, it hadn't prevented a handful of people getting ahold of it. Just like whoever had tracked down her personal email address to send those Facebook messages. She'd had more than a few crazies call her direct with theories, several rival podcasts angling to get in on the action, and one marriage proposal. She answered with a cautious hello.

There was a long pause. Just as she was about to hang up, a female voice spoke.

'Is that Chrissie Chung?'

'Who's asking?'

'I'm calling because ... this is quite difficult. It's about the Molly Donaldson thing you're covering.'

'No kidding,' she said. At the same time, she thought that the voice sounded familiar. She couldn't quite place it. She had spoken to so many people over the last three days.

'I ... I have reason to believe the witness who saw that man shoot at them was lying.'

'What makes you think that?' Chrissie asked. It was on the tip of her tongue. The caller was...

'Well – Edward Da Costa is my husband. I spoke to you the other day. You gave me this number.'

72

Jake walked east, through the Tenderloin. The crowds on the sidewalks were thicker than they had been a few hours before, but in a way the weight of numbers made him feel less exposed. Up-to-date facial composites of him and Molly had been flashed up on the news earlier, no doubt based on descriptions from the agent who almost caught him last night, but the computer reconstruction had the usual uncanny valley feel. The image was technically accurate, but without giving a real likeness. Now, he was wearing Diehl's sunglasses and a wool hat he had bought when they changed at the Martinez stop, and nobody gave him a second glance. As far as anyone following the case knew, he was hundreds of miles north of here.

Every few yards, there was a homeless person lying in a doorway or sitting up against the wall with a handwritten begging sign. A stretch of the sidewalk on Turk Street was so crowded with people that he had to step over bodies to get through. He passed by tents and motionless bodies beneath sleeping bags. He passed a portable grill. He passed a straggly bearded man sitting against the window of a liquor store, openly shooting up.

He knew better than most that the authorities were under budget pressure, and some areas had been left to rot. He knew he wasn't the first police officer to walk by people openly doing drugs on this street today, and he wouldn't be the last. They wouldn't be challenged as long as they kept their distance from Union Square and the Wharf. And every morning, the dealers would arrive on the BART, to serve their regular customers.

The city's homelessness problem had gotten really bad in the past few years. He didn't remember there being so many people on the streets a decade ago. It had crept up. He watched people stream past one guy as if he were invisible. He was on his knees, back perfectly straight, hand held out. Without thinking about it, Jake pressed one of his last dollar bills into the guy's hand as he passed. He knew it wouldn't do much good; to this one, or to any of them. Perhaps it was more of a superstition. A meagre offering to the gods of fortune.

The sidewalks started to get clearer as he got closer to the department stores and fashion outlets around Union Square. He reached Grant Avenue and turned north. He passed through the ornate Dragon Gate that marked the southern boundary of Chinatown. He kept to the inside of the sidewalk as the hill began to climb, sticking to the shadows beneath the awnings, squeezing past spinner racks outside the stores and keeping his head down to avoid the glances of passers-by.

The Blue Dragon Hotel was a few blocks north of the gate; a nondescript three-story brick building on a street with rows of brightly colored Chinese lanterns strung between the buildings. The entrance door was beside a restaurant, a glass panel with the faded word *Hotel* etched on it, with steel mesh in the other side. The intermingled smell of peanut oil and seafood from the restaurant reminded Jake he hadn't eaten a hot meal in almost three days. There was an intercom set into the wall. He buzzed it, and a second later, it was answered with a cautious female voice. 'Yes?'

'I have an appointment.'

There was no verbal response. Just the sound of a hang-up, followed by the buzz of the door's lock mechanism. Jake pushed the door open and went inside to find himself in a dimly lit stairwell. He took his sunglasses off and climbed one flight of stairs to the floor the reception was on. On the landing outside, an elderly workman was replacing the window frame. He had to move his toolbox out of the way to let Jake pass. Jake murmured a thank-you as he hurried past, hoping it was just his imagination that the man's eyes had lingered on his face a second too long.

He pushed at the door to the reception and found it was locked too. He knocked twice and, after a few seconds, heard another lock disengage. A woman was behind the small wooden reception desk. She didn't look up as he entered, her attention completely on something on her computer screen. She seemed to deliberately not look at him. Perhaps that was part of the job description.

'Room fourteen,' she said, pointing toward the adjoining hallway without looking up.

He walked down the hallway and didn't have to count the doors to find 14. It was the one with the big man outside. He was tall as well as wide. Dirty-looking shoulder-length brown hair. His bulk took up most of the corridor, his legs and hands spread wide, ready to move quickly. Jake didn't plan on giving him a reason.

He gestured in the direction of Jake's chest. Slowly, Jake opened his jacket to show the butt of the SIG Sauer. The big guy stiffened and reached a hand out, palm up. Jake reached for the gun and the big guy moved forward. Jake slowed down and lifted the gun out of his pocket slowly, before handing it over. The big guy checked the safety and pocketed the gun, then quickly patted Jake down. He paused as he felt something on the opposite side, and Jake was momentarily surprised until he remembered he was still carrying Rachel's phone and the detached battery. The guy took the phone out, gave it a cursory examination, and put it back in the pocket.

When he was satisfied, he straightened up and knocked twice on the door to room 14.

A muted voice responded from inside. 'Come in.'

73

When Chrissie finished talking, Sean kept staring at her, waiting for more.

'Well?' she prompted finally.

'Well what?'

'What the fuck do we do?'

He considered for a moment. 'I don't know. You think it could be on the level? That Ellis is innocent? Like, actually innocent?'

'Think about it. Everything started with this guy Da Costa saying Ellis shot Rachel and Steve Holdcroft. If that's fabricated, then what does that mean?'

'So why did Ellis run? And what about the messages? The arguments?'

'What does that prove? That he's a bad boyfriend?' She stopped and considered. 'Agent Lark really wanted to know who leaked those to us... What if whoever did it wanted to make sure Ellis looked as bad as possible?'

'They weren't faked, the FBI had them too, that's why they were so pissed.' He thought about it. 'Unless they didn't know they were faked?'

Chrissie was warming to the theory. 'Everyone assumed it's him because it's the obvious answer. It's always the husband or the boyfriend. But I got the feeling Agent Lark thought the witness was lying about seeing him. Remember how interested she was in the motorcycle thing?'

'Why would a witness lie about this?'

'Are you kidding? People lie about this stuff all the time – we have a database full of fantasists getting in touch with us to tell us they know who did it. Hell, we have people who say *they* did it. Why would Da Costa lie about it? A hundred reasons, starting with he wants attention, maybe.' She stopped, and a realization came to her. 'Lark thinks he's innocent.'

Sean puffed his cheeks out and blew. 'We need to go to Agent Lark with this,' he said. 'Tell her that Da Costa's wife contacted us.'

'We don't have anything, yet,' Chrissie said. 'Let's go interview the wife first. Get the details. We have her address.'

'Chrissie ...'

'She's willing to talk to us right now. Us. Not the cops or the FBI. If we call them in now, she'll shut down. This is a chance to get her on the record. If Da Costa was lying from the beginning, then it blows this thing wide open.'

Sean relented. 'Okay. We record her, then we talk to Agent Lark. Before we put it out there.'

'Scout's honor.'

74

'Jake Ellis, welcome.'

Carl Dolan didn't look like anyone's idea of a gangster. He was young, for a start. Late thirties. He wore a black suit with a white, collarless shirt. His hair was jet-black, slicked back. He looked more like the manager of a hipster cocktail bar, or maybe one of the latest generation of tech billionaires reacting against the hoodie-and-jeans uniform of their forebears with a more formal approach to business attire. He was handsome, but in the manner of a seventies movie star. Sharply defined cheekbones and dark eyes.

'Thank you, Paul,' Dolan said.

The big guy nodded deferentially and stepped out of the room, closing the door behind him. Dolan's accent sounded slightly mid-Atlantic. Jake wondered how long he had been in California.

Jake appraised the room. The Blue Dragon was nominally a hotel, but this room clearly hadn't seen regular guests in some time. There was no bed, for a start. Not much furniture of any kind. Just a small desk, on which Dolan was perching. There was a MacBook open on its surface, and a swivel chair behind it. There were two chairs angled in to face the desk. Nothing else. It was a small room, but the sparsity of furniture meant that it didn't seem cramped. Almost-fully closed venetian blinds let in sharp blades of sunlight that striped the dark-shaded carpet.

'How does it feel to be famous?' Dolan asked, when Jake hadn't spoken.

'It's good to be wanted, I suppose,' Jake said.

Dolan favored that with a low chuckle. 'That you are, Jake. That you are. Take a seat.' He gestured at the chair closest to Jake. He sat down, not taking his eyes off Dolan.

'You know, you could get fifty grand just for picking up the phone right now.'

Dolan shrugged, as though the amount was a trifle. 'Actually, I believe it's up to seventy-five thousand. Where's the girl?'

'Safe.'

'Did you do it?'

'You already know I didn't do it,' Jake said. 'Somebody set me up, and they did a great job.'

'Which, I'm assuming, explains why you've walked in to see me today.'

'Who hired him? Your guy, the one on the bike.'

'The man on the motorcycle was indeed the person you thought he was. Wade Lang. One of my regular contractors.'

'Who hired him?'

'My business is built on absolute confidentiality, Jake. If somebody had made an arrangement with me, I would not divulge the details. No matter what.'

It took Jake a moment to think through the implications.

'They didn't hire him through you.'

Dolan said nothing.

'Then why the hell am I here?'

'Like everyone else, I had been following this story with some interest. Yesterday afternoon, I received news that Wade Lang had been killed. A shame, but these things happen. And then, out of the blue, you got in touch, asking about Wade Lang. At first, I thought, why is he making his life even harder for himself? I made some inquiries overnight, and I found my contractor had been working with another party. We were unable to identify the person who hired Wade. We did find something that may be of use.'

Without taking his eyes from Jake, Dolan reached into his pocket and took out a cotton handkerchief. Then he reached into his inside pocket and withdrew a phone, taking care to handle it with the handkerchief. Making sure his fingerprints weren't on anything, as usual.

Dolan put the phone on the desk and replaced the handkerchief in his pocket. Jake picked it up and examined it. It was a cheap burner, not too dissimilar from the one he had bought from the gas station in False Klamath.

'This has the hit order on it?'

Dolan nodded.

'Why are you giving it to me?'

Dolan smiled. 'My good deed for today.' The smile vanished. 'And Wade was a good employee. I don't like people fucking with my business.'

Jake tapped the power button and the screen woke up.

'It's only been used for that one job,' Dolan said. 'The text messages and call history are all that's there.'

Jake thumbed through the call log first. Four incoming calls, all from the same number, in the two days leading up to Saturday, then one outgoing call to that number at 07.36. That would have been the one where the shooter broke the bad news, that he'd lost one of the targets.

The text history was short. A two-way conversation between unlabeled numbers, starting on Saturday morning.

07.22 – All go. Corner of Brown and Sullivan.
07.23 – Red Ford Escape 2 females driver & passenger

07.23 – 6WDG927
07.24 – retrieve all phones etc.
   07.25 – K
07.29 – they're turning onto Sullivan now
07.31 – ?
   07.31 – confirm both?
07.31 – confirmed

Jake felt a tightness in his chest and a rising nausea as he read through the kill order on Rachel and Molly. It seemed even more cold-blooded laid out in abbreviated form, the abbreviations, the euphemism of 'confirmed'. The nausea evaporated to be replaced with a boiling rage so sudden he had to stop himself from throwing the phone at the wall.

'It might not help you,' Dolan said, watching his reaction with a detached interest. 'No names or anything. But I wanted you to have it.'

'Thank you,' Jake said quietly. He turned to leave and stopped when he got to the door. He turned around. 'It wasn't your contract.'

'No.'

'Would you have taken it, if someone had hired you? A woman and a kid?'

Dolan stared back at Jake, not blinking. Then he raised his voice. 'Paul.'

Immediately, the door was thrust open. The big guy – Paul, apparently – stood in the doorway, gun in his hand. His beady eyes took in the situation in a split second. He relaxed a little as he saw his boss wasn't in danger but kept the gun on Jake.

'My guest is leaving. Escort him outside, then ask Gina to call for my car.'

Paul took Jake down the stairs. The workman on the landing had gone, leaving his toolbox and the window frame still empty, but Jake barely noticed. He was too busy thinking about the phone. If location services were turned on, it could prove that the phone was at the scene of the shooting. Would that help him, though? If the phone sending the messages could somehow be traced… He knew there was something else niggling him about the text exchange, but he couldn't put his finger on it.

He reached the ground floor and the big guy handed him his gun. He almost forgot to put his sunglasses back on before he stepped out onto the bustling street with the bright-colored lanterns.

As the door closed behind him and the lock clicked into place, he had it. It was the only thing that made sense.

Rachel's words from the fight last week came back to him.

Everything isn't about you, Jake.

75

Sean pulled his car into a visitor space in the basement parking garage beneath Edward Da Costa's building and killed the engine. They had talked it through on the way over. Shelley Da Costa had sounded rattled on the phone. She had to know something. Chrissie didn't want to take the chance of spooking her. Sean, sweetheart though he was, was tall and brooding, and could look intimidating to people who didn't know him.

'You sure about this?'

'Yep. Go get us a couple of coffees. As soon as I'm done, we'll head over to the FBI and talk to Lark.'

She got out of the car and hurried across the near-empty lot to the door to the stairwell. In truth, she still wasn't sure about going to Agent Lark before they posted the interview. What if she told them to wait until after they had spoken to Shelley? Wouldn't it be better to get forgiveness than permission?

She pushed through the door and moved up the bare concrete stairs, taking her phone out to confirm Shelley Da Costa's apartment number as a man in a black coat passed her on the way down.

She passed by the ground-level door that led out onto the street and kept climbing to the third floor. She rang the doorbell underneath the Da Costa nameplate and waited. After a minute, she knocked three times. No response. She looked down at her phone and checked the message. Yep, right address, and she had told Shelley she was coming straight over. Had she had a change of heart?

Chrissie tried the door handle. It was unlocked.

She stepped inside the narrow entrance hall. 'Hello?'

There were four doors leading off the hall: two on the left, one on the right, one straight ahead.

She began to walk toward the door at the far end. 'Shelley? It's Chrissie, from *Untraceable*.'

What if Shelley's husband had come home and didn't like the idea of her talking to someone about this? She felt a tingle at the base of her neck and started to wish she had agreed to let Sean accompany her after all. Briefly, she thought about calling him to come up here, before curiosity got the better of her. She turned the handle and the door swung open. She clamped her hand to her mouth as she saw what was inside.

And then she was running, back out of the door, back down the three flights of stairs. She fumbled for her phone and got it out. Ready to dial 911 as soon as she got to the car. She opened the door at the bottom, then stopped on the threshold.

There was a man standing by the driver's-side window of Sean's car. He had his back to her. As she watched, he turned. It was the man she had passed without a second look in the stairwell. The man who had been coming down from upstairs.

A smile broke out on his face, as though he recognized her. 'Chrissie?'

Something was off about the way he had turned around. The guy looked like he'd been caught in the middle of something. Oh my God, Sean...

The man had short, dark hair. A military or police cut. He wore a black coat over a black T-shirt. He started walking toward her. His angle of approach put him in the middle of her line of sight to the front of Sean's car, so she couldn't see if he was okay.

'Chrissie, I'm Special Agent Valenti, I work with Agent Lark.'

Chrissie shrank back, ignoring him. She had to make a decision.

'Sean?' she called out.

There was no answer. The man walking toward her stopped, the smile fading from his face. 'It's okay, Chrissie, I'm here to take you to Catherine. I'm going to get my ID out now, okay?'

His right hand was reaching toward the inside of his coat.

It was at that moment she saw it. Maybe she had seen it when she opened the door but not registered what it meant; maybe that was what had seemed wrong. She barely noticed the phone slip from her hand and smack onto the ground as she lifted her hand to her mouth again.

There was broken glass on the ground on the opposite side of the car, just visible beyond the hood. Like someone had broken the passenger-side window from the inside. Or like someone had fired a bullet that passed through the open driver's window and out the other side. She had a better view of the car now. There was something dark spattered over the inside of the windshield.

The man who had called himself Valenti hesitated a second. Then a look came into his eyes that terrified Chrissie, as he reached the rest of the way into his jacket and pulled out a gun, aiming it at her.

She turned back to the stairs and let the door swing shut behind her. A moment later, she heard a gunshot, echoing against the concrete walls. She scrambled up the stairs, taking them three at a time.

The door slammed open behind her, bouncing off the wall. She ducked as he fired again. The bullet hit the wall just above where her head had been.

She reached ground level. Turned away from the stairs and pushed on the door to the street. Stumbled out onto the sidewalk, praying that she would see a cop, but there was no one in sight.

She passed by the spot where she had spoken to the homeless guy on Saturday, hoping she could reach the next alley before Sean's killer reached street level. It was a hundred yards; too far.

And then she remembered the little basement-level entrance, the homeless guy on Saturday had been warming his hands on the vents. A hidden nook, easy to miss if you were in a hurry.

Without thinking, she ducked down the stairs.

At the same moment, she heard the door to the basement parking garage bang open just as she got her head below the level of the sidewalk.

She hunched down, moved across the strewn trash that had collected in the trench at the bottom of the stairs. She took care not to step on any crushed cans or broken glass. The merest sound would signpost her position. She heard running footsteps approaching and pushed herself back against the wall.

The footsteps passed above her and then stopped. She waited. After a moment, the killer made a decision and started running again. He had decided to take the alley.

She waited a long time before she dared climb the first two steps and lift her head above sidewalk level. The street was empty again.

76

The more they looked into Edward Da Costa, the shadier the whole setup seemed. Lark was on the phone, trying to nail down a warrant to search Da Costa's apartment, when Garcia appeared at her desk, looking ready to burst. Before she could ask what it was, he held up his phone.

There was a picture of a man standing at the top of a flight of stairs. He was wearing a hat and his face was turned slightly away, but there was no mistake. It was Jake Ellis.

Garcia explained that the call had come into the tip line a half-hour ago. The caller's name was Walter Yick. It took a little longer to filter through the system, because Mr Yick spoke only Cantonese. Initially, the tip was assigned to the low-priority stream, because the location didn't match up with the most recent intelligence. The details were taken by a Cantonese speaker, translated and entered into the system.

At that point, the case was immediately flagged twice: once because of the location, which was a suspected front for criminal operations. Then again by one of the standard queries Lark had asked to be added following False Klamath, because Yick's description matched Jake Ellis as he had looked when Lark saw him last night, not as he looked on the early photographs. At that point, somebody finally took a look at the photo Yick had sent through when requested.

The photo had been taken in a cheap hotel in Chinatown. The Blue Dragon was frequently used to conduct drug deals, gun sales, contracted hits. What the hell had Ellis been doing there? And where was Molly?

Lark stood up and tapped her steel fountain pen against her mug loudly, until a temporary quiet descended on the office.

'We have a good sighting of Ellis. Right here in the city. A handyman called in with a pic of somebody who is either Jake Ellis or his identical twin. The Blue Dragon Hotel in Chinatown, thirty minutes ago.'

She fielded a couple of questions, which didn't take long, because she had just told them everything she knew. The team got to work, feeding the information out to agents in the field, notifying the SFPD, and reallocating resources to Chinatown. If they were lucky, Ellis would still be at the hotel. If not, they would have a much tighter location for the next Amber Alert.

77

Retrieve all phones.

Jake knew there had to be a good reason behind the instruction. The fact that the person who had ordered the murders of Rachel and Molly Donaldson had felt it necessary to send a last-minute reminder on this specific point.

Molly had told him she had left her phone behind in the car, along with her bag. If the shooter had had time, he would have taken that phone. But Jake knew for a fact that the order had not been carried out in full, because Rachel's phone had not been taken. Molly had been holding it as she fled the scene. She had stopped Jake from tossing it away as they left the city. It had been switched off for the last two days, and for most of that time, it had lain in the inside pocket of his jacket, all but forgotten until now.

A specific instruction. To make the attack look like a robbery? No, because in that case the instruction would have been to take Rachel's bag. The text hadn't said that. It had said, *Retrieve all phones.* They weren't taking any chances.

It suggested that the person who had planned this didn't want anyone else to have Rachel's phone. There was only one problem. He couldn't turn the phone on, for the same reason he hadn't been able to turn it on since Saturday morning.

As Jake crossed O'Farrell Street, he heard a low rumble from below and felt the vibration through the soles of his shoes. He stopped. A man coming the other way glanced at him, and he quickly inclined his head to prevent him getting a clear look at his face. He picked up speed and turned right onto Market Street. Powell Street station was a few hundred yards away. The Powell Street BART platform was three levels down, better than thirty feet beneath street level.

Perhaps there was a way he could see what was on the phone.

78

Evening traffic was heavier than usual. Lark made a call to the SFPD liaison while Kelly Paxon drove, running red lights and weaving in and out of traffic. The PD had two cars at the hotel already, and they were bringing in more officers. Every officer in the vicinity had been told to look out for Ellis, and they were bringing more in.

They reached the turn onto Clay Street in under five minutes. Grant Avenue was two blocks away, and beyond that, the Dragon Gate and Chinatown.

When they got to the hotel, the building and most of the block was locked down already. As requested, SFPD officers had already gone room to room, finding no sign of Ellis. It was a small hotel, so it hadn't taken long. There were only two people in the building: a diminutive receptionist with a quietly furious demeanor, and a shady-looking big man with the chemically augmented build of a pro-wrestler. Both were tight-lipped. There were no guests in the entire place. If Lark had needed another reason to find this place suspicious, that would have done it. Both claimed never to have seen a man answering Ellis's description.

They went back outside and looked up and down the street. 'It was definitely him,' Lark said. 'He was here.'

'I can't believe he came back to the city,' Paxon said. 'Why the hell would he do that? He could've gotten away clean.'

'Why indeed?' Lark said. She thought about the picture of Ellis. 'He looked like he was going in, not leaving. How much time did he spend in there? We could have missed him by minutes again.'

She had her phone in her hand, absently flipping it over and over in her palm. Email notifications aplenty. Lots of chatter on the team Slack channel too. But nothing new.

And where was Molly? The handyman hadn't seen her here with him. Put together with the apparently reckless behavior of returning to the city, she could see from the posts on Slack that it had a lot of people in the team worried.

Paxon took a call, her lips moving as she followed what was being said. She turned to Lark.

'All set. They're waiting for the word.'

Lark hesitated. She looked up and down Grant Avenue, calculating how much distance a man on foot could have covered in between fifteen minutes and half an hour. The latest composite image of Ellis had been sent out to every cop in the area, and every available federal agent in the city was either here or on their way. She had hoped one of them would have spotted Ellis by now.

There were two-person teams from the bureau spreading out across the city, with a concentration here. The SFPD were coordinating with them and were funneling uniformed and plain-clothes officers into Chinatown and the surrounding streets. The big advantage they had this time was that there was no need to spread manpower across the map, no big journey times to chase down a credible sighting. Which again begged the question: why had he come back?

'Agent Lark?'

Lark let Paxon's prompt hang in the air for a moment as

she watched the people pass by, some of them glancing at the police presence at the hotel with interest. Gawkers. Normally they irritated her. Right now, they needed to use that morbid interest.

'All right,' she said finally, turning back to Paxon. 'Once more, with feeling.'

Paxon put her finger to her ear and told them it was a go.

Thirty seconds later, Paxon's and Lark's phones trilled simultaneously with the alert. Lark watched the street, seeing people staring down at their phones already. A couple pushing their kid in a buggy had stopped to look back at her, the woman holding the phone, the man pointing out the police car parked next to the hotel. In a matter of moments, they would start to get feedback from the handling center.

The starting gun had been fired; the race was on.

AMBER ALERT: San Francisco,CA
CHILD:13 Cauc F 5'0 110 Donaldson, Molly
1SUSP:41 Cauc M 5'10 185 Ellis, Jake
On foot, vicinity of Grant Avenue
Suspect armed, do not approach
415-553-0123

79

Jake had turned around and was making his way north again. He was keeping his head down, staying close to the storefronts, making sure not to meet the eyes of any of the other pedestrians. His plan to descend to the subterranean station of the Powell Street BART had run aground when he rounded the corner and saw two cops standing in front of the entrance, watching everyone who passed by.

He saw another SFPD black-and-white parked at the curb up ahead and turned back onto Grant Avenue again before he got too close. He would work out a way to safely turn on Rachel's phone later. He didn't think it was his imagination that there seemed to be more cops appearing on the street. He had managed to keep clear of them so far, but all of a sudden the rented room where Molly was waiting felt a lot farther away than it had twenty minutes ago.

The sidewalk was blocked up ahead by a group of men standing outside a pool hall, all but one vaping; the other leaning back against the doorway with his hands in his pockets. Jake stepped out into the street to pass them, glancing behind him to check there were no oncoming cars. He angled farther out to keep a parked pickup between him and the group of men and almost walked right into a short blond woman coming in the other direction. She was smiling, staring down at her phone as she walked, and they would have collided with one another if Jake hadn't been paying attention and sidestepped.

She glanced up at him, startled, and gave him an apologetic look.

'Oh I'm so sorry, I was—'

Jake snapped his head away from her as she paused.

'No problem,' he called back, facing straight ahead and quickening his pace.

Had she recognized him? He couldn't be sure, but he didn't think she had made the connection in that moment. Her expression was of someone trying to remember if they've met you somewhere. When you see someone familiar-looking but can't quite place them.

He felt her eyes burning into his back. Probably just his imagination, but turning around to check if she was watching him would only look more suspicious. There was another knot of people up ahead: tourists eating at the tables outside a restaurant, digging into cartons of noodles with chopsticks.

There was a young couple on the table nearest the curb. The man wore a blue Warriors jacket and had his back to Jake. The woman wore a black leather jacket, her hair was in ringlets, dyed a bright magenta. She glanced at him but didn't really see him, looking almost immediately back down at her phone. She swiped the screen with the fingers of her left hand while eating with her right.

He passed by quickly; he couldn't let someone else get a good look at him from up close. Up ahead, he saw a uniformed officer had appeared at the corner. He was scanning the sidewalks at the intersection. Jake risked a glance back.

The blond woman seemed to have advanced a little farther from where they had almost walked into each other but had stopped and turned around, was staring right at him.

She didn't react when he looked back. Perhaps she was still

just trying to place him. It would come to her soon, he just hoped he had put some distance between them by that time. There was an alley entrance up ahead. It would take him in the wrong direction, but he decided he could cut through and join the parallel street. It would cost him a couple of minutes, but he didn't want to give the blond woman any more time to put a name to the face.

That was when it happened.

A familiar long tone whined from the phone held by the woman outside the restaurant. Jake froze, slowed his pace unconsciously. A Pavlovian reaction. He had been hearing that sound in the back of his head since Saturday morning at 8.27. The burner phone in his pocket buzzed a second later.

He heard a murmur of conversation from the couple at the table.

'What is it?'

'Amber Alert,' she answered, the tone matter-of-fact. Then her breath caught as she read more. 'Oh my God...'

'What?'

'He's here.'

'Here in the city?'

'No, like right here.'

Jake quickened his pace. The alley was fifty yards away.

'Hey!'

He glanced back and saw the blond pointing at him, the phone still in her other hand. Already, the men outside the pool hall had started to drift toward her, wondering what she was yelling about.

'It's him!' she yelled.

It seemed like time stopped for a second.

The men from outside the pool hall turned as one to look at where she was pointing. The couple from the restaurant turned, the woman's hand clapped over her mouth as she looked at him properly now.

And then the men at the pool hall started running, and the boyfriend of the magenta-haired woman stood up so quickly his chair overturned, and the cop at the end of the street turned to look at what the yelling was about.

Jake ran.

80

This seemed like a pacing sort of moment.

In some of the books Molly had read, characters who were anxiously waiting for someone always seemed to pass the time by pacing. Good for your step count, perhaps, but not so great when your chest was a little tight.

She hadn't fully gotten over the bad attack at the house in False Klamath. She had been okay once the doctor had issued her the Ventolin, but there was a raspy noise in her chest that she could feel as well as hear, and it felt like it was getting worse. Her head was light from taking more of it than she was used to. She hadn't told Jake, didn't want to add another worry to his list. She rattled the inhaler for the hundredth time. Already it felt half empty. She would have to ration herself better; she didn't know how long it might be until she could get a replacement.

It didn't help that the room was dusty. The roof window was open, but in the heart of the city, she didn't think that could be called fresh air, exactly. Her mom had told her that San Francisco was in the top ten worst cities for short-term particle pollution. She thought that was partly to blame for Molly's asthma. It was one of the reasons she wanted to move to Santa Rosa.

Molly felt the sick feeling again at that thought and forced it down.

Don't think about Mom.

She was getting better at it, at blocking out the emotion. She didn't want to think about the fact she was getting better at it, because it made her feel guiltier. But it allowed her to function. To focus on breathing.

She had been watching an *Adventure Time* marathon on Cartoon Network, but every so often she would flick back to ABC to see if there were any updates on Mom. It had been ten minutes since the last time she had checked, probably a new record.

She switched over and saw there had been some development, but it wasn't immediately possible to tell what. The headline said only, *Molly Donaldson Hunt.* The images were from here in San Francisco, so she knew they must have worked out they had come back to the city, but the ticker along the bottom was running through other stories. She hoped Jake hadn't been caught. Impatient, she watched the text scroll by beneath a rolling montage of stony-faced police officers manning barriers, cars being stopped, the familiar split-screen shot showing Jake's police mugshot and the picture of her from Disneyland. She had long since become inured to the weirdness of seeing herself on TV.

'Come on,' she grumbled, waiting for the ticker to roll past stupid updates about Congress and sports.

She told herself the images on the screen were positive. If her mom's condition had changed, there would be a picture of her. If Jake had been caught, there would be video footage of him being bundled into a police car or something, surely.

Then she heard the creak of the third stair outside the door and felt a rush of relief. She got up to let Jake in, and then stopped when she remembered what he had said. She waited, and finally the footsteps reached the top of the stairs and there was a pair of sharp knocks on the door.

Only two knocks.

81

Jake could hear the yells and the footsteps hitting the sidewalk as he raced around the corner into the alley.

He covered the distance between the two streets quickly. As he approached the far end, he could see a steady crowd of people passing by on the street. He burst out of the mouth of the alley, slowing so as not to collide with the crowd, which was advancing along the sidewalk and the road itself.

Not a crowd, a procession. A funeral parade.

People lined both sides of the street, watching the parade as it advanced south. Some dressed smartly, others in casual wear. The shadows were long, the setting sun blinding where it touched the rooftops on its descent.

Jake didn't stop moving, slipped into the flow of the procession. He could see the coffin up ahead, the shiny black veneer bobbing above the heads of the people in front of him, resting on the shoulders of the pallbearers. The second funeral he'd crashed this week. He heard voices behind him as the men from the next street reached the mouth of the alley and encountered the same scene he had found a moment before. He couldn't hear individual words but knew they were looking for him.

The dense mass of people made it much easier to blend in than it would be to find an individual face among the crowd. He shrugged off his jacket, grateful he was wearing a white long-sleeved shirt underneath. Another gift from Diehl. Many of the other mourners wore white shirts. More formal, in most cases, but the difference wouldn't be noticeable at a distance. The walkers on either side of him paid him no notice. By pure chance, he had stumbled onto the one street in the city where nobody was looking at their phones.

He didn't risk looking back this time, just quickened his pace, overtaking some of the slower people while staying consistent with the rhythm of the procession.

A brass band was leading the procession. He recognized the hymn, took a second to identify it as 'Just a Closer Walk With Thee'.

Shit. He was putting distance between himself and his pursuers, but the street was angling north, taking him farther from the route back to the rented room. He thought about dropping out of the procession when it reached the next cross street. He nixed that idea when he saw the intersection was crawling with cops. And then he looked ahead and saw more uniforms were starting to gather on the sidewalks, scanning the procession.

He cursed under his breath and kept his expression blank, staring straight ahead, matching his pace to the mourners around him.

Somebody must have seen him and called it in. What the hell had he expected? Coming back to the city, it was only a matter of time. He had given up the advantage of the open country. His eyes darted around, looking for a way out. Everywhere he looked, there seemed to be more and more cops. Some of the other mourners in the procession had noticed it too, some of them exchanging curious comments about what was going on. A couple of walkers had surreptitiously taken out their phones to find out what was happening.

Eventually one of them would spot him. Or one of the officers on the sidewalk, who was scanning the faces in the crowd for one just like his, would get lucky. He had to get out of the procession. But how? The moment he stepped out of line, he would cease to be one of the crowd. He would be noticeable, distinct.

And then he saw his chance.

A delivery truck had tried to turn out of an alley barely bigger than its width and had stopped with its front end jutting out when the driver saw the road was blocked by the procession. The driver was gripping the wheel tightly, an exasperated look on his face. But the truck was now blocking the view of anyone on the sidewalk beyond.

Jake started bearing toward the truck. He brushed past an old man as he cut diagonally across, hearing a grunt of annoyance. He held up a hand and muttered an apology, without looking back.

The truck was close now. Twenty feet away. Fifteen. Another couple of seconds. He stepped out of the procession, ready to edge past the vehicle and into the alley.

At the same moment, the delivery driver threw up his hands in surrender and then gripped the wheel again, starting to reverse back.

The truck drew back into the alley like a curtain sweeping back from the stage. A uniformed officer was standing just beyond it. He half turned as he registered the movement of the truck. He looked right at Jake. The eye contact lasted for a split second, but it seemed like time stood still. Jake didn't recognize him, but the officer sure as hell knew who he was.

He blinked, his mouth started to drop open, and then he started to move, his hand reaching to his holster, the open mouth of surprise twisting into a yell.

'Hold it!'

82

Molly snuck over to the window, avoiding the loose board, and carefully slipped her sneakers on. She tucked her inhaler into the pocket of her jeans and started to swing the window open farther.

She hoped whoever was out the door would either knock and wait again or give up, but she took an intake of breath when she heard the handle being rattled.

'Open up, it's the police.'

She climbed onto the desk beneath the window. She pushed it wide open and put her hands out on the roof tiles. It was steeper than she had expected. There was another banging on the door and she flinched. She kept going through the tight space, having to stop and angle herself around. As she did, her left foot contacted the glass of water she had left on the desk and knocked it over. It rolled across the desk and fell to the ground, smashing.

She wriggled faster, the urgency making her rush. The next sound she heard was a loud crack as something slammed into the door. As she finally drew her whole body out onto the sloping roof, she heard another crack as the door gave way.

She started crawling across the roof, staying side-on, with her feet toward the edge. She kept her focus on the rough tiles beneath her hands and on the next patch of roof horizontally along from her. She didn't look down at the edge a few inches below her sneakers, tried not to even think about the four-story drop beyond that. She could hear sirens in the distance, traffic rumbling by on the street.

There was a fire escape on the other end of the building. She remembered that from earlier. She just had to focus on making it there in one piece. The second time she had done this in the last few days. No sweat. Except that the last roof had been flat.

She heard the creak of the window as someone leaned out, but she didn't look back.

Whoever it was didn't yell after her, and when she didn't hear anything for another couple of minutes, she knew he wasn't following her out onto the roof.

She was almost there. Another few feet. A pigeon took flight with a sudden flutter of its wings from the crest of the roof just above her. She didn't flinch, just kept inching to the side.

'Almost there, almost there, keep going,' she murmured under her breath. The edge of the roof was almost within reach now. The fire escape was definitely on this side, right? 'Keep going, almost the—'

She screamed as the tile below her right foot slipped away like it had been greased. She felt gravity yank her toward the edge. She flattened her palms and spread herself out to stop the inexorable slide to the edge and managed to slow herself just enough to be able to stop diagonally, one foot dangling into the void, spread out like she was doing a star jump.

She could hear nothing except the sound of her pulse thudding in her ear. She wondered if it would hurt when she hit the ground, or if the fall would kill her instantly. She didn't dare move, in case another tile gave way, or the merest change in balance sent her toppling the rest of the way off the roof.

But she had to. She couldn't stay here waiting to fall. So she inched her right foot up, bending at the knee, moving painfully slowly. After what felt like an eternity, she got the foot back on the roof. She braced herself and inched upward. A little, then a little more. She moved her right hand, found purchase. Her left hand. Then her right foot, then her left foot. It was okay. It was going to take her a little longer, but she was going to make it.

And then the tile under her left foot gave way.

She screamed as she slid down again, once more barely managing to keep hold.

'Molly.'

Carefully, she raised her head. There was a man hanging over the edge of the roof, the fingers of both hands gripping tightly to the edge underneath his chin. He had close-cropped dark hair and a thin, angular face. She could see the collar of what looked like a police uniform, like Jake's.

'Stay still, I got you.'

She couldn't move. All she could think about was the drop.

'Molly, I'm going to need you to move your right hand a little closer to me.' The man's voice was calm. It almost reminded her of a teacher explaining a math problem.

When she didn't move, he glanced down toward her feet, then looked back at her.

'Okay, just stay put for a second.'

His face disappeared from the edge and, after what seemed like a long pause, she heard a grunt and he appeared again farther up. He pulled himself up the whole way this time, getting his palms flat on the roof and then raising his upper body until he could get a knee over, and then the rest of him. The tile four spaces along from Molly cracked when he stood on it, making a sound like a branch snapping, and Molly gritted her teeth and said, 'No.'

The officer didn't answer this time, he was surveying the other tiles, looking for a good place to plant his feet. When he was satisfied, he spread his feet apart, one of them facing down toward Molly, the other bent beneath him. He gripped the ridge on the crest of the roof with his left hand, and then reached out his other hand toward Molly's.

She shook her head carefully. 'I can't.'

'You gotta, Molly. Just reach up, real slow.'

He was right. She knew he was right. So how come she couldn't make her arm move?

'I'm a friend of Jake's. I'm going to get you down from here.'

That reminded her. What about the person who had broken into the room? She glanced back and saw the window still hanging open. No sign of anyone.

'Somebody there,' she said from between gritted teeth, not wasting a word, as though the words themselves might carry a weight and their absence might alter her balance, displace her from this precarious perch.

His eyes didn't waver from her. 'We'll worry about that in a minute, when we get you down. Molly, my name's Marty. I know Jake didn't do it.'

That made her glance up again. She didn't dare raise her head the whole way, but by rolling her eyes up as far as they would go, she saw his gray eyes looking back at her, and she believed he was telling the truth.

She started to shift her weight and felt her hand slide a little on the surface. There was a high, whining sound and it took her a second to realize it came from herself.

'Molly, just reach up.'

She took a breath, bit her bottom lip between her teeth and let go with her right hand, reaching up. She felt herself begin to slide immediately and in that second knew this was it, she was going to fall.

And then she felt strong fingers around her wrist, digging in, and her slide stopped. Her legs kicked in the air and a second later she heard a tile smash into fragments in the alley below.

'I got you,' Marty gasped, his voice only now losing its calm. He braced himself with his left hand and slowly began to pull Molly up from the edge, until she could reach the crest of the roof herself. She grabbed it with her free hand and pulled herself up, finally letting out a breath. He waited until she had swung a leg over the ridge and was sitting perched on the crest of the roof until he let go, then puffed out his cheeks and laughed in relief. 'You had me worried there,' he said.

'Did you mean it? You know Jake didn't do it?'

Marty nodded. 'Hundred percent.'

83

The delivery truck had backed up quickly, was already twenty yards down the alley. The problem was, it took up virtually the whole space. Maybe six inches on each side between the wing mirrors and the brick walls. Not enough room to squeeze past.

Without thinking, Jake charged at it. The driver wasn't looking, his eyes darting between the mirrors to negotiate the tight space. As Jake approached, he noticed him and furrowed his brow. Jake lip-read the start of something that might have been 'What the fuck?'

'Freeze! Police! Stop or I'll shoot!'

Jake didn't look back, didn't slow. There was no way the cop was shooting with that driver slap bang in the middle of the line of fire. The truck had stopped as the driver eased off the gas, and Jake planted one foot on the hood and launched himself up. The next step planted in the middle of the sloping windshield, the third took him onto the roof of the truck. Some part of his brain told him he had now made himself a clear target, and he hit the roof in a foot-first lunge, like sliding into home plate, just as he heard the gunshots from behind him. The shots passed over his head with an audible snap as he dropped off the rear of the truck, hitting the ground hard and rolling.

He heard more yelling from behind him and glanced back. The truck was completely blocking the alley. No clear shot for the officer back there, and it would take him, or anyone else, a while to squeeze past side-on.

The alley opened out onto another street. He flew out onto the sidewalk and started running north, stopping when he saw two more cops standing at the corner of California Street, facing in the opposite direction, talking into their radios. He turned and headed the other way, passing a tourist stall with over-packed racks of wares lining the sidewalk. The vendor, a short Latino guy, was engaged in a negotiation with a couple of young guys in backpacks. Without breaking stride, Jake reached out and grabbed a white baseball hat with *I ♡ SF* emblazoned across the front. He dropped his own hat on the street and fitted the replacement over his head, pulling the brim down low.

'Hey, man, you got a dollar?'

Jake glanced down at the homeless guy in the long army surplus coat bundled in the doorway with his knees against his chest. There was an empty coffee cup from McDonald's between his feet, a couple of coins at the bottom of it. A thought came back to him from earlier. About how some people were invisible.

Jake paused and glanced back along the street. The two cops were speaking to the driver of a tan sedan. He put a hand up to cover his face as he turned back to the homeless guy, making as though he was scratching an itch. It was probably an over-precaution. The guy's eyes were unfocused, and he probably hadn't been near a smartphone lately, if ever.

'I'll give you twenty bucks for the coat,' Jake said quietly.

The guy's eyes widened. 'For real?'

'For real.'

Jake glanced back the way he had come, hoping he could complete this transaction before the cops turned back this way. He took out the bill. The last of his money. The guy surprised him with his speed. From his crouched position, he was on his

330

feet and holding the coat out to Jake within a couple of seconds. He snatched the twenty from Jake's hands and sat back down again, slipping the bill into his hip pocket. He tipped a finger to his head in a little salute.

'Nice doin' business with you.'

Jake mumbled his thanks and pulled the coat on. The coat had a number of competing scents, the best of which seemed to be body odor and cheap wine, but it certainly changed his look. He started walking quickly again, tugging the brim of his hat down. He passed within arm's length of the two cops, close enough to hear his description and last known direction of travel on the closest one's radio.

The sidewalk started to get a little more crowded as he walked. Many of the people he passed were looking down at their phones, reacting to the Amber Alert.

But this time, no one gave him a second glance.

84

Jake's friend Marty kept a hand on Molly's arm to steady her as they descended the fire escape. She didn't feel completely steady until her feet touched down on the pitted concrete of the alley. She took a puff from her inhaler and sat on the bottom step. Marty followed and stood in front of her. She felt an involuntary shiver when she saw the gun holstered on his belt. If she didn't see another gun for the rest of her life, she would be happy.

'Where's Jake?' he asked. She could tell he was trying to be patient with her. 'It's okay, honey, you're safe now. You can tell me.'

'He went to meet someone. He'll be back soon,' she said. 'There was someone up there.'

Marty looked up, his gaze following the rusting steel fire escape climbing the wall.

'Up on the roof?'

Molly shook her head impatiently. It was taking a lot of effort to keep her breathing regular, and this man kept making her speak.

'No. I was in the apartment up there. Somebody came to the door. I knew it wasn't...' She stopped and took a slow breath.

'Wasn't Jake?' Marty suggested. 'It's okay.'

'I knew it wasn't him, so I crawled out the skylight. Whoever it was kicked the door down. They didn't follow me out on the roof.'

Marty took a minute to think it over, then glanced up again. 'Can you take me up to the apartment? We can check they're gone.'

Molly looked at the gun on Marty's belt again. This time he snapped the button from the holster and patted it, smiling. 'Nobody's going to mess with us, don't worry.'

She tried to talk him out of it, but Marty was insistent. The two of them climbed the stairs to the top floor. The door was open, the jamb splintered. Marty stepped inside the room first, gun in his hand, looking around.

Molly lingered by the door, not wanting to go back in and be cornered again. Marty examined the scene, taking in the open skylight window, the smashed glass lying in a puddle of water on the floor.

He kneeled on the desk and took a look out of the window, whistling. 'You got some guts, kid. You wouldn't catch me climbing out there.'

'How did you find us?' she asked, the thought only now occurring to her.

'Jake. He told me where you were.'

He climbed back down and dusted off his hands.

'Are we going to see Jake?'

He nodded. 'Soon.' He surveyed the room. Molly guessed he was looking for clues. He opened the drawer under the desk and closed it again, then looked her up and down. He circled around her and Molly suddenly felt a little uneasy. She glanced at the doorway. As she looked back, Marty stepped past her and turned to stand right in front of the doorway. Had he done that because he saw her looking at it? It was almost as though he wanted to block the way out.

'Say, did you take your mom's phone the other day? We never found it at the scene.'

85

Lark and Paxon were on the move. They had been watching the live tip feed and the first sighting of Jake had come in three minutes after the Amber Alert. He had been spotted by multiple people on Montgomery Street.

Paxon had her phone to her ear as they turned onto Montgomery, talking to Taylor back at Golden Gate Avenue. She put her hand over the speaker to talk to Lark as they walked.

'They're saying he's on Columbus Avenue now. Wait, we got another sighting over on Vallejo.'

'That's impossible,' Lark said, through gritted teeth. 'Only one of those can be right.'

This was the problem. Later on, it might be possible to work out which were real sightings and which were hysteria, but right now, Columbus Avenue was as likely as Vallejo Street. Could be either, could be neither.

Lark's phone buzzed and she answered it without looking at the caller, her eyes scanning the sidewalks on either side of Montgomery Street for a familiar face. She could see a half-dozen uniforms and two federal agents on this street alone. At least they had numbers on their side this time.

'Agent Lark, it's about Edward Da Costa…'

'The warrant came through?' she cut in. 'Good. Can we spare anyone to—'

'No, it's not the warrant. Edward Da Costa's been killed.'

That brought Lark to an abrupt stop on the sidewalk. Paxon continued at a fast clip for another five paces before she noticed Lark had stopped.

'What the hell do you mean "killed"?'

'Somebody shot him and his wife. There's another DOA in the parking garage at his building, we're—'

'Shit,' Lark said.

Paxon was frowning. 'What is it?'

Lark took the phone from her ear and waved her forward. 'Go. Head for Columbus, I'll call you in five.' She put the phone back to her ear. 'What's Da Costa's address? I'll be right down there.'

She turned and retraced her steps, running back to where she had parked the car around the corner from the Blue Dragon. Twenty minutes ago this street had been crawling with cops, but now she couldn't see a single blue uniform. They had all moved east as the sightings of Ellis poured in. As she rounded the corner, she passed by a bum in a long, ratty-looking coat and a white baseball cap.

She dug in her pocket for the car key and then paused, as a thought struck her.

She turned to take a closer look at the guy in the white hat. It was too white; too new. Didn't go with the coat at all. Now she was looking, he had a familiar build and gait. And unless it was her imagination, he had quickened his pace after passing her.

86

Jake rounded the corner and slowed as he saw the woman approaching a gray Chevy Impala. She was wearing a suit and walking with purpose, and he had a bad feeling he recognized her.

And then she turned her head slightly to glance across the road, and he saw enough of her face to be sure. The angular jawline, the dark eyes. He recognized her from last night, and he knew her name from the press conference on Saturday. Special Agent Catherine Lark.

He wanted to turn and start walking back the way he had come, but he knew that would draw more attention than continuing onward. There were some moving cars on the street, most of it heading south toward him. He stepped out into the road and crossed diagonally, in front of a red Chevy as it slowed to let him pass. There was a Sichuan restaurant right around the corner where Jake ate once a month. It was usually fairly quiet. The tables at the back, farthest from the window, were usually available. There was a back exit. He could—

'Sir?'

He didn't slow at the sound of the female voice from behind him. He knew it was Lark. He forced himself to keep to the same pace. Just a regular guy going about his day, not thinking the 'Sir' was directed at him. Why would he? He wasn't the only person on the street.

'Excuse me,' louder now, a more commanding tone, 'I heart San Francisco – the man in the hat.'

He waved his left hand in a way that could have been an acknowledgment or just a gesture to say he didn't have time to stop. Forget about the restaurant, he would break into a run as soon as he rounded the corner.

Just then, a shuffling, bearded figure lunged out from a shuttered doorway right in front of him. He stepped straight into Jake's path, his hand held out. He wore a dirty gray hooded jacket and a blue baseball cap, his hand already outstretched.

'Hey, man, you got a dollar?'

Jake averted his eyes and sidestepped, but the man stepped in front of him, cutting him off.

'Sir, hold on a second. FBI.' The voice behind him was closer now, she was crossing the street.

Jake put a hand on the man's shoulder and firmly pushed him out of the way, but the guy wasn't backing off.

'Fuck you doin', man?'

He grabbed Jake's wrist with his left hand, his grip surprisingly tight.

Jake pushed ahead, barging past him and wrenching his hand away, but in the scuffle, his hat came off, just as he had to angle around to squeeze past him.

He saw Lark, maybe ten paces from him, halfway across the road. She was looking right at him, in no doubt.

'Freeze!' Lark was raising her gun.

Jake pushed the bearded man out of his way and moved. He ignored the yelled curses of the bum and Lark's warning and sprinted for the corner, rounding it to see a black-and-white SFPD car making the turn onto the road at the next block.

He ignored the blast of horns as he ran across the street and

337

ducked into an alley. The heavy coat, useless now as a disguise, could only slow him down. He wrestled it off and let it fall in his wake. A group of teenagers, two males and one female, were coming in the other direction. One of them glanced in his direction as he ran past, and he saw her pull a double take as he passed by.

'Hey … I think that's the guy—'

The voice faded out as Jake cut across the next street and into another alley.

He heard a second set of footsteps echoing off the walls of the alley and threw a backward glance, saw Lark in pursuit, gun in her right hand. He turned left at the end, then ran between traffic, crossing diagonally to the next alley. He heard more horns, followed by a second burst of horns a moment later as Lark crossed.

Another street, this one quieter. He looked back to see if Lark was gaining and collided with a teenage boy in a backpack who had been passing the mouth of the alley, staring down at his phone. Jake stumbled and stayed on his feet as he spun away from the collision. He glanced back as he started moving again and saw that the teenager hadn't fared as well. He was staggering from the sidewalk. As Jake hesitated, the boy tripped over his feet and fell down into the road, breaking his fall with both hands, his phone clattering away across the street.

Jake's eyes widened as he saw the hulking garbage truck bearing down from behind the fallen figure. He saw it all in a split second, a terrible freeze-frame tableau. The boy, still stunned, prostrate on the ground, facing away from the thirty-ton hunk of metal that was about to smear him across the blacktop. The lights and grille of the truck, cruising toward him at a pace that would make stopping in time impossible, even if the driver was paying attention, which he wasn't. Jake could see his eyes focused far above the small bundle in the road directly in front of him, trained on the lights at the next intersection.

Jake lunged toward the boy, grabbing him around the waist and rolling, praying his momentum would be enough to take them both out of the way of the truck. At the last second, the driver must have seen him dive out into the road, because he heard a squeal of tires and a hiss of air brakes as his right shoulder connected with the ground and he rolled over on his back, pulling the kid over on top as he let out a surprised yelp. It seemed to happen in slow motion. He had time to wonder how it could possibly be taking this long to roll over, before the bumper of the truck glanced off his right foot just as he cleared the space in front of it.

He continued rolling over until the two of them were sprawled across the opposite lane. Both of them still – just – intact.

'What—?' the boy began before looking back at the spot he had just been and seeing the garbage truck, which was only just coming to a stop, twenty feet beyond the place where he had been. Black stripes of rubber ran straight across the spot where he had fallen. His phone was in pieces where one of the big tires had rolled over it.

He looked okay: scraped and stunned, but okay. Jake didn't waste any time on words, just scrambled to his feet. As he was turning, a figure stepped out from behind the truck, gun pointed straight at his chest.

'Don't move,' Special Agent Lark said. 'I will shoot, Jake. Hands on your head, slowly.'

He believed her. Slowly, he raised his hands and knitted the fingers together around the back of his head. He winced, realizing the roll in front of the garbage truck had stripped the skin from the side of his right hand.

He could hear sirens in the distance. 'I didn't do it. I didn't shoot Rachel.'

Lark was approaching, doing everything right. Keeping her distance, keeping the gun trained on his center mass. Not taking any chances this time. Without taking her eyes from him, she reached down with her left hand, around to the back of her belt. When her hand appeared again, it was holding a set of cuffs.

'Hands behind your back.'

The teenager had just gotten to his feet, was looking from Lark to Jake in confusion.

'Officer, it was an accident, he saved my—'

'Quiet, son,' Lark said.

Jake had moved his hands behind his back. He might have a chance to make a move when she got in close to put the cuffs on. But if he was going to do something, he would have to go all in. Hit her hard enough to put her out of action. He didn't want to do that, and besides, he wasn't anywhere near sure he could do so without her putting a bullet in him first.

'I didn't do it,' he said again.

Lark circled him, keeping him outside arm's length until she got around his back. He tensed, still not sure if he was going to do anything or not.

'I know,' she said quietly.

It was a second before Jake could process the words.

'What?' he asked, just as he felt the cuffs closing around his wrists.

87

The last of the evening sun was bleeding from the sky as Lark took a wary glance around and opened the door of the back seat of the Impala. She put her hand on top of Ellis's head to keep it down as he got into the car. It had been a while since she had personally guided a suspect into the back seat, but the muscle memory was still there. She glanced around. Nobody in the street seemed to be looking at her. There had been no struggle, no yelling. Just one person helping another into the back of a car. Unless you looked closely, you might not notice that the second person had both hands behind his back. She closed the back door and got into the driver's seat. Ellis was sitting directly behind her.

'Move over,' she said, indicating the seat on the opposite side with her eyes.

Ellis shuffled over.

Her phone buzzed, Paxon's number on the screen. She answered it.

'Hey, are you okay?'

She held eye contact with her prisoner in the rearview mirror as she replied. 'I'm fine, where are you?'

'Uh…' There was a pause as Paxon looked for a street sign. 'Montgomery and Clay.'

'No sign of him down here,' Lark said. 'I need to check something out. I'll see you back at the office later.'

'All right, see you soon.'

She hung up and turned around to face Jake. His eyes were questioning.

'In two minutes, I'm going to call my people and let them know I'm bringing you in. If you have anything to say to me that might help your case, you better say it now.'

'Did you mean it? That you know I didn't do it?'

She hesitated, then answered, 'Yes.'

'How do you know?'

She let out a breath. 'I didn't have any doubt it was you, at first. Then some things didn't seem to add up. The fact Molly didn't take the chance to get away at False Klamath. When somebody tried to kill Rachel in the hospital, I knew it couldn't have been you. And if it was someone else that did that, I figured there was a good chance it was someone else who shot her in the first place. And then what happened a minute ago. You could have gotten away, if you hadn't helped that kid.'

Jake had had the look of a cornered animal in his gray eyes since she had caught up with him at the garbage truck. For the first time, she saw him start to hope. 'I didn't do it,' he said again.

'This afternoon, I talked to the witness who IDd you on Saturday.'

'He's lying. I just don't know why, yet,' Jake said.

'We might not get to know. Somebody just shot him and his wife at his apartment. That's where I was headed when I saw you.'

'They're trying to clear up the mess,' Jake said. 'Whoever framed me must have killed him too.'

'Hold on,' Lark said quickly. 'Maybe I believe you, but that's a long way from convincing anybody else. You didn't help yourself, running like that.'

'I had to protect Molly. They wanted to kill her, too.'

So many questions. Like who exactly are *they*? But one question took precedence over all others, part of the reason Lark had chosen to wait before calling this in.

'Where is she?'

'I rented a room in Pacific Heights. She's waiting there. I was trying to get back to—'

Just then, Lark's phone rang. She turned away from Jake to answer the call. He could see her right eye in the rearview as she spoke. As he watched, it widened.

'*What?* Where are you?'

It didn't sound like it was a cop on the other end of the line. Jake couldn't hear distinct words, but it sounded like a woman was talking fast, barely pausing for breath.

Lark leaned forward to confirm what street they were on from the signs at the crosswalk. 'Got it. Stay there, Chrissie, I'll be there in five minutes.'

She hung up and dropped the phone on the passenger side, turning the key in the ignition. She turned her lights on against the gathering dusk. 'Lay down on the back seat and keep your head down until I say it's okay.'

'We're going somewhere?' Jake asked.

Lark waited until she had maneuvered out of the spot and merged into the traffic before she answered.

'This day keeps getting more and more interesting.'

88

Chrissie did exactly as Lark had told her and waited under the shelter of the awning outside Larry's Bar. It had been the first place that had come into her mind when she finally worked up the nerve to leave her hiding place. She hated Larry's, had declared more than once that she wouldn't be caught dead there. Maybe that was why it called to her now. If someone from the FBI really wanted her dead, it was best to avoid her usual haunts. Plus, it was quiet on a Monday evening, and dimly lit, and they left you alone if you sat in the back and kept buying drinks.

When the gray car rounded the corner, she didn't move. She shrank back into the shadows, keeping her eyes on the windshield. When it got close enough, she recognized Lark at the wheel. She hoped she was making the right decision. But she had to trust someone, and she didn't believe Lark was involved with what had happened to Sean.

The car was traveling fast, but slammed on the brakes outside of Larry's, angling in to stop at the curb. Agent Lark got out and glanced back at the back seat. She started moving toward the front door of the bar.

Chrissie stepped out into the light cast by the green neon sign outside Larry's and called Lark's name.

Lark glanced around the street before putting a hand on Chrissie's shoulder and guiding her toward the passenger side of the car. She opened the door, giving another furtive look around the street.

'Get in. There's no one in the back seat. It's your imagination.'

Chrissie frowned and then started to get in.

She took a sharp breath when she saw Jake Ellis staring back at her from the back seat.

Ten minutes later, she had finished going through the story for the second time. The phone ringing earlier that afternoon, Edward Da Costa's wife wanting to speak on the record: she thought her husband had lied about witnessing Jake shoot Rachel Donaldson and Steve Holdcroft. How she had gone up to the apartment and found the door unlocked and the bodies of Edward and Shelley Da Costa lying sprawled on the kitchen floor, gunshot wounds to their heads. Running back downstairs in time to see . . .

'If I hadn't insisted on going up alone, if Sean had gone instead of me . . .' She started to choke on her words. 'Why couldn't we both have—'

Lark put a hand on top of hers. 'If you had stayed in the car, you would be dead.'

She knew Lark's words were intended to be comforting. They didn't do anything to erase the memory of the glass on the ground, the blood on the windshield, the way Sean was slumped over the wheel.

'Chrissie, can you describe the guy who did this?'

She noticed that Lark looked skeptical. She had told her that the killer claimed to be an FBI agent. That he knew Lark's first name.

'I didn't see him up close. He was a ways off, and he was turned toward the car. When he started coming for me, I just ran.'

'Tall, short? White, black?'

345

'White guy. Average height.'

Lark exchanged a frustrated glance with Jake Ellis, and suddenly Chrissie had the name that she had been trying to remember ever since the basement.

'Valenti. He said his name was Valenti, and he was working with you.'

Lark's head snapped back around to look at her. 'Mitch Valenti?'

'He just said he was Agent Valenti and he was going to take me to see you. He knew your first name. He sounded like he knew what he was talking about.'

Jake Ellis leaned forward in the back seat. His hands were still cuffed behind him. 'One of yours?'

Lark shot him an irritated glance. She opened her mouth to say something, then seemed to change her mind.

'Chrissie, what color hair did the guy have?'

She thought back, closing her eyes to concentrate. It had been so fast.

'I don't know. It looked dark, maybe? Yeah, dark and cut short.'

Lark nodded. 'Sean was in the driver's side.'

'That's right.'

'I want you to picture the scene again. You open the door to the lot and see ...'

Chrissie closed her eyes again. 'I see the guy standing by Sean's car, like he's talking to him.'

'And he doesn't see you at this point?'

She shook her head. It was horrible, reliving it, but she knew it was important. 'I'm just standing there, the phone in my hand to call nine one one, holding the door with my other hand. The guy turns and sees me. He says hi, but I know something's wrong. Apart from the two dead people upstairs, I mean. That's when I see the broken glass.'

346

'Go on.'

'I freeze. It's like I can't move. I know I should do something, but it all happens before I can process it. I step back into the stairwell. And that's when he takes the gun out.'

She felt Lark's hand on her own again and looked up, suddenly realizing she was shaking. She cleared her throat and steadied her voice. This was important. She couldn't help Sean now, but she could help to catch the guy who had murdered him.

Lark kept prompting. 'He's coming after you. He's pointing the gun at you? Or holding it by his side?'

'Pointing at me.'

'One or two hands?'

'One.'

Lark paused. 'Left or right hand?'

Chrissie was surprised at how much detail she could remember, with the right questions guiding her. She knew the answer right away, could see the image clearly.

'Right hand.'

'You're sure?'

'Sure.'

Lark sat back in her seat. 'Valenti's a lefty. It wasn't him.'

Jake Ellis leaned forward. 'Well, who the fuck was it?'

Lark seemed to think of something. Her mouth dropped open and she spoke quietly, as if talking to herself. 'Not one of my minions.' She grabbed her phone from the dash.

89

Shit.

Lark had been racking her brains trying to work out who the mystery gunman had been. It had felt like an unexpected static shock when Chrissie had said the guy had identified himself as Valenti. She knew Valenti hadn't been in the office at the time of the shooting. She had sent him to speak to the guy who had reported seeing the bike on Saturday morning. Of all the people on the team, he was the one she knew least about. Could it have been him?

If Chrissie was remembering correctly, the right-handed shooting suggested it wasn't Valenti. But if it wasn't him, she knew it still had to be someone else close to the investigation. The shooter knew Valenti was on the task force, he knew that Lark was the agent running the investigation, and he even knew her first name.

And then something had unlocked when Jake had asked, 'One of yours?' a minute ago. He had reminded her of Hartzler then. The other day in the bar, the smartass, dismissive way he had asked if Valenti was one of her 'minions' when he saw the name flash up on the phone screen. Maybe it didn't mean anything, but…

'Chrissie, the guy who shot Sean…' She stopped and glanced down at her phone, remembering the picture Hartzler had sent her. The one of him and Jake with the female officer who had been injured in the line of duty. She scrolled back through her messages until she found it. Hartzler was facing the camera. A good, clear picture.

She stretched the screen to blow up his face and held the phone up so that Chrissie could see it. Jake leaned in to see it too and his eyes widened.

'Was this the guy?'

Chrissie put a hand to her mouth. 'That's the guy.'

'Motherfucker ...'

She looked around at Jake, who was still staring at the photo of Hartzler. He looked in shock, but already he was starting to realize it all made sense. And then the color drained from his face.

'What? What is it?'

'We have to get back to Molly, now.'

90

Lark told Jake to get in the trunk this time. She followed his directions to the rented room on Jackson Street, taking the hill fast and beating two sets of lights. Luckily, they didn't have to go through Chinatown. The route took them just far enough away from the focus of the hunt. Lark smiled grimly as she thought about the crazy fact that she was driving around the city, desperately hoping none of the hundreds of cops on the streets would find out that she was carrying their wanted fugitive in the trunk. If somebody on Saturday morning had asked her where she expected to be in three days' time, this would have been pretty low on the list. At least they had cover of darkness now.

She stopped at the intersection with Mason Street to wait for a cable car to rattle past and tapped her fingers on the wheel impatiently, thinking about the revelations of the last half-hour. She had been wary of Hartzler all along but, she realized now, for completely the wrong reasons. She had suspected he might be trying to help Ellis from the inside, divert the investigation. Instead, he had tried to use her to get to Ellis. That was why he had put her on the right track with the man who turned out to be Walter Diehl – the bastard had relied on the FBI doing the legwork in tracking Ellis down, and then planned to silence him before he could talk. Even though she had never entirely trusted Hartzler, she couldn't help feeling a sting of betrayal.

And if that was how she was feeling, she could imagine how hard it was hitting Jake Ellis.

She reached Jackson Street a couple of minutes later and parked around the side of the building, near the fire escape. She checked the coast was clear before popping the trunk. She told Chrissie to stay in the car while they went up.

They made their way up the stairs, Jake leading the way, still with his hands cuffed, running up the stairs at full pelt, heedless of the risk of tripping. The door was broken down at the top of the last steep flight of stairs.

The room was unlit and empty. The skylight wide open. Lark flicked the lights on, then moved to the window and looked out. The roof sloped down for about four feet and then it was a sheer drop to the street.

Lark heard a guttural growl behind her and instinctively turned, tightening her grip on her gun. Jake slammed his body hard into the cheap drywall partition at the door. His cuffed hands meant that he was unable even to punch it in frustration.

'Stupid...'

'What? How did Hartzler know?'

'I called him yesterday. He offered to help. He wired money to a prepay credit card.'

Lark caught up quickly. 'Which you used to book this place.'

'I didn't have any money. I couldn't use my own cards, and we needed somewhere.'

'Hartzler was counting on it. He must have checked the online billing. He could have gotten the address from the apartment broker if he was down as the cardholder. He used the money to find you. Jake – what the hell does he want? What is this about?'

Jake seemed to remember something. 'Uncuff me.'

She gave him a wary look.

'Fine, there's a phone in my pocket. Take it out.'

Jake leaned back so that his jacket fell open. Lark reached into the inside pocket and withdrew a phone and battery. She regarded it for a second on the flat of her palm.

'Rachel's phone?'

'Rachel's phone,' Jake confirmed. 'I think this is what he wants. There's something on here that he doesn't want anyone to see. The man who shot Rachel was told to take her phone.'

'We wondered why you – why the shooter had taken this,' Lark said. And then she realized they had a problem. 'If we turn this phone on, my people are going to know about it.'

'I know, I was going to go underground to do it. Before I was interrupted by your latest Amber Alert.'

She glanced around the room. There was an empty bag of Doritos in the trash can under the desk. She pulled it out and shook the crumbs from the foil bag. 'I hope this works.' She put the battery in, slid the phone into the bag, and switched it on. 'It basically creates a Faraday cage. I saw someone do it on TV once. If it works, the phone won't get any kind of signal.'

'And if it doesn't work?'

'Then we can talk about what we did wrong in the cell we're sharing.'

The phone screen lit up. The wallpaper showed Jake and Rachel, dressed up, smiling for the camera.

'That was the wedding we went to last month, in Santa Rosa,' Jake said. There was a plaintive quality in his voice, like he was wishing he could turn back the clock a month.

Lark tapped the screen and the code entry appeared. 'Any idea of her pin?'

'Her birthday, I think. No, Molly's. It's ...' He looked like he would be scratching his head, if his hands hadn't been cuffed. 'June sometime.'

'June twenty-second, 2006,' Lark said, starting to tap it in.

'How do you know that?'

'I've spent a lot of the last three days looking into the background of all three of you, Ellis. I could probably beat you in a general knowledge quiz about your own life at this point.'

62206 failed. She tried 062206. It worked.

'So what are we looking for?' she asked.

'Hartzler wanted something on that phone. Or he didn't want anybody else to see something. A picture?'

Lark shook her head in frustration. 'It could take hours to do this properly.' She scrolled through the first few photographs in the gallery. Nothing that stood out. Lots of pictures of Molly, some Instagram-filtered food pics, a long-range shot of the Golden Gate Bridge with the city in the foreground that looked like it had been taken from the window of Rachel's office on Van Ness.

'Try the texts.'

There were five conversations in the message app. One between Rachel and Molly, one with Jake. The other three were names Lark recognized as Rachel's friends or work colleagues: Karen Lewis, Jane Kelly and William McMurtry.

'McMurtry. That's her boss,' Jake said.

'I know. We talked to him,' Lark said, tapping in. 'He was very keen to help.'

When she read the last few messages in the trail, she knew this was it.

91

The text conversation between Rachel and her boss stretched over a number of days, and related to concerns Rachel had about one of her clients. A client whose name Lark didn't remember appearing on the list McMurtry had given her the other day.

Rachel mentioned the Driscoll file in one of the first messages. McMurtry attempted to blow her off early on, saying that there was a mistake in the filing, and immediately offered to take over the task. But Rachel kept at it. A few days later, there were more questions, about a large, unexplained hole in the accounts. A hole that someone had attempted to hide.

The last three messages sent a shiver down Lark's spine:

Rachel Donaldson: I really think we need to go to the police about this.

William McMurtry: Rachel, let's talk about this in person tomorrow. If you're not satisfied, we'll go together.

Rachel Donaldson: Okay. See you at 8.

'The son of a bitch set her up,' Jake said. 'Or, at least, he knew what was going to happen. What is this?'

Lark was thinking. 'Driscoll' sounded familiar, but she didn't think it had been on the list of clients McMurtry had given her. She swapped Rachel's phone for her own and found the picture of Rachel's client list. The name Driscoll was nowhere to be seen.

'Maybe it was one of the big-ticket clients,' Jake said. 'Has to be a big gun if it's this important.'

Lark remembered it all at once. The name didn't belong to anyone involved with the investigation, it belonged to someone who had very publicly commented on it. 'Driscoll is George G. Driscoll.'

It took Jake a second to place the name. 'The politician?'

'Yeah. He's a rising star on the Board of Supervisors. Gunning to be mayor someday. Or maybe skip straight to governor. He went on TV the day you and Molly disappeared, saying he wanted you dead or alive.'

'I saw it,' Jake said. 'But why would he care about someone like me?'

'He doesn't. He just wants some loose ends tied up. And it doesn't hurt his career prospects to look like a hard-ass – cracking down on the homeless problem, wanting child abductors dead or alive, it all plays to his base.' Lark read the exchange over again. 'This doesn't make sense, though. He's willing to have people murdered over some ... financial irregularities? Who the hell is going to care about that? Scandals don't bring people like this down any more. Like the president saying he could shoot somebody on Fifth ... What?' She tailed off when she saw the look on Jake's face.

'I think I know what it is.'

'What?'

'The homeless activist guy.' Jake was snapping his fingers. 'Annoying guy, yappy. He was on the news all the time about

355

the South Beach homeless shelter development, before it got canned. He was killed in a mugging a couple of months back.'

'Michael Gregg,' Lark said. The same name she had remembered a few hours before. She didn't know the intimate details of the case, only what had been reported in the news. The FBI didn't investigate common or garden street killings. That was strictly the local police's territory. The *Chronicle* had run a half-page obituary on Gregg, she remembered. 'Death of a Dreamer', something like that. She could see where Jake was going with this.

'Michael Gregg, right,' Jake said. 'He was shot after leaving a club in Mission one night. It was down as a mugging gone wrong. They never caught the perp. His body was found—'

'Under the Central Freeway,' Lark finished. 'Just like Wade Lang yesterday morning. And it wasn't long after that that the homeless shelter was reassigned to another area. Unrelated to the murder, but they would have found it easier to do when the loudest voice was silenced. Are you suggesting Driscoll—'

'That's exactly what I'm suggesting,' Jake said. 'And do you want to take a guess who was the first cop on the scene that night?'

92

Jake dialed the number while holding eye contact with Lark. He listened to the ringtone. In his other ear, he heard distant sirens through the open window. They would only get one shot at this. If he screwed it up...

'Who is this?' Hartzler's voice was wary. He sounded like he was indoors somewhere. There was no noise in the background. An apartment? A hotel room?

'It's Jake.'

There was a long pause. 'Where are you, buddy? They're saying you've been spotted in the city.'

'I'm here,' Jake said. 'And I've got what you want.'

'I'm not sure what you mean, partner.' He overdid the confused tone, and there was an edge of steel in his reply. He knew.

'I know it was you, Marty. You set me up.'

There was no reply. He was surprised, and he wasn't denying it, but he was too smart to confess to anything over the phone.

'Where is she?' Jake said, barely unclenching his teeth between words.

Hartzler's voice was all business when he spoke again. 'You're back at the room, and no one's home. And you'd like to know where your traveling companion has gone.'

Lark's eyes met Jake's and he saw her really believe it for the first time. He was being careful not to say anything incriminating, while letting them know he knew exactly what this was about. This was no misunderstanding.

'I'm at the room on Jackson Street. I have the phone. Rachel's phone. You can have it if you let Molly go.'

'I have no idea what you're talking about, buddy. And I have to advise you, you should turn yourself in.'

Jake waited.

'That said, maybe we can come to an arrangement. It's nine-fifteen now. Get to the corner of Guerrero and Sixteenth by ten o'clock and I'll call you back.'

'All right.'

'And Jake? Come alone, and unarmed. I'll be watching.'

'I've been alone for a long time, Marty. I didn't know how alone until now.'

'Life's a bitch, my friend,' Hartzler said, without a hint of sympathy. And then the line went dead.

Lark was watching Jake. 'What do we do?'

'Only thing we can do. Exactly what he says. He thinks he's made sure I don't have a friend in the world. Is he right?'

93

'Pull over here, ma'am?'

The eyes of the youthful-looking officer manning the barrier at South Van Ness and Mission Street scanned the back seat of the Impala as he spoke. Lark had been waiting with bated breath as she watched the traffic move slowly beyond the checkpoint. It looked like they were stopping one out of every three cars, letting others through with a cursory glance. It was a belt-and-braces move – they knew Jake was on foot, but if he had somehow acquired a vehicle, a quick visual check would be enough to spot him, or notice a driver in distress. She had hoped they would just wave her through.

'It's okay, Officer,' Lark said, holding up her FBI ID.

He blinked and looked at the ID, this unexpected break from the routine requiring a moment to reconfigure his spiel. He looked from the photo to Lark's face. He looked uncertain. She guessed he was used to running DUI checkpoints and had a 'no exceptions' rule drummed into him.

'Oh, okay. I was just going to check your trunk.'

Lark gave him a frustrated look. 'I genuinely appreciate your diligence, Officer, but I really have to be in a press briefing like five minutes ago, so ...'

He was wavering, but still didn't look convinced.

She fixed him with a glare and kept her tone completely polite. 'Perhaps I could speak to your lieutenant?'

He looked uneasy, glanced around, and then shrugged, gesturing for her to go ahead. 'All right, then. Good luck with your briefing.'

She smiled a thank-you and drove past the barrier. Only once she had traveled a couple of blocks from the cordon did she relax a little. There were no cops in evidence here; they were all occupied to the north and east. Jake Ellis had slipped through the net one more time, with a little help from the agent who always got her man.

She was doubly glad they had convinced Chrissie to let them drop her off at a friend's place on Fillmore Street. She had protested at first, but when Jake had explained where they were going, she had demurred. Lark told her to sit tight, and that she would call with an update soon. If things went wrong at the rendezvous, she knew Hartzler would be looking for Chrissie next. Were other members of the police department involved? There was no way to know right now. Chrissie didn't need much convincing to lay low until they could attempt to get Molly back.

They passed beneath the Central Freeway, where both Wade Lang and Michael Gregg had met their deaths. Two very different people. One killer?

A couple of minutes later, Lark turned into a narrow alley off 16th Street and parked, then walked around to the trunk and opened it. Jake Ellis looked up at her, clearly in discomfort after riding three slow miles in the confined space.

'Problems?'

'Very nearly,' she said. 'I have to be insane to go along with this.'

'If it goes wrong, you can say you got a tip-off and got there after everything went down.'

'If this goes wrong, I might not be around to make bullshit stories up, Jake.'

94

The Elizabeth Theater was one of the neglected gems of post-earthquake reconstruction. Built in 1922, it kept packing houses through the studio era and late into the seventies. Sold to developers in 1981, it had fallen foul of restrictive planning laws and lain dormant ever since. It was tucked away on a quiet stretch of 16th street, in the south of Mission District. Its whitewashed Spanish Colonial Baroque facade had been dulled by a century of pollution and damp northern Californian weather. It was a quiet part of town, far from the focus of the manhunt. That was good news for Jake, but Lark remembered it was also the reason Hartzler must have picked it.

'My mom and dad used to go to this place,' she commented, as she and Jake examined the map of the streets around the theater on her phone. 'We used to drive by it when I was a kid. They saw *Star Wars* there.'

It hadn't taken them long to narrow down the Elizabeth as the number one probability for Hartzler's location. He had to be somewhere secluded and sheltered. Somewhere he could observe the rendezvous point he'd given Jake without being seen himself. The derelict movie palace was the only candidate in the area. Lark just hoped they were right, because it would be difficult to adapt once they had started to move.

She felt a sinking feeling in her stomach as she weighed

everything up. Any decision she made right now could have disastrous consequences.

'You know, in ten minutes I can have a tactical team and negotiators down here. We don't have to risk this.'

'Yes we do,' Jake said. 'This only works if Hartzler thinks this is between me and him. As long as he believes he can get the phone back and cover his ass, Molly's safe. As soon as he realizes the game's up, everything changes. Maybe he gives it up and lets Molly go, or maybe he decides to kill her and eat a bullet. It's out of our hands. This is the only way I can get close enough to get Molly. I'm counting on you to make sure we walk out of there.'

He held her gaze for a long moment, and she knew there was no turning back now. He was right about Molly. This gamble was more dangerous for the two of them, but it gave Molly the best chance of survival. If Lark had wanted to play it by the book, she would have had to make the decision back in the room on Jackson Street, before she unlocked Jake's cuffs. The look in his eyes told her there was no way she would be able to stop him from walking in there now. She would have to shoot him first.

Lark gave a resigned sigh. She looked back down at the screen and zoomed in on the alley running behind the back of the theater. 'There'll be a back exit, I'll go in that way.'

'Thank you,' he said.

She reached over to the glove box and opened it.

Jake's SIG Sauer pistol was there, where she had put it after cuffing him. He regarded the gun with indecision in his eyes. 'He said to come unarmed.'

'Do you know why he said that?'

He shook his head. 'It's too risky. He'll frisk me anyway, before I can get close to Molly. But he can't shoot me until he's sure this is really Rachel's phone. If I'm going to have a secret weapon, it's you, Lark.'

They went over the plan one more time, and then got out of the car. Lark popped the trunk again and took out the tire iron, hoping it would be enough to deal with whatever lock she found at the Elizabeth's back exit. It was 9.43. Jake would wait another few minutes and walk out onto 16th Street, exactly on the hour, to wait for the call. Lark would get into position to move at the stroke of ten.

She jogged to the far end of the alley, backtracked to the crosswalk at Dolores Street, and hurried past a half-dozen storefronts until she found the alley that headed back down behind the Elizabeth Theater. The buildings, of a similar period, all looked the same from behind. The good news was there were fewer windows back here. Their plan hinged on Hartzler being alone and not expecting anyone to be with Jake. He couldn't watch both entrances, and he would have to be watching the front at ten o'clock.

95

'Get over there in the corner and don't move.'

Marty was at the small window, holding back the dusty curtain and looking down on the street. The room was in darkness, lit only by the streetlights through the gaps in the curtain. They were in a room behind the balcony on the upper floor of the old theater. It was a small space, littered with broken furniture and wooden crates. He had his gun in his right hand. As Molly watched, he pushed a button on the handle and the magazine slid out. He examined it with a consternated look on his face, then slid it back into place with a click. He looked up and saw Molly hadn't moved.

'I said get in the corner, Molly.'

The spot Marty had indicated was the farthest point in the room from the door. Molly obeyed. She noticed that, by the corner, there was a small alcove in the wall, lined with shelves. As she passed by it, her foot crossed through a narrow shard of light.

She glanced back to see if Marty had seen it, but he was still looking down at the street. Molly shook her inhaler. Marty glanced back at her when he heard the rattle.

'You need that?' he said, eyeing the inhaler.

She took another puff, feeling her chest loosen a little, and nodded. Marty looked back out at the street. She slid down the wall so she was sitting down. From this angle, she could see where the shaft of light had come from. Behind a waterlogged cardboard box tucked beneath the bottom shelf, there was a gap in the drywall, maybe a foot high. It wasn't visible when you were standing up, obscured by the bottom shelf. The edges of the gap were rough and crumbling. The space through there was lighter, maybe another room without curtains.

Marty looked out at the street again, then back at her, a look on his face that wasn't so much concern as, 'This is all I need.'

'Rough couple of days for you, I guess,' he said. 'I don't suppose it would do much good for me to say I'm sorry.'

Molly didn't say anything. It was dusty in here. Much, much dustier than Jake's friend's place had been. She was putting fifty percent of her concentration into controlling her breathing. The other fifty percent was focused on a chance to get out of here. The cardboard box in front of the hole seemed to be full of newspapers. It looked heavy, but if she could somehow get it out of the way without Marty noticing, she might be able to squeeze through. What if it was a dead end? She could worry about that later.

Slowly, she moved her right foot to rest on the box, hoping it would look like she was just adjusting her position.

'I mean, not that any of this is my fault, you understand,' Marty continued. 'I'm just caught up in this clusterfuck, same as you. Of course, if your mom had minded her own business—'

He stopped, and then peered out of the gap in the felt curtains at something, then looked back as Molly coughed lightly. She slumped back against the wall. Laying it on a little thick, but not that much. She really did feel almost as bad as she was acting.

Marty looked back at her. 'You okay?'

'Dusty,' she said.

He shook his head. 'If she had minded her own business,

you wouldn't be here. I wouldn't be here. We'd all be nice and happy, enjoying the delights of a normal Monday night. But she didn't, and here we are.'

He looked back down at the street and squinted. He'd definitely seen something of interest this time. He took his phone out and held it up, waiting. After ten seconds, he muttered something under his breath and tapped the screen of his phone, holding it up to his ear.

Molly took the chance to give the box a solid push with her foot. The soggy cardboard tore, but it moved. One of the sides sagged and burst and some of the contents spilled onto the floor with a soft crumpling sound. She looked up, fearful, but Marty hadn't heard it. He was absorbed by whatever was down there, and whoever was on the phone.

There was a murmur on the other end of the line, too quiet for Molly to make out.

'I know,' Marty replied. 'I see you. Do you have the phone? Hold it up.'

He kept talking. Issuing instructions. To Jake, she assumed. He hadn't been caught. He had come to save her. But if this worked, she might not need saving.

Marty told Jake to lift his shirt and turn around slowly. Molly assumed it was to prove that he was unarmed. Molly tensed and adjusted the position of her legs. It was now or never. She looked back at Marty. He was still focused on looking out of the gap in the curtain.

'You see the movie theater across the road and down? The door's unlocked.'

He was winding up. Molly took as deep a breath as she was able to, slid down on her hands and knees, and crawled through the gap.

96

It was 9.56 when Lark reached the back of the theater. Right on schedule. The rusting fire door had the word ELIZABETH stenciled on it in faded lettering. She put a hand out to test the door and heard a scuffing sound from behind her.

She dropped the tire iron with a clang and whirled around, pulling her Glock from its holster. A figure emerged from the inky shadows of a doorway on the opposite side of the alley. Lark had started to squeeze the trigger when the man stopped and put his hands up. She eased the pressure off the trigger, but kept the gun level.

The man was dressed in dirty jeans and a ragged black sweater, with a gray beanie over his dirty hair. He stood in the doorway, holding up his hands. 'Whoa there.'

'FBI,' Lark said, keeping her voice hushed. She jerked her head in the direction back the way she had come. 'Get out of here.'

The man carefully lowered his hands and picked up a plastic bag laden with what looked like tin cans, before shuffling off down the alley. Lark cast her eyes around the rest of the alley to see if there were any more surprises waiting. She was pissed at herself. She should have seen him. But they blend in, don't they? It's how Hartzler and Driscoll and the others had been able to do what they had done and get away with it up until now.

She turned her attention to the door again and pushed tentatively, then more firmly. It didn't budge. She stepped back and examined the hinges to confirm it opened outward. There was no exterior keyhole; the door was just a flat sheet of steel.

So much for the stealthy approach. She had never been inside this building, and they hadn't been able to find a floor plan online, so it was impossible to know for sure what the layout was behind the door.

She knocked softly down the side opposite the hinges until she found the solid echo where the lock was. She carefully wedged the prying end of the iron in the gap between the door and the jamb.

She glanced at her phone again just in time to see it click from 21.59 to 22.00. Jake would be taking the call now.

She started to push, angling the tire iron backward and forward until it started to warp the metal, getting in behind the lock. It was hard work; she winced every time the metal let out a squeak. After a minute, the tool was wedged behind the lock, the handle sticking out diagonally, held in place even when she let it go. She laid her gun down on the ground, out of the way of the swing of the door, and gripped the iron with both hands. She took a breath and pushed hard.

The door bent outward for a second, and she was certain it wasn't going to break. But then the lock burst with a loud crack and the door swung open on rusty hinges.

The noises echoed into the dark, musty-smelling space within. The crack and the moan of hinges were like a concise sentence, telling anyone within earshot exactly what had just happened.

97

Jake crossed 16th Street and moved quickly toward the awning of the theater, keeping his eyes on the boarded-up arched windows on the second floor. Hartzler was up there somewhere, maybe still watching.

The awning outside still had enough letters to identify that the last film exhibited had been the original *Amityville Horror*. There was a shutter across the entrance, and as he approached, he could see that there was no padlock in the hasp, just as Hartzler had advised. He reached the awning and glanced around the street. There was a guy sweeping the sidewalk outside of the Asian market fifty yards down the street, but he was facing in the other direction. Jake lifted the shutter and stepped inside.

It was dark, smelled of mildew. He activated the flashlight on his phone and saw that the entrance doors were set inside a vestibule that also contained a small ticket booth. Thick swirls of dust motes danced around in the air displaced by the shutter opening. He cleared his throat and covered his mouth with his hand to avoid a coughing fit.

The door farthest from the shutter was unlocked. He stepped inside and found himself in a narrow foyer: doors to the auditorium ahead, and a spiral staircase up to the top level. He paused, his eyes and the beam of his flashlight trained on the door up there.

Where the hell was Hartzler?

He gritted his teeth. Either something had gone wrong or Marty had something unexpected planned.

He cleared his throat and called out, 'Marty? I'm here. Let's get this over with.'

98

Molly heard a crack and the squeaking of hinges from some-where down below. Jake making his way in? The sound seemed like it came from farther away, though.

She tried to control her breathing.

Hartzler's footsteps stopped. He was so close to her that she could hear the faint creak of the floorboards as he shifted his weight to look toward the direction the sound had come from. Another squeak and he took two more steps forward. She could see his boots on the ground. All he had to do was take another step forward and look over the barrier and he would see her. Could he hear the soft rasp of her breathing?

The room she had crawled into had only one door, and it had taken her out into the balcony seat area. She had been making for the door that she hoped would lead down to the ground level when she heard a surprised yell from Marty Hartzler as he realized his prisoner had slipped away. A split-second decision: run for the door or hide behind a four-foot-high barrier at the edge of the balcony. At first, she thought she had made the right choice, ducking down a second before Hartzler barreled out into the balcony, shining a flashlight around the seats. He would have been able to cut her off before she got close to the door. But now, a minute later, she wondered if she should have taken the chance. Now she was utterly cornered, waiting for him to shine that light over the barrier.

'Come on out, Molly.' His voice was still commanding, confident, but he had lowered it a little.

She held still, holding her breath, ignoring the tightness in her chest. He was bluffing. Had to be. And if he wasn't? Then it didn't matter, did it? So stay still, try not to breathe.

She heard some more sounds from down below. For what seemed like an eternity, she waited. Could he have moved without her hearing? She didn't dare look up. She sat perfectly still, her lungs burning.

And then she heard the floorboard squeak again and braced herself for discovery. One footstep, then another. And then another, and another. The light clicked off. He was moving away from her, gaining in speed.

99

As soon as the lock burst open, Lark bent and retrieved her gun with her right hand. She moved into the darkness. There were no windows, but the open door let in just enough light to see. The fire door led into a small corridor that dead-ended just after the door, then extended thirty feet to where she could see the handrail of a stairwell. She waited for a second, listening. No sounds, no movement. She moved forward down the corridor, staying close to the wall.

When she reached the stairwell, she saw a short flight of stairs down to the basement, and another going up. She started to climb. There was a door at the top of the stairs at ground level. She opened the door and saw it opened out onto the main auditorium.

It was a little lighter in here. A yellow sodium glow was filtering in through the open doorway out to the foyer.

Lark kept her gun steady as she closed the door again softly and started to walk up toward the space through to the foyer. The felt-lined seats were arranged in a rainbow shape, split by a central aisle. Extending out halfway over the auditorium was a balcony floor. Where was Hartzler? Was Jake inside already?

As if in answer, she heard his voice from somewhere above. 'Lark – behind you!'

She whirled and saw a figure rise from in front of the front row of seats, between the seats and the stage. She ducked just as she saw the muzzle flash. Lark counted three shots. Heard the first two bullets impact somewhere on the walls. The third one smashed right through the back of the seat next to the one she was sheltered behind.

She raised her head and loosed a volley of shots as she saw Hartzler disappear behind the curtain at the side of the screen.

100

Lark kept her gun on the spot where Hartzler had disappeared behind the curtain, ready to switch to another focal point at the first sign of movement. She glanced up at the balcony. Jake was up there. He pointed toward the ground, indicating he was coming down. She nodded and he disappeared from view.

She advanced down the right-hand side of the theater, keeping her gun trained on the spot where Hartzler had disappeared. She moved up the stairs on the side of the stage, treading as softly as she could. After the non-stop noise and bustle of the last three days, it was like walking into a deserted church. The silence was absolute. The eye of the storm.

She took a breath and pulled the curtain aside, ducking through and scanning the space behind the screen. It was empty: just a long strip of bare floorboards extending another fifteen feet, up to the rear wall of the building. A door on the right-hand side was open. She approached it steadily, tensing and waiting for a figure to suddenly appear. She reached the door and found a corridor that led along the edge of the building and finished with a set of stairs going up to the balcony.

She climbed the stairs. The pads of her footsteps echoed in the tight space, no matter how softly she tried to tread. She reached the top of the stairs and pushed the door open, ready to fire.

She found herself on the upper balcony, where Jake had been a couple of minutes before. There was no sign of him now. There were more rows of seats up here, a railed balcony at the front looking down onto the bottom floor. She started moving toward the front.

Then she heard the movement from behind her and whirled around, her finger tightening on the trigger.

'Don't shoot!'

She had been a heartbeat away from putting two bullets in the silhouette before she registered that the voice wasn't a man's.

She took her phone out and the screen lit up enough to see Molly Donaldson's tear-stained face.

She rushed forward and kneeled down beside her. 'Are you okay, Molly?'

Her voice sounded like she was borderline hysterical. 'He says his name is Marty, he tried to—'

'I know, Molly. But you're safe now. He can't hurt you.'

That was when she felt the hard metal of the gun prodding into the back of her head.

'I wouldn't go that far, Agent Lark.'

Lark let her body go loose. Started to raise her hands.

And then she moved.

101

Jake had retraced his steps, heading back down the spiral stairs to the foyer. He was entering the auditorium when he heard the gunshot. It was followed by a yell and the sounds of a struggle, from what sounded like directly above him.

He looked up, and was almost hit in the face by something dropping from the balcony. He got his arm up just in time and it deflected off his elbow. He saw a hand and a forearm on the rail, and then another hand grab the first and pull it back out of view.

He glanced down at what had fallen and saw it was Lark's Glock. As he stooped to pick it up, he heard his name yelled from above.

He glanced up, knowing it was already too late for the gun in his hand to be of any use, but Hartzler wasn't leaning over the rail. He was yelling into space. He didn't know where he was. Jake stepped back beneath the cover of the balcony before Hartzler decided to take a look over the edge.

'Jake, get your ass out here or I kill this Fed bitch. You know what has to happen.'

Quickly, Jake moved back the way he had come. Up the spiral staircase and over to the door. He edged close and risked a glance around the edge of the doorway that led to the balcony. Hartzler was in the same position at the edge of the balcony.

He was holding Lark with his left hand across her throat, gun to her head. He was peering down into the auditorium, looking for movement in the gloom.

Jake moved forward silently as Hartzler manhandled Lark toward the edge. He could see Molly, over to the side. She made eye contact with him but didn't make any sound.

He drew a bead on Hartzler, but it was impossible to get a clear shot with the way Lark was struggling.

'You're surrounded, Hartzler. Don't make it worse,' Lark said. Jake was impressed with her tone, which made it sound like she was dispassionately stating a fact. It didn't sound like what it was: a desperate bluff.

'Give me a break. If he's here, then you're the only one who knows about it. You think I'm an idiot?' He laughed humorlessly. 'Of course you think that. You're so superior, aren't you? And yet...' He raised his voice to address Jake, 'I'm going to count to three, then I do it. You know I'll do it. I got nothing to lose, and I got another hostage if you don't like this one.'

Jake tensed.

'One.'

For a split second, he had a clear shot at Hartzler's head, but he hesitated. Hartzler shifted position and Lark was too close to him again.

'Two.'

What was that weird crack in Hartzler's voice? He was going to do it. He was really going to do it. Jake took a step forward, hoping he would get a clear shot again. No good.

'Thr—'

'Okay!' Jake cut in.

Hartzler spun around to see Jake, less than ten feet from him. 'Not bad, Jake. Drop it.'

'Don't do it, he'll kill us both anyway,' Lark said.

Jake hesitated. Hartzler jerked Lark closer and dug the muzzle of his gun hard into her cheek.

'Jake—' Lark prompted.

'Save your breath, Lark. He believes me. Don't you, Jake?'

'All right.' Jake bent down and laid his gun on the ground. He hadn't thought much about the action, but in his peripheral vision, he saw Hartzler's expression twitch.

'Kick it. Hard. Toward me.'

Jake grimaced and did as he was told. The gun scuffed across the carpet and came to rest two thirds of the way to Hartzler.

'Why did you do it?' he asked.

Hartzler shook his head. 'This isn't my fault. It isn't your fault either, brother. If your goddamn girlfriend had kept her nose out of it, none of this would have happened.'

'Whatever it takes, huh?'

He opened his mouth to protest, and then just shrugged, conceding the point. 'Whatever it takes, that's right.'

'You made your choices,' Jake said, unable to keep the anger out of his voice. 'Nobody forced you.'

'Maybe that's true. Doesn't change things, though, does it?' He switched his gaze from Jake to Molly. 'Okay, Molly, come over here.'

'Leave her out of it.'

He sighed. 'Do we have to go through this again?'

For a split second, Hartzler glanced at the gun on the floor, and then back at Molly. Jake knew then why he was telling Molly to come over. Hartzler's gun was empty. He needed the other gun, but he couldn't risk letting Lark go. But how could he be sure?

Jake looked from Hartzler to the gun to Molly. And then he held eye contact with Lark. She looked back at him, unblinking, and he knew he could rely on her to do what had to be done, whether that gun was loaded or not.

'It's okay,' Jake said, fixing Molly with a stare. He tried to make his voice sound resigned, defeated. 'It's okay, carrot-top, do what he says.'

Molly blinked, and he thought she got the message. She moved forward, toward Hartzler.

As she got close, Hartzler told her to stop. Then he confirmed Jake's hunch.

'Pick up the gun by the barrel, then hand it to me.'

She glanced at Jake. He didn't look back at her, didn't want to give Hartzler the slightest warning of what was coming. She looked down at the gun and stepped forward, then she moved quickly and punched him hard in the kidneys.

Hartzler wasn't expecting it. He yelled in surprise and flinched back enough to give Lark an opening. She moved like she was starring in one of the bureau's close-combat training videos, like it had been choreographed. As Hartzler stumbled, she ducked out of the way of the gun, grabbed it and twisted around.

Hartzler let go of the gun without a struggle, just as Jake had expected. He stumbled forward as Lark brought the gun up and squeezed the trigger.

The hammer came down on an empty chamber.

Hartzler was moving faster than Jake had anticipated, diving for the floor. His hand was reaching for Lark's gun. Jake had thought he could be on it before him, but Hartzler was going to reach it first.

Hartzler got to the gun first. Raised it.

Just as Jake slammed into him. He grabbed him around the midsection and pushed, taking the both of them over the edge of the balcony. The gun went off. The world flipped upside down, and somewhere, someone screamed.

Untraceable

Excerpt from Untraceable – Season 4, Episode 6, April 27

Welcome to the final episode of *Untraceable*. I'm Chrissie Chung, and this episode is dedicated to the memory of my producer, Sean Tramel.

When we started this new season of the podcast last week, it was an experiment; something that had never been done before. We wanted to cover a live case as it unfolded. We wanted to use the skills and the resources we had developed over the years to tell the story as it happened, and perhaps even to help deliver a positive outcome. We couldn't have imagined that we would become part of the case.

Tragically, as many of you know, Sean was murdered on Monday April 20. Killed by a San Francisco police officer named Martin Hartzler, as part of the cover-up of a series of major crimes that goes all the way to the San Francisco Board of Supervisors.

It started with a homeless shelter; a symptom of a growing social problem in San Francisco. It finished with a cover-up and a series of murders and the biggest manhunt in recent California history.

But there was one bright spot in the darkness. The lost girl was found. This is the story of the people who paid the ultimate price to find her.

102

One week after what had happened at the Elizabeth Theater, Special Agent Catherine Lark climbed the thirteen flights to the office at 450 Golden Gate Avenue. It was a beautiful morning, barely a cloud in the sky. She could see the sun glinting off the windows of the buildings on Alcatraz Island. She sipped her coffee and thought about the day ahead. Normally, the positive resolution of a child abduction case meant some time to unwind and take care of the copious amounts of paperwork. That wasn't an option this time.

The text messages on Rachel Donaldson's phone had done exactly what the people who had tried to kill her had been worried about. They had opened up a Pandora's box.

It had begun three weeks before, when Rachel Donaldson went to her boss, William McMurtry, with concerns about a hole in the accounts of a company owned by one of the firm's major clients: George G. Driscoll. What had at first looked like an error had started to look increasingly suspicious the more Rachel began to untangle the accounts.

Driscoll had positioned himself as one of the leading voices railing against a major new homeless shelter due to be constructed in one of the many neighborhoods of San Francisco where property prices had been steadily rising for years. The residents didn't want to reverse that trend. Lark had remembered reading about the controversy a while ago. The plans had been shelved following a series of problems. The last straw had been when Michael Gregg, the activist leading the charge, had been killed in a mugging.

As it turned out, there was much more to it than that.

Warrants to search the homes of Martin Hartzler and the home and office of William McMurtry were issued straight after what had happened at the Elizabeth Theater. Those searches led directly to a warrant being issued for the home and office of George Driscoll himself.

The evidence discovered as a result revealed the detail of what had happened, and how it had spiraled out of control after last Saturday morning.

Driscoll had ordered the killing of Michael Gregg, along with three other homeless people whose deaths didn't make the news. He had an arrangement with Officer Martin Hartzler, who had carried out some low-profile strong-arm work for him in the past and was only too willing to graduate to murder for the additional fee. Hartzler helped broker the hit on Gregg himself and ensured that it was set up so that he was first on the scene and could help to establish the narrative.

But Driscoll made a mistake. The cash payments to Hartzler and his subcontractors were supposed to be hidden. They weren't hidden well enough. When Rachel Donaldson started asking questions, and McMurtry passed on his concerns to Driscoll, they decided they had no option. One more hit, and the problems would go away. They even had an ideal patsy: Rachel Donaldson's new boyfriend was well known to Hartzler and had recently had some career problems. An eyewitness would help, and Hartzler happened to know that a college lecturer by the name of Edward Da Costa lived in the area and had a sideline selling cocaine to students. Under pressure of losing everything, he agreed to fabricate a credible witness statement to Hartzler's specifications.

A little bit of computer-assisted friction added to the relationship would mean nobody would question it. A disgraced cop murders his partner and her child, before turning the gun on himself and leaving a confession. Nice and tidy.

Only it hadn't gone smoothly, and they had been forced to improvise.

A dead woman and kid would have been news, of course, but with an identified culprit and a narrative, it would have been over quickly. An abducted kid and an Amber Alert turned it into a major story.

Driscoll panicked, but Hartzler told him to stay calm. He would deal with it. He had almost managed it, too, winning Lark's wary trust in order to get closer to the task force and capitalizing on the stroke of good luck that Jake had reached out to him.

Ballistics matching the bullets to Hartzler's gun suggested he had killed Wade Lang on Sunday, before attempting to finish the job on Rachel in the hospital on Sunday night. When Edward Da Costa showed signs of cracking under pressure, he and his wife had to be killed too. Sean and Chrissie had just been in the wrong place at the wrong time. By that time, of course, he had to have known it was way too late to take care of this under the radar. Lark speculated that, at some point, Hartzler had decided his best shot was to kill anyone who could talk. She had a strong suspicion William McMurtry would have been next on his list. Driscoll, he would probably have reached a financial settlement with, since the two of them were equally compromised.

But Hartzler was dead, as was Wade Lang, the man he had hired to kill Rachel and Molly. McMurtry and Driscoll had been arrested on suspicion of conspiracy to commit murder.

And now the hard work began, making sure all of this evidence was built into an iron-clad case.

She supposed she should be grateful to still be in a position to build that case. The official story, backed up by Jake and Molly, was that she had arranged to meet Hartzler at the theater on 16th Street because he had information about Ellis, and had arrived early, in time to disrupt his plan to kill Molly. The story had more holes in it than a net curtain, and she had half expected SAC Finn to suspend her on the spot. He hadn't though. He had kept a perfectly straight face, offered a couple of softball questions, and then asked when she would be ready for the press conference. She guessed the combination of a positive outcome and a heroic story to give to the press went a long way.

She had told Joe everything when she had finally stumbled through the front door at home at 3 a.m. He had listened sympathetically, run her a hot bath, fixed her a strong mojito, and told her never to even think of doing anything like that again. 'I'm okay with that suggestion,' she had said after a moment's thought.

Now it was a week later, and the pressure hadn't let up yet. Lark hit send on the last of a dozen emails, then sat back in her chair and rubbed her eyes.

'You need to take a break,' Kelly Paxon said, looking across from her own desk.

'I've got a vacation penciled in for October next year,' Lark said, smiling.

Just then, her phone rang.

'Good morning, this is Doctor Callister over at Zuckerberg.' Lark felt a sinking feeling in her stomach. 'Yes?'

'You asked to be updated on Rachel Donaldson's condition.' Lark took a deep breath. 'Go ahead.'

103

The hospital was almost too bright and clean. After her days on the run, it felt to Molly like stepping into a different world.

Agent Lark led the way along the corridor, showing her ID to the officer on guard outside the ICU.

She stopped at the door and turned around to look at Molly. 'You ready?'

'Ready,' Molly answered, though she wasn't sure that was the truth. She wanted to see her mom more than anything, of course, and yet... it felt like it would take more nerve to walk through that door than it had to climb out on the roof four stories up.

'She's going to look a little different. There's swelling, and her head is all bandaged up, of course.' Lark touched her left hand to the side of her head. Molly looked away, remembering broken glass and a gunshot louder than the voice of God. When she looked back, Lark was smiling supportively. 'She's really looking forward to seeing you, Molly.'

Molly reached out and pushed the door open. The ICU was even whiter and even brighter than the rest of the hospital.

There were four beds in the room. Two were unoccupied, and the closest held a large, unconscious man. Her mother was in the bed at the farthest side of the room. The room smelled like bleach and warm plastic. Lark lingered by the door, and Molly approached the bed.

Her mom was lying back, her head in the middle of the pillow. Lark had only been the most recent of the people warning Molly about her mother's appearance, but actually, she didn't look too bad. The left side of her head was covered with a gauze bandage, which partially covered one of her closed eyes. Yellow and purple bruising extended out from underneath the pure white of the bandage. Her hands were placed on her chest, one on top of the other. It reminded Molly of hieroglyphics: Egyptian mummies prepared for burial. She hesitated a couple of steps from the bed. What if she touched her hand to her mother's and they were cold and dead?

But no. The machines she was connected to bleeped away with a reassuring regularity. The waves on the monitor rose and fell like an orderly mountain range. And now that she looked, she could see the chest rising and falling shallowly beneath her hands.

As she watched, the patient's eyes opened.

'Molly?'

She rushed forward, her instinct to grab her mother and hold her tight, and then stopped, remembering how fragile she was. Instead, she reached out and touched her hand. Slowly, her mother raised her right hand and grasped Molly's weakly.

'You look thin,' she said quietly. Then her brow furrowed. 'What did you do to your hair?'

Molly smiled.

'You're all right, though,' Rachel continued. 'They told me someone shot at us.'

'That's right,' Molly said. 'But you're going to be okay.'

'You weren't hurt?'

She shook her head, and then felt tears well in her eyes. 'I thought you were dead, Mom.' She felt the weak fingers on her hand tighten a little.

'Hey, it's okay, I'm fine,' Rachel said.

Molly choked back the tears and nodded seriously in agreement.

'I mean ... I've felt better...'

Molly laughed. A sudden guffaw that came as a surprise to herself, more than anyone.

Her mom's eyes defocused, as though she was miles away. 'Where's Jake?'

Molly turned around and looked at Lark. She stepped forward.

'He got into a little scrape. He can't be here right now.'

But then the door opened. And a familiar figure stood there, the officer guarding the door a step in front of him.

'They wouldn't let me bring flowers, I'm afraid.'

Lark nodded at the officer, who stepped out of the way and let Jake into the room. He was wearing a cast over his right arm where he had broken it in the fall from the balcony. Marty Hartzler hadn't been so lucky. He had been beneath Jake when they fell and took the brunt of it, breaking his neck as they crashed into the seats.

Jake approached the bed, moving slowly, in pain. He saw Molly looking at him with concern and winked, gently clapping her on the shoulder with his good hand as he reached the bed.

'What happened?' Rachel said slowly.

Molly glanced back at Lark, just in time to see her slipping out of the door, a smile on her face.

'It's a long story,' Jake said. He looked over at Molly and they exchanged a meaningful look. 'But I think we have enough time to tell you all about it.'

Acknowledgements

There's only one name on the cover, but if you know anything about writing, you know it takes a lot more than one person to create a book.

I'm grateful to Luigi Bonomi for advice, support, and doing his usual brilliant agent thing, and to Alison Bonomi for helping me untie a particularly knotty plot problem.

Thanks to my wonderful editor Francesca Pathak, and to the whole team at Orion, including (but not limited to) Lucy Frederick, Alex Layt and Emad Akhtar. Thanks for making sure this book was as good as it could be.

Thanks as always to my advance readers and to everyone who helped me out with research. This is a work of fiction. I've used some real places, and made some up. You can find False Klamath on a map, but the town I've put there doesn't exist. I just couldn't resist the name.

Shout-out to all the booksellers, bloggers, librarians and, obviously, the readers. You guys are the whole reason we do this.

Lastly, thanks most of all to Laura, Ava, Scarlett and Max for inspiration, support, and making me appreciate alone time.

Credits

Alex Knight and Orion Fiction would like to thank everyone at Orion who worked on the publication of *Hunted* in the UK.

Editorial
Francesca Pathak
Lucy Frederick

Copy Editor
Marian Reid

Proof Reader
Jade Craddock

Audio
Paul Stark
Amber Bates

Design
Debbie Holmes
Joanna Ridley
Nick May

Editorial Management
Charlie Panayiotou
Jane Hughes
Alice Davis

Production
Hannah Cox

Marketing
Folayemi Adebayo

Publicity
Will O'Mullane

Finance
Jasdip Nandra
Afeera Ahmed
Elizabeth Beaumont
Sue Baker

Rights
Susan Howe
Krystyna Kujawinska
Jessica Purdue
Richard King
Louise Henderson

Contracts
Anne Goddard
Paul Bulos
Jake Alderson

Operations
Jo Jacobs
Sharon Willis
Lisa Pryde
Lucy Brem

Sales
Jen Wilson
Esther Waters
Victoria Laws
Rachael Hum
Ellie Kyrke-Smith
Frances Doyle
Georgina Cutler

If you loved *Hunted*, don't miss the gripping, nail-biting new thriller from Alex Knight:

DARKNESS FALLS

Twenty years ago, her brother was murdered.

Tonight, she's found his killer.

Turn the page now for an exclusive sneak preview...

Part 1

Thessaly

I

Thursday, February 4

Rain, beating down like it had always been raining, and always would be.

The windshield wipers struggled to keep up, even on their fastest setting. The reflections of the lane markers and the taillights of the truck ahead would become clear for the briefest instant, before being submerged again in a thick sheet of water. Melting into blurry, untrustworthy hints of themselves, shifted an inch this way or that, becoming unreal.

Thessaly risked taking her hand from the wheel for a second to rub her eyelids, one at a time. She didn't dare risk letting the road out of her sight for a second.

Impossibly, the downpour seemed to step up a pitch, and she saw the brake lights of the truck flash as the driver slowed down, facing the same visibility challenge. Thessaly braked a little harder than necessary, saw the needle drop to thirty, and then gradually eased the pedal down again to match the removal truck's forty-five miles an hour. *Rolling Movers*, the livery on the rear door had read, back when visibility had been good enough to make it out. Some family's earthly possessions making their slow way across America through the night. It was attractive.

The thought of a blank slate. Starting again somewhere completely new.

But for the moment, she had no choice but to head back home. She wished she could have stayed over in Reading, but she couldn't cancel the editorial meeting tomorrow morning. It had been a straight choice between going and driving back after the post-service get together, or missing the funeral entirely. It had sounded like a good compromise a couple of days before, but the weather meant a three-hour drive was looking like extending to four or five hours, if the periodically readjusting ETA on her GPS was anything to go by. Barely halfway home, and she was already tired. So tired.

The day had taken more out of her than she had expected. Still, she was glad she had made the trip. Nate had been one of the best friends she had made in her time on the magazine. He had always been so much more full of life than any of the others. Always the first at the bar, always the first to suggest a beer on a Friday. If any of Nate's contemporaries had been asked to bet on his eventual cause of death – and Thessaly thought Nate would have enthusiastically approved of such a poor-taste suggestion – it would have been liver failure or alcohol poisoning. Suicide? She thought that would be the last thing anyone considered. Nate had always seemed so ... together. Like a lot of her former colleagues, she had lost touch with him after *Inside NY* had finally shut down in 2017.

The sign for an exit flashed by. She had a momentary panic as she read 'Greenville', because that would have put her a couple hundred miles west of where she thought she was, but she reread it and saw that the sign said 'Grenville'. Only one E. Also derived from 'green village', she supposed. Or perhaps just named after some long-dead British guy.

The removal truck was crawling now, down to thirty-five. If the rain didn't let up, she wouldn't make it back in time for the meeting in the morning. At this rate, she would get there sometime in late July.

A third light source suddenly appeared in the darkness. Up ahead and on the right-hand side, a red glow beyond the tail-lights of the truck.

The wipers swept the wash aside for another moment and she could see that it was a sign. A big red circle with some words beneath. It blurred again before she could read it.

A second of clarity. She saw that the circle was an 'O', and below it the word

OLYMPIA

and a series of smaller words beneath, two of which might have been 'All-Nite'.

Blur. A third sweep would take her past the sign.

In the spur of the moment, she slowed and signaled, getting ready to take the turn when she could see it properly. She pulled into the almost-empty parking lot as the wipers cleared and the rest of the sign revealed itself.

OLYMPIA DINER

ALL NITE
FOOD ★ COFFEE ★ LIQUOR

At least two of those sounded like a very good idea.

There were only two other vehicles in the lot: a silver sedan and a black BMW SUV. Thessaly parked beside the BMW. She watched the road as the taillights of the removal truck slowly retreated from view. Her wipers were still on. Blur. Clear. Blur. Clear. Eventually the twin red points of light vanished. Perhaps the rain would stop while she took a break. It didn't seem likely, but her eyes needed a break. She turned off the wipers and the engine and steeled herself for the run to the door of the diner.

She was drenched in the ten seconds it took her to get there. She opened the door and stepped out of the February night chill and into the warmth, blinking in the bright light of the interior. A sign by the entrance said, *Please wait here to be seated*, so she did. She wiped the rainwater from her forehead and looked around. It was an old-fashioned diner, but not old-fashioned in the fashionable sense. It wasn't a Disney reproduction of some kind of 1950s ideal, with checkerboard floor tiles or chrome fittings or red leather upholstery, but all the basics were there. A stainless-steel lunch counter down one side, booths arranged along the opposite wall. A mix of fake vintage and humorous signs on the walls. *If My Music Is Too Loud, You're Too Old*. An old Coca Cola ad with two ladies in Victorian-looking bathing suits. She could smell coffee and hot oil.

There was only one other customer in the place. A middle-aged bald man in a worn gray suit, looking down at a notebook, a cleared plate to one side. He glanced up at Thessaly as she entered, then looked back down again.

Salesman, she decided. Was travelling salesman still a profession? Or another thing the internet had killed, like magazines. She thought about Nate again, and the others. She had been luckier than most, snagging her first book deal right before the final round of redundancies. But perhaps the universe owed her that luck.

A door behind the lunch counter opened and a waitress stepped out. She was young, with brown freckles and dark hair tied back in a ponytail with a yellow ribbon. She didn't greet Thessaly with a hello or a how can I help you, just raised her eyebrows expectantly.

'Just for one,' Thessaly said.

Her name tag said, *Kayla*. Kayla turned her gaze to the row of booths, thought about it for longer than seemed strictly necessary, and then gestured at the one closest to the bald man.

Thessaly noticed that there was a plate on the opposite side of his table. The remains of somebody's meal on it; bacon offcuts and an ignored pile of hash browns. She sat down with her back to the other booth.

She ordered a black coffee when Kayla came around and glanced at the menu, quickly opting for French toast and bacon before she departed again. She shivered involuntarily as a drop of icy rainwater dripped suddenly down the back of her neck. She ran her fingers through her hair to strain some of it out.

She leaned forward and put her face in her hands, massaging her eyelids with her fingers. The urge to doze off was powerful. She didn't fight it too much. Better here than behind the wheel. Still well over a hundred miles to go.

She breathed through her nose and listened to the sound of the rain beating rhythmically off the roof, and then splashing into puddles at the side of the building. She listened to the hum of the coffee machine or the milkshake dispenser or whatever it was, behind the lunch counter. Underneath that, she heard the muffled sound of plates and skillets clattering and rattling in the kitchen.

'So are we done here? I guess I should tell you good luck.'

She started and opened her eyes before she realized the man in the next booth wasn't addressing her. She felt a bump through the back of her seat as someone sat down behind her and adjusted their position.

She blinked the tiredness out of her eyes and saw that the coffee she had ordered had already appeared. She must have been closer to sleep than she realized.

And then she heard something that made her wonder if she would ever sleep again. The voice of the person sitting opposite the bald man.

'You ever hear that old saying? Waiting for luck is like waiting for death.'

Thessaly felt an icy chill travel the length of her spine that was nothing to do with rainwater.

She knew that voice better than she knew her own mother's voice. She had been hearing it in her dreams for half a lifetime.

The voice of the man in the booth behind her belonged to a man named Casper Sturgis.

The man who had murdered her brother twenty years ago.

2

Waiting for luck is like waiting for death.

Thessaly straightened up in the booth seat like somebody had yanked her strings.

The words were as painfully familiar as the voice. Mitch's killer had told Mitch it wasn't his lucky day. Then he had used those exact words before he pulled the trigger.

She didn't turn around. She stared straight ahead, at the vintage Coke poster on the far wall. It felt like she wasn't in the diner anymore. It was twenty years ago, and she was still in the Redlands Mall. She had never left Deadlands.

The guy who looked like a salesman was talking quietly. She couldn't make out individual words over the thump of her pulse in her head. And then she heard the voice again. Cold and deep. So deep that if she heard it on a song, she would assume the producer had looped in some kind of effect. Like the voice of a bad dream. Like the feeling of a partly healed wound being scratched at with ragged fingernails. She felt her head begin to swim, and the two Victorian ladies on the Coke poster looked like they were moving. She gripped the edge of the table and closed her eyes.

'You okay there?'

Kayla, the waitress, was examining her with a mildly concerned expression. She was carrying Thessaly's order in her right hand. Her left was poised for action, as though she expected Thessaly to topple onto the tile floor at any moment.

'Fine,' she mouthed, but no sound came out. She cleared her throat. 'Maybe a glass of water?'

Kayla nodded and then looked up as one of the men in the other booth caught her eye. Had to be the bald man. The killer was facing the other direction.

'You fellas okay?'

'Just the check when you got a minute, thank you.'

Thessaly reached for her phone. It was lying face down on the table. When she turned it over and looked down at the screen, she was almost surprised to see the slender black mirror of a Samsung Galaxy, and not the chunky gray Nokia 3310 she had thought was pretty nifty back in 2001.

She risked glancing around. She could only see the back of his head. Dark blond hair with some gray. The collar of a plaid shirt.

Beyond where they were sitting, on the far wall of the diner, there was a neon arrow pointing toward the restrooms. She gripped the edge of the table and slid out. Her legs were unsteady as she moved quickly past the two men. She passed a mirror sign advertising Budweiser and her reflection told her why the waitress had looked so concerned. She looked as though she was auditioning for a vampire movie.

When she had made it three booths down, she risked stopping and turning around. The two men were continuing their conversation, neither looking up.

She couldn't see the man on the other side of the table at first. The salesman's head got in the way. But then he shifted position to take his wallet out and she had a clear line of sight.

Dark blond hair. A dusting of stubble that was a little gray now. A white T-shirt under a plaid shirt. He noticed her staring and glanced in her direction. She looked down quickly, pretending to examine her phone screen. When she stole another glance, he had looked away again and was talking to his companion.

Him.

It was him.

She turned and made the turn for the restrooms. Relieved to be out of the line of sight of the man in the seat, but not wanting to take her eyes off him. How long did she have? They had already asked for the check, and the waitress didn't have anything else to delay her other than Thessaly's glass of water.

She tapped the three numbers on her phone and held it to her ear.

'Nine-one-one emergency, which service do y—'

'Police.'

'Putting you through.'

The line wasn't great. Weather making the sound glitchy. She glanced around the corner and saw that the waitress had left the check on the table the two men were sitting at. The salesman was leaving cash.

'Pennsylvania State Police, are you reporting an emergency?'

'Yes. I mean … I think so.'

'What is the nature of your emergency, ma'am?'

'I think I saw a murderer. I mean, I know I did. He's here now. His name is—'

'You're reporting a murder?'

'No, a murderer. The person who committed a murder.'

'Ma'am are you in danger at this moment? Where are you?'

'No, he doesn't know I'm here. His name is Casper Sturgis. He killed my brother, and I just saw him.'

'Somebody's hurt?'

She gripped the phone tighter and tried to speak slowly without raising her voice.

'No, he killed my brother twenty years ago.'

'Twenty years ago?'

'I think he's leaving. You need to send someone now.'

There was a long pause, and Thessaly wondered if the dispatcher was going to admonish her for wasting police time. Too late, she realized she shouldn't have been specific. Send a cop. Any reason. She could explain when they got here.

'What's your location?'

'Can't you tell from my phone? I'm at some diner on the seventy-eight.'

'The location I'm getting is no good. Looks like you're somewhere in Northampton County, but I can't see specifically.'

Her mind went blank for a second. What the hell was this place called again? Something about sports? No – the Olympics. Olympia. 'I'm at the Olympia diner on the seventy-eight eastbound. Please hurry.'

She looked out again and saw that the two men were already leaving.

'Sit tight, ma'am. We'll have somebody with you in about fifteen minutes.'

She hung up and looked around the corner. The booth was empty, the door at the exit slowly swinging shut. By the time the cops got there, they would both be long gone. She made the decision in a second and headed for the door. If she could get a license plate, she would have something to give them.

She hurried outside and saw that she was too late. The silver sedan at the far side of the lot had started up, its headlights bright in her eyes. It started moving out and turned right onto the highway. The BMW followed it out, turning in the opposite direction, crossing over to the opposite side and heading west.

Thessaly ran for her own car. She had left her jacket in the booth inside, and she was soaked to the skin by the time she got into the driver's seat. She reversed out of the space and accelerated out of the lot, sending a shower of muddy rainwater over the windshield as she bumped in and out of a big pothole at the exit. She turned into the westbound lane and pushed the pedal down as far as she dared. The needle climbed above seventy before she was rewarded with the sight of taillights ahead of her. She switched the wipers to full and risked going a little faster, feeling the wind buffet her as the rain poured down like she was in a car wash.

She was gaining. Soon she would be close enough to read the BMW's license plate. And then the other car seemed to widen the gap a little. Did he know he was being followed? Had he noticed her coming out of the diner right after he did?

She gritted her teeth and pressed the pedal all the way to the floor. The needle jumped over eighty and kept rising. This was insane. She never drove this fast on a cloudless summer's day in the middle of nowhere. She was closing the gap though, the other car slowing a little as the road began to climb. Almost there. She could make out the contrast between the white plate and the blue numbers now. Another two seconds and—

A truck appeared over the crest of the hill in the opposite lane, full brights on. She braked and squeezed her eyes to slits as she tried to keep her car in the lane. The truck dimmed his lights and blew past her with a thunder of eighteen wheels. She opened her eyes full, but it was too late. The other car had disappeared over the crest of the hill and the needle had dropped to forty. She floored it again, the transmission taking its time to shift and the engine grumbling as she tried to accelerate uphill.

She crested the hill, wondering how much the gap would have widened, and saw ... nothing.

Just blackness ahead, the strip down the center of the road the only feature she could make out. The other car had vanished. The highway curved around and she hoped it would straighten out and she would see a set of taillights, but there was nothing.

She passed a sign.

Had he turned off? There was no place else to go. The GPS map showed a straight road ahead. This exit was the only one for miles.

She slowed and took the exit.